The Dante Legacy: Passion

DAY LECLAIRE

MILLS
BOON

Published in Great Britain 2015
by Mills & Boon, an imprint of Harlequin (UK) Limited,
Eton House, 18-24 Paradise Road, Richmond, Surrey, TW9 1SR

THE DANTE LEGACY: PASSION © 2015 Harlequin Books S.A.

Dante's Contract Marriage, *Dante's Ultimate Gamble* and *Dante's Temporary Fiancée* were first published in Great Britain by Harlequin (UK) Limited.

Dante's Contract Marriage © 2008 Day Totton Smith
Dante's Ultimate Gamble © 2010 Day Totton Smith
Dante's Temporary Fiancée © 2010 Day Totton Smith

ISBN: 978-0-263-25198-2
eBook ISBN: 978-1-474-00377-3

05-0115

Harlequin (UK) Limited's policy is to use papers that are natural, renewable and recyclable products and made from wood grown in sustainable forests. The logging and manufacturing processes conform to the legal environmental regulations of the country of origin.

Printed and bound in Spain
by CPI, Barcelona

Day Leclaire lives and works in the perfect setting—on an island off the North Carolina coast. Living in an environment where she can connect with primal elements that meld the moodiness of an ever-changing ocean, unfettered wetlands teeming with every creature imaginable, and the ferocity of both hurricanes and nor'easters that batter the fragile island, she's discovered the perfect setting for writing passionate books that offer a unique combination of humour, emotion and unforgettable characters.

Day is a three-time winner of both The Colorado Award of Excellence and The Golden Quill Award. She's won *RT Book Reviews* magazine's Career Achievement Award and Love and Laughter Award, a Holt Medallion, a Booksellers' Best Award, and has received an impressive ten nominations for the prestigious Romance Writers of America RITA® Award.

Day's romances touch the heart and make you care about her characters as much as she does. In Day's own words, "I adore writing romances, and can't think of a better way to spend each day." For more information, visit Day on her website at www.dayleclaire.com.

DANTE'S CONTRACT MARRIAGE

BY
DAY LECLAIRE

To Nancy Cecelia Totton.
You've been missed for far too long.

Prologue

"Cut it out, Ariana." Lazzaro Dante glared at the pesky five-year-old. "I don't like it when you do that."

"But I can zap you," she protested. "And I don't even have to rub my socks on the carpet first. See?"

She proved it by poking him again. A faint sizzle rippled along his arm, one that caused all the hairs to stand up on end. He jerked back from her and rubbed the spot. "I said cut it out."

Hurt blossomed in chocolate-brown eyes that seemed to fill half her face. "I'm just playing. Don't you want to play with me?"

Was she nuts? Of course he didn't want to play with her. He was twelve, nearly a teenager. She was little more than a baby. "Go ask Marco. He likes those kinds of games."

She pouted. "It's not the same. I can't shock him. I tried already. I can only shock you."

"Well, I don't like it."

Her dark brows drew together in a worried frown. "Does it hurt?"

"No." And it didn't. He just felt uncomfortable, like ants were racing beneath his skin and making him itchy and jumpy and confused, all at the same time. But maybe if he claimed it hurt, she'd stop touching him. "A little, okay? So don't do it anymore."

Contrition swept across her face. Heck, she even looked as if she might cry, which filled him with a pang of guilt. Having grown up with brothers and male cousins—with the exception of Gianna, who acted as though she were one of the guys—he wasn't used to dealing with girls. If you weren't happy with something a brother or cousin did, you just slugged them until they stopped. But he didn't dare treat Ariana that way.

He regarded her uneasily. For one thing, she was tiny and looked as if she might break if he stepped wrong. And some idiot had dressed her in a pink dress covered in bows with layers of petticoats. She even wore little lace socks with her shiny black shoes. How did you play in that sort of getup? In fact, now that he thought about it, she looked more like a doll than a girl. Somebody ought to stick her on a shelf someplace where she wouldn't get hurt.

"Ariana, come here, please."

Lazz sighed in relief at the sound of Vittorio Romano's voice. Good. Her dad would take care of her now, put her away so she wouldn't get dirty or broken. He waited until she'd been lifted into her father's arms

before making good his escape. Tossing aside his book
of logic puzzles, he joined his brothers. Maybe if he
hung around his twin, Marco, she'd get them mixed up
and bug his brother instead of him.

Ariana wrapped her arms around her father's neck
and buried her face against his shoulder. "He doesn't
like me," she said. "Fix it, Papa."

Vittorio chuckled, shooting a swift grin toward
Dominic Dante, surprised when his friend didn't share
his amusement. "You want me to make Lazz like you?"

"Yes."

"I'm sorry, *bambolina,* it doesn't work that way." He
signaled for his daughter's nanny. "Go with Rosa now.
She'll play with you. Or you can ask Grandmother Penelope to read you your favorite Mrs. Pennywinkle
book. She's in the garden painting or writing."

Ariana didn't protest. She struggled to master her
tears before giving her father a dutiful kiss on the
cheek. With a final forlorn glance in Lazz's direction,
she took Rosa's hand and trotted off.

Vittorio turned to Dominic, stiffening at his friend's
expression. "What's wrong? You look quite ill. Can I
get you something?"

Dominic shook his head. "No, no. There's nothing
you can get me. Damn it to hell. It's The Inferno," he
murmured. "My God. It may not be how it's experienced as adults, but I'll bet every last fire diamond the
Dantes possess that we just witnessed the beginnings
of The Inferno."

"You mean that silly zapping game? Don't be ridiculous, Dom. Ariana is still a baby and Lazz a boy." Vittorio hesitated, striving for delicacy. "I know you said

something about The Inferno in passing when we were in college, but—"

A reminiscent smile flickered across Dominic's face before fading to grimness. "I believe we were blind drunk at the time or I'd never have mentioned it. We don't speak of it, except with other Dantes. I'm surprised you remember."

"The concept of The Inferno is a bit hard to forget," Vittorio said drily. He tilted his head to one side. "But surely you don't believe it? You claimed it was nothing more than a Dante family myth."

"It's no myth, despite what I told you. I felt it myself not many years later."

Vittorio smiled. "I believe that's called love, though some call it lust. Or infatuation. A lightning bolt from heaven…or as it eventually turns out, from hell." He slapped Dominic on the back. "Your family has simply chosen a more clever name for it. But everyone has those romantic stirrings toward their wife."

"It wasn't with Laura," Dominic instantly denied. "I decided to ignore what I felt toward the woman The Inferno chose for me and married for business reasons. As it turns out, my life and marriage have been nothing short of a disaster."

Vittorio stared, shocked. "Surely not."

"My father warned me. He said I'd regret it if I didn't marry where The Inferno struck. I didn't listen."

"It was Primo who put those ideas in your head in the first place," Vittorio argued. "Of course he'd warn you."

"You still don't understand." Dominic spun to confront his friend, his eyes black with a combination of pain and fierce determination. "I didn't listen to The

Inferno, and I've been cursed ever since. I can't allow that to happen to my children. I'll do whatever it takes to make certain they don't suffer my fate."

"I don't like the sound of this."

"I'm not proposing anything that hasn't been done for centuries." Dominic spoke fast and low, with a worrisome underlying urgency. "I want to betroth our children. Draw up a contract to that effect."

"Don't be ridiculous." Vittorio allowed a hint of sharpness to color his words. "Even if I were to consider it, we couldn't force our children to honor such an outrage, not if they were unwilling."

"If I'm right, we won't need to force them. The first time they touch as adults they'll be bonded. They'll be only too happy to marry. And even if there's an initial reluctance, they'll change their minds after a few months of wedded bliss. All we have to do is get them in front of a priest."

Vittorio shook his head. He couldn't believe he was listening to this insane scheme. "And how do you propose we get them to the altar?"

"Like I said. We offer an incentive to sweeten the deal." He hesitated and lowered his voice to a mere whisper. "Have you heard of Brimstone?"

Vittorio stiffened at the mention of the infamous fire diamond. "I've always wondered if it were real or another Dante legend."

A small smile played around Dominic's mouth. "It's real enough."

"I've heard the diamond carries a curse."

"Or a blessing. It depends on your perspective."

"And your perspective is?"

"That it's up to the individual person and how he or she chooses to use the diamond."

"And how do you intend to use it?"

Dominic's smile grew. "Now that my father has given me control of our family business, I also have control of Brimstone. I propose that we make the diamond part of the contract. We'll put the stone in a bank deposit box for safekeeping. If Lazzaro and Ariana marry by the time your daughter turns twenty-five, the diamond will be split between the two families."

"Literally?" Vittorio asked, intrigued.

Dominic shook his head. "No, that would be very bad luck. Dantes will pay you half the worth of the diamond."

"And if the two refuse to marry?"

A fevered expression glittered in Dominic's eyes. "Then Brimstone will be sacrificed, thrown into the deepest part of the ocean."

"You've lost your mind."

Dominic laughed. "My soul, perhaps, but not my mind."

Vittorio hesitated, weighing the pros and cons despite himself. "The truly frightening part of this is that I'm actually considering your offer." The distinctive squeak of a wheelchair came from nearby and Vittorio glanced over his shoulder to make certain his mother-in-law wasn't close enough to overhear. There would be hell to pay if she caught wind of this.

"I'm hoping you'll do more than consider it," Dominic replied. "I'm hoping you'll agree."

"I can't believe I'm saying this, but I agree to your proposal."

A hint of contentment settled on Dominic's face. For the first time since the Dantes had arrived in Italy, Vittorio realized just how stressed his friend had become over the past few years. It saddened him to see Dom change from the charming, carefree schoolboy he'd once known to this hardened businessman. It also filled him with a vague unease. Maybe there was something to his story. Maybe the Dantes were cursed. Perhaps the fates had chosen to balance the Dantes' astonishing good fortune in the business world with a cursed personal life.

Vittorio crossed himself surreptitiously. "I want to make it clear, Dom. I refuse to force Ariana to the altar if she chooses not to marry."

"She'll marry Lazz. They both will agree to it, if only to keep a priceless diamond from being destroyed." He shot Vittorio a confident look. "If I'm right and that spark between children grows to an Inferno between adults, you'll benefit financially while I'll have the greatest gift of all."

"And what's that?"

Dominic stared at where his sons were heaped in a pile with Vittorio's son, Constantine. They formed a squirming mass of arms and legs, heads and tails. Their laughter rang out, the sound more precious than anything else in his life. "I'll have gained peace of mind."

One

From: Lazzaro_Dante@DantesJewelry.com
Date: 2008, August 04 08:02 PDST
To: Bambolina@fornitore.it
Subject: Marriage Contract, Premarital Conditions
Ariana, as discussed in our recent phone conversation, I'm sending my first marital condition.
Condition #1: Absolutely, positively, unequivocally **no secrets**.

August 7, 2008

"I hate secrets."

Lazzaro Dante made the statement so emphatically that it caused Ariana Romano to fall silent. Honesty compelled him to admit to himself that he hated secrets almost as much as he hated The Inferno—a myth his family considered a reality. The Inferno, or rather what his brothers and their wives perceived as some nebulous and fiery connection between soul mates that struck at first touch, had recently formed an exclusive club to which all his family members belonged, except him. As far as he was concerned, the family "curse" didn't exist, and nothing anyone could say or do would change his mind. Ever.

He could hear his fiancée's breath catch through the phone line and sensed her searching for an appropriate reply to his pronouncement. "I realize we've never met, but you are aware you're marrying a woman, yes?" she asked. "Secrets and women go together like handbags and heels."

Her comment caught him off guard. Perhaps it was the way she said it, with a hint of gentle humor sweeping through her odd accent. Her English, which she'd acquired from her British grandmother, carried the upper-crust echo of tea and crumpets and combined with the sunny warmth of her native tongue, an Italian lilt that orchestrated her every word.

"And you do realize I'm not Marco, right?" he reminded her.

"Your brother has explained as much," she replied with far too much equanimity. "He's visited us many times on Dantes business and says that despite being twins, the two of you are as different as night and day."

"True."

"For instance…he's charming and you are not."

Lazz straightened in his chair. "I'm logical."

"He is amusing. You…not so much. I believe that is the way Marco puts it."

"When I see my brother, I'll be sure to explain precisely where he can put it."

If she heard the muttered comment, she didn't respond to it. "Marco is also handsome and intelligent and kind. Not to mention an excellent kisser." A pregnant pause followed the pronouncement. "Should I expect my future husband to be none of those things?"

He locked on to the most vital portion of her comment. An irrational anger exploded in him, an emotion far out of proportion to the situation. *Not again,* an insidious voice whispered. No way would he share another woman with his brother, especially not someone he planned to marry.

He'd been through that with Caitlyn, a woman he'd been on the verge of proposing to, when Marco had tricked her into marriage by posing as Lazz. He wouldn't—*couldn't*—marry Ariana if she expected him to be a stand-in for Marco. Logic be damned, he flat-out refused to be a substitute for any man.

"You and Marco kissed?"

She must have heard the edge in his voice, because she answered promptly. "Before he met Caitlyn, yes. But it didn't rock either of our worlds." Her use of the idiom would have amused him if the circumstances had been different. "Despite his expertise, it was like kissing in the hopes of finding a lover and finding only a good friend. Do you know what I mean?"

"No."

"Ah, well. Perhaps it's never happened to you." Again came that tiny pause, and he had the strong sus-

picion she was laughing at him. "Are you…inexperi-
enced?"

"Hell, no!"

"I thought since you've been so insistent that you're
Marco's complete opposite that perhaps this is another
area in which you are lacking."

She was poking at him, the same as when she'd been
a child, he realized with equal parts amusement and annoyance. "You're playing a dangerous game," he warned.
"Jerk a kitten's tail, and Marco might scratch you. Jerk
my tail, and you're dealing with an entirely different
kind of animal."

Her breath escaped in a soft laugh. "Touché. I have
gathered as much from our negotiations. Your list of
marital demands have been quite…interesting."

"As have yours. Particularly your latest, which is why
I'm calling." Lazz regarded the printout he held with a
basic masculine confusion. "Why do you want your own
room? I can understand your own bedroom, but—"

"I require a room with a lock and a guarantee of
utter privacy. Did I phrase my request in a way that
confused you?"

"Not at all." Suspicion roared to the surface. "You
phrased it in a way that makes me wonder what you're
hiding and why."

"I am not hiding anything. I'm being quite explicit.
This is not a matter for one of your infamous negotiations. Refuse my request and it's a deal-breaker."

"Why?" he repeated.

Her laugh came to him, rich and earthy, and filled
with a honeyed warmth. "How many times must I tell
you? I'm a woman. Women need their privacy."

"Your own bedroom isn't private enough?"

"I can't do what I have in mind in a bedroom."

"That's a relief," he muttered.

Ariana's laughter teased him again, decimating the barriers of logic and rational thought Lazz had worked so hard to erect. He struggled to remember what she looked like, but nothing came to him, possibly because nearly two full decades had passed since he'd last seen her. Maybe he'd ask Marco. His brother had conducted protracted business dealings with the Romano family. Worse, Ariana and Marco had kissed. No question he would be able to describe Ariana. Knowing Marco, he'd be able to do it right down to the last tiny freckle.

Lazz grimaced. Or perhaps he wouldn't ask his brother a damn thing, since he suspected Marco would use the opportunity to either give him some serious grief, or even worse, try and talk him out of honoring the contract their father had signed with Vittorio Romano. And all because of that ridiculous Inferno nonsense.

"Are you going to tell me why you need a private room?" Lazz asked again.

"No."

"You simply expect me to comply with no explanation or clarification?"

"Yes. I expect you to comply the same way you expect me to comply with your marital demands." She paused, before asking delicately, "How many are we up to now? Ten?"

"Five," he corrected. "Six, if you count the one I'm sending you later today about the disposition of Brimstone."

"Of course that one counts. And how many have I made?"

"Three."

"Which leaves me with three to spare, should I choose to use them. And maybe I will. Maybe I'll save my extra three demands for after we're married. You can be the genie to my wishes." Her sigh of pleasure drifted across continents. "I quite like that idea."

For some reason that sigh caused a hunger to gnaw at the pit of his stomach. "That's not how it works."

"It works however we say it does. You claim you're the logical one."

"I *am* the logical one." He always had been, and marriage to Ariana wouldn't change that fact, a point he intended to make crystal clear. He attempted to get them back on topic. "About the room. If you'd just explain—"

"Are you worried that I intend to take a lover? Would you feel better about my request if I tell you I promise to honor my vow to remain faithful to you for the duration of our marriage?"

Yes. He closed his eyes at the silent acknowledgment. He knew where his suspicions came from. Understood his knee-jerk reaction to anything that hinted at a secret or a hidden agenda. He could lay that little issue squarely at Marco's door—and at his own. Just as Marco had used subterfuge to sweep in and carry Caitlyn away, Lazz had been every bit as guilty of a few secrets and deceptions of his own in the course of that entire debacle. Still, it had been quite a blow to his pride when the woman he'd hoped to marry had chosen his twin brother over him.

The entire incident had left a sour taste in Lazz's mouth and created a general distaste for lies and deception. And yet, here he was embroiled in just that. It might have been of his father's making, but he'd chosen to keep the reasons for his impending marriage a secret from two of the people he loved most in his life. And though he attempted to rationalize his decision, there were certain lines that couldn't be smudged.

What he was doing was wrong and he knew it.

"You're not going to tell me why you need a private room, are you?" Lazz asked. "Despite my condition that we not have secrets from each other, you still refuse to explain."

"I'm sorry, Marco."

"Lazz," he corrected softly.

"Now I really am sorry." There was no mistaking her sincerity. "I swear I wasn't 'jerking your tail' as you called it. Using your brother's name was an honest mistake. You sound so much like him."

"I look like him, too," Lazz warned. "But I'd appreciate it if you'd remember my name by the time we marry. My grandparents might find it a bit suspicious if you keep calling me Marco. They believe we met and fell in love the last time you were in San Francisco, and it's imperative that they continue to believe that for the duration of our marriage."

"Of course. You made it a condition, one I heartily approve of." A note of formality stole the summer warmth from her voice. "I will be very careful to play my part. Believe me, I don't wish my grandmother or my mother to find out about this devil's contract any more than you want your grandparents to discover the truth."

"My grandparents would do everything in their power to stop the wedding if they knew about the contract." Primo had once told him that to marry without The Inferno would turn a blessing into a curse. So Lazz had allowed his grandparents to believe that he and Ariana had experienced what he privately denied.

"Don't you find it disturbing that you're marrying a virtual stranger," she asked, "knowing nothing about what sort of person I am?"

"It's not forever, Ariana. And it enables us to achieve the same goal. We both want to prevent Brimstone from being thrown away."

"So we marry for profit."

Her concern came through loud and clear. She sounded on the verge of backing out, something he couldn't allow to happen. "If privacy is what you need in order to make all of this more palatable for you, you can have it. I agree to your third condition. I also promise we won't stay married a minute longer than necessary."

"How can I possibly refuse such a romantic offer?" she asked lightly.

His grin slid into his voice. "I can't imagine. So, when are you coming over?"

"Not until right before the ceremony. Both my grandmother and mother are shrewd women. I'm afraid if they see us together, they won't believe our story of a whirlwind love affair. It took a lot of maneuvering to convince my mother to delay our arrival. She wanted to fly over weeks beforehand. Fortunately, once I explained my problem to my father, he supported my request. We arrive the morning of the rehearsal."

"That makes sense." Lazz glanced at the calendar on his desk. "Not long now. Just three more weeks."

"August 28th. And then we'll be married," she murmured.

"Temporarily." Lazz's mouth tightened. And The Inferno be damned.

"So what's his latest demand?" Constantine asked his sister. Ever since the contract between their father and Dominic Dante had come to light, her brother had scoured the fine print, watching over the negotiations like a hawk.

"He's just reiterating one of his older ones. We're to have no secrets."

Constantine grinned. "Are you serious?"

"No. But he is." She dropped into the chair in front of her brother's desk and lifted her feet to rest on the edge. "I'm beginning to realize that Lazz is nothing like Marco."

"I like Marco. He's fun."

"Maybe a little too much fun, just as his brother is a little too much business." She released her breath in a sigh. "Isn't there a happy medium?"

"You're looking at him."

Ariana chuckled and nudged a stack of files with her bare toe. They cascaded in his direction, creating a flurry of papers that swamped his desk. "Aren't we full of ourselves, especially for virtual paupers."

Constantine busied himself for a moment, straightening the papers she'd knocked over, but Ariana understood. They'd been broke for years due to a series of bad investments their father had made. Since then, they'd lived off their name, as well as off friends who were willing to pick up the tab in order to have the Romanos grace their homes. And though it didn't seem to bother their father, Ariana had watched with serious concern the impact it had on her brother.

Constantine hated being broke. Hated freeloading. Hated having their maternal grandmother, Penelope, use the money from her Mrs. Pennywinkle royalty checks to keep the Romano estate intact. He had a head for business, but so far lacked investors. And the few who'd shown interest didn't plan to allow Constantine to run the concern, but simply wanted the Romano name attached to the project and her brother installed as a figurehead.

This marriage offered salvation for all of them. With their share of Brimstone, it would be more than enough to seed Constantine's business, as well as provide her father with a comfortable retirement.

"Do you think Grandmother suspects anything?" Ariana asked.

"Not at all. She's downright giddy over your wedding."

"I'm so relieved she's well enough to come."

A light tap sounded at the door, and the object of their conversation wheeled herself through the doorway. "Oh, there you are." She beamed at her grandchildren. "I was hoping to find you here. I just wanted a word with Ariana about a few wedding details."

Constantine shoved back his chair. "In that case, I'll make myself scarce." He bent over his frail grandmother and kissed her rose-petal-soft cheek. "You call me if you need anything, Gran," he said before making good his escape.

"Would you like some tea?" Ariana asked. Even though Penelope had left England more than fifty years ago when she'd married her Italian-born husband, she still preferred a cup of hot tea over any other beverage.

"I just had some, thank you." She regarded Ariana with china-blue eyes that sparkled with good humor. "I have to confess, I told a small fib just now."

Ariana grinned. "You didn't want to discuss wedding plans? I'm shocked."

Penelope waved that aside. "You and my dear daughter are more than capable of handling the wedding arrangements on your own. Plus you have all of the Dantes at your disposal."

"So, if this isn't about my wedding…" Ariana tilted her head to one side in question.

"You know perfectly well what this is about."

Ariana blew out a sigh. "Mrs. Pennywinkle."

"Yes, Mrs. Pennywinkle. You can't delay any longer."

The stories her grandmother created were beautifully illustrated tales, all about a china doll named Nancy who passed from needy child to needy child. With each subsequent owner came exciting adventures and heartrending problems for whichever youngster came into possession of the doll. By the end of the book, Nancy had helped resolve the child's problems and magically moved on to the next boy or girl in need. Ariana even owned the very first Nancy doll to come off the production line. It was one of her most treasured possessions.

"Have you finished the sketches the publisher requested?"

"The portfolio's ready to go, as is the storyline,"

Ariana admitted. "But I'm not sure Talbot Publishing is ready for such a significant change to books that have become classics over the years."

"Nonsense."

Ariana curled deeper into her chair. "I'm serious. My artistic style is nothing like yours. I'm not certain children will take to the change."

"It's time the books were revamped. Mrs. Penny-winkle has been in serious need of a face-lift for years now." A tiny frown marred the beauty of Penelope's English rose complexion. "Sales are dropping. If I don't find a way to turn it around—" She broke off with a shrug.

Ariana froze, understanding dawning. "Your money... It's running out?"

"It will if we don't get Mrs. Pennywinkle turned around." She leaned forward, lines of worry furrowing her brow. "Your mother doesn't have the talent or the interest. But you do."

"I definitely have the interest. It hasn't been decided whether I have sufficient talent. Which reminds me..." Ariana hesitated, reluctant to broach the subject. "I asked Lazz for a room where I can work on my illustrations, and he's curious about why I need both the room and such privacy. Would you mind if I tell him about Mrs. Pennywinkle?"

"You mustn't," Penelope cut in, her agitation increasing. "The Dantes attract media attention the way bread attracts butter. It'll get out. People will discover I'm Mrs. Pennywinkle. It'll be like it was after my accident."

Compassion filled Ariana at the mention of the accident that had killed her grandfather and chained Penelope to a wheelchair for the rest of her life. And though she understood why her grandmother preferred to keep her identity private, and respected that decision, Ariana had also made a promise to Lazz. She closed her eyes. There was no question which promise took precedence. Her grandmother's well-being came before all else.

"If you prefer I not tell Lazz what I'm up to, of course I'll respect your wishes," she said gently. "Besides, there's nothing to tell him. Not until your publisher accepts me as the new Mrs. Pennywinkle."

Penelope relaxed ever so slightly. "Since I'm no longer capable of continuing the series, thanks to these arthritic hands of mine, he won't have any choice."

Ariana wasn't as certain. Profit was the bottom line in today's business world, and if Talbot Publishing didn't feel her talent could change the face of Mrs. Pennywinkle in a way that would enhance the bottom line, they'd find someone else or allow the series to end. She'd do just about anything to ensure that didn't happen.

She shot her grandmother a concerned glance. She could only hope it all worked out in the end…and that she could keep the truth from Lazz for the length of their temporary marriage. Besides, it was only one tiny secret. Perhaps he wouldn't mind.

"So, what's her latest demand?" Marco asked.

Lazz scanned the printout of Ariana's e-mail for the umpteenth time. "You're married. Explain this to me. What the hell does it mean when she says she needs a private room? One that I won't invade, no less. Why does she need an entire room in order to be private?"

"And more importantly, why can't you invade it?" Marco asked.

"Yes, exactly. I mean, no, damn it! I wouldn't invade. Much." Lazz winced at his brother's bark of laughter. "Does Caitlyn have a private room?"

"Of course. I call it the bathroom, but she's turned it into some sort of female sanctuary, and God forbid I enter at the wrong time."

"When's the wrong time?"

Marco grinned. "Anytime she's in there."

"You're joking around, and I'm asking a serious question here."

Marco held up his hands in surrender. "Caitlyn has private areas. All women have them. They need places they can go to be alone and enjoy their femininity with all the delightful mystery that entails."

Lazz crumpled the e-mail in his fist. "Apparently, Ariana needs an entire room in order to be feminine."

"If it's such a problem, maybe you should reconsider marrying her."

"So you've said." Lazz's voice cooled. "As has Nicolò, twice. And Sev, at least a half dozen times."

"They're worried about you." Marco attempted to placate. "We all are. You don't have to honor that damnable contract Dad drew up. And you sure as hell don't have to marry Ariana in order to get your hands on Brimstone. No diamond, no matter how valuable, is worth that sort of sacrifice. None of us expect it of you."

Lazz lifted an eyebrow. "I'm surprised you all

aren't worried about the curse if I don't go through with the marriage."

"That diamond is only cursed if we believe it is," Marco said with a hint of unease. "Sev has secured our position in the jewelry world. It's ridiculous to believe that without Brimstone our family will never know true happiness or success. That's just a silly fairy tale."

"Just like it's ridiculous to believe The Inferno is anything more than a silly fairy tale?" Lazz asked pointedly.

Marco's jaw took on a stubborn slant. "That's different. One legend has nothing to do with the other."

"Right."

"Oh, can the sarcasm, will you? You're making a mistake marrying Ariana for business reasons, and you know it."

"So Sev and Nicolò have said." Lazz lobbed the balled e-mail in the direction of the trash can. It bounced off the rim before landing in the basket. "They think it's a mistake to marry Ariana because she's not my Inferno bride."

"I happen to agree with them," Marco said with deceptive mildness.

"Fortunately for all of us, I don't believe in The Inferno or its curse."

"Blessing."

Lazz ignored the interruption. "Ariana and I have e-mailed extensively, and we both agree. We'll marry. We'll put on a show for our grandparents for a few months. And then we'll go our separate ways. At some point, we'll have the marriage terminated."

Marco shook his head in open disgust. "I'm surprised at Dad. Considering how miserable he and Mom were, why would he want to force you into a similar type of marriage?"

"How many times do I have to explain? This isn't a real marriage." Lazz fought to control his impatience with only limited success. "Ariana and I will fulfill the terms of the contract and then have a friendly parting of the ways. Brimstone will be saved, and we'll buy out the Romanos' share of the stone. Nothing could be simpler and, best of all, everyone wins."

"If you really believe it'll be that easy, you're crazy. Primo and Nonna think you're marrying because of The Inferno. You've gone out of your way to give them that impression. Now you're stuck maintaining the pretense for the duration of your marriage. The minute you and Ariana divorce, they'll realize the truth." Marco leaned in, his expression unusually grim. "When that happens, it's going to crush them."

"I don't want them hurt," Lazz admitted. "But better they think I was mistaken about The Inferno than they find out about Dad's contract. In my opinion, that would crush them more than my confusing lust for The Inferno."

"You're wrong. They'd be more hurt to discover you're marrying for any reason other than love."

After a moment's consideration, Lazz was forced to concede the accuracy of his brother's observation. "Then I convince them that Ariana and I were in love when we married and that it simply didn't work out. I thought it was The Inferno and it wasn't. A simple case of wishful thinking. My understanding is that Ariana's grandmother, Penelope, and mother, Carolina, also believe it's a love match and we don't want to disabuse either of them of that notion. The fact that Ariana and I have only met by e-mail will remain our little secret."

"I'll be interested to see your reaction when you two really meet."

"Why?" The question slipped out before Lazz could prevent it.

Marco shook his head with a mocking smile. "I'll just let you find out for yourself."

"You're not going to tell me anything, are you?"

"I'll tell you this much… She's gorgeous. Passionate about life and everything in it. Has a terrific sense of humor. And she has a soft spot when it comes to children."

"You forgot to mention that she's a good kisser."

Marco laughed. "Told you, did she? Yes, she's a good kisser. So, when's the big meet and greet?"

"Ariana and her family are scheduled to come in the day before the ceremony. We'll get together privately right before the rehearsal."

Marco's amusement faded. "You're crazy if you think one brief meeting is going to establish enough of a rapport between you to convince everyone you two are romantically involved. You know nothing about each other and yet you think you can fake an intimate relationship—fake it well enough to convince Primo and Nonna, as well as Ariana's mother and grandmother, that the two of you are madly in love."

"Since it's only for one evening, plus the reception after the wedding, I think we can pull it off, assuming everyone keeps their collective mouths shut."

"Well, good luck. Primo and Nonna will be tough enough. But you're really going to need to watch your step with Penelope. She's a canny old bird. Too bad you don't have my charm."

"Fortunately, I have the brains you lack."

Marco stood. "One last question before I leave you to your facts and figures. Have you warned your bride-to-be about The Inferno yet?"

Lazz regarded his brother in genuine bewilderment. "Why would I want to do that?"

Marco frowned. "Didn't you tell me that one of the conditions of your marriage was that you won't have any secrets from each other?"

"Fairy tales are not secrets." With any luck at all, this was one fairy tale he'd never have cause to repeat.

"A word of warning. You may not consider it a secret, but Ariana may have a different view," Marco said in parting. "Women can be funny about the details."

Lazz groaned. Damn, but he didn't like the sound of that. He could only hope his brother's comment didn't prove to be as prophetic as it felt.

Two

From: Lazzaro_Dante@DantesJewelry.com
Date: 2008, August 04 23:28 PDST
To: Bambolina@fornitore.it
Subject: Marriage Contract, Premarital Conditions…
Addendum
Forgot to mention…I must request that my grand-
parents be kept in the dark about the existence of
the contract between my father and yours.
Condition #2: Maintain a convincing facade of ro-
mantic bliss in the presence of my grandparents.
L.

From: Bambolina@fornitore.it
Date: 2008, August 05 09:17 CEST
To: Lazzaro_Dante@DantesJewelry.com

Subject: Re: Marriage Contract, Premarital Conditions…Addendum

Fine, fine. Both your conditions are acceptable. I would also like to keep the reason for our marriage from my mother, Carolina, and my grandmother, Penelope. Not a secret of course, since you don't believe in them. Just a little white lie (for which we will both go straight to hell). I have told them we met and fell madly, passionately in love on my last visit to San Francisco. Does that work for you?

Ciao! Ariana

August 28, 2008

The morning of her wedding, Ariana woke to a world encased in fog. She wandered out onto the balcony of her hotel room at Le Premier and felt as though she were stepping into a cloud. It blanketed her in cool droplets of moisture that sparkled like a thousand individual diamonds.

Carolina wandered out onto the balcony and handed her daughter a mug of fragrant coffee. "How did you sleep?" she asked with a yawn.

"Really well. Between our flight being delayed all those hours and the jet lag, I fell off the minute I crawled into bed."

"We should have flown in earlier," Carolina said. "I never should have let you talk us into flying in the day before the ceremony."

"I didn't consider the possibility we might get grounded due to weather," Ariana conceded. "And I should have."

Though privately she thought it couldn't have worked out any better if she'd planned it. Not only had they missed the rehearsal, but the rehearsal dinner, as well. Now she only had to face the wedding. Anything between now and then that seemed a bit off or odd would be put down to wedding jitters. After that, she and Lazz just needed to put on a loving front long enough to get through the reception, and they'd be in the clear.

"Will it stay foggy like this? I'd so hoped for sunshine."

"It'll burn off in time," Ariana reassured. She glanced past her mother toward her grandmother. "Come out and look at this. It's amazing."

Penelope wheeled herself onto the balcony. Ariana crouched to wrap an arm around her grandmother while Carolina clutched her other hand, three generations of women united. "It's so strange to think we won't be returning to Italy together," Carolina murmured. "In a few hours you'll be married and living in a strange country with a husband you barely know."

"When it's right, it's right," Ariana replied lightly.

There wasn't time for more chatter. With three women in one hotel suite, every second counted as they prepared for the wedding. Little by little, order gave way to confusion, which gave way to chaos, which gave way to emotion-diffusing drama. Tears were shed, then rinsed away, just as the summertime sunshine rinsed away the final wisps of fog. As the hours ticked by and the time approached for the Romanos to leave for the church, tension turned to laughter and bittersweet reminiscences. Chaos organized itself into mild confusion, which drifted toward a messy sort of order.

At long last, Ariana stood in the middle of the suite, garbed in a gown that all three women had unanimously chosen as their favorite. The pearl-white color complimented her complexion and made her eyes seem deeper and darker, while the fitted bodice drew attention to the trim figure she'd inherited from her mother. The skirt floated around her like the wisps of fog she'd been admiring earlier. And she wore a lace-and-tulle veil that had belonged to her great–grandmother, anchored in place by a fire diamond tiara delivered to their hotel suite only that morning—a wedding gift from Lazz.

Her mother fluttered around her, making final minute adjustments, while Penelope simply sat and beamed. "You look stunning," she stated.

A brief knock sounded at the suite door and then Vittorio and Constantine entered. Tears filled her father's eyes as he embraced her. And concern ripped the stoic mask from her brother's face. "Are you sure you want to go through with this?" he whispered as they embraced.

"I'm positive."

"It's time to go," Vittorio warned.

Ariana barely recalled the ride from Le Premier to the small, intimate church. The stone structure topped a hill close to downtown and offered a tantalizing glimpse of the bay with its dotting of islands and famous red bridge. Her mother and grandmother hugged and kissed her before proceeding into the chapel, leaving Ariana in the garden with her father.

The constant clamor of busy streets and bustling people faded away. In its place, a lush summer wind stirred her veil and voluminous skirts and caused the surrounding trees to creak and rustle. Birdsong rose and fell, sweet and life-affirming. And then came the joyful pealing of bells.

Vittorio tipped her chin up so their eyes met and held. "There's something you need to know before you marry Lazz."

"What is it, Papa? What's wrong?"

He hesitated, conflict rife on his face. "It's about Brimstone. It's—it's gone missing."

It took a second for his words to sink in. Once they had, she fought to breathe. Oh, please let her have misunderstood. "What do you mean…missing? How does a diamond go missing?"

"I can't find it anywhere," he confessed.

"You mean, you've lost it?" At his reluctant nod, she shook her head in distress. "I don't understand. Didn't you have it in a safe deposit box? Isn't it locked up?"

"It was." He glanced over to where the wedding co-ordinator beckoned to them, indicating it was time to enter the chapel. "There's no time to go into the details right now. Just believe me when I say that I'm doing everything I can to recover the stone."

"I still don't understand. Why are we going through with the wedding, Papa? Why didn't you stop it as soon as you realized Brimstone was missing? Why haven't you told the Dantes?"

He rushed into speech. "I just need time. Time to find it."

"We don't have any time," she reminded him. "My birthday is in two days. If Lazz and I aren't married by then, Brimstone will be disposed of—assuming, of course, you can find the diamond in order to dispose of it."

He nodded unhappily. "If you want to cancel the wedding, we will."

It was the only sensible option, Ariana conceded. But it also meant a tremendous loss should her father recover the diamond in the meantime. She thought fast. "What will happen to the family if I back out? How do you think the Dantes will respond?"

"We'd have to explain everything to Primo and your mother and grandmother."

Ariana crossed herself with a moan.

"Don't worry, *bambolina*. We'll find a way to work it out." But she couldn't help noticing he didn't quite meet her gaze. "I'm sure the Dantes will be reasonable about everything."

Right. After all, look how reasonable Lazz had been so far with all of his premarital conditions. Somehow she didn't see him being any more reasonable about the loss of the diamond. Her hands twisted together. What if the Dantes decided to take legal action? It would destroy her family and start a media frenzy. She and her father wouldn't be the only ones affected, either. Constantine would never be able to start his own business. And as for Gran… She'd already been through one media nightmare. She couldn't handle another. Even worse, if the Romanos were put under such intense scrutiny, someone might uncover her grandmother's secret identity.

"I'm going through with it," she informed her father. "That'll give you time to find the diamond. But I beg you, Papa, make it fast."

There wasn't time for more conversation. The wedding coordinator scurried out, grabbed the two by the hands and literally dragged them toward the chapel. "Hurry, please. We're late."

Ariana and Vittorio paused in the vestibule. He bent and kissed her before helping settle a layer of the tulle veil over her face. Together they entered the still coolness of the chapel. The bells gentled, replaced by the sweet welcome of strings heralding her approach.

Ariana struggled against a wave of emotion. In that moment, she didn't care why she'd agreed to this marriage or whether it had been a reasonable decision. Right now, she longed for more. All the trappings were here— the sanctity of the church, the beauty of the music, the warmth and well wishes of her family and Lazz's. But it wasn't real. It lacked the most important ingredient of all.

Love.

A man who looked exactly like Marco stood to one side of the altar, wearing a tux. No, she realized an instant later. He wasn't quite identical to Marco. As she approached, she could detect minute differences. Lazz was every bit as handsome as his twin, but lacked the mischievous twinkle and ready smile. This man remained guarded and implacable, watching her with a deep, penetrating intelligence.

There was depth there and an innate power, as well as a delicious sensuality that tugged at her the closer she came. A hum of tension grew with each step. By the time she joined him at the altar, the hum had escalated to a sizzle of awareness unlike anything she'd ever felt before. She fought to conceal it, to keep from trembling in reaction.

As though experiencing something similar, Lazz stiffened and fixed her with a fierce gaze. His eyes were a similar shade of hazel-green to Marco's, except that the green in Lazz's eyes appeared more intense, the gold highlights slightly tarnished. Somehow his gaze went deeper and saw far more, reflecting the heart of someone who had been badly burned in the past and chose to keep his distance from the flames in the future.

Time seemed to catch its breath as he studied her through the veiling layer of tulle. It felt as though he spoke to her on some private wavelength. As though some part of him called to her, demanding a response. She almost took that final step separating them, intent on wrapping herself around him. Before she could cave to instinct, Lazz cupped her elbow and turned them to face the priest, his touch burning through the satin of her sleeve.

The ceremony passed in a haze, the familiar words settling over her like a comforting mantle. Finally the moment came when they were to speak their vows. The priest blessed their rings and presented hers to Lazz. She watched as he accepted the simple gold band, fascinated by the graceful sweep of his hand. She'd never noticed Marco's hands before, but she did Lazz's. They were long and powerful and unbearably elegant. At the priest's direction, Lazz took her hand in his.

And that's when it happened.

She'd felt the burn of his touch through the satin of her wedding gown. But it was nothing in comparison to the shock that struck her when skin touched skin. It hit with such force that if Lazz hadn't been holding on to her, she'd have fallen. His fingers tightened around hers, and she glanced up, somewhat relieved to see his look of stunned disbelief. It would seem she wasn't the only one to feel it.

"What the hell was that?" he muttered.

"Not quite the first words I'd hoped to hear my husband speak," she whispered back. "But an excellent question. What just happened?"

With a swift glance toward the priest, Lazz shook his head and the ceremony resumed. He repeated his vows in a strong, clear voice. And then it was her turn. Whatever had caused the jolt of electricity had subsided into a bone-deep warmth that seeped inward and lapped through her veins, melting her into irrational want.

She struggled to focus on the words of commitment, but they turned into a meaningless jumble that twisted her tongue and had her switching impatiently to Italian. Sympathetic laughter drifted from those seated in the pews. No doubt they thought wedding jitters were responsible. But this—whatever *this* was— had nothing to do with jitters and everything to do with the man holding her hand.

Minutes flew by and then came the words she'd awaited with equal parts dread and anticipation. The priest pronounced his final blessing then instructed Lazz to kiss his bride. He took his time, driving her to the brink of insanity with his deliberation.

Slowly, he reached for her, capturing her veil and flipping it backward away from her face. He gazed down at her, his expression one of avid curiosity. It confirmed what she'd suspected. He didn't remember her. The time they'd been in Marco's conference room together hadn't made the least impression, no doubt because he'd been focused on his brother and Caitlyn—the woman Marco had tricked into marriage, as well as the woman Lazz had hoped to marry.

Perhaps if circumstances had been different, she'd have found Lazz's stunned reaction to her appearance amusing. Clearly, she met with his approval. As though unable to resist, he lowered his head and kissed her. She sensed he meant to keep it light and impersonal. But the instant their lips touched, heat exploded. His arms closed around her, powerful and possessive, and he locked her against him.

She'd been wrong. Oh, so wrong. Marco might have been a good kisser, but her husband was incredible.

One minute Lazz controlled both his life and destiny, and the next he took a woman he'd never truly met before for his wife and stepped into the vortex of a tornado.

If his life depended on it, he couldn't have said what had happened in the course of the past ten minutes. From the instant he took Ariana's hand in his own, everything changed. His illusion of control was ripped away, shredded in the howling winds of the tornado that tore through him. Reason vanished, as well. One thought consumed him.

Claim this woman. Grab hold of her and never let go.

He needed to make her his in every way possible. To make her understand that they were connected. That they belonged together. He vaguely heard the priest instruct him to kiss Ariana, and he wanted to shout in exultation.

First came the touch that linked them. Then came the kiss. And later, when they were alone, he would complete the bond between them. He would make her his in every sense of the word.

She trembled in his arms, but it wasn't fear that caused it. He could sense a hint of nervousness when he kissed her. Of surprise. Then it changed. The rapid pounding of her heart matched his, the passion blooming within her a mate for his own. Whatever the connection between them, it went both ways, a circuit completed.

And then, as though from a great distance, Lazz heard Marco in his capacity of best man. "I believe that's now Dantes zero," he murmured, just loud enough for Lazz to hear. "The Inferno four for four. Looks like the family blessing wins again."

The instant the words penetrated, he released Ariana and yanked himself free of the flames. No. Not a chance in hell. It couldn't be The Inferno. And yet, what other explanation could there be for what he felt? For his complete and utter loss of control? He'd never set eyes on Ariana before, at least not since she was a child of five, and yet it was as though he knew her. Worse than that, he wanted her with a wanton desperation he'd never experienced toward another woman.

She stared up at him with an expression of dazed bewilderment. "What just happened?" she asked in Italian.

"Absolutely nothing." He refused to even consider any other possibility.

They turned to face the congregation, and he saw a hint of amusement sparkle in her gaze, the same amusement he'd heard in her voice during the phone conversations they'd shared. "If that's 'nothing,' I can't wait to give 'something' a try."

They weren't given the opportunity for further conversation. Church bells rang out, and the strings began a joyous recessional. Ariana slipped her hand through Lazz's arm, and together they made their way down the aisle. As they passed the front pew, he caught a glimpse of his grandparents. Nonna dabbed at tears while Primo regarded him with an expression of such relief that Lazz nearly flinched.

Secrets and lies. He despised them, even as he lived them. He'd spent the last several months trying to convince himself that his reasons were sound, that recovering Brimstone was worth the minor inconvenience of a temporary marriage. But looking at his grandfather, Lazz knew that Primo would never have approved his decision, not if it meant consigning a hundred Brimstones to the deep blue sea. There was only one way of winning Primo's approval.

Lazz would have to marry his Inferno mate.

As though picking up on his thoughts, Ariana leaned in. "What happened when we first touched?" she asked in an undertone.

"Like I said. Nothing." The denial came automatically. It was another lie or, more likely, a hope. He escorted her to the limousine waiting to drive them to their reception at Le Premier. The driver opened the door while Lazz helped his bride in.

The instant the door enclosed them in dusky privacy, she shifted to face him. "That wasn't nothing. When you took my hand, you shocked me," she argued. "And don't try and tell me it was static electricity."

"It was static electricity."

Instead of arguing, she smiled. "Have it your way. When you're ready to tell me the truth, let me know."

"There's nothing to tell."

She leaned closer, and he struggled to keep his hands off her, to keep himself from kissing her again. He longed to see if what they'd experienced before was a onetime deal or an insanity he could expect every time they touched. "In case you haven't noticed," she told him, "you've already broken your first marital condition. No secrets, remember?"

Son of a— "This isn't the appropriate time."

"Of course not," she instantly agreed. "Though your comment suggests there is…something."

"Delicately put. And yes, there is something. But it has nothing to do with us. Nothing to do with what happened at the church." He refused to even consider the possibility.

"And what did happen at the church?"

"We kissed." And time stopped. The gates to heaven opened. And the earth moved—without benefit of an earthquake.

To his relief, the limousine pulled up in front of the hotel, putting an end to their discussion. Their marriage was temporary, he reminded himself. He'd be a fool to expect anything else, to complicate a simple, straightforward agreement with whatever form of lunacy held him in its grip, especially considering Ariana's marital conditions.

Once inside, they joined the wedding party in a receiving line. No sooner were they free from that duty when the orchestra began the opening strands of a waltz. Lazz took Ariana's hand in his and led her out onto the floor for the opening dance. Applause drifted through the assembled guests as the bridal couple circled the room. But Lazz might as well have been deaf and blind to everyone but the woman he held close to his heart.

She fit in his arms as though the universe had deliberately formed her as his perfect counterpart. A deep melding formed where their palms joined, a melding he'd often heard his brothers refer to. Even so, he refused to believe it was The Inferno.

He'd felt a similar tingling before in Caitlyn's presence the day after she'd married Marco. Granted, it hadn't been this strong. Not even close. But he refused to give in to the family delusion, to pretend that whatever he felt toward his temporary wife could be anything more than simple, ordinary lust. He'd accepted long ago that fairy tales weren't meant for him. And who wouldn't have reacted to Ariana? His wife was a beautiful woman.

Lazz gazed down at her. Incredibly beautiful, he corrected. Stunning. Her face contained an intriguing mixture of lushness and delicacy. And while her features were fine-boned and aristocratic, her mouth was full and ripe and the exact color of sun-kissed peaches. She gazed up at him with sweetly wanton eyes that exactly matched the deep, rich brown of bittersweet chocolate. Even her skin revealed the complexity of her nature, passion giving a rosy glow to the creamy white blending of her Latin heritage with her British.

"Have I told you how beautiful you look?" The words escaped of their own volition.

"Thank you. I can't take credit for it. It was an accident of birth."

He laughed. "That was one hell of an accident."

"You appeared surprised when you lifted the veil. Why?"

"I'd never seen you before. Well, not since we were children," he corrected.

An odd expression drifted across her face, part pain and part exasperation. "That's not true. We were in the same room together not so many months ago."

Lazz stared. "Are you serious?"

"Quite serious."

"Not a chance," he denied. "If we'd met that recently, I'd have remembered. When was this? Where?"

Ariana stared at a spot over his shoulder. She'd known at the time that he hadn't noticed her, even as she'd felt the first shimmer of a connection. It hadn't been anywhere near as strong as at the church. But it had definitely been there.

She shouldn't take it personally that he didn't remember her. She'd seen how he'd reacted to the news of Caitlyn's marriage to Marco. It had devastated Lazz, a fact he'd driven home by physically attacking his brother. She wouldn't have been a female worthy of the name if she hadn't understood that both twins had been in love with the same woman.

"Ariana?"

"It was at Dantes. In Marco's conference room." She forced herself to look at him, allowing her gaze to reflect the full depth of her knowledge. "The morning after Caitlyn's marriage to Marco."

It was as though an impenetrable barrier slammed into place. "You were there?"

She couldn't help but laugh, though the sound carried a hint of sorrow. "I believe that explains why you don't remember me. Did you love her very much? Are you still in love with her?"

"She's my sister-in-law."

"That doesn't answer my questions."

"As my wife—as my temporary wife—that subject doesn't concern us. It has nothing to do with our marriage, the contract that brought us together or the conditions we both agreed to before marrying."

So cool. So logical. And yet, she sensed that emotion smoldered just beneath the surface, like dry tinder longing for a hot spark to set it ablaze. "What about our agreement not to keep secrets?"

"Consider the subject of Caitlyn to be the equivalent of your privacy room."

"Ah."

"What does that mean?"

She shrugged. "It just means that I understand." Then she added a gentle, "And sympathize."

"I didn't ask—" He broke off, staring toward a cluster of his relatives. "What's going on over there?"

Ariana turned to look. "That's Nicolò and…Kiley? Do I have her name right?"

"Yes. Aw, hell. They're all crying. We need to get over there. Something's wrong."

A chuckle escaped Ariana. "Nothing's wrong. Not unless having a baby is wrong."

"A baby!"

"See how Nonna is touching Kiley's belly? That's

universal woman-speak. And now Francesca is…" Her laughter grew. "Oh, how sweet. Please, can we go over and congratulate both of them?"

"Both. Both?"

"Francesca and Kiley. I wonder how close their due dates are."

She caught Lazz's hand in hers and urged him toward where the Dantes stood gathered. With everyone talking and laughing at once, it took a moment for them to be absorbed into the group. The minute Ariana reached her sisters-in-law, she gave each a hug in turn.

"I didn't mean to steal your thunder," Kiley instantly said. "But Nonna took one look at me and burst into tears. And as soon as Francesca understood why, she started to cry. And well…"

"Why would you apologize? You have made our special day all the more joyous. May I?" At Kiley's nod, Ariana spread her hand over Kiley's abdomen. "For good luck and God's blessing. Have you been trying long?"

"We weren't trying at all." A blush touched Kiley's cheeks. "I was nearly run down by an SUV when I ran into the street to save Nicolò's dog. Afterward, he and I… Well, one thing led to another and somewhere on our journey between the one thing and the other, we forgot a few vital steps, steps that ended up with me pregnant. Not that I'm complaining."

"You're happy then?"

Kiley reached for Nicolò's hand and tears filled her eyes. "Ecstatic."

Ariana turned to give Francesca another hug of congratulations. "I don't have to ask how you feel. You're glowing."

Francesca chuckled. "I couldn't be happier. Maybe that's because I'm not suffering from morning sickness the way Kiley is."

"It will end soon," Nonna offered.

Primo caught his wife's hand in his. "And do you see boys or girls in their future?"

"Boys for these two." Her gaze landed on Ariana, her eyes eerily similar to Lazz's. Then her face lit up. "But you. You will have a daughter. The only Dante girl of your generation, I'm sad to say."

"Nonna—" Lazz began.

Ariana shushed him before giving Nonna a swift hug. "You have the sight? My great-grandmother Romano did, as well. Everything she predicted always came true. This is her veil I'm wearing."

"Nonna predicted my pregnancy," Francesca warned. "So, I'd start knitting little pink booties, if I were you."

"I'll get right on it. But after the honeymoon if you don't mind," Ariana teased. To her surprise, even Lazz laughed.

"I am glad you mentioned the honeymoon," Primo said. "Penelope, Nonna and I all have a small surprise for the two of you. Lazz, I know you said there is no time for a honeymoon right now, but I have made arrangements for Caitlyn to fill in for you while you and Ariana go away."

Beside her, Lazz stiffened. "You shouldn't have—" he began, before being waved silent by his grandfather.

"These past six months have been long and difficult for you." Fierce golden eyes gazed at his grandson with compassion. "You deserve a break."

"The Romanos are well acquainted with the royal families of Verdonia," Penelope contributed. "So, we've arranged for you to stay there. Your flight leaves tomorrow."

"What a lovely gesture," Ariana said. "Thank you so much. You're all too generous."

Lazz added his thanks to her own, then kissed his grandparents, as well as Penelope. Only Vittorio didn't contribute to the celebration. Ariana sensed his concern and did her best to alleviate it with a cheerful demeanor. So long as he found Brimstone before Lazz uncovered their deception, all would be fine. Otherwise… She shuddered. She didn't want to consider the alternatives.

The minute she and Lazz were alone again, she regarded him with a hint of uncertainty. "You don't seem as upset as I expected you to be."

"I'm not."

"You surprise me."

He lifted a shoulder in a casual shrug. "This gives us time to get to know each other. By the time we return, we'll be more relaxed together."

"Like an old married couple?"

"Something like that." He lifted an eyebrow. "Now you're the one who looks upset. You knew we were going to have to convince our grandparents that we're happily married before gradually going our separate ways. This will help the process along."

"They're going to find out eventually," she murmured.

"They'll find out that the marriage didn't work out. They won't find out why we married in the first place."

"They'd be crushed if they knew."

"Knowing Primo, he'd dispose of Brimstone just to make that point." Lazz inclined his head toward the head table. "Recess is over, I'm afraid. Time to resume our duties."

The rest of the reception passed with a breathtaking swiftness. Before she knew it, Lazz caught her hand and drew her from the ballroom onto a shadow-dipped balcony overlooking downtown San Francisco. When she shot him a questioning glance, he merely smiled.

"They expect us to leave early. We're supposed to be eager newlyweds, remember?"

She shook her head in amusement. "How silly of me. Of course. We'd probably shock our guests if we insisted on dancing the night away. Still…" She crossed to the railing and gazed out at the glittering lights of the city. Fog stretched out stealthy fingers, reaching for the streets closest to the bay. "It was a lovely reception. Thank you for putting it together."

"I didn't—"

"Please, don't." Her smile faltered for an instant before she had it safely back in place. "Please, don't tell me you weren't responsible. I'd like that much of an illusion, if you don't mind."

"Actually, I was going to say that I didn't expect it to turn out as well as it did," he said gently. "And I was responsible, though I had help."

"From Caitlyn?"

"Among others. Come on." He dropped an arm around her shoulders. "Le Premier has reserved the honeymoon suite for us tonight."

"And tomorrow we fly off to Verdonia," she said, hoping her nervousness didn't show. "I guess that means we better get a decent night's sleep. Tomorrow's flight will be a long one."

"Then I suggest we turn in." His face slid into shadow, while ambient light caught in the depths of his hazel eyes. "And when we get to our room, you can decide whether you'd care to break one of your marital conditions."

Three

From: Bambolina@fornitore.it
Date: 2008, August 05 18:41 CEST
To: Lazzaro_Dante@DantesJewelry.com
Subject: Re: Marriage Contract, Premarital Conditions…**mine!**

Dear Lazzaro,

I'm sure you will understand the need for my first counter-condition, especially since our marriage is not permanent.

Counter-Condition #1: No sex.

Short and sweet, yes?

Ciao! Ariana

P.S. I guess that means we'll need separate bedrooms. Do you wish me to make that a separate counter-condition?

Ariana didn't say a word. Not as they left the balcony, nor during the endless elevator ride to their suite. She didn't dare speak in the face of such overwhelming temptation.

She hadn't expected such a strong physical response to Lazz. Perhaps she should have, since she'd been drawn to him every single time she'd been in his presence, starting at the tender age of five. When she'd seen him in Marco's conference room, some part of her had instinctively sensed the connection between them. She'd even told her father that Lazz was the one.

The one she'd cried over at five.

The one who called to her on some visceral level.

The one who'd connected them with a single touch.

"Looks like someone's been here ahead of us," Lazz commented as they entered the suite.

Sure enough, flowers covered every available surface, including the huge canopied bed, although in the case of the bed they were deep velvety red petals, with a pair of long-stem roses decorating the pillows.

"I don't see luggage anywhere," she said. "Should we ring for it?"

A hint of a smile carved a path across Lazz's mouth. "I'm guessing no one thought you would need luggage until tomorrow. Other than this…" He snagged a swath of virtually transparent ivory silk that had been spread across the down duvet topping their bed. He lifted an eyebrow. "Do you need help changing?"

Oh, heaven help her. Surely, she hadn't been left with just her wedding gown and…and that. Ariana cleared her throat. "I think I mentioned that my mother doesn't know that we're not—" She gave an expressive shrug. "I'm sure she meant it as a romantic gesture."

Tossing her nightgown to the bed, he proceeded to strip off his tux jacket. "I don't have any objections. Nor am I offended." He ripped his tie free of its mooring, allowing the ribbon of black silk to flutter to the carpet. "And you still haven't answered my question. Either of my questions, for that matter."

If he'd asked any questions, she'd already forgotten. His unnerving striptease had driven them straight out of her head. "I'm sorry…?"

A hungry smile slipped across his face. He worked the onyx studs free of his shirt and dropped them onto the bedside table. "Do you need help undressing?" he prompted. "And how soon can we break your first marital condition?"

It took a heartbeat to force her gaze from his gaping shirt and the broad expanse of golden chest beneath. Another heartbeat to gather her wits enough to respond. "Yes, as a matter of fact, I do need help undressing."

She crossed to Lazz's side with as much composure as she could summon. There was something about a half-undressed man that struck her as downright dangerous to the female psyche, particularly when the other half was clothed in formal wear. Maybe it was the incongruity she found so appealing. Somehow she'd have to find a way to ignore it, though she didn't have a clue how. Not when a relentless tug of desire attacked all her senses at once, leaving her totally defenseless.

Presenting her back to him, she asked, "Would you mind unbuttoning my gown?"

"My pleasure. And you still haven't answered my other question."

He stroked a hand down the length of her spine. Even through the heavy satin of the material, she could feel the heat of his touch. Feel the tautening of the connection between them. "The answer is never," she managed to say. "I don't intend to break any of my pre-marital conditions."

"Or allow me to?"

"No." Yes, please. Soon and often.

"Are you certain?"

She fought to control her shudder of awareness. More than anything, she wanted to throw herself in his arms and beg him to make love to her. To complete whatever odd bond had formed between them during their wedding ceremony. But she couldn't. She wouldn't.

"I'm positive."

To her relief, he accepted her response without argument though she could sense that he forcibly held himself in check. "I have to admit, this is a first for me," he admitted. "I've never helped a woman out of a wedding gown before."

"I wish you hadn't told me that."

"Why?"

She felt the subtle give of her gown. "It makes me sad."

"Sad, that you're the first I've ever stripped out of a wedding gown?" A hint of amusement ran through his words. The back of his hand brushed against her skin, eliciting a shiver she couldn't quite suppress. "I would think that would make you happy."

"I'm not your true bride, or it would. It makes me sad thinking of your future wife and the fact that all the things that should be a first with her are a first with me, instead." She twisted around, holding her gown against her breasts. In the short time her back had been to him, a darkness had wiped all emotion from his face, turning it remote and forbidding. "Perhaps I'm not phrasing it well," she murmured.

"You phrased it just fine."

"I've annoyed you. I am sorry."

"Not at all." He made a circle with his finger, a silent demand that she turn around again. "I'm not quite done."

"Oh, of course." She did as he requested, forcing herself to stand perfectly still while he finished unbuttoning her gown. "It's just that these little memories should be special. I don't want to tarnish them."

He'd reached the last button, but instead of releasing her, he cupped her hips and slid her tight against him. Her breath escaped in a silent gasp, and she froze as his bare chest pressed against her bare back, heat against heat. One hand slid from her hip to settle low on her abdomen where one day she hoped a child would nestle. Desire intensified, driving her nearly insane with need. She could feel the strong, tensed muscles of his thighs and knew he was aroused. Seriously aroused. Knew that she'd done that to him, just as he'd done the same to her.

"What about you?" he asked. An almost guttural quality slid through his voice. "Am I tarnishing sacred memories for you and your future husband?"

"No, because this isn't real." But it felt real. His

hands on her. Their partial nudity. The want that thickened the air and made it difficult to breathe. A wedding night waiting to happen. It felt all too real. "Someday I'll have a real marriage. But this isn't it. It can't be."

"It can, if you let it." He spun her around. "Let's start with that kiss we shared. Let's find out whether that was real…or pure imagination."

And then he took her mouth in a kiss reserved for lovers, one that claimed, just as it seduced. A kiss that proved that what they'd felt earlier hadn't been imagination, not unless they were both experiencing the exact same fantasy. Time seemed to halt, to give them endless seconds to wallow in the moment. This man could have brought stone to life, Ariana decided, and she was far from stone. If she could have melded her body to his, she would have. Instead, she simply gave everything she had within her. And then she gave more.

He slid his fingers deep into her hair as he consumed her, tumbling them from one delicious connection into the next. "I don't give a damn what we agreed. I need you."

And she needed him. Needed the hardness of his mouth over hers. Needed the delicious blaze of heat. She wanted to fill her lungs with his breath, to inhale his scent and taste and revel in the very air that sustained him.

Every nerve in her body screamed in surrender, making it almost impossible to resist the inevitable. Somehow she managed. "We have an agreement." The words were barely more than a whisper.

He pulled back just far enough to allow sanity to slip between them. "An agreement…or a suggestion?"

"It was an agreement you promised to honor," she insisted. "Please let go of me."

He bent his head and buried a final kiss in the sensitive curve between her neck and shoulder. Fire flashed through her, arrowing from her breasts straight to the warm feminine core of her, and a deep yearning threatened all she held most dear. "No one needs to know." The words hovered, tantalizing with possibility.

"I would know." Could he feel how she trembled? Could he sense her longing? She needed to stop him while she could still stop herself. She spoke with difficulty, fighting to translate her thoughts into English. And still her tongue stumbled over the words. "And it would prevent us from getting an annulment. Since we were married in the church, and since Romanos don't believe in divorce, we can't take this any further."

To her profound relief—or was it regret?—he released her. "If that's your preference."

She clutched the bodice of her gown to her breasts to keep it from slipping. "It is." Not. Most decidedly, not. She didn't dare look at him in case her conflicted emotions showed on her face. "I'll use the bathroom first, if you don't mind."

"Fine." He stopped her with a touch, one that raced across her skin like wildfire. "Fair warning, Mrs. Dante. There's only one bed, and I'm not feeling terribly chivalrous, particularly with the flight we have to look forward to tomorrow. I hope you don't mind sharing."

"Not at all." She spared the bed a brief, wistful glance. "It's large enough to house an entire family. We'll just stake out opposite sides."

By the time she removed her wedding gown and used the toiletries supplied by the hotel, she managed to gather up the tattered remains of her equilibrium. She also managed to silence her wayward body and the wicked suggestions it screamed by drowning every hungry inch in an icy shower. Though she attempted to convince herself otherwise, the remnants of his touch remained, soft echoes of helpless passion.

She smothered the echoes beneath a luxurious Le Premier bathrobe, one that enveloped her sheer nightgown. She emerged from the bathroom to find Lazz relaxing in the bed, reading a newspaper. The fact that he was quite likely nude beneath the sheets—after all, her mother hadn't left any nighttime garments for him—threw her enough that she spoke in Italian instead of English.

"Ah, the perfect picture of domestic bliss," she teased.

He glanced up and returned her grin, though she suspected it had more to do with the voluminous bathrobe than her comment. "I put a buffer between us," he said, indicating the line of pillows that divided the bed. "I hope it will make you feel more comfortable."

"I assume you're a man of your word?"

"Of course."

She grabbed the pillows and tossed them to the floor. "Then I trust you without these."

As soon as she'd stripped off the bathrobe and climbed into bed, he turned out the light. At first the darkness seemed impenetrable. But gradually her eyesight adjusted, and she managed to make out the various pieces of furniture scattered around the suite. She also managed to make out her husband's form. Other than tossing aside the newspaper, he hadn't altered his position. He continued to lounge against a mountain of pillows, his arms folded behind his head. In the darkness his breathing seemed deep and heavy. Hungry. Teetering on the edge of action.

She rushed into speech before opportunity became deed. "You know, you never explained what happened in the church. What caused that shock when we touched?"

"As I said before, it wasn't anything."

She sat up in order to plump her pillows and adjust the bedding. Nerves. Nerves were making her restless and chatty. Maybe she should have had that second glass of champagne she'd been offered during the endless round of toasts. It might have helped her sleep. She spared Lazz a swift glance. Or maybe not. No telling what foolish decisions she'd be tempted to make while under the influence.

"And yet, you also said there was something you weren't telling me," she persisted. "When we were in the limousine, remember?"

"It's nothing. A family legend."

"A legend? That sounds interesting." She wriggled around in an effort to find a comfortable spot in the massive bed. Since the most comfortable spot was in Lazz's arms, she didn't expect to meet with much success. Exasperated, she said, "Since I'm not sleeping and you're not sleeping, why don't you tell me about it."

"I'm surprised you haven't already heard. But perhaps you don't read gossip magazines."

"I have read a few," she admitted. "*The Snitch*. But

when Papa came across it, he was furious and banned the paper from the estate. Since then I've been gossip free."

"Well, that explains it." Lazz fell silent, and for a brief moment Ariana wondered if he'd decided against telling her his "secret." Not that she didn't sympathize, considering she had a few of her own. And then he spoke. "Our family claims an odd sort of legacy. I consider it a not-so-charming fairy tale."

"But some of your family think this legacy is real?"

"Yes. It's called The Inferno."

She instantly clicked on the play on words. "Dantes' Inferno? I love it. What is this Inferno? And who in your family believes in it?"

"Most of them," he admitted. Reluctance tore through his words. "I don't know about my cousins, but all of my brothers claim to have experienced it. In fact, Primo and Nonna are under the impression we're marrying because of The Inferno, and I intend to keep it that way."

"I gather you don't believe in it?"

"Not even a little."

"Yet, you expect us to pretend we feel it?"

"Yes."

Ariana rubbed her thumb against the center of her palm where the spark between them had first originated and where the heat from it still seemed to dwell. That spark hadn't been nothing, despite what Lazz might claim. Could it be from this Inferno Lazz insisted didn't exist? It would certainly explain a lot.

"How can I pretend to feel The Inferno if I don't know what it is?" she asked with a touch of his logic. "Won't your grandparents expect me to know?"

"Yeah. I didn't think of that, but they will expect it." He shifted in the bed, rolling over to face her. Darkness hid his expression from her, but not his scent. Not his size. Not the fascinating ridges and valleys his body created beneath the sheets. Those were all too apparent. "It's…it's a connection. A bond. My brothers claim they experienced it the first time they touched their wives."

Ariana's breath caught in sudden understanding. "And if I asked them, would they say The Inferno felt something like an electric shock?"

"They might," Lazz conceded. "According to my brothers, after they touched, they were so overcome with desire, they couldn't think straight."

"Unlike what we felt in church. You were completely in control when you kissed me, right?"

She could practically hear him grind his teeth at her irony. "You're a beautiful woman. It's only natural that I'd be sexually attracted to you. It has nothing to do with The Inferno. The Inferno isn't real."

"Is it that The Inferno isn't real? Or is it that you consider yourself too logical to experience it?"

"It isn't real. I am logical. Therefore, how could I possibly experience it? What my brothers felt toward their wives is simple lust, nothing more. They chose to call it The Inferno because it puts a polite word to emotions that are more carnal than romantic."

She pounced on the flaw in his argument. "Then explain what happened when we first touched. Or didn't you feel what I did?"

"I felt something. But it wasn't because of some ridiculous legend."

A sudden idea occurred to Ariana, and she fought

to speak without inflection. "Do you deny it because you experienced this Inferno with Caitlyn? Do you believe you can't feel that with another woman?"

"It's only supposed to happen with one woman. I thought I felt something with her," Lazz confessed. "Once. It happened—" He broke off, swearing beneath his breath.

"What?" She sat up in bed. "I don't understand. When did it happen?"

"It doesn't matter."

"It does matter," she insisted. "When did it happen?"

"The morning after she married Marco."

"In the conference room? When you attacked your brother?" When she and her father had been there to witness the fight? When she'd been seized by that overpowering attraction to Lazz?

"Yes. But what happened that day doesn't have anything to do with us or our situation. Or, God forbid, The Inferno."

His words shouldn't hurt. For some reason, they did. "Because ours is a temporary marriage, right?" She didn't wait for a response. "Just out of curiosity, what are you looking for in a wife, if not The Inferno?"

Lazz hesitated long enough that Ariana thought he wouldn't answer. And then he said, "I'd rather have a marriage based on compatibility. On reason. On mutual likes and dislikes. Once emotion subsides, there has to be something to keep the marriage together. All The Inferno offers is physical desire. I want more than that."

Is that what he'd found with Caitlyn? "And yet, it seems to have worked out for your brothers. I gather you believe you have some sort of special immunity, is that it?"

Lazz moved with lightning speed. One minute he lounged safely next to her and the next Ariana found herself caged beneath him. He interlaced their fingers, and she felt again that odd burn within her palm. Not that he seemed to notice. But then, maybe he was distracted by the way he anchored her body to the mattress, filling her soft contours with hard male angles, forcing her to give to his take. His take of space. His take of control. He even seemed to take the air she fought to pull into her lungs.

"Listen to me, Ariana. What you and I felt earlier was a natural desire. If you want to pursue that desire to its natural conclusion, I'd be delighted to accommodate you." He freed a hand and used it to cup her breast. His thumb drifted across the hardened peak, showing her without words how easily and how well that accommodation would be. "But don't expect anything more than the conditions we both agreed to."

His words doused the desire screaming through her body. "Thank you for making that clear." She made the mistake of speaking in Italian again and deliberately switched to English. "If you don't mind, I think I'll go to sleep now."

His tantalizing movements stilled. "I assume you prefer to do that without me on top of you?"

"You assume correctly."

He lowered his head and skated his mouth across hers. Just a light, tender brush of lips against lips. Her groan slipped out as he slipped in. He told her without words how it could be between them, showed her with a simple mating of their mouths and tongues how he would turn her world upside down.

But where would that leave her afterward? She'd have given everything and been left with nothing but heartache. Lazz didn't believe in the possibilities or in the connection that had sparked to life between them. And a night in his arms, no matter how blissful, wouldn't change that.

"I gather the answer is still no."

Ariana didn't trust herself to speak, not with the frantic words fighting for release. Words that would beg him to hold her. To make love to her. To give her a wedding night she'd never forget. But it would only add complications on top of complications, especially with Brimstone missing. She pushed against his shoulders, still unable to reply. He rolled off of her without another word.

She didn't expect to sleep, not considering her intense awareness of the man beside her and not with her emotions in such turmoil. Not only did she long to give in to base instinct but she also knew that part of her, a secret childish part, wished that she could experience The Inferno with Lazz.

She couldn't help but wonder if maybe, just maybe, the reaction she had to his touch—and his response to hers—might mean that her secret wish had come true. What if the odd sensations they'd shared were from The Inferno? How would that change her plans for the future?

And how did she convince her husband that his plans for the future should change, too?

The instant Lazz and Ariana's plane touched down in Verdonia, they were whisked by limousine through the mountainous principality of Avernos to the private estate of the newly elected king, Brandt von Folke.

"According to my grandmother, King Brandt was elected about eighteen months ago," Ariana said.

Lazz lifted an eyebrow . "Elected? I gather succession doesn't follow hereditary lines in Verdonia."

"No, it doesn't. Here, they gather up all the eligible royals and have an election by the people. King Brandt won. My grandparents knew his grandfather, King Grandon. We used to visit when I was a child."

"Which explains your family's ability to pull a few royal strings and arrange our honeymoon trip."

"Exactly."

The car pulled up to the front of an enormous structure, part palace and part fortress. Hewn from local stone, it offered a hard, cold welcome in complete opposition to their reception by Brandt and Miri von Folke, both of whom Ariana remembered having met as a child.

After the formal introductions, Brandt arranged for refreshments and then surprised them by waving aside their use of his title. "There's no need," he insisted. "This isn't a state function, and I have as little interest in titles as my grandfather."

A baby of close to a year crawled over to Ariana and held out his arms imperiously. The minute she acquiesced and gathered him up, he gazed around and beamed in delight. "And who is this little one?" she asked in amusement.

"Thomas Grandon," Miri replied. "He's named after Brandt's father and grandfather. My brother, Lander, and his wife, Juliana, have a little girl the same age.

And we're expecting a call any minute from my brother, Merrick, about his wife, Alyssa. When he phoned a few hours ago, she was in labor."

As though in response to her comment, the door opened and a huge man appeared in the doorway. "A call for you, Your Highness. It's Prince Merrick."

"Thanks, Tolken." Miri shot to her feet. "This is it. I'll be right back. Oh, I hope Alyssa and the baby are safe and healthy."

Brandt reassured her with a simple touch. "They're fine. Now go and find out whether we have a new niece or nephew." He smiled at Ariana and Lazz. "They decided to be old-fashioned and keep the sex a surprise. Miri's been on pins and needles for months."

"I hope our arrival hasn't inconvenienced you," Lazz said. "We appreciate your allowing us to use your private cabin for our honeymoon."

Brandt waved that aside. "It's the perfect spot. The original cabin burned down a while back. We've replaced it, though this one is a bit snug."

Ariana shot a nervous glance in Lazz's direction. Just how snug was snug? "I'm sure it'll be perfect."

"I have fond memories of the place. Miri and I…" He broke off with a smile that turned his face from austere to warm and approachable. "Well, let's just say that our stay there changed our lives."

"Thank you so much for sharing it with us," Ariana murmured.

"Our pleasure." He rubbed his hands together. "Now, let me just go over a few particulars. The cabin is fully stocked for the week you'll be there. We've had electricity installed, but it goes down at the least provocation. There's a generator and propane to fuel it." He lifted an eyebrow in Lazz's direction. "Are you familiar with running a generator?"

"My family has a cabin that requires a generator. We were all taught how to work it—as well as maintain it—from an early age."

"Perfect. The generator is powerful enough to keep the refrigerator and freezer going, should you lose power. Tolken will arrange to provide you with cell phones. Again, the mountains make reception spotty, and this time of year our mountains send us some rather spectacular storms. I should warn you that they hit fast and hard. But I'll have someone call in a warning so they don't catch you off guard."

Lazz inclined his head. "Much appreciated."

"As soon as you're refreshed, I've arranged for my helicopter to fly you out and drop you off."

Ariana stiffened, fighting to conceal her alarm. "The cabin isn't accessible by car?"

"By four-wheel and even then with difficulty." He lifted a single eyebrow, and Ariana was painfully aware of his royal status. "Is that a problem?"

"Not at all," Lazz interrupted smoothly. "I can't think of a better way to spend our honeymoon."

Ariana forced an enthusiastic smile. "Nor can I."

Miri appeared just then, saving them from an awkward moment. "A boy. Eight pounds, two ounces," she announced in a breathless rush. Tears gathered in her eyes. "They've named him Stefan, after our father."

"He was our former king," Brandt explained in a low tone. "And succeeded my grandfather. His death was a great loss to all of us."

"I'm sure he would have been so proud to have his legacy continue," Ariana offered gently.

Brandt gave her a look of quiet approval before turning to his wife and gathering her close. "Would you care to freshen up before your departure?" he asked them.

It was clearly a dismissal, though one Ariana completely understood. This was an intimate moment. A time for family. For some reason, it caused her to slip her hand into Lazz's. She could feel the tug of the peculiar bond that had formed between them. He might deny that it was The Inferno, but whatever the link, it hummed with urgency.

"We can freshen up at the cabin," Lazz said. "We'll go ahead and leave you now."

The comment made Ariana smile, since she'd been about to say the same thing. "Please extend our good wishes to Prince Merrick and Princess Alyssa. It was a pleasure to see you both again after all these years." She crouched beside Thomas and ruffled his dark hair. "And it was especially nice to meet you, Prince Thomas."

Tolken returned a few minutes later and escorted them to the waiting chopper. "Your luggage is already loaded." He handed them a leather satchel. "This contains a pair of cell phones with emergency contact numbers. Don't hesitate to call if you need anything. King Brandt has put me entirely at your disposal."

Lazz offered his hand. "Thank you. If you don't hear from us, we'll see you in a week."

Tolken shook hands and then assisted Ariana into her seat and helped her strap in. A few minutes later, the helicopter lifted off the ground. It hovered over the estate for a few minutes, affording them a gorgeous bird's-eye view of the palace and grounds before banking northward.

The surrounding mountains were a deep, lush green with towering conifers and a scattering of oak, beech and alder. Eventually, they soared over one of the higher mountain peaks and drifted down toward a large clearing beside a sparkling green lake. White imported sand cupped the side closest to a small cabin. A very small cabin, Ariana noticed.

After touchdown, the pilot gave them a hand with their luggage. "Is there anything else I can do for you before heading back?" he asked.

"I think we can manage from here," Lazz assured him.

"The generator is housed in the shed over there." The pilot pointed toward a structure that abutted the edge of the forest. "And you'll find fishing gear in the boathouse down by the lake."

"Sounds fantastic."

The pilot lifted two fingers to his brow in a casual salute. "Enjoy yourself. If you need anything, I'm only a phone call away."

Lazz opened the door to the cabin and carried the luggage inside, but Ariana waited, watching as their only connection to civilization slowly rose. Its blades flattened the grass and kicked up small dirt devils before it tilted to one side and zipped southward on its return flight. A moment later, the earsplitting thump of the blade faded away as the helicopter vanished over the nearest mountaintop.

Ariana released her breath in a sigh and turned to

enter the cabin. It took her eyes a moment to adjust from the bright sunlight to the shadowed duskiness of the interior. The minute her vision cleared, she shook her head in disbelief.

"Call him back," she demanded in Italian. "There's no way I'm staying here."

Four

From: Lazzaro_Dante@DantesJewelry.com
Date: 2008, August 05 09:54 PDST
To: Bambolina@fornitore.it
Subject: Marriage Contract, Premarital Conditions, Additional

I think you're kidding yourself if you think either of us can go without sex for three whole months. I suggest you reconsider. And no, you don't need to make separate bedrooms a separate counter-condition. That's a given. In the meantime, here's my next premarital condition.

Condition #3: Occasional displays of public affection may be necessary in order to maintain the facade of a "normal" marriage.

L.

From: Bambolina@fornitore.it
Date: 2008, August 05 19:06 CEST
To: Lazzaro_Dante@DantesJewelry.com
Subject: Re: Marriage Contract, Premarital Conditions, Additional
Allow me to assure you that I am not kidding myself. I take sex very seriously. My first condition stands. *Capito?*
As for condition #3... Just what sort of public displays do you have in mind? I have the distinct impression your idea of a "normal" marriage and mine are quite different.
Ciao! Ariana

Lazz folded his arms across his chest. "We are not calling him back."

"I can't stay here with you." She waved her hand to indicate the interior of the cabin. "It's too... Too..."

"Intimate?"

"Yes!" She glanced at the bed and swiftly away again. "That mattress is barely big enough for one, let alone two. I thought kings had giant beds. *King-size* beds."

Lazz lifted an eyebrow at her phrasing, and a broad smile came and went. "Never having been a king, I can't say. I assume, considering how isolated this place is, they elected to stick with sizes that were easily transported. Or maybe Brandt and Miri prefer sleeping on top of each other."

She spared the bed a final, uneasy look. "Lazz—" she began.

He shook his head, adamant. "Forget it, Ariana. We're not going to refuse von Folke's hospitality. It would be rude, and word of it would get back to our grandparents."

That stopped her. She stared at him, stricken. "But what are we going to do?"

"We're going to do just what we agreed before our marriage. We're going to make the best of it."

"I can't even turn around without bumping into you."

"Bump into me as much as you like. I can live with it."

In fact, the idea appealed. A lot. The tension between them had already climbed to unbearable levels. At some point one of them would trip over that condition of hers and they'd both take a fall—preferably onto the nearest bed, no matter how narrow. As far as he was concerned, the sooner, the better.

She hesitated, no doubt wanting to react to the comment. He sensed his darling wife—and how he stumbled over *that* word—felt as edgy as he did. Their wedding night had been rough, the awareness they'd felt toward each other both unexpected and surprising, and not an issue either of them had anticipated dealing with. Although, if he were honest, he should have anticipated it. When two people were locked in a marriage, it was only natural that a severe case of intimacy was bound to break out at some point or another.

Now they'd gotten themselves into a situation they couldn't escape…a situation that threatened to break more than one of the conditions the two of them had made before their marriage. He could only hope his lasted longer than hers. Lazz studied Ariana and realized with a kick of amusement that she continued to hover by the door.

"You look like you're on the verge of running," he said.

"I'm considering it."

"Why don't you come on in and take a look around?"

Her expression soured. "I think I can pretty much see everything from here."

"It's supposed to be a romantic getaway, which may explain why there's more bedroom than anything else." He inclined his head toward the shadowed interior. "There's a small kitchen and a huge bathroom with a tiled shower stall and a tub that's larger than the bed."

"Maybe I can sleep in there." She turned her attention to the stone fireplace and the small sitting area that contained a deep love seat and a striking table made of a variety of inlaid hardwoods. "Very cozy."

"It's only for a week."

"I'm being ungracious, aren't I? That's considered a deadly sin for a Romano. I think I'll blame it on exhaustion." She took a deep breath and surprised him with a serene smile. "I'm sure this will be fine. Why don't I check out the kitchen and fix us some coffee?"

"I'll get it."

"In that case, I'll unpack our suitcases." Her smile turned teasing. "Maybe that'll give us more room to maneuver."

Considering the bags for their honeymoon trip had shown up in their bridal suite at the same time as their breakfast, their luggage fully packed and ready to go, he had no idea what they contained. "Let's hope whoever packed them for us threw in some swimsuits." And sleepwear that covered a bit more of Ariana than the night-gown she'd worn on their wedding night. Otherwise, he wouldn't survive the first night, let alone a full week.

While he prepared the coffee, Ariana unzipped the first suitcase. "Tons of casual wear and—hallelujah—a bathing suit."

After transferring the clothes from the suitcase to the dresser, she unearthed a sketch pad and pencils. He eyed it curiously as he offered her a lightly steaming mug. "Do you draw?"

"I do, yes." She accepted the mug and inhaled the fragrant scent of the coffee. Then she let out a low sigh of pleasure, one that wreaked havoc with his self-control. "What little talent I have, I inherited from my grandmother," she confessed.

He lifted an eyebrow in surprise. "Penelope?"

"Mmm. So what would you like to do first?" Her deliberate change of subject roused his curiosity, but he let it go for the time being. "After that flight, I wouldn't mind taking a short hike."

"Before jet lag hits?"

"Actually, my internal time clock will adjust faster than yours, since I'm now back in the same time zone as Italy."

"With all the traveling I've done for Dantes, I've discovered that a solid workout helps most." And maybe it would douse the tiny sparks of arousal that grew hotter and more pervasive the longer he remained cooped up in the cabin with her. "I'm up for a hike if you are. We can get a feel for the surroundings."

She smiled brightly. "Give me a second to change into a pair of shorts, and I'll be ready to go."

He worked them hard, following a trail that wound around the lake. At one point, he glanced over at Ariana. Realizing he was setting a blistering pace, he deliberately slowed down. It took her less than a dozen steps before she clued in. Throwing him a challenging look, she dashed ahead, her teasing laughter drifting back to him. He lagged behind, allowing her to build up a decent lead before pouring on the power. The instant she heard his footsteps pounding closer, she sped up.

She had glorious legs, long and toned and shapely. He quickly discovered just how she kept them in shape. She ran like she'd been born to do nothing else, moving with a supple grace. The ease with which she hurdled obstacles in their path would have done a gazelle proud. And as far as he was concerned, the view was spectacular. Not only did he get to admire her legs, but a gloriously rounded backside, as well.

He waited until they reached the final curve of the lake before overtaking her. The instant the dirt path turned to sand, he swooped in and snatched her high into his arms. Her shriek echoed across the lake, sending a brace of ducks airborne. He carried her a half dozen steps before flinging himself and his delectable armful into the shallows.

"How about a swim?" he suggested when she surfaced, sputtering.

For an instant, she simply stared at him. Then a laugh broke free. "You are insane."

Ariana flipped her hair back from her face, the dark length streaming down her back like an ebony waterfall. The bright sunlight reflected off the strands, catching in ruby highlights that Lazz had never noticed before. His gaze slipped lower, and the breath stopped dead in his lungs. She wore a thin, very wet, cotton shirt. The brilliant red clung to her upper torso, molding itself to generous breasts that were a fantasy come true.

He struggled to do the honorable thing and look away. But somehow his eyeballs had become disconnected from his brain. "Do me a favor, will you?" he asked politely.

She planted her hands on her hips. "You just threw me in the water, and now you want *me* to do *you* a favor?"

"Or not."

She relented with a smile. "What's the favor?"

"I seem to be having trouble controlling my caveman genes. Would you mind ducking down a little?"

Fate rewarded him with a few more seconds of visual bliss before comprehension set in. With a gasp, she sank downward so the water lapped around her shoulders. "Did your caveman genes enjoy the view?" she asked acerbically, her accent a bit more pronounced than before.

"They did. They really did."

She spared him a disgruntled look, one that took on an appreciative glint. "I must admit, my cavewoman genes are having some enjoyment, as well. Maybe too much enjoyment. If you don't mind, I think I'll go in and change."

He nodded. "Feel free."

She lifted an eyebrow in a manner as regal as it was pure Romano. "Would you mind turning around?"

"I'm afraid I would mind. But don't let that stop you."

Her mouth twitched and she splashed water at him. "You are a rotten man."

"Not rotten. But definitely all man."

He lunged at her, catching her around the waist and yanking her into his arms. He didn't give her time to catch her breath, let alone protest. He took her mouth in a kiss as thorough and urgent as the one they'd shared on their wedding night.

Her mouth was warm and wet and the most delicious thing he'd ever tasted. This time there weren't any witnesses to the embrace, and he could take his time and explore at his leisure. He half expected her to resist, to slap him or give him hell in Italian.

To his surprise, her curiosity matched his own. Her hands slipped upward to trace the contours of his face before sliding into his hair and tugging. But it wasn't a demand for release. It was a silent appeal for more.

With a harsh groan, he mated her mouth with his, deepening the kiss until their breath became one. His hands swept up and under her shirt and closed over her breasts. They were every bit as full and lush as they'd appeared through her wet shirt, the skin like velvet against his palms. The peaks turned to hard nubs beneath his touch, and he captured them between his fingers, torturing a moan of sheer pleasure from her.

For a tantalizing moment she pressed herself more fully into his embrace, giving with the soft want that was uniquely woman. Water swirled between them, carrying them together so their hips fit male to female. A groan snagged in his throat. It would be so easy to strip away the thin layers of clothing separating them and mate more than just their mouths. His hands swept downward, his thumbs hooking into the waistband of her shorts. Before he could slip them off her hips, she twisted free.

Wrapping her arms around herself, she dragged air into her lungs. "We shouldn't have done that," she informed him the instant she could speak.

"It was bound to happen, if only for curiosity's sake."

"Is your curiosity satisfied?"

"My curiosity's satisfied. But it hasn't done a damn thing for the rest of me."

"No, it hasn't done a damn thing for my rest, either." She slid her hands across her face as though to scrub the lingering traces of passion from it. "I would like to go inside and change. Would you mind staying here for a few minutes so I might have some privacy?"

"Of course."

He tormented himself a bit more by watching her wade from the lake before working off his libido with a long, hard swim. By the time he'd finished, all he could think about was food and sleep. Okay, he thought about Ariana, too. Most of all, he wondered how long it would take to talk her out of her first condition and into bed.

By the time he'd showered himself human again and changed into dry clothes, she had dinner prepared. "I'm not very good in the kitchen," she warned.

"That makes two of us."

She shrugged. "In that case, we'll take turns poisoning each other."

She'd done a reasonable job, punching up the canned soup with grated cheese, spinach, and roasted garlic. She'd also warmed up a loaf of bread and thrown together an olive oil and herb dipping sauce. Finally, she served them a salad topped with grilled chicken.

"I thought you said you didn't cook well," he commented as he polished off the last of the bread.

She lifted a shoulder. "You'll see. It's all downhill from here."

He grinned. "That's only because I fix dinner next."

"You know, I'm discovering you have a very nice sense of humor," she observed. "I like that about you. I worried during our negotiations because you were very…serious. Very autocratic."

His grin faded. "Having a sense of humor doesn't turn me into Marco."

"And I'm not Caitlyn." She shrugged again. "If we were honest, I think we'd both admit that we wouldn't want it otherwise. Even though my grandmother adored your brother, she was concerned that I might fall in love with him."

"I gather she didn't like that idea."

Ariana shook her head. "Not at all. She said he was all wrong for me. Charming, yes. A heart bigger than all of Italy, true. But he was missing something a husband should have."

"And what's that?" He couldn't have stopped the question if his life depended on it.

"She said a woman should only marry someone who has a clear sense of right and wrong and that sliver of gray that divides the two. In that sliver lies compassion, she always claimed. It was a quality my grandfather had. Before we left for Verdonia, she told me she saw that sliver in you."

He couldn't think of a higher compliment, though he

doubted Penelope would still be of that opinion if she knew the real reason he and Ariana had married. "I like the way your grandmother thinks." He tilted his head to one side. "How did she end up in a wheelchair?"

"It was from a car accident. She and my grandfather went over an embankment on a remote mountain road while touring Germany. They weren't located for two days. It was in all the newspapers at the time."

He stared, shocked. "My God."

"It was a hideous tragedy. My family kept the worst of the details from me, but I read copies of the reports on the Internet." It took her a moment to continue. "They said my grandfather was thrown clear of the car, but was badly injured. He died shortly before the rescuers found them. If they'd gotten there sooner, he'd have survived."

"And your grandmother?"

"She was trapped in the car. Her spine was damaged. She rarely speaks of the incident. I gather the only thing that kept her going was my grandfather. He couldn't get to her and she couldn't get to him, but they encouraged each other for those two days."

It made him see Penelope in an entirely new light. "How old were you when it happened?"

"Just a year."

"So, you don't remember your grandfather?"

"No."

He covered her hand with his. "I hope you'll find time to get to know Primo. I realize it won't be the same, but maybe you can get a feel for what it would have been like to have had a grandfather in your life."

Tears welled up in her eyes. "Thank you. I'd like that,

even if it's only temporary." She stood, strain showing on her face. "If you don't mind, I think I'll read for a little bit before turning in. It's been a long day."

"No problem."

Silence descended on the cabin as night fell. The temperature dropped, bringing a refreshing coolness. When he finally decided to turn in he discovered that Ariana had fallen asleep on the love seat. He debated picking her up and carrying her to bed. But he couldn't count on his self-control being strong enough to keep him from taking advantage of the situation. Stripping the blanket off the bed, he covered her with it. And then he turned away before he did something he'd regret.

The next several days passed in a similar manner. They ate, hiked, swam and threw fishing lines in the water. They told amusing stories about their family and discussed endless topics of interest. Lazz even managed to convince himself that their honeymoon getaway was spacious enough for two, though he noticed that they never stayed inside longer than absolutely necessary. Not while the bed remained the centerpiece of the cabin.

All the while they circled each other, pretending not to feel the sexual tension that grew with each passing hour of each passing day. It seemed to loom just over the horizon, like a storm rumbling in the distance. The worst hours were while he waited for Ariana to fall asleep on the love seat, hours during which he waged a private war to keep from scooping her up and putting an end to their stalemate.

Two days before they were scheduled to leave, he joined her on the stretch of imported sand by the lake.

She sat curled up on a towel, hard at work on her sketch pad. He handed her a bottle of ice-cold water.

"Do you mind?" he asked, inclining his head toward her sketch pad.

"Not at all." She handed it over, then cracked open the bottle and tilted back her head to take a long swallow of water.

Lazz forced himself to look away from that endless length of neck and the tantalizing curve of breast and focus on the drawings. There were page after page of them, mostly of the local flora and fauna. But his face had somehow found its way in there and in the most peculiar places. Peeking out from under a bush. In the spots of a fawn. On the tail of a fish. In the downy feathers of a duck. There was an irresistible whimsy to her art form that left him grinning.

"These are really outstanding. Very clever."

"Thanks."

"Have you ever thought of having a showing?"

She lifted a shoulder in a gesture that had become endearingly familiar over the past few days. "Not really."

"Would your family frown on it?"

"It's not that. It's just…" She made a face. "My drawings aren't to everyone's taste."

"Well, they're to *my* taste."

She held out her hand for her sketch pad. He started to pass it to her, but then surprised them both by taking her hand in his. The connection between them flared, hotter and stronger than ever before, mocking their efforts to keep it subdued. Lazz swore beneath his breath. He'd done everything he could to bury the attraction he felt, to keep it under control. But now it seemed to explode in great messy waves of need.

Ariana stiffened, as though sensing how close he'd come to the end of his restraint. "We can't," she whispered.

"Yes, we can. And yes, we will."

"You say that as though I have no choice in the matter."

"You have the choice of when and where. But this is going to happen. You know it. You just haven't reconciled yourself to it yet."

She snatched up her sketch pad and pencil. "We only have two more days, Lazz. We can hold out that long."

"Possibly. But then what?" he pressed. "What happens when we return to San Francisco?"

"We'll have more room." She shot a frustrated glance at the cabin. "We won't be living on top of each other like we are here. We can go our separate ways."

"And at night? When we're lying in bed filled with want?"

She shuddered, and he could see her teetering, poised on the verge of tumbling. With an exclamation of frustration, she tossed aside the bottle of water and shot to her feet. "I'm going for a walk."

He slowly stood. "You do that." He pulled one of the cell phones from his pocket and tossed it to her. "But I'll still be here when you return. And so will that bed."

Without a word, she spun on her heel and walked away. But this time she looked back. This time he saw the coming surrender.

Lazz checked his watch for the umpteenth time. Damn it. Ariana had been gone for hours, and a call had just come through warning of an impending storm. He shot an uneasy glance toward the sky. Threatening clouds gathered with unnerving speed, descending on the peaks of the surrounding mountains in a great, boiling mass, like an army preparing to sweep down and invade the valley below. Lightning shot through the bruise-colored center of the storm mass.

He reached for the cell phone that was a mate to Ariana's and punched in her number again. The last half dozen times he'd tried, the call hadn't gone through. No doubt it had something to do with the approaching storm. This time, he was in luck. The call connected.

"Lazz?" he heard Ariana's voice say. He also realized she was speaking in Italian, a dead giveaway as to her emotional state. He could barely hear her through the static. But what he did hear had his blood turning to ice. "I'm lost."

He spoke swiftly, not sure how long the connection would last. "What direction were you heading when you left?"

"Along the stream away from the cabin. After a while there was a path that cut off to the right. There were these really gorgeous purplish-blue flowers. I wanted to sketch them. I just kept following the flowers. Then I fell down an incline and twisted my ankle. When I climbed back out I couldn't find the flowers or the path or the stream or anything."

He could hear the incipient thread of panic weaving through her voice. "Leave your cell phone on," he instructed. "I'll call Tolken and see if he can get a GPS lock on—"

The connection cut out and Lazz swore. No signal

and no time. He needed to find Ariana and fast. First things first. If she'd twisted her ankle he'd have to wrap it. Some food and water would be helpful if they were caught out in the storm. He could use one of the backpacks he'd noticed in the boathouse, along with a couple of the rain slickers stored there. She'd also be cold from either fear or shock, so a sweater wouldn't be a bad idea. Five minutes later he had everything he needed, including a pair of flashlights and a compass.

Jogging around the lake, he hit the trail that paralleled the stream just as the first boom of thunder rumbled down the hillside like cannon fire. He picked up his pace, keeping a sharp eye out for the path Ariana had indicated. He found it less than a mile along. The flowers she'd described trembled beneath a gust of rain-laden wind, but he paused long enough to check his compass before continuing on. He took off again, watching the path for any section that tumbled down a hillside. Unfortunately, since they were in the mountains, there were endless drop-offs.

A quick glance behind warned that the storm would break soon. The sky turned nighttime dark, and a curtain of rain cut him off from where he'd left the path along the stream. The curtain marched steadily in his direction. He continued onward, calling Ariana's name as he went.

Five minutes farther along he came across a grassy expanse covered in a colorful banquet of flowers. On the far side of the area, the grass ended abruptly in a steep bank, where dirt and rocks mixed with uprooted flowers cascaded into a deep ravine. There wasn't a doubt in his mind that his wife had slid down the hillside into that dark pocket. He couldn't say how he knew; he simply did.

"Ariana? Can you hear me?"

Overhead the storm broke, rain slamming against the ground so hard he couldn't hear his own voice, let alone any response from Ariana. Cautiously, he climbed down into the ravine, slipping and sliding as the rain turned the dirt to an avalanche of mud. The instant he reached the bottom, his awareness of her grew stronger, along with the certainty that she'd been here not too long ago. He shone the flashlight around until he found the proof he needed, the spot where she must have landed. Part of a snapped pencil rested on top of a broken boulder, and the torn remnants of her sketch pad blew toward a narrow channel of water that cut the ravine in two.

After rescuing the sketch pad, he carefully circled the area a second time until he spotted where she'd climbed back out of the gully. Unfortunately, it was on the opposite side from where she'd fallen in, which explained why she'd been unable to find her way back to the stream.

He followed in Ariana's footsteps. Below him, the ravine rapidly filled with water, the narrow channel that bisected the ravine becoming a churning river of mud, rock and mountain runoff. Worse, the rain was turning the loose dirt beneath his hands and feet into a mudslide that threatened to send him right back down the hillside. He had no idea how long it took him to work his way to the top. By the time he hauled himself over the ridge, he was up to his eyeballs in mud and soaked to the skin, despite his rain gear.

"Ariana?" he shouted. She was close. He could feel her now. Hell, he could practically taste her.

Above the sound of the rain, he heard her faint cry. "Here! I'm over here."

The beam from his flashlight cut through the gloom and landed on her. His wife sat huddled at the base of a towering pine, her knees drawn tight to her chest and her arms wrapped around her legs. He broke into a run. When he reached her side, he didn't say a word. He simply pulled her into his arms and kissed her.

Five

From:	Lazzaro_Dante@DantesJewelry.com
Date:	2008, August 05 10:34 PDST
To:	Bambolina@fornitore.it
Subject:	Marriage Contract, Premarital Conditions…
Next

Now that we've dealt with the public aspects of our marriage, perhaps we should deal with the private. Condition #4: No intermingling. We'll keep our private lives separate on all levels…financial, physical, social, etc.

L.

From:	Bambolina@fornitore.it
Date:	2008, August 05 19:59 CEST
To:	Lazzaro_Dante@DantesJewelry.com

Subject: Re: Marriage Contract, Premarital Conditions…Next

I actually had to look up the word *intermingling*. Okay, okay. I get it. In public we are joined hips to lips. And in private, my high heels stay out of your closet. Ciao! Ariana

One second Ariana's mouth was cold and wet and the next it turned to liquid warmth. Lazz sank inward, driven to tell her without words everything he felt. Traces of his fear and concern made the kiss hard and urgent. He forked his hands into her damp hair while she met him kiss for kiss, the need for reassurance unrelenting.

Minutes slid by and the tenor changed, the embrace easing into a joyful mating. His relief at finding her alive and relatively unhurt blunted the edginess from moments before. It grew softer, gentler, as he drank his fill. Until passion pushed the kiss back into the danger zone.

The sharp crack of thunder and an answering sizzle of lightning brought him to his senses. Reluctantly, Lazz drew back. "Sit tight."

"Trust me, I'm not going anywhere."

Stripping off his slicker, he spread it across the branches directly above Ariana to provide some protection from the rain. He ducked beneath the temporary canopy and crouched beside her.

"How are you holding up?"

"I'm cold. Scared. I hurt my ankle when I fell. But other than that, I'm fine." Her eyes were huge and dark in her pale face, and her gaze clung to his, practically eating him alive. "Better now that you're here."

"Let's see what we can do to fix you up." He opened

his backpack and pulled out the sweater and the extra slicker he'd brought for her. Helping her to her feet, he spread the slicker on the wet ground directly under their makeshift canopy. "Take off your shirt."

To his surprise, she didn't question him, let alone protest. She simple grabbed the hem of her shirt and yanked it over her head and off. Without waiting for him to suggest it, she also removed her bra before taking the sweater and pulling it on. He had enough time—and was still male enough, despite the circumstances—to admire the beauty of her shape and to realize that reality far exceeded what he'd seen up to this point.

She sighed in pleasure. "I didn't think I'd ever get warm again."

"Enjoy it while it lasts. It's a long hike back to the cabin."

"Especially with my ankle the way it is." Taking the hand he offered, she resumed her seat beneath the tree. "I can't believe you found me."

"I have a feeling finding you was the easy part." He glanced over his shoulder. "We can't go back the way we came. The ravine's filling up with water."

"Is there another path we can take?"

"Let's hope so. I've got a fairly good idea which direction we need to go."

"That's an excellent start."

He settled down beside her and grinned. "I like your confidence." He dipped into the backpack again and pulled out a bottle of water and a candy bar. "Have something to eat and drink while I check your ankle."

To his amusement, she devoured the chocolate with unmistakable greed, even licking her fingers to make certain she consumed every last morsel. While she sipped the water, he examined her ankle. Some nasty bruising and swelling, he decided, but not broken, thank God. And not as bad as he feared, though bad enough that it would make for a long and difficult return trip.

He dug into the backpack again and pulled out the bandage he'd unearthed in the emergency kit at the cabin. "I'm going to wrap your ankle with your shoe on to give it some extra support."

"Good idea." She flinched as thunder crashed overhead. "The storm's getting worse, isn't it?"

"A little."

"Is it safe to move?"

"Not for a bit." He finished wrapping her foot and settled in next to her. "We're in a pocket between two hillsides, under a stand of fairly short trees. Sitting here is better than being out in the open. I want to wait until the storm moves off a little and then see if we can't make it back to the cabin before nightfall."

She capped the water and handed it back to him. "Thank you for coming to find me."

Did she think he wouldn't? He tucked her close to help warm her up. "You're my wife."

"Not really."

His mouth tightened. "You're my wife," he repeated, more strongly this time. "I wouldn't leave you out alone in this."

Ariana fell silent for a few minutes. Then she said, "I could feel you, you know. I could feel you coming for me."

Just as he'd felt her. Lazz didn't want to admit that

what he considered instinct might have been enhanced by something else. Something more. Something that caused his palm to itch and desire to cling to him like a second skin. Something that made him want to sweep her into his arms and carry her to safety. To strip off her clothes and warm her with his touch. To complete what remained incomplete between them.

"You must have heard me," he attempted to explain away her reaction. "Or seen the flashlight beam."

She continued as though he'd never spoken. "I was afraid and alone. And then I sensed you coming, and the fear and loneliness melted away. I knew that if I just waited a few more minutes you'd find me. And you did."

He wanted to deny her words, to deny the suggestion that whatever connected them might be The Inferno. The Inferno was a lie, the proof of that lie evident in his own parents' marriage. His brothers might have been deluded into believing, into creating romantic fantasies out of plain, old-fashioned lust, but he was the most pragmatic of all the Dantes and he refused—*refused*—to allow his life to be controlled or dictated by a fantasy that could vanish as quickly as it had appeared.

"You gave excellent directions, Ariana. It wasn't hard to find you. In fact, if you hadn't gotten turned around when you fell into that ravine, you'd have found your own way back to the cabin. It was just bad luck."

"Did you love her very much?" She waited a heartbeat before adding, "Caitlyn. Is that why you don't believe me?"

"Caitlyn is Marco's wife."

"That doesn't answer my question."

"No, I didn't love her. Not really. Not the way Marco did." He forced himself to admit the truth. "And not the way Caitlyn loves Marco."

"But you believed she was your Inferno match, even if for a short time. You said you felt something for her once."

He dismissed Ariana's comment with a restless shrug. "Yes, I felt something. And I deluded myself into thinking it might be The Inferno and that she might be responsible. I was wrong."

"You told me it happened in Marco's conference room, the morning after they were married. The day I was there with my father," she added pointedly.

"Yes."

"But you still don't believe in The Inferno, do you? You refuse to consider that maybe what you felt was for me and not Caitlyn."

"I don't believe, Ariana." Thunder underscored his response. He continued to look at her, so she could read the truth in his gaze. "I never have and I never will."

"You must sense something," she insisted. "I can't be the only one of us experiencing whatever this is."

"It's simple desire. We're physically attracted to each other. We're two people—two *married* people—confined in a limited space. To make matters more difficult, we made sex a condition of our marriage."

Her lush mouth twisted into a wry, self-deprecating smile. "I believe I made *no* sex a condition of our marriage."

"Am I sensing regret?"

Lightning sizzled from the sky, striking close enough to fill the air with a sharp, metallic scent. He felt rather than heard Ariana's swift inhalation. And then she curled into him, burying her face against his shoulder.

"Yes, you sense regret," came her muffled voice. "I regret every last one of those ridiculous conditions we agreed to. I regret not having met you instead of Marco all those months ago. I regret that our parents ever signed that hideous contract. I regret that the first time we touched, the first time we kissed, was standing at the altar on our wedding day."

"I couldn't agree more." Lazz held her close, wrapping himself around her so she stayed safe and warm. "I've always wondered why Dad drafted that contract. Do you have any idea?"

"None. If my father knows, he hasn't said."

"I find it odd that Vittorio agreed to Dad's proposition. Was it just the money?"

She winced. "I'm sure that was part of it." Pain bled into the words, and he realized that on some level she must feel as though her father had betrayed her, allowing avarice to outweigh his love for his daughter. "He said it was something your father told him that finally convinced him to sign, but he refused to explain what. He claimed it wasn't the right time."

Lightning flashed in the distance, and the thunder took a moment to rumble a response. Though the rain remained steady, it didn't pound the ground the way it had only moments before. A deep gray seeped into the hillside, warning of the advent of dusk. Lazz stood and stripped the slicker off the branches above them. Shaking it out, he passed it down to Ariana.

"Here, put this on."

"Are we leaving?" she asked in relief.

"We're going to give it a shot." He checked his compass. "I'm hoping we can parallel the path on the other side of the ravine. The stream shouldn't be too far along. Once we find that, we'll be back to the cabin in no time."

After donning the slicker they'd been sitting on, he searched the underbrush for a sturdy branch Ariana could use as a walking stick. Then he slung the backpack over one shoulder while bracing his wife with the other. It had taken him a mere five minutes to traverse the distance from the stream to the ravine. Returning to that spot took a full thirty.

Pain and weariness lined Ariana's face as they rested on a mossy boulder near the stream. "I would never have made it without you. Thank you." She regarded the stone-strewn path ahead of them, and her chin set into a determined line. "What do you say we tackle this next part before it gets any darker?"

"I'd say you were pretty damn amazing, Mrs. Dante." He dug in his backpack for another candy bar and handed it to her. "Eat this first, and then we'll push off."

It took them two more hours to reach the cabin. Ariana's legs buckled mere steps from the porch, and Lazz swung her into his arms. "Just another minute," he reassured, "and I'll have you in a nice hot tub."

She moaned in response. "Who knew I'd want to be any wetter than I already am. But a hot bath…"

He shoved open the front door and carried her inside. "With bubbles."

"Stop. You're killing me."

He reached for the light switch and flicked it on.

Nothing happened. "Hell. It just figures." He gently set Ariana down, helping her balance on her one good foot. "Looks like the storm knocked out the power."

"No bath?" she asked with surprising equanimity.

"There should be enough hot water," he reassured. "And as soon as I get the generator going, there'll be more than enough."

Using his flashlight to guide him, Lazz carried her through to the bathroom and turned on the faucet. Sure enough, hot water came pouring out. He upended a jar of bath crystals, watching with interest as they exploded into bubbles. Then he shone the beam of light in Ariana's direction. She stood awkwardly on one leg, laughter dancing in her dark eyes.

"Too much bubble?"

"A bit," she conceded.

"Do you need help getting in?"

"You sound entirely too hopeful." She shook her head. "If you'd leave me one of the flashlights, I should be fine."

"I can do better than that." He shone the light toward a trio of squat candles grouped on the tile ledge that surrounded the tub. "Will that do?"

Her sigh of pleasure was answer enough. "Perfect."

He left her to it while he powered up the generator. To his relief, it started with ease. Finally, he went to the freezer and removed a bag of frozen corn, poured two glasses of wine and returned to the bathroom. He paused outside the door.

"Cover up with bubbles. I'm coming in." He heard a feminine yelp, followed by a soft splash. Grinning, he pushed open the door. "Hope you don't mind."

"I do, as a matter of fact."

"Maybe this will help." He handed her the wine. "Rest your ankle on the edge of the tub."

"Corn?"

"Frozen corn." Draping it across her ankle, he headed for the shower stall and began to strip.

"What are you doing now?" Nervousness cascaded through her voice. She glanced over her shoulder and then whipped around again. "You're taking your clothes off."

"True." He paused deliberately. "I'm wet, filthy and tired. I'm taking a shower, assuming there's any hot water left. And if there's not, I'll be wet, cold and tired. But at least I'll be clean."

"Yes, of course," she murmured in Italian. "I wasn't thinking."

He smiled. Did she have any idea how much she gave away when she switched languages? "I could always join you in the tub," he suggested.

"Or not."

"There are enough bubbles in there for two. And considering the size of that thing, there's more than enough room for both of us."

She sank lower in the tub. "You choose the oddest times to display your sense of humor."

"Huh. I could have sworn I was being dead serious."

He turned on the shower and braced himself. To his relief, it wasn't as bad as he feared. Lukewarm, at best, but the illusion of warmth lasted long enough for him to scrub down. Once he'd dried off, he regarded his wife. Only the top of her head was visible above the dissipating layer of bubbles, not to mention one shapely leg.

He grabbed a stack of towels and piled them within reach of the tub. "I'm going to start a fire. Are you okay?"

"I'm fine. Thank you, Lazz."

She'd switched back to English, and when she glanced up, she managed to regard him with the sort of regal poise that must have been drummed into her from infancy. And yet, he could feel the want sizzling behind the facade.

Something had changed as a result of what they'd gone through during the storm. They'd come out the other side and everything had been different. There'd always been a strong, sexual awareness between them—not The Inferno. Not a chance. But definitely an awareness. Now, that awareness had sharpened to a keen edge. One that was going to cut them if they didn't do something to blunt it.

"Call me if you need help getting out." He paused at the door and shot her a wicked grin, one he hoped disguised how he really felt. "Looks like I should have used more bubble bath, not less."

Ariana glanced down and gasped. Embarrassing gaps had appeared in the bubbles. The tips of her breasts peeked through one of those gaps, while the curve of her hip and belly could clearly be seen through another.

She shivered despite the warmth of the water. Humorous remarks aside, she'd never seen that look in Lazz's eyes before. Sure, she'd seen awareness. Desire. But not to this extent. Not that bone-deep hunger that had turned his eyes to jade. He wanted her. Badly. It showed in the tautness of his face and the ferocity of his gaze, as well as the rigid play of muscles across his impressive chest. It suggested a man hovering on the edge, clawing to hold himself in check.

This time she shivered for real. The bathwater had gone from toasty to cool, and the bubbles were little more than a delicious memory. Even the bag of frozen corn had turned warm and soggy.

Levering herself onto the edge of the platform surrounding the tub, she grabbed a towel for her hair and wrapped a second one around herself. Her ankle felt better, at least enough for her to hobble out of the bathroom in search of clean clothes. The central portion of the cabin remained in darkness with only the flickering light from the fireplace to pierce the shadows.

Lazz stood as she limped into the room. "You should have called me."

"I managed."

"Do you need help dressing?"

Absolutely not. "I don't think so, thanks."

He moved from his stance by the fireplace, and she lost him in the darkness, tracking him by voice alone. "I'll go top off the generator while you change. Feel free to turn on a light if you want. I left them off to conserve fuel so we could keep the refrigerator and freezer running."

She offered a self-conscious smile. "Not to mention the hot water heater."

There was a stillness about him that unnerved her. A purposefulness. And she could practically taste the tension thickening the air. "That, too."

She clung to the edges of her damp towel. She couldn't remember the last time she'd felt this awkward. Lazz must have sensed as much because he left the cabin without another word. Ariana didn't waste any time. She limped to the dresser as quickly as her ankle would allow and dug through the drawers. She yanked out clothing at random, anything that would give her adequate coverage.

She'd just finished dressing when an unearthly screech split the air, followed by a boom so violent it jolted the cabin right down to its foundations and literally knocked her off her feet. She lay on the floor, fighting for breath, not daring to move. Whatever just happened, it had killed the generator.

The instant the thought entered her mind, she bolted upright and shrieked, "Lazz!"

She scrambled to her feet and hobbled to the back door of the cabin. Turning the knob, she attempted to open it, but it wouldn't budge no matter how hard she shoved. She threw her full weight against it, horrified when her actions made absolutely no impact. Something had wedged the door shut. She hammered on the wooden surface and shouted for Lazz, panic sweeping through her.

He was out there. Whatever had caused that hideous noise and knocked out the generator, Lazz had been there when it had happened. The flashlight. Where had she put her flashlight? She stumbled back toward the fireplace and found it on the table that fronted the love seat. Switching it on, she hurried to the front door and threw it open. The storm had circled back on itself and continued unabated, lashing the clearing and forest with wind and rain. Thunder rumbled, the rolling boom a far different sound than the one that had knocked her off her feet. Lightning forked a jagged path across the sky, and that's when she saw him.

Lazz came toward her through the rain, tall and broad and—as far as she could tell—undamaged. Ignoring the stab of pain from her ankle, Ariana shot across the porch, down the steps and into the storm. He broke into a run as she made a beeline for him. The next instant, he scooped her up into his arms.

"Are you all right?" he demanded, urgency underscoring the question.

"Fine. I'm fine. What about you?" Her hands raced over his face and down across the breadth of his shoulders, searching for any signs of injury. "Are you hurt?"

"Nothing serious." He hustled toward the porch. "Though it was a close call."

She knew she was crying, but hoped he attributed it to rain instead of tears. "What happened? What made that horrible sound?"

"Tree came down. Took out the generator shed a few seconds before I got there."

The tears came faster. "It didn't hit you? You're sure you're not hurt?"

His arms tightened around her, holding her snug against his heart. She could feel the calming beat, the steady reassurance that he'd survived and was here with her, safe and sound. "I got brushed back by a few of the smaller branches. Nothing serious. But the tree blocked off the back of the cabin."

He carried her across the threshold and inside. The symbolism of his actions didn't strike her until much, much later. "Show me. Show me this 'nothing serious.'" Struggling free of his hold, she shoved at his jacket, tugging it off his shoulders, not even aware of her actions. "Show me where you were hit," she demanded.

He didn't fight her. He must have understood her fear and concern. "Across the shoulder. Right arm."

"Take off your shirt. Let me see." She aimed the flashlight at his torso and waited. When he didn't immediately move to comply, she added, "I'm serious, Lazz. Do it."

He gripped the bottom of his shirt and whipped it up and off. For some reason, he focused on a point over her shoulder, almost as though standing there before her, stripped to the waist, had left him vulnerable on some level. She understood the feeling all too well, considering that not an hour ago their positions had been reversed. Now it was her turn to care for him.

It took her a moment to regain her focus. She'd seen him bare chested any number of times. It still had the power to steal her breath away. Heaven help her but he was built. His jeans rode low on narrow hips, offering her plenty of viewing room.

Strong, lean muscle rippled across the endless expanse of golden skin, begging for her touch. Soft against hard. Gentle overlaying power. She felt the piercing siren's call of The Inferno—*no,* not The Inferno. Lazz had insisted it was lust, nothing more. No matter how she might long for it to be different, their feelings for one another weren't the stuff of legend.

Ariana forced herself to put aside foolish dreams and examine Lazz for any signs of injury. She found evidence almost immediately. Several gouges streaked across his shoulder and down his chest, while a bruise was already forming across his right bicep.

The beam from the flashlight trembled. "You *were* hurt."

He glanced down and shrugged. "It's nothing. Just a scratch."

Tentatively, she reached for him, stroking his chest with trembling fingertips. The instant she touched him, he froze. A harsh sound rumbled in his throat, and he closed his eyes. A tense second passed. And then he looked at her again, and she realized that he'd lost the battle to hold himself in check. Gently, he reached for her. And just as gently, she surrendered.

Six

From: Bambolina@fornitore.it
Date: 2008, August 05 22:08 CEST
To: Lazzaro_Dante@DantesJewelry.com
Subject: Marriage Contract, Premarital Conditions…
My turn ;)
Lazz, I'm a little concerned about how we will eventually end our marriage. Romanos don't believe in divorce, and I have no intention of becoming the first to change that.
Counter-Condition #2: I would like to have our marriage annulled when the time comes.
Ciao! Ariana

From: Lazzaro_Dante@DantesJewelry.com
Date: 2008, August 05 14:36 PDST

To: Bambolina@fornitore.it
Subject: Re: Marriage Contract, Premarital Conditions…My turn ;)
Is this open for negotiation?
L.

From: Bambolina@fornitore.it
Date: 2008, August 06 00:19 CEST
To: Lazzaro_Dante@DantesJewelry.com
Subject: Re: Marriage Contract, Premarital Conditions…My turn ;)
Not even a little.

Lazz cupped Ariana's hips and locked her against him, a delicious slide of male against female. Before she could do more than catch her breath in a soft gasp, he slid under her shirt and upward until he hit hot, satiny skin.

"I've tried." His voice contained the same raw, gritty quality as sandpaper. "I've done my best to leave you alone. But I can't. If you still want me to honor your request, you need to say so. Now. While I can still stop what's about to happen."

Common sense struggled to override base desire. Her motives for refusing to make love to her husband were sound. They were part of her core values, as vital to her well-being as her heartbeat. In addition, Brimstone was missing. How would Lazz view her actions tonight if her father was unable to recover the stone?

It didn't take any consideration at all. He'd be furious and might even wonder if she'd sacrificed herself on the altar, as it were, in order to protect her family. But in this moment, her need to complete the bond between them overrode every last sensible thought. Whatever connection had formed when they stood before the altar and first joined hands had slipped into her heart and soul and become as much a part of her as those values.

As hard as she tried to resist, she'd have an easier time convincing the tide not to turn or the sun to dim its flames. She wanted him. Wanted his hands on her. Wanted their clothes off. "Don't stop. Please, Lazz. Make love to me."

He shook his head, regret reflected in his expression. "I don't think I know how to love." He swept her up into his arms once again and carried her to the bed. He settled her onto the mattress and followed her down. "But you make me want to try. And I swear what I feel for you is unlike anything I've ever felt before."

He didn't give her time to respond, but lowered his head and took her mouth in a kiss so tender, so warm and life-affirming that any remaining resistance slipped away. She opened to him, welcoming him inward.

A delicious humming darted through her veins. "More," she murmured.

"Anything you want."

"You. I just want you."

He reached for her, then hesitated at the last minute. "I just realized. I have no way of protecting you."

She stared blankly. "Protecting me?"

"From pregnancy," he clarified.

She struggled to think straight, to admit—even to herself—that she'd considered that possibility over the course of the past week, despite her marital conditions. That she'd done the mental arithmetic…just in case. "It's safe."

He accepted her at her word. "Thank heaven for small miracles."

He grasped the hem of her cotton shirt and drew it up and over her head. She emerged breathless and rumpled. Lightning burned the room in hard white light, spotlighting her partial nudity. She heard Lazz's sharp inhalation and caught a glimpse of the undisguised desire that cut sharp grooves on either side of his mouth. Green and gold fire flashed in his eyes as he looked at her, igniting a scorching path across her skin.

Darkness consumed them once again, alleviated only by the banked glow emanating from the fireplace. Thunder rattled the windows, but this time she didn't flinch at the sound, not while Lazz held her safe within the protective warmth of his arms. His hands glided across the silken curve of her abdomen and upward to cup her breast.

Her heartbeat stuttered before catching and echoing the beat of his, and frantic need exploded deep in the pit of her stomach. She arched farther into his embrace, a low moan disturbing the air between them.

"I've never touched anything so soft," he murmured. "Or so warm."

"I think I'm melting into the mattress."

He chuckled, the sound deliciously intimate. "That makes two of us. It's either melt, or set the sheets on fire."

"Yes, please."

"I'll get right on that."

And he did. He caught her nipple between his teeth and tugged. She didn't have a hope of concealing her response, not when it shuddered through her. He absorbed her reaction and excited another as he followed a velveteen path downward.

The breath escaped her lungs in a desperate rush. "What are you doing?"

He paused, tracing the indent of her belly with his mouth and then with his tongue. "You can't say that in English, can you?"

She groaned. "No. Please, Lazz."

"Let me in, Ariana. I want to know every part of you."

"Don't. I can't—"

Reason fled and so did any capacity to speak. He slid his hands beneath her backside and lifted her. He touched her with surprising delicacy, a slow, thorough exploration that had her clutching fistfuls of the sheet beneath them. Her thighs tensed as he delved into the damp heat of her, and she would have jackknifed off the bed if he hadn't held her in place. Again he touched her, the tip of his tongue skating ruthlessly along its predetermined path.

The muscles in her belly drew taut, and she literally lost the ability to see or hear or reason. A deep quaking struck, the epicenter just beneath his tongue and radiating outward in great, rolling waves. She'd never experienced anything like it before, couldn't seem to process what he'd done to her.

But he wasn't finished. Before the aftermath of the final quake had fully died away, he surged upward and sank into her with a single, unerring stroke. She froze at the unexpected pain and fullness, catching her lip between her teeth so she wouldn't cry out.

"What's wrong?"

She took a deep, careful breath. "It's a bit uncomfortable," she admitted.

"I assume it's been a while?"

"A while," she confirmed. "If never is a while."

"Never?" A moment of stunned silence followed. "Are you telling me you've never made love before?" he asked carefully.

Did he even realize he referred to it as lovemaking? Until that moment he'd always called it sex. "No, I've never made love before. I once heard some friends of Constantine's—ex-friends—taking bets to see who could relieve me of my virginity first."

"Bastards."

She shrugged. "It was because I'm a Romano. It would have given them bragging rights to have been the first. But perhaps I should have mentioned it to you sooner."

He rested his forehead against hers. "That might have been a good idea."

"Has this deflated your interest?" she asked politely.

A rough laugh escaped him. "Not even a little. I almost wish it had."

"It shouldn't be a problem if you go slowly."

"Give me a minute and I'll see what I can do. Right now, it's taking all my self-control not to move."

"What if I move?" Cautiously, she arched upward, absorbing a bit more of him, before sinking back down again. "How's that?"

He groaned. "Yes."

"More?"

He didn't answer. He simply took her mouth with his. His tongue slid inward before withdrawing in a leisurely rhythm. Understanding what he wanted, she shifted her hips upward, matching stroke for stroke. Little by little the rhythm picked up, increasing in speed and depth until she'd fully sheathed him.

She couldn't say when he joined the dance. One moment she was leading, and the next they matched each other move for move. Scorching heat slicked across her skin and sank into her pores, radiating through her. She could feel the quickening approach again and moved to chase it.

Lazz raced with her, encouraging her with word and touch. Then he was driving their movements, driving her. They climbed, fast and hard, teetering breathlessly at the very peak. The air exploded from her in a sharp cry and she felt his final push to join her as she tumbled over. He stiffened within her embrace, frozen for a timeless moment.

She'd never seen anything more soul-shattering than his expression in that intensely personal moment. She'd brought him to this. It showed in his eyes, a knowledge that whatever connected them was utterly unique and all-consuming. That her touch, her embrace, had fulfilled him in ways he'd never experienced before. That no matter who or what had come before, she had changed him.

As though aware of how much he'd given away, he closed his eyes. "I'm sorry, Ariana."

"Sorry?" She stared in bewilderment. "Why are you sorry?"

"You deserve more than I can give you." The admission was torn from him. "Your first time should have been with someone you loved."

"How do you know it wasn't?"

A muscle jerked in his jaw. "Love doesn't guarantee a happily-ever-after marriage. It didn't for my parents. In fact, they set a spectacular example of love gone wrong. I'd rather not follow in their footsteps. I'd rather not build our relationship into some ridiculous fantasy. Because when the fall comes, it's going to be long and hard."

"What about your grandparents?" she protested. "Your brothers? Haven't they shown that a marriage can endure? That love can, as well?"

"It's early days for my brothers. And my grandparents are merely the exception that proves the rule." He took her hand in his as he rolled off of her. She doubted he was even aware of the way he interlaced their fingers so their palms were joined. "Right before my father died, I remember him telling me how alike we were. That I got my logical bent from him and that it would make a successful marriage more difficult for me than my brothers."

"And you think that means you can't love?" she asked, stunned.

"I think it means he discovered The Inferno wasn't real. He didn't believe in it any more than I do. I think he was telling me that it didn't exist, no matter what Primo claimed to the contrary. That I shouldn't go looking for what couldn't be found."

She stared, appalled. "Did your father actually say that?"

Lazz's mouth twisted. "Not in so many words. But I'm logical, which makes me fairly good at connecting the dots." He released her hand and cupped her face. "Do you realize you speak in Italian whenever you're upset?"

"Like now?"

"Like now." He traced a fingertip from the hollow of her throat to the tip of her breast. "Of course, you also speak Italian when you're aroused."

Her eyes fluttered shut. "Like now?"

"Oh, yeah."

She slid into helpless surrender, enjoying the delicious give of female to male. "This wasn't supposed to happen. And it's definitely not supposed to happen again."

"It was inevitable."

"You don't understand."

"I understand perfectly. You don't believe in divorce, and I don't believe in love." He feathered a kiss across her mouth. And then another. "So where does that leave us, Ariana? Do you want to change the conditions we agreed to?"

A bittersweet laugh escaped her. "In case you didn't notice, the conditions have already been changed."

Lazz conceded her point with a brief smile. "What do you want from me?"

Love. A home. A real marriage, she wanted to say. But he wasn't capable of providing any of those things. "I'm not asking you for anything."

"Aren't you?"

She flinched. Was she so easy to read? Could he really see into her heart, see the dreams and hopes she kept safely tucked away there? Had she left herself so open and vulnerable? One careless touch and he could shatter all she held most dear. Assuming he hadn't already. She needed to protect herself and pull back before he hurt her more than he had already. At the very least she needed to pull back until her father had found Brimstone. Because if Lazz ever found out that she'd known it was missing and had still gone through with their wedding, he'd never forgive the betrayal. Not after what Caitlyn and Marco had done to him.

She slid from his embrace and escaped the bed. Snatching up the sheet, she wound it around herself. "This—" She gestured toward the rumpled bed. "We need to agree that our sexual encounter never occurred."

He raised an eyebrow. "Sexual encounter?"

Her chin shot up. "Would you prefer I call it love-making?"

"Touché." He lifted onto an elbow, not in the least concerned about his nudity, and regarded her through narrowed eyes. "You think we can just pretend tonight never happened?"

She kicked the trailing end of the sheet to one side. "Yes."

"And if we pretend hard enough, we can have our marriage annulled?" he asked in a neutral voice.

Pain filled her, a soul-deep ache. "I don't know."

He hesitated. "We don't have to annul it. Or divorce. There's a third option."

She froze. "What do you mean?"

"I mean we can stay married."

"Because I was a virgin? Because we had sex?"

He shook his head. "Just because I don't believe in love doesn't mean that I don't believe in marriage. I want to have children someday."

She drew in a sharp breath. Did he have any idea

how insulting she found his offer? "And since we find each other physically compatible, why not?"

"That was more than physical compatibility. Way more."

"So, I'll do? Physically, intellectually, socially, I meet all the criteria for a wife?"

He swore. "I'm suggesting we consider turning our marriage into something more than what we originally discussed. If you're not interested—"

"No. I'm not."

Not on his terms. Not in such a cold-blooded, *logical* fashion. She closed her eyes, fighting tears. Was he really so emotionally detached that he didn't understand how his "suggestion" came across? That he didn't see how she ached for him to consider the possibility—even if for one tiny second—that fantasy could become reality? That his Dante family legacy might be alive and well and burning within them both?

She gathered up the shreds of her self-control. "Here's what we're going to do. Since the generator shed has been smashed, first thing in the morning we're going to call Tolken and ask to be flown out of here. Then we're returning home. When we get back to San Francisco, you're going to go your way and I'm going mine."

He climbed off the bed and stood before her in all his glory. She struggled not to look, but couldn't seem to help herself. He had the most magnificent body she'd ever seen. And for a short time it had been hers to touch and taste and take deep inside herself.

It didn't seem to matter that they were worlds apart emotionally. It didn't dim the want. Desire still hammered away at her, tempting her to bend. To give. To tumble again into an embrace she wanted more than anything, even though it promised nothing in return. At least, nothing permanent.

"You're right," he surprised her by saying. "First thing in the morning we are leaving. But when we return to San Francisco your way is the same as mine. You made a commitment to me and you will honor it."

"And you promised not to touch me," she shot back. "It looks like we were both disappointed."

Instead of rousing his anger, her comment provoked a laugh. "You gave me permission to break that agreement. And I wasn't the least disappointed." He took a step closer. And then he did something totally unfair. He swept his hand along the side of her face. Just that. Just that single touch. So gentle. So tender. Sincere regret darkened his eyes. "But I'm sorry if you were, especially considering it was your first time. I'd like to change that, if you'll let me."

She stared at him in desperate silence. She couldn't have answered him if her life depended on it. Her first time hadn't been a disappointment. Far from it. It had been the most incredible night in her life, one she wanted to relive as often as possible. But that would mean surrendering. And surrender meant heartache.

"Tell me, sweetheart. Tell me what you want." He reached for the sheet and loosened the knot. "Do you want me to kiss you more? Touch you in a different way? Would you prefer I go slower? Go faster?"

"Not again," she managed to say. "We're not having sex again."

Something slammed through his gaze, something

fierce and determined. "Then we won't." He snatched her free of the sheet and swept her into his arms. "What happened in that bed... What's going to happen again, is something far more than sex."

"But it's not love." She groaned when his mouth closed over her throat, his teeth scraping the sensitive skin just beneath her ear. "This isn't The Inferno."

He tumbled to the bed with her. "There's no such thing as The Inferno," he insisted. Even as he spoke the words, he interlaced their hands until the heat erupted palm against palm. "And we've only known each other mere days. How could it be love?"

He slid over top of her, mating their bodies in one delicious stroke. She groaned, coherent thought fast becoming an impossibility. "Then what is this?" The words escaped in a choked gasp.

"I don't know. But I never want it to stop."

His movements escalated and he drove into her, hard and fast, racing toward that incredible peak he'd shown her earlier. How could the passion they shared be so strong and relentless, consuming them in great greedy gulps, and not last for all eternity? He didn't believe, and yet she felt the fire within him. He burned for her just as she burned for him, her body like dry tinder to his scorching touch.

They'd been together such a short time, and yet to be with him, surrounding him, inhaling him, inflamed for him, had become as vital to her as the air she breathed. Her feelings terrified her. They seemed to melt her down to her bare essence and reform her into something infinitely more.

Her climax caught her by surprise, slamming into

her and threatening to shatter her to the core. It ripped her apart, leaving her utterly exposed, every thought, every feeling there for him to see. And he must have seen, because he closed his eyes and covered her mouth with his, as though to keep the words unspoken.

And yet the kiss they shared said far more than any words could have expressed. The tenderness. The joy. The helpless want. The undeniable connection that existed between them. It was all there in that gentle benediction. Perhaps he sensed it, as well.

"We'll return home tomorrow," he told her again. "But we definitely won't be going our separate ways."

"So, how's married life treating you? You're celebrating your…what? Three-week anniversary?"

"To the day." Lazz flipped open the menu the waitress handed him and glanced across it at his brother. "And married life is fine."

"Fine," Sev repeated. "That's it…fine? Most men who've been married so short a time would describe it a bit differently. Incredible, maybe. Fantastic."

Lazz dropped the menu to the linen-draped tabletop. "My marriage to Ariana isn't real, as you damn well know." And wasn't that the biggest crock of manure he'd ever attempted to shovel.

"But you are still planning to keep that fact from Primo and Nonna, right?"

"Yes." Impatience edged Lazz's voice. "Penelope, too. Why the inquisition? What's going on?"

Sev turned to the waitress hovering at his elbow and placed his order, then waited while Lazz placed his, before answering. "No inquisition. I just wondered why you chose to have lunch with me instead of your beautiful wife."

"Ariana made plans with friends. In fact, she asked me which restaurant would afford the most privacy and best view, and I suggested Fruits de Mer. I expect she's around here someplace."

In fact, he knew it. He'd sensed his wife's presence the moment he'd walked in. The need to go in search of her had been nearly overwhelming, which was why he'd done just the opposite and taken a chair that kept his back to temptation. Not that he'd confess that small detail to his brother. It irritated Lazz enough that he had such a strong awareness of Ariana. He wasn't about to give Sev the opportunity to go off on one of his Inferno rants.

"You know, I brought Francesca to Fruits de Mer on our first official date." Humor drifted through Sev's eyes, turning them a burnished gold. "I think we lasted an entire five minutes before we went tearing over to my Pacific Heights place. We couldn't control ourselves."

"I assume you're going to blame that on The Inferno?"

"It was definitely a contributing factor." Sev's gaze dropped to Lazz's hands. "Wouldn't you agree?"

Lazz froze, suddenly aware that he was kneading his palm the same way his brothers and grandfather did. They'd always claimed it was one of the side effects of The Inferno, that when the connection formed during that first touch, it caused the bone-deep itch he'd been unable to suppress. Without a word, he picked up his glass of beer and took a long swallow.

To Lazz's relief, Sev changed the subject. "You didn't say who Ariana was lunching with."

"Maybe because I don't know. Friends." He shot his brother an inquiring glance. "Is she with Francesca?"

"Ariana isn't with any of the wives."

Lazz struggled to shove back a wave of irritation. "And you know this…how?"

"Because she's a half dozen tables behind you by the window. And her luncheon companion definitely isn't female."

Lazz stiffened and slowly turned. Ariana sat in a snug table for two close to a window perched above the Marina District. The sun plunged into the dense darkness of her hair, just as his hands had plunged into that silken mass during their time in Verdonia. She tilted her head in a way he'd seen countless times on their honeymoon, and the days since, and shards of ruby erupted from the ebony of her hair. From the back, her trim figure was showcased in a formfitting blaze of red that sculpted to her slender waist before cupping the curves of her hips and backside.

Oh, yeah. The woman was definitely Ariana. Which begged the question… Who the holy hell was the man with her?

The view from the window beside the two was one of the most incredible in the world, offering a stunning panorama of San Francisco Bay extending from the Golden Gate Bridge to Alcatraz. Not that either his wife or the man who so thoroughly held her attention noticed. Lazz caught the sound of her quick, husky laugh and watched as she reached out and squeezed the man's hand.

He heard a low, dangerous growl and didn't even realize he'd made the sound, any more than he remembered shooting to his feet. His hands collapsed into fists, and it took every ounce of self-control to keep them at his side. His focus narrowed, centering on his wife's back. Without a word to Sev, he stalked toward her table.

Seven

From: Lazzaro_Dante@DantesJewelry.com
Date: 2008, August 06 08:36 PDST
To: Bambolina@fornitore.it
Subject: Marriage Contract, Premarital Conditions…
Ad Nauseum
It occurs to me that I never asked whether you were romantically involved with someone else. In case you are…
Condition #5: We will both honor our vows for the duration of our marriage.
L.

From: Bambolina@fornitore.it
Date: 2008, August 06 17:45 CEST
To: Lazzaro_Dante@DantesJewelry.com

Subject: Re: Marriage Contract, Premarital Conditions…Ad Nauseam
Oh, Lazz. Allow me to ease your mind. I'm not currently involved with anyone. Are you?? Your fifth condition is not necessary. I would never cheat on my
husband, even if he's a husband in name only. So no
need to worry on that account or have an attack of
the male jealousies.
Ciao! Ariana

From: Lazzaro_Dante@DantesJewelry.com
Date: 2008, August 06 08:49 PDST
To: Bambolina@fornitore.it
Subject: Re: Marriage Contract, Premarital Condi-
tions…Ad Nauseum
No, I'm not involved with anyone, either. And FYI, I
don't have male jealousies. It's not in my nature.
L.

"I'm serious, Ariana," the man said as Lazz approached. "You're going to have to make some changes
or this won't work. I told you what I want, and you
refuse to give it to me."

"You don't understand, Aaron. I can't. It's not who
I am."

The man flicked a glance in Lazz's direction, the
casual look changing to curiosity when Lazz paused
beside their table. His wife glanced up at him, alarm
blossoming in her widened eyes.

"Lazz? What are you doing here?"

He opened his mouth, planning to give his caveman
impulses a voice. To his relief, he managed a more civ-

ilized response. "I'm having lunch with Sev." He kept his gaze fixed on her lunch companion as he addressed him. "Lazzaro Dante. I'm Ariana's husband."

The man climbed to his feet and offered his hand. "I'm Aaron Talbot. I'm—" Ariana gave a tiny shake of her head, and after a telling hesitation, he continued with barely a hitch. "I'm an old family friend. My father and Ariana's grandmother go way back."

If Sev hadn't chosen that moment to approach, Lazz didn't have any doubt that he'd have done or said something he'd have thoroughly enjoyed in the short term and eventually regretted given time. A lot of time.

"Hello, Ariana. Good to see you." Sev greeted his sister-in-law with a cool smile. He dropped a heavy hand on Lazz's shoulders. "Our lunch just arrived. You're coming, aren't you?"

Lazz resisted the pull for a full ten seconds. His attention switched to his wife. "Later," he promised.

Gathering up his self-control, he returned to their table. Sev motioned to the waitress, and a moment later she showed up with a tumbler containing two fingers of Jack Daniel's. She set it down in front of Sev, who shoved the glass across the table toward Lazz.

"Drink. Then tell me again that you don't believe in The Inferno."

"My reaction is perfectly logical," Lazz gritted out.

"And I'll testify to that at your murder trial." Sev speared a scallop. "Interesting."

Lazz closed his eyes. "I know I'm going to regret asking… What's interesting?"

"I didn't think The Inferno could only go in one direction. I guess I was wrong."

Lazz downed his drink in a single swallow, welcoming the burning heat as it shot straight to his stomach and poured through his veins. "I'm going to say this one last time. Ariana and I have not, nor will we ever, experience The Inferno. And there's an excellent reason for that."

"You're an idiot?"

The tumbler hit the table with a dull thud. "It doesn't exist. And what you've mistaken for jealousy is irritation that Ariana would conduct her…friendships—" and how the word scalded his tongue "—with such flagrant disregard. I'll suggest she be more discreet in the future so our marriage isn't exposed for the sham it's clearly become."

Sev leaned forward. "You might want to make that suggestion in a quieter voice than you're currently using and well outside of your wife's throwing range."

"This isn't a joke."

"No, marriage isn't. Nor is it a business proposition. I wish Dad had lived long enough to explain that fact to you. Since he didn't, I guess I'm stuck with the job."

Lazz frowned. Maybe he shouldn't have downed that whiskey quite so fast. "Now what are you talking about?"

"Haven't you ever wondered why Dad entered into that contract with Vittorio?"

Actually, he had. But with all the rush to slip the wedding in before Ariana turned twenty-five, he hadn't had time to pursue that aspect of the whole business. "The Romanos are broke, right? I assumed this was Dad's odd way of offering them a helping hand."

Skepticism swept across Sev's face. "A helping hand that's delayed for twenty years? A helping hand that's dependent on you and Ariana marrying?"

"No, you're right," Lazz said. "That doesn't make any sense."

"And why make Brimstone a part of the contract? Hell, why make a contract at all?" Sev pressed. "Just give Romano the damn stone."

Lazz shook his head. "I doubt Vittorio would have taken it. He may not have money, but he has more than his fair share of the Romano pride."

"And yet he sold his daughter to Dad. Why?"

Lazz winced at the harsh description. "I have no idea why he signed that contract. Ariana doesn't know, either. She said that Vittorio claimed it was Dad's idea, that he couldn't be talked out of it."

"Dad was so determined to have Vittorio sign that contract that he made Brimstone part of the deal. He was so determined to see you two married, that if you *didn't* marry, Brimstone would be disposed of. Why, Lazz?"

"How the hell should I know? Dad's gone."

"But Vittorio isn't. He must have some clue as to what Dad was thinking." Satisfied that he'd made his point, Sev leaned back in his seat. "I suggest you look into it."

Lazz studied his brother. He knew something—something he wasn't telling. "Why are you bringing this up now, after the fact? Why didn't you ask me to pursue it before Ariana and I married?" Understanding hit. "You know why Dad did it, don't you?"

"I have my suspicions. But since you're Mr. Facts and Figures, I'd rather you investigate this in your own meticulous fashion. Just be careful that when you add one and one together, that you don't come up with three."

"I'd rather you just told—"

Lazz caught a flash of red out of the corner of his eyes and turned. Ariana and Talbot had finished their lunch and were departing. As they wended their way through the tables, they spoke in low, furious voices, their heads close together. Not once did she look his way. Based on the intensity of her conversation, there wasn't a doubt in his mind that she'd forgotten all about him.

Time to remind her.

"Take care of the bill, will you?" Lazz shoved back his chair and stood. "And let them know at the office that I won't be in for the rest of the day."

Laughter glittered in Sev's eyes. "Last-minute change in plans?"

"A business meeting I forgot to attend," he corrected coolly. "A few contractual obligations I've neglected to address."

"Or undress?"

"Stuff it, Sev."

His wife and Talbot stood in the foyer where they exchanged a few final words. Then Talbot inclined his head and left the restaurant. Ariana stood there watching him, looking utterly devastated. Lazz came up behind her. Cupping her elbow, he ushered her outside into the brilliant early fall sunshine. Since they'd driven to the restaurant in Sev's car, he was without a vehicle, so he lifted an arm to summon a cab.

"What do you think you're doing?" she demanded in Italian.

A cab pulled up and Lazz opened the door. "I'm escorting my wife home."

"What if I don't want to go home?"

"I'd say that's too damn bad," he answered, switching to Italian.

He rattled off the address to the driver as he helped Ariana into the backseat. To his relief, she didn't fight him, possibly because she didn't want to cause a scene. Fumbling in her purse, she yanked out a pair of sunglasses and perched them on the end of her nose. Turning her head to look out the window, she didn't say another word until they reached an elegant apartment building.

They took the elevator to the penthouse, again in silence. Although the floor had originally housed two apartments, he'd taken them both over when he'd purchased the building and remodeled the space to better suit his needs. Unlocking the door, he stepped to one side. Ariana swept in ahead of him. Tossing her purse and sunglasses onto the foyer table, she swiveled to confront him.

"You are rude."

"And you, *wife,* are keeping secrets. Who is Talbot?"

She lifted a shoulder in a careless shrug. "Like he told you. He's an old family friend."

"So, if I pick up the phone and ask Vittorio or Constantine about Talbot, they'd describe him that way, too?" Her split-second hesitation gave her away. "I gather that would be a no."

"He's a family friend of Grandmother Penelope's. And yes, she would describe him just that way. Or rather, she'd describe his father that way."

His questions came rapid-fire. "You met the son through the father?"

"Yes."

"Is it serious between you?"

"We're not personally involved."

"Funny. You looked personally involved. In fact, you looked like you were having a lover's spat."

"Funny. That's what I thought *we* were doing." She turned on her heel with a graceful swing of her hips and crossed to the living room, affording him an exquisite view of a derriere lovingly outlined in red silk.

"This isn't a lover's spat," he replied, following her. "This is a termination discussion. As in, termination of our contract."

That caught her attention. She spun around to face him. "You wouldn't. The contract our parents signed requires that we remain together for three months. If you leave now, we lose the diamond. After all we've been through in order to preserve Brimstone, why would you throw it away at this late date?"

"Because I don't like being made a fool of. If you'd told me you had a lover—"

Angry color swept across her elegant cheekbones. "I don't. Haven't, as you know damn well."

"And is he the reason you didn't want to enter into a sexual relationship with me? I thought you understood that I don't like secrets." He approached, impressed by the way she continued to hold her ground. She lifted her chin, glaring through a sheen of tears that she was too proud to let fall. He felt the hum of tension gather strength, could feel the irresistible tug of it, demanding a surrender he refused to make. "Who is he, Ariana?"

This time she didn't bother with pretense. "I'm sorry, Lazz, but I can't tell you. I promised Penelope

I wouldn't discuss it long before you and I began our negotiations. But I assure you, he's not my lover."

"I want to believe you."

"But because of Marco and Caitlyn you find that difficult." It wasn't a question.

"Very difficult." He considered various options before reaching a decision. "I want your promise that you won't see him again."

She stared in dismay. "I…I don't think I can make that promise."

A wintry coldness settled over him. "Our marriage needs to remain intact for a little more than two months. If you want to resume your association with Talbot at that point, there's nothing I can or will say about it. But until then we have to act the part of newlyweds. That fiction isn't going to work if you're seen having intimate luncheons with another man."

"We were in public."

"You put your hands on him."

She stared blankly. "I did?"

"You put your hand over his and squeezed it."

"I—I don't remember." She closed her eyes and shook her head. "I'm sorry, Lazz. I'm a demonstrative person. I hug. I kiss. I touch people. It's who I am. Who I've always been."

"Not with Talbot. At least, not for the next nine weeks."

She looked at him then. He didn't want to notice how bone-white she'd gone. Or how her eyes grew black with pain. Clearly, Talbot meant something to her. Who would she have married, if not for that damnable contract? Who would have been her first lover?

The mere idea of Talbot putting his hands on Ariana shredded every ounce of Lazz's self-control.

He'd always prided himself on his ability to reason his way through any situation. Even with Caitlyn, after that one outburst in Marco's office, he'd been able to consider the situation from all angles and come to terms with it. He had a knack for compartmentalizing. He could logic his way through even the most emotional issues. He had an innate talent for tallying things up in tidy rows and columns. It took little-to-no effort to draw a line separating X from Y, a line that didn't allow any Zs to slip from one side to the other. But with Ariana…

He rubbed a hand along the back of his neck. Damn it to hell. Ariana sent his Zs all over the place.

"And if I refuse to stay away from Aaron?" she finally asked. "What will you do then?"

Aaron. Lazz's tidy columns melted right along with his temper. "Then I will personally take Brimstone and consign it to the deep blue. I won't be made a fool of by my wife. I won't allow the woman I married to sleep with another man while my ring is on her finger." He fought his way past a flood of emotions, unwanted emotions that ripped away every shred of civilized behavior. "I can't handle any more deception, Ariana. I won't tolerate any more secrets. This is the end."

Pain turned to temper, sparking a fire in Ariana's dark eyes. "Oh, please. You have as many secrets as I do. All people have them." The Italian lilt grew heavy in her voice. She approached—stalked—toward him, her anger growing with every step. "You made this 'no secrets' business a part of our marriage before we ever met. You demanded I confide in you before I had any idea what sort of man you are. How did I know I could trust you? Why should I open myself to such a risk?"

"Because those are the rules I play by."

"Rules? I'm talking about our marriage and you're spouting rules at me?" She flung her arms wide. "You expect me to walk into this contract marriage and strip myself bare for you. Have you done as much for me? I think not."

His own temper made a swift return, no matter how hard he attempted to tamp it down. "What secrets have I kept from you? I've answered every question you've asked, been as honest as I can."

"You kept The Inferno a secret." She cut off his incipient reply with a sweep of her hand. "And you lie to yourself, as well as to me, when you claim it doesn't exist. One touch from you and I'm ruined for any other man."

"Ruined?" He couldn't disguise how the word appealed to him. Apparently it didn't appeal to his wife quite as much.

Tears vied with temper. "Yes, ruined! But did you bother to warn me of that possibility? No!"

"The Inferno is the lie, not my denial of it."

"You think so?" She closed the distance between them and interlaced her fingers with his, sliding into the burn of palm against palm. Her hand tightened around his, deepening the connection. "Deny this, husband of mine. Deny your Dante heritage and whatever created this bond. Like it or not, we're stuck with each other."

The rush hit him, stronger than ever before. Like it? What a watered-down word to describe what he felt.

It wasn't just physical anymore. If that were the only connection between them, he wouldn't have been so furious when he'd discovered Ariana dining with another man. "It's lust." Truth became jumbled with self-preservation. "Desire."

Her fingers trembled within his. "You repeat those words like a mantra, when the truth is you're so determined to be logical that you can't see what's right in front of your nose. You are afraid of losing control. You are afraid that your heart will overrule your head. You are afraid to give yourself, fully, to another person."

"I'm not afraid," he denied. And he wasn't. He simply knew what he wanted in his life and, more importantly, what he didn't. "I'm pragmatic. Being pragmatic means I refuse to allow myself to be controlled by my emotions."

A hint of a smile curved a path across the lushness of her mouth. "So I noticed at lunch."

"I believe that proves my point," he bit back. "Don't you get it? I come from a passionate family, all of whom allow their emotions to overrule their common sense. And how has it benefited them?"

"The last time I looked, they all had strong, happy marriages."

"I'm sure my parents' marriage was the same when it first started out. But it doesn't last. And when it goes wrong, it goes very wrong. The minute you put your well-being in someone else's hands, you're going to get hurt."

Anger eased into compassion. "Life hurts, Lazz. You can't protect yourself from the bruises it doles out. Your relationship with Caitlyn is a perfect example of that. But you can allow someone else in, someone who's willing to share all of that with you. The pain. The joy. The sorrow. The laughter. Can't you open the door a crack? Allow nature to take its course and see where we end up in a few months."

"If we allow nature to take its course one more time, in a few months our twosome risks becoming a three-some," he said drily.

Soft color streaked across Ariana's cheekbones. "What's happened between us wasn't supposed to happen at all."

"It was inevitable," he said gently. "The only one who didn't know it was you."

"Lazz—"

"Shall I prove it to you?"

He didn't give her time to respond. He hooked his fingers around the lapels of her suit jacket and tugged. She didn't resist. Couldn't resist. It was beyond either of them. She came into his arms, fitting herself to him, a lock to a key. She'd asked him to let go of his control, to allow nature to take its course. He didn't have any other choice. Common sense vanished whenever he touched Ariana.

His hands eased into her hair, destroying the sophis-ticated little twist as he gave in to temptation. Her ir-resistible siren's call grew more powerful with each passing day. Did she even realize it emanated from her in the way she walked, in the way she looked at him, in every word she spoke? That despite what either of them claimed, their hunger for one another overrode every thought and intent?

He fell into the kiss. Fell into her warmth and the

generosity of her welcome. He never understood how she could open so utterly to him. And yet, she had from the very beginning. How did she allow herself such intense vulnerability when it was the one thing he most wanted to avoid? She gave so unstintingly that he couldn't just take. More than anything, he was driven to give back.

In that instant, the quality of their lovemaking changed. Slowed. Became more than a physical expression. One by one, he released the buttons of her suit jacket. It parted, revealing a scrap of black lace that cupped her breasts, the play of ebony against cream providing a visual feast.

"It's going to happen again, isn't it?" she asked.

"Without question."

A smile sweetened her expression, creating a fascinating dichotomy to her lush earthiness. She was a woman of endless facets and contradictions. An innocent sophisticate. A practical dreamer. An open mystery. And he wanted to know and explore each and every one of those facets.

He unclipped the front fastening of her bra and palmed the silken weight of her breasts. Her breath escaped in a low moan, and her head fell back. He swept his thumbs across the tips of her breasts, watching as desire caused them to flush and tighten. He couldn't remember the last time he'd seen anything that aroused him more. Lowering his head, he dragged his teeth across her nipple, then soothed it with his tongue.

Italian erupted from her, a strangled stream of plea and demand. He'd planned to keep the pace slow and leisurely. But she didn't give him that option. She tore at his shirt and tie, stripping them off him with impressive speed.

"Are we doing this here?" she demanded. "Now?"

He refused to make love to her again without proper protection. "No. We're doing this in my bedroom."

"Fine. The bedroom it is."

After kicking off her heels, she unzipped her narrow skirt and shimmied out of it. She straightened, standing before him in a black thong, garter belt and stockings. He must have groaned because laughter competed with the passion in her gaze. She threw herself against him and practically leaped into his arms. Her head nestled against his shoulder and waves of heavy, dark hair spilled across his arm in a silken curtain.

"Take me to your bedroom," she ordered. "Now."

He gathered her close. "If not sooner."

It was difficult enough to walk with the fullness of her breasts pressing against his chest. But her thighs— round, sleek thighs—wriggled within his grasp while her hip and the curve of her backside flirted with his groin. He had no idea how he made it the short distance from the living room to the bedroom without dumping them both on the floor and losing himself in her. Every step was sheer torture.

Lazz kicked the door closed behind him, enclosing them in dusky solitude. Muted sunshine filtered through the blinds, chasing after them as they reached the bed. He dropped Ariana to the mattress, not bothering to pull back the comforter. It was almost painful to strip off his trousers and shorts. At the last minute he remembered protection.

He yanked open the bedside drawer, pulling it free

of its mooring and dumping it onto the floor. He swore in frustration and then swore again when Ariana slipped off the bed. "Wait," he said. "Let me—"

"I've got it."

She gathered up one of the foil squares and fumbled slightly with the wrapper, betraying her inexperience and rousing a fierce wave of tenderness in him. Then she ripped it open and removed the circle of latex. There was a hint of curiosity in her expression as she examined it, before turning her attention to him.

She shook her head in dismay. "This will never fit. Have you nothing larger?"

If his need hadn't been so dire, he'd have laughed. "It fits," he said. "Give it to me. I'll do it."

"No, no. Let me." She fit the latex over him and cautiously rolled it down his length. She caught her lip between her teeth. "Am I hurting you?"

"You're killing me."

She froze. "Should I stop?"

"No. Not unless you want to drive me straight out of my mind."

A tiny laugh slipped free. She struggled to contain it, without success. "I'm not laughing at you, I promise. It's…" She waved a hand as though to summon the right words. "Look at us. We have no clothes. All we want is to make love. We are desperate."

"Very desperate."

"If we don't make love right this instant, you have assured me we will either expire or go insane."

"Any second now it'll be over," he confirmed.

"And I haven't a clue what I'm doing."

He grinned. "You're making me laugh at a totally inappropriate time. That's never happened to me before."

"Me, neither." His gorgeous, sophisticated wife grinned like a street urchin. "It is funny, yes?"

"Oh, yeah."

"Give me a minute and I'll be serious again."

"I don't want you serious." And he didn't. "Just be yourself."

For some reason that caused her laughter to fade. He'd already bared her, physically. Now he watched as she bared her emotions, betraying the gentle want, the soft hunger. The need for him, and him alone.

Slowly, her hands moved again, stroking him into hardness. When she was done, she bent slightly to remove her garter and stockings, and her hair swirled forward across her shoulders. The sheer grace and sensuality of her impacted like a blow. Unable to help himself he caressed the vulnerable spot at the nape of her neck and followed the pure silken line from there down to the base of her spine.

She shuddered beneath his touch and whispered something in Italian. Whether plea or confession, he didn't quite catch it. But when she straightened, the last of her clothing formed a dark pool at their feet. Together they fell back onto the comforter, and he mated their bodies.

They moved slowly at first, taking those first few moments to reacquaint themselves with the fit and feel and flow of one into the other. "Oh, yes. Like that," she murmured.

He gave to her. And then he gave more, taking the

time to unlock the subtle secrets of her body, the movements and caresses that were unique to her and caused
her to soar to places she'd never been before. The burn
came. The flame that connected them exploded with
heat and light and pleasure as it consumed them.

Lazz felt her quiver beneath him, teetering for an
endless second on that pinnacle between climb and
tumble. Her breath caught, held, and then burst from
her lungs as she shot up and over into a helpless free
fall. He didn't hesitate. He leapt with her.

And he lost himself in her. In this woman. In his
wife. Within that intense release came a shattering, and
all he could do was surrender to it.

Eight

From: Bambolina@fornitore.it
Date: 2008, August 07 11:22 CEST
To: Lazzaro_Dante@DantesJewelry.com
Subject: Marriage Contract, Premarital Conditions...
me again!
I just thought of one more thing. I hope you don't
mind. And I hope your apartment is big enough!
Counter-Condition #3: I require a room for my
private use, one that you promise not to enter.
Ciao! Ariana

From: Lazzaro_Dante@DantesJewelry.com
Date: 2008, August 07 09:04 PDST
To: Bambolina@fornitore.it
Subject: Re: Marriage Contract, Premarital Condi-
tions...me again!

What the hell is this about? I'm serious. What do you
need a private room for? I'm going to call. We need
to discuss this.
L.

Ariana regarded her grandmother with a hint of exasperation. "I can't believe I agreed to this."

"And I can't thank you enough, especially considering you're still practically on your honeymoon." Penelope said.

"One month tomorrow," Ariana confirmed before
shaking her head. "What in the world made you suggest I attend this benefit in your place? Mrs. Pennywinkle has never made a public appearance before.
Nor has she ever had a representative."

"They caught me at a weak moment," Penelope confessed. "It's for children who are burn victims. Once they
promised no media attendance, how could I refuse?"

Ariana softened. "You couldn't, of course. Are you
certain you don't want to go yourself?"

One look at her grandmother's face answered that
question. "I can't run the risk I'll have a panic attack
and frighten the children."

"Never mind," Ariana soothed. "I'm happy to stand
in for you."

"Thank you. I was hoping you'd say that." A hint
of mischief glittered in Penelope's eyes. "I also had an
ulterior motive for my request."

"You thought it would convince me to do everything
in my power to become the new Mrs. Pennywinkle?"

"I can't fool you, can I? I even had your Nancy doll
flown in for the occasion. I thought it would make a nice

prop. You have no idea how much I've longed to attend a charity event—" Penelope broke off with a sigh.

"Don't." Ariana stooped beside Penelope and enfolded her in a tight embrace. "You've done so much for the family. Worked so hard. I just wish you'd let me explain to Lazz. It's been weeks since he saw me with Aaron. Even though he doesn't mention it, it's still there between us."

Penelope shook her head, adamant. "The Dantes are under constant media scrutiny. I know they'd agree to keep my secret." She gazed intently at her granddaughter. "But secrets have a way of getting out."

Ariana flinched. She sincerely hoped not. At least, she hoped certain secrets didn't get out. "He's my husband, Gran," she insisted gently. "He has a right to know."

"Maybe once Aaron Talbot agrees to take you on as the new Mrs. Pennywinkle, we could reconsider."

"*If* Aaron agrees," Ariana corrected. "After our luncheon meeting, I'd have to say it's going to be difficult to convince him. He's determined to keep Mrs. Pennywinkle sacrosanct."

Penelope dismissed that with a wave of her hand. "He'll give in. He won't have any choice if he wants more Mrs. Pennywinkle books. And once you're the new Mrs. P, the media attention will be on you. They might have a passing interest in me, but once I'm back with Carolina and Vittorio on the Romano estate, they won't have the opportunity to approach me unless I choose to let them." Pain and fear added definition to her wrinkles. "It won't be like it was after the accident."

"No, it won't." Ariana kissed her grandmother's cheek and straightened. "I'd better go or I'll be late."

"Will you come back to the hotel room afterward and tell me how it went?" Penelope asked.

Ariana shook her head. "I'll have to fill you in tomorrow. I'm supposed to meet Lazz for dinner, and that won't give me much time to get back to the apartment before he returns from work."

"Be careful with your doll. I'd be crushed if it were lost or damaged. She's the very first one ever made."

Ariana smiled indulgently. "I remember. I wouldn't dream of allowing any harm to come to her."

Penelope nodded in relief. "Try and have fun."

That would be a stretch. Still, she would do everything in her power to make it a special occasion for the children. Giving her grandmother a final hug and kiss, Ariana picked up the Nancy doll Penelope had given her as a child and left the hotel room.

"Are we all set?" Lazz asked one of the benefit organizers. "I'm hoping this Pennywinkle representative will be an acceptable substitute for the author. Fortunately, the publisher sent free autographed copies of Pennywinkle's book, so that should please the children."

He also hoped the representative didn't have an adverse reaction to some of the more severely deformed burn victims. Of all the Dantes, he was the most passionate about this particular organization and worked tirelessly on its behalf. He'd hate to think what should have been a special treat for the children might turn into a nightmare of rejection.

"I believe the rep just arrived," the organizer replied, nodding toward the ballroom doorway.

Lazz turned to look, then grinned. "That's not Pennywinkle's rep. That's my wife."

"Oh, of course," the man hastened to say. "I guess it was the Nancy doll that fooled me."

Lazz took a second look. Ariana stood near the doorway, shaking hands with the assistant he'd assigned as the "official greeter" for Mrs. Pennywinkle's representative. And in her arms she cuddled a Nancy doll. After excusing himself, he left the small group of organizers to their last-minute details and joined his wife.

"Fancy meeting you here," he greeted her.

For some reason she didn't look thrilled to see him. Shocked might be a more appropriate description. "Lazz? What are you doing here?"

"I sit on the board of the organization. I'm the one responsible for today's benefit." He cocked his head to one side. "And you?"

She hesitated for a telling moment. "Mrs. Pennywinkle is an old family friend. She asked if I'd represent her."

Interesting. There wasn't time to ask further questions, but he had to admit he was curious to know more about the reclusive author. "I'm glad you're here," he said simply. "Let me introduce you to the children."

She linked her fingers with his, and the distinctive tug hit the instant their palms joined, a ribbon of desire that continued to connect them even as the program began. Over the next hour, lunch was served. While everyone ate, Ariana read from the latest Mrs. Pennywinkle book and cuddled one of the children on her lap. Lazz held the book and turned the pages for her.

He wondered if she realized her emotional reactions to the situation caused a hint of an Italian lilt to weave its way through her voice. If anyone else picked up on it, they didn't let on. But he noticed. He noticed something else, as well. He noticed how his wife maneuvered from table to table, never seeming to rush. Never seeming too busy to speak to or hug or laugh with each and every child.

Toward the end of the event, she joined the very last table and sat with one of the more severely burned children, a painfully shy little girl. Although the child carried a tattered Mrs. Pennywinkle book, she was the only one so far who didn't also have a Nancy doll clutched in her arms.

"Does Cecelia not like dolls?" Ariana whispered to the mother at one point.

Bright color swept across the woman's cheekbones as she shook her head. "We can't afford one," she replied stiffly. "Maybe for Christmas."

Lazz watched as tears gathered in his wife's eyes. Turning to the little girl, Ariana indicated the doll she'd brought with her to the event. "Did you know this is the first Nancy doll ever made?"

Cecelia stared, wide-eyed. "The very first?" She reached toward the doll's ruffled skirt before jerking her hand back. "I'm sorry," she whispered.

"You can touch her. In fact…" Ariana settled the doll carefully in Cecelia's arms. "This Nancy doll is magical, maybe because she was the first. Her job is to live her life the same way she does in the storybooks. She wants to be with someone she can help. Otherwise her magic will fade away."

Cecelia froze, hardly daring to breathe. "She wants to be with someone like me?"

"Just like you," Ariana confirmed. "She's to stay with you until you don't need her any longer."

Cecelia bit down on her lip. "What if that's a long, long time? What if the operations take years and years?"

It took Ariana a moment to reply. "Nancy will stay with you for as long as necessary. And when you don't need her any longer, then it's your job to pass her on to someone else who does."

The little girl stared up at Ariana, a mixture of adoration and determination reflected in her ruined face. "I will," she promised fervently. "I'll give her to someone who needs her as bad as me."

Lazz could only imagine how difficult it must have been for his wife to give away her treasured doll. But when it was done, she stood, smiled at everyone and then walked away without once looking back. After excusing himself, he went after her and took her arm. She didn't require his physical support, but there wasn't a question in his mind that she desperately needed him emotionally.

"Hang on just a minute. It's almost over."

He stopped at the dais long enough to give a brief speech thanking everyone for attending and wrapping up the event. He didn't have a moment's doubt that the children would remember this occasion for years to come. Finally, he gestured toward the side door.

"Let's go."

"I can manage," she insisted.

He could hear the strain dragging through each

word. He didn't reply. He simply ushered her into the hallway. The minute the door closed behind them, he wrapped her up in a tight embrace and kissed her. She stiffened within his hold, resisting him for all of five seconds before dissolving, responding to him as passionately as every other time he touched her.

Eventually he pulled back and regarded her with a tender expression.

"Are you all right? I imagine giving that doll away was one of the most difficult things you've ever done."

She didn't deny it. "Helping others, paying it forward. It's what Mrs. Pennywinkle stands for. It's the message that underscores every single one of her books. How could I not honor the true meaning of the Nancy doll by passing her along the same way all the children do between the pages of the Pennywinkle books?"

"You couldn't. It's not in your nature." He draped a comforting arm around her shoulders. "Come on. What do you say we go home?"

"Sounds perfect."

When they reached the apartment, Ariana took Lazz's hand in hers. Instead of leading him to the nearest bed, she paused by the door to the room she'd requested for her third marital condition. She opened it without a word and flipped on the lights.

He walked in and stared, stunned. "My God." He took his time, moving through the room, examining painting after painting. "You did these, didn't you? I'd recognize your artwork anywhere."

"Yes, they're mine. Most of them I painted while in Italy. They're for a new Pennywinkle book. At least, they might be, depending on what Aaron decides." She took a deep breath and faced him. "Aaron Talbot publishes the Mrs. Pennywinkle series. That's why we were meeting at lunch the other day. He's considering me as a replacement for the previous Mrs. Pennywinkle."

"It was a business meeting?" Lazz winced. That finally answered his question about Talbot, and he couldn't begin to express the relief he felt, as well as his remorse over his earlier suspicions. "I'm so sorry, Ariana. I really am an ass, aren't I?"

"Occasionally." She smiled to soften her response. "And your apology is accepted. Sometimes it's hard to reach an accurate conclusion when you don't have all the facts."

"Sev warned me of that. But that still doesn't excuse my reaction." Lazz studied the paintings and shook his head. "These are amazing. I assume Talbot has agreed to take you on?"

"Not yet."

That caught him by surprise. "He hasn't already snapped you up as the new Pennywinkle? Is he crazy?"

Ariana laughed, though he heard a hint of anguish underscoring her amusement. "I happen to think so. So does Gran."

Just like that, it clicked. "Penelope. Penny. Pennywinkle. *She's* Mrs. Pennywinkle."

Ariana nodded. "She started painting as a form of therapy after her car accident. Now that her arthritis makes it too difficult to continue, she wants me to take over."

"I don't understand." He glanced over his shoulder

at her. "If Penelope's the real Pennywinkle, why didn't she attend the benefit?"

"One of the side effects of being trapped for two days in a wrecked car is that she suffers from panic attacks. The intense media attention afterward only made her more fearful. She refuses to make appearances in case she has an attack and frightens the children."

Compassion swept through him. "Losing control like that would be difficult for anyone, but it must be especially tough for a woman of her strength of character."

"Extremely."

Lazz returned his attention to his wife's artwork. He'd been impressed when he'd seen the sketches she'd done while on their honeymoon. He'd even gone out of his way to rescue and salvage her sketch pad because he couldn't bear the thought of losing such amazing drawings. But those were mere shadows of what she'd accomplished here.

"You've actually shown these to Talbot? And he rejected them?"

"Not exactly. I showed him a portfolio of my work. He rejected that. He says my illustrations are too whimsical. And those are nowhere near as whimsical as these. What he really wants is for me to copy my grandmother's style so no one knows there's been a change in authorship. I tried to do what he asked." She crossed to a stack of canvasses leaning against the wall and removed one of them, pulling back the cloth covering. "This is how they come out."

"Ouch."

"My reaction, exactly."

"There are other publishers, Ariana, any number of whom would be delighted to produce a new, updated Mrs. Pennywinkle. Have you considered approaching someone else?"

"According to Aaron, our contract prohibits it."

"Why don't you give me a copy of the contract, and I'll have my lawyers take a look? If they don't see an out, we'll hire a literary attorney."

"I'm not sure my grandmother will agree. She has a long history with Aaron's father. But I'll ask her." Ariana gave Lazz a quick kiss, just a swift brush of her lips against his. "Thank you."

That one fleeting caress was all it took. If he lived to be a hundred, he didn't think he'd ever understand exactly what it was about Ariana that moved him so. That took him from down-to-earth common sense and shot him straight into molten need.

He didn't say a word. He didn't have to. He heard the slight hitch in her breathing, saw comprehension darken her eyes to ebony. A light flush gave definition to her cheekbones. And the air around them thickened, grew heavy and scented with the perfume of their want.

Without taking his eyes off her, he tugged at the knot in his tie and yanked it free. Ariana followed suit, stripping out of the clothes she'd changed into after their return to the apartment. And yet, still they didn't touch, not until the last bit of silk and cotton carpeted the floor.

Then they came together. Slowly. Gently. Softly. There in a room that contained his wife's soul, he joined with her. Gave to her. Gifted her with all he had within him. Just as she had sacrificed her doll, he sacrificed his disbelief. He gave himself up to her, gave himself up to The Inferno.

He gave himself up to love.

Ariana moaned. "I don't think I can move."

"Join the club."

"I'm also starving," she confessed. "Why don't we order in? That way we don't have to move any farther than the phone."

"Dinner? Is it that late?" He checked his watch and swore. "You're going to have to move a lot farther than that. And faster, too. Your father is due over any minute."

She bolted upright, panic shooting through her. The past month had been sheer agony while she'd waited for either the phone call from her father informing her that he'd found Brimstone and saved her from guaranteed damnation or for her world to come crashing down when Lazz discovered how she'd deceived him. It would appear the wait was over.

She burst into nervous Italian. "Papa? Here? Why is he coming here? I thought he was back home."

"I asked him to bring Brimstone over."

She went absolutely rigid. "Now? But… Aren't we supposed to split Brimstone on our three-month anniversary? What's the rush?"

Lazz shot her a curious look. "In order to determine the diamond's value, I need to have it appraised. That doesn't happen overnight. I asked Vittorio to bring the diamond to San Francisco sometime this week."

"And Papa agreed? He brought it?" she asked tautly.

"He flew in today."

She relaxed slightly and drew a slow, calming breath. "I wonder why he didn't let me know. That's good news." She grinned, reveling in the joyful relief that washed over her. "Actually, that's great news."

He scooped her close. "And we're not splitting the stone, remember? The Dantes are buying you out. Very bad luck to split Brimstone."

"Really?" she asked, intrigued. "Why is that?"

"According to legend, the only way Brimstone can be split is if—"

She lifted an eyebrow. "Hell freezes over?"

He grinned at the play on words. "Close enough. No, according to legend, Brimstone has to split on its own. And diamonds don't normally do that. Not without a bit of help.

"So, until that happens, your family plans to keep it intact?" At his nod, she asked, "What do you get when it splits on its own? You do get something, right?"

"Rich."

She smothered a laugh. "That's what the legend says?"

"No, that's what I say. The legend says we'll receive good fortune and God's favor until the Dante line is no more. The Dantes are big on superstition, if not reality. Everything from The Inferno to Brimstone."

Before she could argue the point, the doorbell sounded and they both jumped to their feet, yanking on clothes with careless haste. Lazz finished dressing first. "Take your time," he told Ariana. "I'll delay your father."

She joined them just as Vittorio greeted Lazz with a handshake that didn't quite hide his nervousness. "I hope you don't mind that I'm a few minutes early."

"Not at all." Lazz gestured toward the wet bar. "Can I get you something to drink?"

"Scotch and water," Vittorio requested. "A double."

The request had Ariana's heart stuttering. She tried to catch his eye, but he refused to look at her. And that's when she knew. He hadn't found the diamond, and he'd come here to confess his sins. She shut her eyes. Please, no. Please let her be mistaken. Please don't let her marriage end before it had fully begun.

Lazz fixed the drink and offered it to Vittorio. "What's wrong?" he asked quietly.

"I was hoping to delay this conversation for a while longer. But clearly, I cannot."

"I assume that means that you don't have Brimstone," Lazz said without inflection. "Is that what you're here to tell me?"

"Yes." Vittorio downed his drink in a single swallow. "That's what I'm here to tell you."

Ariana closed her eyes. "Oh, Papa," she murmured.

"I tried to call and warn you, *bambolina,* but—"

Lazz cut in, fighting to keep his voice level. "What happened to the diamond? Where is it?"

Vittorio hesitated. "After Dominic's death, I removed the stone from the safety deposit box where we'd agreed to keep it," he confessed.

Ariana dropped into the nearest chair. "After Dominic died?" she repeated in disbelief. No. No, that wasn't what he'd told her before the wedding. He'd said… She struggled to recall. He'd *implied* that he'd only recently lost it. "It's been gone all these years?"

"I'm afraid so." Vittorio cleared his throat. "Primo had no idea Dominic had taken the diamond in the first place, so after his death I wanted to return it and explain how it came to be in my possession."

"Of course," Lazz said evenly. "It was the only option available to you since disposing of the diamond in any other manner would have been unethical."

Vittorio had the grace to redden. "This was my feeling, as well," he was quick to assure. "But before I could return it, it went missing. I searched everywhere for it. It was as though it had vanished into thin air. I can only assume one of the servants…" He trailed off with a lifted shoulder.

"And you've spent the last dozen or more years searching for it? I assume you called in the authorities?" Lazz lifted an eyebrow. "No?"

"No," Vittorio admitted. "I didn't say anything when I lost Brimstone because I was too ashamed to admit to my carelessness. On top of that there would have been a scandal." He spared Lazz an apprehensive glance. "But there's another reason. A more important reason I allowed the wedding to go through."

Ariana crossed to his side and took her father's hand in hers. "What, Papa?"

He caressed his daughter's cheek. "Dominic wanted this marriage with all his heart. He insisted on the contract, even over my express objections." He addressed Lazz again. "He did it to protect you, my boy. And he made Brimstone part of the deal because he knew it was the only way to convince me to go along with his crazy scheme. Now that he's gone—" Vittorio broke off and gathered himself before continuing. "I wish to honor his wishes."

"I'm sure your reasons for insisting Ariana and I go

through with the marriage were totally altruistic." Lazz made the comment in a wintry voice.

"It was because of The Inferno," Vittorio continued doggedly. "Out of respect for your privacy I haven't wanted to mention something so personal, but your father saw a spark between you and my daughter all those years ago. That's why he insisted on the contract."

"Enough," Lazz snapped.

Ariana gazed at him, stricken. "Lazz, please," she whispered.

He glared at Vittorio. "I can make a fairly logical guess why you didn't tell my family you lost Brimstone. You were hoping that despicable contract never came to light. After all, my father was dead, and supposedly none of the other Dantes knew about it, any more than they knew what happened to Brimstone. Its whereabouts died with my father."

"No, I—"

Lazz cut him off. "Of course, if the agreement did turn up, you hoped it wouldn't happen until after Ariana's twenty-fifth birthday so that you could claim the diamond had been disposed of as per the terms of the contract. But when Caitlyn unexpectedly came across Dad's copy of the agreement in a box of old family papers and brought it to my attention *before* Ariana turned twenty-five, it didn't leave you any choice."

"You seem to have all the answers," Vittorio said with a dispirited shrug. "Feel free to finish it."

"Very well." Lazz addressed his remarks to Ariana. "Your father had two options. He could either admit the truth and deal with the suspicion and fury of the Dantes.

And I guarantee, not only would Primo have been livid over that contract, he'd have also been highly skeptical about the diamond's convenient disappearance, especially considering the Romanos' precarious financial situation. Or your father had a second option. He could pretend that Brimstone was still safe and sound. He could allow the marriage to go through and...hope. Hope that our marriage worked out and all would be forgiven. Hope that the Dantes wouldn't want to cause a scandal involving the Romanos, especially now that the two families were connected by marriage. Hope that a miracle would happen and Brimstone would be found."

"Actually, you're wrong about that last part," Ariana corrected. "My father didn't hope any such thing."

Lazz shot a sharp look at his wife, and she could see suspicion take hold, one he visibly fought to suppress. "I was wrong about Aaron, so I don't want to make that same mistake again," he told her. "But how do you know what your father thought or didn't think?"

She lifted her chin and looked straight at him. "Because *he* didn't take those possibilities into consideration before we married. *I* did. I married you to protect my family from the Dantes."

Nine

From: Lazzaro_Dante@DantesJewelry.com
Date: 2008, August 07 10:57 PDST
To: Bambolina@fornitore.it
Subject: Marriage Contract, Premarital Conditions…
Final

As per our phone conversation, I'm sending you my final premarital condition.

Condition #6: Dantes will have Brimstone appraised by two (2) independent sources. Dantes will retain possession of Brimstone. The Romanos will receive a cash settlement of one half the appraised value of the diamond.

I hope this meets with your approval. Looking forward to the 28th.

L.

From: Bambolina@fornitore.it
Date: 2008, August 07 20:20 CEST
To: Lazzaro_Dante@DantesJewelry.com
Subject: Re: Marriage Contract, Premarital Conditions…Final

Oh, Lazz. You make me laugh. I, too, am looking forward to the 28th. However you decide to divide Brimstone is fine with me and my family.

Ciao! Ariana

Ariana's confession hung in the air for an endless minute.

Then Lazz turned to her father. "Please excuse us," he said with biting formality. "Your daughter and I need to speak in private."

Alarm flared in Vittorio's dark eyes. "I won't leave her alone with you. Not while you're so furious."

"He won't hurt me," Ariana reassured. "And he's right, Papa. This is between the two of us."

Lazz didn't wait for an argument to erupt. He simply opened the front door and stood there. Without another word, Vittorio left. Hanging on to his self-control through sheer willpower, Lazz gently closed the door. "Just to clarify, you knew before we married that Brimstone was missing?" he asked.

Ariana nodded. "My father told me right before the ceremony." She retreated behind a facade of calm poise. If the circumstances had been different, it would have impressed the hell out of him. "He neglected to mention how long the diamond had been missing, or I might have made a different decision."

"So, you've been lying to me from the start."

She didn't spare herself. "Yes. At the time I found out about Brimstone, I didn't know you other than through a few terse e-mails and a stilted phone conversation or two. What little I did know warned that you wouldn't react well to the news. So I did what I felt I had to."

"You were right," he said. Her head jerked up at that. "I'm not reacting well to the news."

She was foolish enough to cross the room toward him. "Try and see this from my point of view, Lazz. I hoped my father would find the diamond before anyone discovered it was missing. What I didn't count on was The Inferno." Her thumb traced a shaky path across her palm as she confessed with devastating honesty. "I also didn't count on falling in love with you."

"Don't," he bit out. He took a step back, putting some distance between them and the relentless pull that even now urged him to surrender to his feelings for Ariana. The connection should have broken. It should have shattered when she confessed what she'd done. But it hadn't. If anything, the more he resisted, the more unrelenting it grew. "You expect me to believe you love me when everything about our relationship has been a lie? Every condition of our marriage a joke?"

Her chin shot up. "The only thing I lied about was Brimstone," she insisted. "The rest was real."

"It's all been a lie. Mrs. Pennywinkle. Brimstone." He fixed a wintry gaze on her. "The Inferno."

Anger flared, turning her eyes to jet. "Fine. I didn't tell you about Mrs. Pennywinkle and Brimstone. I was protecting my family, and I refuse to apologize for that, especially considering that in my position, you'd have done the same thing. But the rest…" She held out her hand, palm up. "The rest of it is real. My feelings for you are real. The Inferno is real."

Ice encased him. "I was betrayed before. You knew that. And yet, you still chose to betray me again. I won't stay with a woman I can't trust."

She turned deathly pale. "We can work through this. Please, Lazz, won't you try?"

He wavered for a brief moment. Only hours earlier, for a brief, shining moment, he'd believed. The Inferno had lived in him, even if it had been an illusion. He wanted the dream again, was desperate for another taste of the fantasy, regardless of the personal cost.

He forced himself to take another step back before he lost all he held most dear. Reason. Common sense. Clear-cut lines and tidy columns. "We married for business," he informed her. "That business has now been concluded."

Her arm dropped to her side, and her fingers curled inward on her palm, like a flower blossom closing against the chill night air. "There's no longer any reason for our marriage to continue, is there?" She asked the question in Italian.

"No logical reason."

He flinched as he witnessed the death of hope. She lifted her chin, hanging on to her dignity by a shred. "I realize this is your apartment, but if you'd give me an hour or two of privacy, I'll remove my things."

"Ariana—"

"Please, Lazz."

Her voice broke apart on his name, a shattering that

went from voice to heart to spirit. He started to say
something, then changed his mind. There was nothing
left to be said. Without another word, he turned on his
heel and walked out.

Ariana stood in the middle of Lazz's apartment less
than an hour later and stared at her grandmother. All
around her were the bits and pieces of the life she'd
shared with Lazz, like flotsam adrift after a shipwreck.
"I'm really happy to see you, Gran, so don't misunderstand my question," she said. She fought a wave of
exhaustion that threatened to knock her off her feet.
"But why are you here?"

"Lazz called. He said I should come over immediately. He's filled me in on most of what's happened."

"He called you?" Ariana couldn't hold back her
tears. Considering how they'd parted, it was an incredibly kind gesture on his part. "Why would he do that?"

"I assume he's worried about you. It's an excellent
quality to have in a husband." She wheeled herself
farther into the living room. "Since I'd already arranged for my driver to transport me over here, it
worked out well for all concerned."

"You were coming for a visit?" Ariana asked. Unan-
nounced? That wasn't like Penelope. She wouldn't
intrude without calling first. "You're welcome, of
course. I just don't understand why…"

"I have two items to discuss with you. I was going
to postpone them both until I heard your father had
flown in to see Lazz. There could only be one reason.
He was finally going to admit the truth about Brimstone. As soon as I heard that, I rushed over." She gave

her wheelchair a disgruntled smack. "Not that either of us can actually rush anymore."

Ariana froze, zeroing in on the most critical of her grandmother's comments. "You know about Brimstone?"

"I do." Fire flashed in her grandmother's blue eyes. "I know about both Brimstone and that despicable contract. I've known for years. How your father could do something so unconscionable I'll never understand."

"He says—"

Penelope cut her off. "I know what excuses he's given. All that nonsense about The Inferno."

Ariana closed her eyes. "It's not nonsense," she said softly.

"No?" A hint of humor mitigated her grandmother's fury. "I was hoping you'd say that. It must be the romantic in me. Not that it matters. If what you and Lazz felt as children really was a form of The Inferno, then Vittorio and Dominic should have waited and let nature take its course. Your parents should have separated you two until you were old enough to meet as fully grown adults. At that point, you could have formed an attachment—or not—without involving contracts and diamonds and temporary marriages. Instead they decided to give new depth and definition to the word 'idiotic' and mucked up the entire affair."

"It's too late to change anything now, Gran. What's done is done."

Penelope lifted an eyebrow. "So nature hasn't taken its course?" she asked delicately.

Ariana bit back a tear-laden laugh. "Oh, it's taken

its course. But because Papa lost the diamond and I knew it before we married, Lazz doesn't trust me anymore. With some justification, I have to admit."

"Hmm." Penelope's mouth compressed in annoyance. "I suspect I've contributed to that problem, as well. Or at least Mrs. Pennywinkle has."

Ariana sank into a chair next to her grandmother and joined hands with her. "There were a lot of contributing factors. Secrets on top of secrets. Aaron and Mrs. Pennywinkle. Papa and Dominic. Brimstone. Now that the diamond's gone, it gives him the excuse he needs to pull away before he gets burned."

Penelope patted Ariana's hand. "Yes, well. That can be dealt with in time. But first things first. Brimstone isn't gone. I have it." She gave a little shrug. "Well, technically, you have it."

Ariana stared in shock. "I have it? Where?"

"In your Nancy doll. When your father removed the diamond from the safe deposit box and brought it home, it gave me the opportunity to put paid to that disgraceful contract once and for all. I took the diamond and sewed it inside the doll. I decided that if there was no diamond, there wouldn't be a marriage." She sniffed. "Little did I know your father would prove more determined than I anticipated."

Ariana struggled to draw breath. "Wait, wait. Go back." Please, please let there have been a mistake. "You put Brimstone in my Nancy doll? The one you had flown out here for the charity event? *That* Nancy doll?"

"Of course *that* Nancy doll. What other one is there? To be honest, I had it couriered out here because I knew that at some point Vittorio would be forced to produce the diamond. When he couldn't, he'd have to admit what he'd done." Her smile would have done a canary-swallowing cat proud. "I've been looking forward to that moment for years. I'm just sorry I missed it."

"Why would you allow me to take that doll to the charity function, knowing it contained a diamond worth millions?" Ariana could barely articulate the question. "Why would you allow me to take such a risk?"

Penelope stirred uneasily. "You'd never let anything happen to that doll. It means more to you than anything you've ever owned. If the entire villa were aflame, Nancy would be the one possession you'd grab on your way out the door." Something in Ariana's expression must have given her away. Penelope turned chalk-white. "You do still have the doll, don't you?

Ariana shook her head. "No." The word was barely more than a whisper. "I gave her away. I gave Nancy away."

"What do you mean? What are you talking about?"

"There was a little girl at the charity event. A burn victim. She was the only child without a doll. So…so I gave her mine and told her to pass the doll along when she didn't need it any longer."

"Oh, Ariana, how could you do such a thing?"

Ariana stiffened. "I don't care how many diamonds are hidden in that doll," she snapped. "It was the right thing to do. If you'd met Cecelia, you'd have done the same."

Penelope held up her hands. "You're right. Of course, you're right. Maybe I'd have removed the diamond first, but nevertheless." She waved that aside. "That still doesn't solve our problem. What are we going to do?"

Ariana folded her arms across her chest. "Absolutely nothing. I refuse to take the doll away from that child or attempt to substitute it with another. If Lazz or one of the Dantes wants to approach her, that's on them. But as far as I'm concerned, it was fate. That diamond should have been thrown in the ocean long ago, right along with that hideous contract." Not to mention every last one of the conditions she and Lazz had negotiated.

"I can't say I disagree. Even so…" Penelope frowned. "Is your marriage really over, dearest? Can nothing be done to salvage it?"

Ariana's bravado faded. "With Brimstone gone, so is my reason for marrying Lazz. The only excuse I have for remaining in San Francisco is if Aaron wants me to write and illustrate the Mrs. Pennywinkle books. Maybe if that happens, Lazz and I will have time—" The expression on Penelope's face had Ariana closing her eyes in distress. "You told me there were two reasons you were on your way over here. One was Brimstone. I assume the other was to tell me you heard from Aaron."

"He's rejected you as my replacement. I'm so sorry."

"Lazz planned to have some lawyers look over your contract." Ariana gave a humorless laugh. "I don't think that's likely to happen anytime soon. Do you?"

Her grandmother shook her head. "No, I guess not. So, what now?"

Ariana looked around the apartment in silent farewell. "The only logical alternative available. I'll return to Italy." Penelope started to say something then hesitated. An odd expression drifted across her face, one Ariana recognized all too well and which caused her to warn, "You're not to interfere, Gran. There's been enough of that already."

Penelope smiled blandly. "I agree," she surprised Ariana by saying. "And I wouldn't dream of interfering. Pack a bag. You can stay with me at Le Premier until we return home. I'll ask your father to gather up the rest of your belongings here. It's the least he can do given the circumstances."

Ariana didn't argue. She didn't think she had any argument left in her. No emotions. No tears. No hope. She kneaded her palm. No Inferno. Without Lazz, the burn would cool, fading to no more than a memory. Any minute now, it would ease. It had to. She didn't think she could live with the heartache, otherwise.

She headed for her bedroom and, once there, closed the door and sagged against it. Who was she kidding? She'd have to find a way to live with it. Because, no matter how hard she might try and wish The Inferno away, it wasn't going anywhere anytime soon.

Sev opened the door to his Pacific Heights home and stepped back. "I thought you might show up here," he informed Lazz. "Come on in."

"How did you—"

"Penelope called, though I gather it was against your wife's express wishes. She filled me in on what happened between you and Ariana."

Lazz took a moment to digest that. "Did she also tell you Brimstone is gone?"

"No, she told me Brimstone's been found." Sev

chuckled, his eyes turning a rich, dark gold. "Judging by your expression, I gather that's news to you. Come on. I think you could use a drink."

"Explain first," Lazz ordered.

"Okay, Mr. Logic. See if you can follow this." Sev led the way to his study while he gave his brother the shorthand version of what Penelope had done with the diamond and how Ariana had unwittingly disposed of it.

When Sev finished, Lazz held out his hand. "Give me that drink," he ordered. He snatched the tumbler from Sev and tossed back the generous finger of whiskey in a single swallow. "Well, hell."

"I'd say that pretty much sums it up," Sev concurred. "Which leaves us with a choice. We can go after the diamond, assuming it hasn't already been passed along. Or we can let it go and allow fate to control its destiny."

Lazz grimaced. "If my vote counts for anything, I say let it go. That damn rock has been nothing but bad luck since the day it was ripped from the ground." He fixed his brother with a wary eye. "You've done a fantastic job of returning Dantes to its former position in the jewelry world. We don't need Brimstone to solidify our financial or business position, do we?"

"No, we don't. And it may interest you to know that your vote makes it unanimous."

Lazz couldn't conceal his surprise. "You discussed this with Nicolò and Marco?"

"I just got off the phone with them. If you choose not to try and recover the diamond, the rest of us will go along with your decision."

No question. No hesitation. "Let it go. If the Romanos want to track it down, let them. But my opinion is that no one should benefit from that rock."

After helping himself to a drink and refreshing Lazz's, Sev settled on the couch and waved his brother toward a nearby chair. "Next order of business. Now that all the secrets are out in the open, what do you plan to do about Ariana?"

"What we agreed from the beginning. End the marriage."

Compassion tarnished Sev's gaze. "She made a mistake, Lazz."

"She betrayed me."

"She was protecting her family. No doubt it's been drummed into her the same way it's been drummed into us. That doesn't mean she's not your soul mate. That doesn't mean you didn't experience The Inferno with her."

"Don't."

"You still don't believe, do you?" Sev leaned forward and rested his forearms on his knees. "Why, Lazz? You're the most logical of us all. How can you deny its existence when the evidence is all around you?"

"You're forgetting one vital piece of that evidence." Lazz's mouth compressed. "You're forgetting that Dad and I share similar personalities. You're forgetting that The Inferno didn't work for him and Mom."

Sev tilted his head back and swore. "Of course. I am *such* an idiot. I had no idea you thought that or I'd have set you straight years ago. But you were only a teenager when our parents died, and I didn't want to destroy your memories of them." He released his breath in a sigh. "Dad absolutely believed in The Inferno. But he and Mom never felt it toward each other."

Lazz froze. *"What?"*

"After they died, I found letters indicating that Dad had experienced The Inferno with one of his designers. He chose to ignore what he felt, despite Primo's warnings. He married Mom for her business contacts...and regretted it for the rest of his life. That's why he drafted that contract with Vittorio. He saw an incipient form of The Inferno spark when you and Ariana first touched as children, and he wanted to be certain that the son who most shared his logical bent wouldn't make the same mistake he made."

"How do you know this?"

"From the letters. And I've spoken to Primo and Vittorio about it." Sev paused. "And because you're sitting there attempting to rub a hole in your palm."

Silence reigned for five solid minutes before Lazz spoke again. "I don't know if I can let go," he confessed. "I don't know if I can choose the possibility over the reality."

Sev took a second to gather his arguments. "I understand what you're going through. So do Marco and Nicolò, since we've all been there. We've sat right where you're sitting now and faced the same decision. You have two choices, Lazz. You can forgive your wife, surrender to The Inferno and have a life fuller and richer than you can possibly imagine. Or you can make the same mistake our father made and die in perpetual regret. I suggest you choose fast, before it's too late." He stood. "Now get the hell out of here before I beat your decision into that ugly mug of yours."

Lazz had no memory of returning to his apartment. When he opened the door, he could feel the lack of connection, the sense of emptiness that signaled his wife's absence. Even so, he called to her, praying she'd respond with an enthusiastic volley of Italian. Of course, there was no answer. But there was a message from Vittorio.

I've collected all of Ariana's belongings except her paintings. Will return later tonight for those.

At a loss, Lazz wandered through the empty apartment. He couldn't help but notice that the bits and pieces that Ariana had contributed to his home—and his life—had been stripped away, leaving it cold and sterile. He fought against a pain he had no hope of easing. Had he really lived like this before Ariana? How the hell had he survived it?

Eventually, he found himself in the Mrs. Pennywinkle room. He glanced around, absorbing the beauty and whimsy of his wife's artwork. It was a beauty and whimsy that had slipped into the other areas of his apartment and into all aspects of his life. Into his heart and mind and body. And straight into his soul.

Sev was right. He could reject it, reject The Inferno, along with his wife. Or he could embrace the true meaning of the legend. He could embrace the love that Ariana had given him so unstintingly. The joy and laughter and passion. And he could give it back to her just as unstintingly. He could have love, or he could cling to his common sense and reason and return to the barren existence he'd known before.

It didn't take any thought at all.

He bent down and picked up a piece of paper that had missed the trash can, realizing as he started to ball it up that it was a letter. Aaron Talbot's name leapt off the page and Lazz stiffened as he read. Son of a— He pulled out his cell phone and punched in Penelope's number. She answered on the first ring.

"Talbot rejected Ariana?" he asked tersely.

"Yes," she confirmed. "Ever since Aaron took control of his father's publishing firm, he's been fanatical about preserving the sanctity of Mrs. Pennywinkle. Young fool. At least Jonah would have been more open to change."

"I can fix this," he offered. "I just need time."

There was a brief pause. "What's the point, since Ariana's returning to Italy? Your marriage is over, isn't it? Isn't that what you told her?"

He didn't hesitate. "Not by a long shot."

"It took you long enough to come to your senses," she said with a touch of acid. "Now, what are you going to do to straighten out this mess?"

He grinned as he glanced around the room at his wife's paintings. His gaze narrowed as an idea came to him. Maybe. Just maybe… "First, I need you to delay Ariana for a day or two," he said. "Assuming you're willing."

"I could be talked into it," she graciously conceded.

"Next, I'm going to get my digital camera and take a few pictures. And then you're going to tell me how to get in touch with Aaron's father."

"Ma'am?" The bellboy hovered by the open door to the hotel room. "Your grandmother is waiting in the limousine. She asked if you'd come now."

Ariana gathered up her handbag and gave the suite a final check. "I'm ready."

Lazz stepped into the room. "Actually, she's not.

Tell the limo driver he can leave now. I'll escort Mrs. Dante to the airport."

It took Ariana an instant to react, just long enough for Lazz to hand the bellboy a bill and jerk his head toward the door. With a cheeky grin, the boy snagged the Do Not Disturb sign and hung it on the outside handle before closing the door behind him.

"You can't do that," she protested. "I have a plane to catch."

He crossed to the sitting area and dropped his brief-case onto the coffee table. "There will be other flights if you miss this one. But there might not be another opportunity for us."

She wanted to resist. Wanted to turn and run before he hurt her again. But something kept her from leaving. Maybe it was the sincerity in his eyes and voice. Or maybe it was something else. Something that caused a fragile seedling of hope to blossom with new life. "Okay, I'm listening."

He opened the briefcase he carried and pulled out a sheaf of papers. "I assume you recognize this."

"Is that the contract our parents signed?"

He nodded. "As well as the list of conditions we agreed to."

"That's why you've come?" she demanded, outraged. "You're going to throw those in my face? Try and bind me to you with a pile of documents that never should have been drafted in the first place? You think you're going to keep me here with rules and logic and paper?"

"Not even a little." In one swift motion, he ripped the papers in half and tossed them to the carpet in a flurry of black and white. "I'm hoping to keep you here because of a marriage. Our marriage."

The seedling that had taken root unfurled, its roots grappling to anchor into good, strong soil, while its leaves reached toward the warmth of the sun, toward an Inferno of light and heat. "Go on." She couldn't contain the smile flirting with her mouth. "I'm back to listening."

He reached into his briefcase again and pulled out more papers that reeked of "contract." "And then there's this," he said.

She was tempted to follow his example and rip those apart, as well. "What is it with you Dantes and contracts?" she muttered.

"I think this is one contract you're going to like. It's for a new Mrs. Pennywinkle book." He held it out. "It's yours, if you want it. All you have to do is sign."

She shook her head, stunned. "I don't understand. Aaron rejected me as my grandmother's replacement. How did you manage this, Lazz? What have you done?" Her eyes widened in dismay. "Tell me you didn't bribe him."

He chuckled, the sound deep and rich, causing tendrils of desire to slip through her and grab hold. "I didn't bribe him with anything more than your own artwork."

"How?"

He removed the mock-up of the book he'd created and handed it her. "With this."

She took it from him and flipped through it. Tears filled her eyes. "You made this and showed it to Aaron? It must have taken you forever to put together."

"It didn't take forever. Just a very long twenty-four hours."

It took her a moment before she could speak through her tears. "And it convinced Aaron to give me a contract?"

"There might have been a tiny bit of prodding from Aaron's father. But you got the contract through your own hard work and talent. Your illustrations sold you, not me. They just needed to see the evidence in a more recognizable form. And now that they have they've realized what I did from the start. You, Mrs. Pennywinkle, are amazing." He took the book from her and set it aside. Then he gathered her close. He ran his thumbs along her cheekbones, brushing away the tears. "Does this give you enough reason to stay in San Francisco, instead of returning to Italy?"

She shook her head. "I can be Mrs. Pennywinkle in Italy just as easily as here," she pointed out. "If you want me to stay, give me a better reason."

"I thought you might say that. And my response is…" His voice altered, softened. The words were filled with unwavering certainty and a passion she couldn't mistake. "Stay because of me. Because of us. Not because of a diamond, or a contract or family obligations. Let's start over, for the right reasons this time."

"And what reasons are those?"

He didn't hesitate. "Because we belong together. We have from the very first touch. My world exploded around me that day and it's never been the same since."

"Exploded?"

The expression that swept across his face dazzled her. "Burst into flames?" he dared to tease.

She stilled. "Are you telling me you believe in The Inferno now?"

"I believe in this..." He threaded his fingers through hers until their palms met and the warmth came. "If this is The Inferno, then yes. I believe in The Inferno."

It took her a moment to gather herself enough to respond. "Even though it defies logic and common sense?" she managed to ask.

His smile turned tender. "I sacrificed those the moment we first joined hands. And I would much rather have what I found as a replacement."

"And what's that?" she whispered, daring to hope. Daring to believe.

"Love. I love you, Ariana Dante."

It was all she wanted him to say and everything she needed to hear. "And I love you."

Her arms tightened around his neck and she kissed him. Kissed him until the fires burned and they were consumed in the flames. He swept her into his arms and carried her to the bed. He lowered her into a nest of down and butter-soft cotton, his weight a delicious dichotomy to the smoothness beneath her.

He feathered a kiss across her lips, just a quiet, fleeting pressure that still managed to push her ever closer to that delicious edge between reason and insanity. Between need and desperation.

"I can't imagine my life without you," he admitted between kisses.

"But if I'd left..."

He smoothed her hair back from her face. "I'd have come after you. You are..." He lowered his head, burying his face in the crook of her shoulder. He inhaled her scent before pressing a string of kisses along the length of her neck. Then he found her mouth again, his hunger for her taking on a sharp edge. "You are everything to me. You are my life."

"Oh, Lazz." She cupped his face. "Haven't you figured it out yet? Don't you realize that it's the same for me?"

"I'd hoped," he admitted gruffly.

They moved in concert, their clothing slipping away in a slow, sweet process interrupted by kisses and filled with intimate laughter. When nothing remained between them, she reached for him, surprised when he stopped her at the last moment.

"I didn't come prepared. Is it safe to make love?" he asked.

"Not even a little," she warned.

Satisfaction swept across his face. "I was hoping you'd say that. Do you mind?"

She didn't hesitate. "Not even a little," she repeated softly.

They didn't speak again for a long, long time. This time when they came together it was different. It was as if those other occasions had been mere shadows of the real thing. Preludes to a song as yet unsung. As though they'd experienced only the disparate parts without ever knowing the whole. This time all the pieces came together, locking into place and creating a union of intense color and light and rightness. This time they surrendered everything they had, giving themselves up to love.

And in that ultimate joining, the Inferno had fulfilled its promise. The last Dante man fell. In fact, the last Dante man didn't just fall into the flames.

He leapt.

* * * * *

DANTE'S
ULTIMATE GAMBLE

BY
DAY LECLAIRE

To Mom, whose encouragement is unwavering
and who has always believed in me.

Prologue

"**I** need your help."

If it had been anyone other than his grandmother uttering those words, Luc Dante would have walked away. But coming from a woman he loved with all his heart, he found himself replying, "What can I do?"

Beautiful hazel eyes, wise from the weight of her years, held a wealth of compassion. There was also a twinkling of the irrepressible humor that was so much a part of her character. She hesitated just long enough for a faint warning bell to sound, an internal alarm he'd long-ago learned to listen for…and respond to with all due haste. "The truth is, it is a friend of mine who needs your help," she admitted.

"Nonna—"

"Hear me out, Luciano." In her own way, his grandmother could be as autocratic as his grandfather, Primo. At his nod, she continued. "You remember my dear friend Marietta de Luca, do you not? We all vacationed together one summer at the cabin when you were a boy. You children all called her Madam. Even her grandchildren address her by that name."

It took a moment to summon the memory from his childhood. Then it popped into crisp focus. The Dante family summer home. The lake. His three brothers, sister and four cousins all running rampant. And three little girls—Madam de Luca's grandchildren—with frizzy black hair and pitch eyes whom they'd secretly dubbed the three witches.

There'd been a fourth girl, he recalled, with bright red hair, white, white skin and intense eyes, who'd drifted from shadow to shadow and rarely spoke. Most of the time, she had a nose in a book. Showing stunning originality, they'd dubbed her Red.

Even more oddly, she made him…itch. It was the only way he could describe it, that vague jittery reaction he had whenever she came too close. It made him want to poke at her, to try to elicit a reaction. But she'd shied away from all of them, vanishing like a ghost whenever they approached, showing up at mealtimes long enough to nibble at her food before slipping away again. For some reason, her behavior had irritated him. He might have done something about it if not for the watchful eye of his grandparents.

Luc shook off the memory. "I remember Madam," he admitted. He also remembered thinking that it would make the perfect name for a dog, but decided—even at such a tender age—that it might be wise to keep that particular tidbit to himself. A brief image flashed through his head of an elegant, aristocratic woman with coloring to match her dark-haired grandchildren, a woman who could command obedience with a single black look. "What about her?"

"Her eldest granddaughter, Téa, needs your assistance for a few weeks."

He wondered briefly which of the witches was Téa, but the bell inside his head sounded another warning, this one louder than before and he focused on that, instead. "What sort of assistance?" he asked suspiciously.

"Well…" Nonna released her breath in a sigh. "To be honest, she needs a bodyguard."

Luc shot to his feet, his knee screaming in protest at the unexpected jolt. Damn it to hell! "No."

"Now, Luciano—"

He limped to the bank of windows of Dantes conference room where his grandmother had cornered him and stared out at the city of San Francisco. Any other day, he'd have admired the crystal clear spring morning that offered a stunning view of San Francisco Bay and the startling backwash from a crisp blue sky. Not today. Not this moment. Not when memories tried to crowd their way into his thoughts and heart.

"I can't." The words came out far harsher than he'd intended. "Don't ask me to go through that again."

"It was not your fault," Nonna said quietly.

He pivoted on his good leg, struggling to hold the nightmare at bay. But flashes crept through, no matter how hard he worked to keep them compartmentalized. The urgent rush to escape their pursuers. The SUV coming out of nowhere. The car crash. The child. Oh, God, the child. The husband, gone. The wife, broken. The sound of her weeping. Her pathetic pleas. "Let me die! Just let me die so I can be with them!"

He closed his eyes and forced the memories into the

furthest recesses of his mind. "I can't do it, Nonna. I won't."

"It is not that sort of job," she said with such gentleness that it threatened to overwhelm him.

He waited until he regained his self-control. "It is that sort of job if I need to guard her," he corrected with amazing calm.

"Attend to me, *cucciolo mio*. Téa is to receive a large inheritance when she turns twenty-five." Nonna raised her eyes to the heavens in clear benediction. "*If* she turns twenty-five."

Facts first. Refuse later. "Someone wants to prevent that from happening?"

"No, no. Nothing like that. Téa is…oblivious." Nonna made a tsking sound with her tongue and then switched to Italian. "The girl is highly focused."

Luc lifted an eyebrow and followed suit, switching to Italian. "Which is it? Oblivious or focused?"

Nonna gave a speaking shrug. "Both. She is very organized and focused on that which holds her attention. Such organization and attention to detail causes her to be somewhat oblivious to all else. It has gotten to the point where she has become seriously accident prone."

"So, lock her up in a room somewhere for—" He tilted his head to one side. "How long?"

"Six weeks."

"For six weeks."

"First, the de Lucas would have to get her to agree, which she will not. Secondly, she is the main support of her family. She cannot afford to take a six-week leave of absence. They are in serious financial straits."

"Why does that change when…Téa?" He lifted an eyebrow and at his grandmother's nod, he continued. "When Téa turns twenty-five?"

"On her next birthday, she receives a huge trust fund and ownership in a business which will support the entire family for the rest of their lives. If she does not…" Nonna shrugged again. "The money does not."

"I already have a job."

And he did. Sort of. As head of security for Dantes Courier Service, the branch of the business which handled the day-to-day operations of safely transporting Dantes fabulous fire diamonds, gemstones and jewelry, he wouldn't normally have time for this. But there had been a recent robbery of one of the shipments and while the police and insurance company were investigating, DCS had been temporarily shut down.

Nonna's eyes flashed with hazel fire. "Do not insult my intelligence."

Luc sighed, hearing the painful snap of the trap closing around him. "Let me get this straight. You want me to safeguard a klutz so she makes it to her twenty-fifth birthday? That's it? No danger. No actual bodyguarding. You just want a… What? A babysitter?"

Nonna smiled in relief. "Exactly. Téa de Luca needs a babysitter for the next six weeks and I promised Madam that you would sit on her baby."

One

Luc lounged—as best as a six foot three inch man could lounge—in the dainty chair at the small bistro table outside a trendy downtown San Francisco restaurant. He struggled to control his impatience. Beside him Nonna and Madam chatted happily in Italian while they awaited the arrival of Téa de Luca, or Witch Girl #1 as Luc had privately dubbed her. Because she was late, a trait that—quite literally—drove him out of his mind, he was in hurry up and wait mode, one of his least favorite memories of his military service.

It was rude. It was self-indulgent. And it gave the underlying message, "It's all about *me*." He despised women who adopted that sort of attitude and avoided them like the proverbial plague.

He reached for a breadstick and pulverized it between his teeth. Where the *hell* was she? It wasn't like he had all day to sit around waiting on Her Witchiness.

Well, actually, he supposed he did now that he was temporarily out of a job while the cops and insurance company looked into the fire diamond heist. But there were plenty of other things he'd rather do. Like drive a spike between his ears, or tie himself to a railroad track in front of an oncoming freight train, or swim with a pack of voracious Great White sharks.

He cleared his throat and leaned toward Madam. "Where the he—" He broke off beneath the withering glare emanating from his grandmother and rethought his choice of words. "Would you mind trying Téa's cell again, Madam?"

"Do you have another appointment, Luciano?" Nonna asked. Her tone came across sweet enough, but a hint of hazel fire flashed through her eyes. A warning message he pretended not to notice.

"As a matter of fact, I do," he lied without remorse.

Madam picked up the pretty lavender cell phone she'd set on the table as gingerly as if it were a landmine. Peering through a pair of reading glasses hanging from a crystal beaded necklace around her neck, she carefully punched in a number. "No, no. That's not right," she murmured, her brow furrowing.

"I think if you just hit send several times it dials the last number," Nonna explained helpfully.

"Would you like me to take care of it?" Luc offered.

Madam passed him the cell with an amusing combination of relief and hauteur, reminding him again why she'd been given her particular moniker. "If you wouldn't mind, I would appreciate it."

"Happy to help."

He pushed the speed dial and waited for the call to connect. While it rang he automatically scanned the busy sidewalk just past the frilly wrought iron fence that separated the outdoor section of the café from the rest of humanity. It was an occupational hazard he'd developed first during his military career, and then when he'd opened his own personal security business. And it had spilled over into his current—he grimaced—or rather *former* job as head of security for Dantes Courier Service. With luck, the case would soon be resolved and he'd be back doing something useful instead of babysitting Witch Girl #1.

Pedestrians scurried across the intersection adjacent to the café. All except one lone woman who paused dead center in the crosswalk, juggling a briefcase and a voluminous shoulder bag from which she extracted three cell phones. Without quite knowing why, Luc shoved back his chair and stood, the phone still pressed to his ear.

The pedestrian warning signal guarding the intersection began to blink, indicating that the light would soon change. To his concern, the redhead remained oblivious as she sorted through the cell phones she'd unearthed before selecting one that, even from the distance separating them, he could see was a distinctive lavender. A distinctive lavender matching the one in his hand. She flipped it open.

A breathless greeting sounded in his ear. "Hello? Madam?"

Alarm bells clamored with painful intensity. He dropped the cell to the table, took a single step toward the waist-high wrought iron gate separating the outdoor portion of the café from the sidewalk and vaulted over it, careful to land on his good leg. He forced himself to attempt a swift jog, ignoring the red-hot stab of pain

that shot from knee to hip. The light changed just then
and cars began to move forward.

Get the woman!

The urgent demand roared through him, deafening
him to everything else. He remembered his cousin,
Nicolò, describing how his wife had been hit by a cab
shortly after they'd first met. The driver had changed
lanes to avoid a slow-moving vehicle and sped into the
intersection, hitting Kiley. Even now, her past remained
a blank as a result of the accident, although she and
Nicolò were busy building new memories and creating a
new life together—which included a baby due sometime
in the next few weeks.

Get the woman now!

Luc watched helplessly as history decided to repeat
itself. A cab swerved around a delivery truck who'd
unexpectedly double parked outside a mom-and-pop
market. With a blare of its horn, the cab accelerated
directly toward the intersection. Clearly the driver didn't
realize the woman was there, probably because he was
intent on cursing at the truck driver, while the woman
remained oblivious to her danger as she pressed buttons
on her cell.

Get the woman now before you lose her forever!

Luc thought he shouted a warning and forced himself
into a limping run, cursing a leg that would prevent him
from reaching her before the cab. The driver didn't spot
the hazard until the very last instant. He slammed on the
brakes with an ear-splitting scream of metal and rubber.
Luc forced himself to move even faster, praying his leg
would hold him, but he knew he'd never be in time.

A split second before the cab hit the woman, it
swerved a few precious feet. It was enough. Just enough.
Luc snatched her clear and dove toward the safety of the

sidewalk. He twisted so he'd absorb most of the impact, landing hard on his bad hip. Raw pain exploded through him.

"Son of a *bitch!*"

The woman shoved against his chest, surfacing in a tangle of deep auburn curls, lean ivory arms and legs and countless files and papers. Three cell phones rained down around them. A pair of rimless reading glasses dangled from one ear while teal-blue eyes regarded him in open outrage.

"Did you just call me a bitch?"

"Not exactly." Wincing, he grasped the woman around the waist and levered her to one side. Cautiously he sat up. His hip screamed in protest. Aw, hell. Not broken, but not in good shape, either. "Do you always stand in the middle of an intersection daring cars to hit you?" His injury gave the question more of a bite than he intended.

She wrapped herself in indignation while straightening her glasses. One of the fragile bits of wire connecting the two lenses across the bridge of her nose was severely bent, causing the lenses to sit cockeyed on her face. "I was answering a call from my grandmother." As though the explanation reminded her, she scrambled through the paraphernalia littered around them until she unearthed a lavender cell phone identical to Madam's. "Hello? Madam, are you still there?"

"Téa! Oh, my dear. Are you all right?"

The voice didn't come from the phone, but from a few feet away. Madam and Nonna hurried down the sidewalk toward them. Groaning, Luc cautiously climbed to his feet, then offered Téa a hand. And that's when it hit. A powerful spark, followed by a bone-deep burn shot from her palm to his. It flew through his veins, sinking into him, absorbed on the deepest level.

His internal alarm bells went berserk, clamoring and clashing and shrieking so loudly it destroyed all sensation but one—a desire so strong and powerful he literally shook from the desperate need to snatch this woman into his arms and carry her off. Sweep her away to someplace private where he could put his mark on her. Claim her in every way that a man claims a woman.

She stared at him in open shock and he had to assume she'd felt it, as well. Her lips parted, as though begging for his kiss, and her eyes seemed to smolder with blue-green fire. Every scrap of color drained from her face leaving behind a tiny pinprick smattering of freckles dusting her elegant nose. The foam of deep red curls tumbled down her back in bewitching disarray and provided a blazing frame for her upturned face—a face that mirrored every single emotion from bewilderment to disbelief.

She tore her gaze from his and looked at their joined hands. "What… What was that?" she whispered.

Deep down he knew, though he couldn't quite give it credence. Not yet. Not when it defied logic and understanding. Not when every fiber of his being resisted admitting the possibility of its existence. And yet… It was exactly as his grandfather had described. Exactly as his parents had told him. Exactly as what his cousins claimed happened to them. And exactly what he'd hoped would never happen to him.

"*That* was impossible," he answered.

"Téa?" Madam's apprehensive voice cut through the wash of desire. "Téa, I asked if you were all right."

Jerking her hand free of Luc's grasp, she turned to her

grandmother. "I'm fine," she assured. "A little shaken and manhandled, but otherwise unhurt."

Luc's brows gathered into a scowl. Manhandled? *Manhandled?* How about snatched from the jaws of death? How about saved by the generosity of a stranger? How about rescued from a metal dragon by a poor battered knight who could have used some freaking shining armor to protect himself from injury?

Before he could argue the point, pedestrians paused to help gather up Téa's belongings which she carefully organized, tucking everything away into her briefcase and voluminous purse. The desire that had overwhelmed him minutes before eased, at least enough for him to recover her cell phones. One of them was chirping at great volume, urging, "Answer me. Answer me. Answer me, me, *me!*" over and over. Even these had individual slots in her handbag.

By the time she finished, reaction set in. Madam appeared on the verge of tears. Nonna's brow was lined in worry. Only Téa seemed blissfully unconcerned.

Luc, on the other hand, found it difficult to even think straight, other than to resent like hell the events of the past several moments. Pain radiated from every muscle in his body. Between his banged up knee and hip, Téa's apparent obliviousness to her near-death experience, and that undeniable sizzle of physical attraction when they'd first touched flesh-to-flesh, he was *not* a happy man. And the fact that Téa was ignoring the significance of each and every part of all that, only made it worse.

Luc was a man of action. Someone who took charge. Granted, he had finely tuned instincts. But he backed them with logic and split-second decisiveness that had saved his hide countless times in the past. It had also saved Téa's, though she didn't seem to quite get that fact.

Whatever had just happened had done a number on him and he resented it like hell.

Determined to revert to type, he regained control by gathering up the three women and urging them toward the café. After seeing them seated, he went in search of their waiter and ordered a new round of drinks, adding a black ale for himself. If they'd had anything stronger, he'd have chosen that instead, but until he could down a dozen anti-inflammatories chased by a stiff couple of fingers of whiskey, the beer would have to do.

"Thank goodness you were there to rescue Téa from that crazed cab driver," Madam said the minute he returned to the table.

Luc took a seat and fixed Téa with a hard gaze. "Perhaps if your granddaughter wouldn't answer her cell phone in the middle of the intersection, she wouldn't have to worry about being mowed down by crazed cab drivers."

Téa smiled sweetly. "My grandmother tells me that *you* were the one who phoned me. I believe that means this is *your* fault."

"*My* fault?" The waiter appeared with their drinks, but froze at Luc's tone, one he used when dressing down some gomer over his latest FUBAR. "How is it my fault that you chose to answer your phone in the middle of a busy intersection?"

"If you hadn't called—"

"Which I wouldn't have needed to do if you'd been on time—"

"—I wouldn't have answered my cell in the middle of the intersection."

"—I wouldn't have had to call you. But you're welcome."

He glanced at the waiter and gave an impatient jerk

of his head toward the table. Scrambling, the waiter deposited the drinks, scribbled down their orders and made a hasty retreat.

"You're welcome?" Téa repeated.

She blinked, her eyes huge from behind the bent lenses of her reading glasses. As though suddenly aware she had them on, she shoved them into the curls on top of her head. Then her expression blossomed into a wide smile, completely transforming her face. What had been pretty before became stunning.

Heat exploded low in his gut. The urge to carry her off grew stronger, more compelling than before. He snatched up his lager and took a long swallow, praying it would douse the flames. Instead it seemed to make them more intense. All he could think about was finding a way to extract her from this ridiculous meeting and take her off someplace private. To explain in a manner as physically graphic as possible that whatever was happening between them needed to be completed. Several times, if necessary. Whatever it took until the rage of fire and need cooled and he could think rationally again.

"I'm sorry," she said. "Maybe we could start over? Thank you for saving me from being run down. I'm sorry I was late for our lunch meeting. I assure you, it was unavoidable. I don't usually answer my cell phones in the middle of a busy intersection, but it was Madam's and I *always* take her call, regardless of time and place."

She'd ticked off her points with the speed and precision of a drill sergeant. Where before he'd considered her scattered, now he saw what Nonna had meant by her description of Téa de Luca. It would appear she was a woman who existed in organized chaos and operated in focused oblivion.

Luc inclined his head. "Fair enough."

"That said," she continued, "I don't see the point in this meeting." She spared her grandmother a warm smile. "I appreciate your concern, but I don't need a bodyguard."

"Funny," Luc muttered. "Considering what happened just five minutes ago, I'd say that was precisely what you need."

She waved that aside. "It could have happened to anyone. Besides, he would have missed me."

It took Luc a split second to find his voice. "Have you lost your mind?"

She patted his arm, then snatched her hand away. Maybe it had something to do with the arc of electricity that flashed between them. Or the throb that shot through the palm of his hand and quite probably her own. With each new touch, whatever existed between them grew stronger, the tendrils binding tighter and more completely. It gave him some measure of satisfaction to see that it took her several seconds to recover her poise sufficiently to speak. During the few moments of silence the waiter approached and deposited their luncheon choices. He didn't linger.

"You played the hero quite well and I appreciate your efforts on my behalf," Téa said in a stilted voice. She splashed some oil and vinegar on her salad. "But the cab swerved at the last second."

He leaned in, emphasizing each word with a steak fry. "Which gave me just the extra time and room I needed to keep you from getting clipped by his bumper and turned into roadkill." He popped the fry into his mouth. "He would have hit you if I hadn't pulled you clear."

"Luciano…" Nonna murmured.

He glanced first at his grandmother and then at Madam. They both wore identical expressions, a wrenching combination of fear and shock. Not cool, he realized. He'd way overplayed his hand. He pulled back and gathered Madam's hand within his own.

"She's safe and I promise I'll keep her that way."

"Thank you." Tears flooded her dark eyes. "I can't tell you how much this means to me."

"Wait a minute," Téa interrupted. "I haven't agreed to anything."

He shot her a quelling look. Not that she quelled, which amused almost as much as it frustrated him. He excelled at quell. Any of the men who served beneath him or currently worked with him could attest to that simple fact. "Not even for your grandmother's peace of mind?" he asked.

It was her turn to be both amused and frustrated. "Oh, very good," she murmured. "Very clever."

"You will agree, won't you, Téa?" Madam's request sounded more like a demand. "It will make all of us feel so much better. Juliann can concentrate on her wedding. Davida can focus on her studies. And Katrina can…" She hesitated, clearly at a loss.

"Can continue getting into trouble?" Téa inserted dryly.

"She means well," Madam said with a sigh. "She's just a magnet for disaster."

As though to underscore the comment, Téa's handbag began to chirp again. A youthful, feminine voice demanded, "Answer me. Answer me. Answer me, me, me!" Téa smiled blandly. "Speak of the devil."

"So we agree." Luc struggled to be heard over the shrill tones of another ringtone as it added its personalized demand to the first. "I'm your baby—" He cleared his throat. "Your bodyguard for the next six weeks?"

She wanted to argue some more. He suspected the trait was as much a part of her as her red hair. He lifted an eyebrow in Madam's direction and waited, not a bit surprised when Téa caved. "Fine." She lowered her voice so only he could hear. "And don't think I missed that babysitter slip."

He kept his expression unreadable. "I have no idea what you're talking about."

Reaching into the bag, she went through each of her three phones and set them on vibrate. Lunch proceeded at a leisurely pace after that and he noticed with some amusement that everyone went out of their way to stick to innocuous topics. Schooling himself to patience, he guided the women through the conversation and the meal, before he could finally pick up the check and pay for their lunch. All the while he watched Téa.

Although she chatted with the grandmothers, Luc could tell that her thoughts were elsewhere. He could practically see the wheels spinning away, analyzing her problem—*him*—while searching for a satisfactory solution.

"Figured it out, yet?" he asked in an amused undertone.

She stared blankly. "Figured what out?"

"What you're going to do about me."

"Not quite." Then she hesitated and a hint of relief caused her eyes to glitter like gemstones. He didn't need the blazing light bulb that flashed over her head to tell him that she'd come up with a plan to escape her predicament. "Madam, quick question…"

"Yes, dear?"

"How are we compensating Mr. Dante for his time and expertise?" She actually smiled at Madam's small inhalation of alarm. "Bodyguards don't come cheap. And you know we're under serious budgetary constraints for the next six weeks."

"Well, I—"

"Didn't Nonna explain?" Luc offered smoothly. "Consider it your twenty-fifth birthday present from all the Dantes."

"How generous." He could hear the grit through the politeness. "But I couldn't possibly accept such an expensive gift."

He allowed irony to slide through his words. "No, no. Don't thank us. It's our pleasure. Besides, babysitters charge far less than bodyguards. Even if you were to refuse, it wouldn't cost you much at all to hire me." He pushed back his chair and stood. "I'll tell you what. Why don't we continue this meeting in private in order to settle the particulars?"

"Excellent suggestion," she replied crisply and gathered up her briefcase and shoulder bag. "My office?"

Not private enough for what he had in mind. Not nearly private enough. "I have an apartment close by."

"I'm not sure that's such a good idea."

Ignoring her, he gave Nonna and Madam each a kiss. Then draping a powerful arm around Téa's shoulders, he swept her from the restaurant. A cab lingered just outside the door and he bundled her inside, protesting all the way. He gave the driver the address to his apartment complex and settled back against the seat.

All the while, Téa bristled with feminine outrage. With her rioting red curls and flashing eyes she looked like a cat who'd been rubbed the wrong way. He couldn't quite help taking a certain pleasure in having upset her tidy little world. Considering the ease with which she'd upended his, it seemed only fair.

The cab had barely pulled away from the curb before she started protesting. "I have to get back to work. I don't have time for this. I don't know what sort of game you're playing, Luciano Dante, but I'm not in the mood for it."

"I'm giving our grandmothers what they asked for. If I can spare six weeks out of my life to make sure you reach twenty-five, you can put up with having me around."

"Well, shoot."

He'd clearly gotten her with that one. She took a moment to call the office and inform them of her change in schedule before turning her jumble of cell phones from vibrate to ring, meticulously checking each for messages before stowing it away. Not that she was through arguing. Not this one.

The minute she finished fussing with her phones, she pushed a tumble of curls from her eyes and glared at him. "And another thing… What was that weird zap you gave to me when we first shook hands?"

He gave an "I'm clueless" shrug, hoping it would satisfy. It didn't.

"Don't give me that. I've heard that you Dantes have some bizarre touch thing you use on women. It knocks them right off their feet and into your bed." A sudden thought struck and her eyes widened. "Is that what you have planned with me?"

Two

"Do you want me to zap you into my bed?" Luc pretended not to notice the cab driver's shocked gaze darting to the rearview mirror.

"No! Of course not."

"Too bad. I'd give it a try even though…" He allowed a hint of bewilderment to drift across his face and lied through his teeth. "To be honest, Téa, I have no idea what sort of bizarre touch thing you're talking about."

"Don't give me that." She brushed his denial aside with a graceful sweep of her hand. "Rumors have been flying all over the city about your cousins and how they acquired their wives."

Luc's eyes narrowed. Heaven help him. The woman was like a dog with a bone. He wasn't accustomed to people arguing with him. Damn it. Didn't she know she should be intimidated? That when he spoke others leaped to obey? Why the hell wasn't she leaping? "I would have thought you too intelligent to give credence to a bunch of lurid gossip magazines, like *The Snitch*."

A hint of telltale color underscored the delicate arch of her cheekbones. "It wasn't just the rags. I believe that whole Dante thing was demonstrated on television with Marco's wife."

He dismissed that with a shrug. "Easily explained."

"I'm listening. Explain away," she challenged.

Son of a— "A publicity stunt. Marco and Caitlyn were married. Of course she'd recognize her husband, even blindfolded."

He didn't need to see Téa's skeptical expression to know she wasn't buying it. "And that weird electrical shock we experienced? Or do you try that with every woman just to see how she'll react?"

"That's never happened to me," he admitted.

She honed in and Luc began to understand what Nonna had meant about her being focused, though he'd call it borderline obsessive. "What was it? What caused it?"

"Static electricity."

"That was *not* static electricity."

As far as Luc was concerned, they'd given their driver more than enough entertainment. "We'll discuss it when we get to my place," he said, hoping that would put an end to the conversation.

It didn't.

"I'd like to know now," she insisted.

"We'll wait." He inclined his head in the direction of the cabbie and gave her a pointed look. "Until then, tell me what you do for a living."

She turned her gaze toward the front seat, blinked, then smoothly switched gears. "I work for Bling." It was a nickname for Billings, who supplied the Dantes

Jewelry empire with their gold and silver needs. "Actually, I sort of own it."

Interesting. "Sort of?" he prompted.

"My grandfather, Daniel Billings, left it to me when he died a few months ago."

"That's your mother's father?" he hazarded a guess.

"No. Mom was married to Danny Billings—Daniel's son—who was killed in a plane wreck when I was a baby. Then, when I turned nine she married my father—my stepfather," Téa clarified. "That's when we were at the lake with Madam. Mom and Dad were on their honeymoon. We de Lucas are a blended family. My sisters are his and I'm hers, but we became theirs and us and ours. All de Lucas in the end with a bit of Billings thrown in for good measure."

The pieces came together. "Got it. Téa seems a rather unusual name for a Billings. Actually it sounds more Italian."

"It comes from a Billings ancestor from way back when. Téadora. It became tradition that the first daughter of the eldest son be given that name."

He tilted his head to one side. "It suits. Or at least, the shortened version does."

"Thanks."

"And you take control of your Billings inheritance in six weeks."

She nodded. "Until then I'm learning the ropes."

A soft bell rang in the back of his head, just the vaguest of alarms. "Who's running the show while you learn the ropes?"

"My second cousin, Conway Billings."

"And if something happens to you before you turn twenty-five?"

She turned her megawatt smile on him again, nearly blowing his circuits offline. "You think my cousin's out to do me in?" she teased.

He took the question seriously. "You'd be amazed what people will do for money. Trust me. I've seen it all."

"Not Connie."

"Connie?"

Téa lifted a shoulder in a careless shrug. "That's what everyone calls Conway. As a bodyguard, you're probably used to looking for trouble, even where it doesn't exist. But that's not the case with me."

She patted his arm in a reassuring manner, the same as she had at the restaurant, then once again whipped back her hand. He found the idea of anyone attempting to reassure *him* disconcerting. It had always been the other way around. She rubbed the surface of her palm as though it itched or tingled, and he wondered if she even noticed her actions. It took every ounce of self-control not to imitate her gesture. Snatching a quick breath, she glanced out the window.

"Are we almost there?"

"Almost." And it wouldn't be a minute too soon. "Tell me about these accidents you're experiencing."

"I'm not experiencing any accidents." That brilliant smile flashed again. "I'm experiencing a failure to walk and talk at the same time."

It wouldn't be the first time he'd come across a recruit with that problem. He'd get her straightened out soon enough. "You're a klutz."

Her breath escaped in a sigh. "I wish I could deny it. But that's pretty close to the truth. I guess I'm distracted."

"Because of your financial problems?" he hazarded a guess.

"That's part of it. I'm also struggling to learn everything I possibly can before I take over Bling. I never expected to inherit the place, so it hasn't been easy," she confessed. "There's a lot to learn that wasn't covered in my business degree at Stanford."

"And you're certain that Connie doesn't have a hidden agenda to ensure you don't make it to twenty-five?"

No hesitation. "I'm positive. He's actually planning to start his own business as soon as I'm able to take over the reins. He can't wait to get out from under his responsibilities."

The cab pulled up just then and Luc handed over the fare. Then he led the way up the front steps of the apartment complex to the door. He swept his keycard across the lock and gestured her in. They crossed the foyer and he rang for the elevator. The doors slid open almost immediately and he used his card again to access the top floor. The instant they were enclosed within the suffocating confines of the car, Téa returned to their earlier topic of conversation.

"So now we're alone," she began.

"We are."

Ignoring proper elevator etiquette, she turned to confront him. "Tell me why we keep getting zapped every time we touch. What's going on?"

He watched the digital numbers tick off one by one. After all, *someone* had to follow proper protocol, especially if it helped him keep his hands to himself. "Magnetic attraction?"

"Not a chance."

"My electric personality?"

She dismissed the suggestion with a delicate snort.

He allowed the silence to consume them while the elevator finished its ascent. The doors slid open directly into the foyer of his suite and she stepped out of the car before freezing. "Good Lord, is all this yours?"

"Yes."

To his relief, her interest in his living accommodations sidelined her questions about The Inferno. "You live here alone?"

"I'm a bit of a hermit." At least, these days he was.

She took her time looking around, examining the Spartan interior, the over-the-top electronics, and the smattering of photos from family gatherings on his walls that offered a few reluctant peeks into his past. She studied each in turn. First the ones of his Dante-filled childhood and those carefree years of raw emotion and puppylike wildness. Then the group shot of his unit revealing his transition to manhood—as evidenced by his uniform and military bearing—with its loss of innocence and rendering of character and spirit until all that remained was sheer grit and the drive to survive. Where life ended or continued based on a confusing combination of fate and experience. And finally, the professional man and the men who'd worked with him, the lone wolf standing ever so slightly apart from the others, who still carried the taint and scars of what had gone before, closed now to the emotional openness of youth. Innocence twisted to cynicism. Joy and hope tempered by reality. Normal, everyday dreams for the future layered beneath caution.

She took it all in, absorbed it without a word, then moved on. And yet, he saw the comprehension in her gaze and realized she understood what so few others had when they'd looked at all those group shots. She'd seen the emotions that existed behind the two-dimensional photos, seen his pain, as well as his determination. She wandered deeper into his sanctuary, forcing him to regard it with fresh eyes. The place would have come across as too austere if not for the warm redwood trim that accented the twenty-five-foot ceilings and the parts of the floor not covered by carpet. She paused in front of the floor-to-ceiling windows and the spectacular view of the bay they afforded with a deeply appreciative expression. Apparently she approved of the uncluttered look. Somehow that didn't surprise him.

Nor did it surprise him when she gathered herself up and transitioned back to business. "Okay, time for answers," she announced, swiveling to face him. "Before we discuss this bodyguard business, I want to know one thing."

"Funny. So do I."

He approached, impressed that she simply stood and waited for him. Allowed him to reach for her. To take her hands in his while desire exploded around them and through them.

"What is that?" she whispered, dazed.

"*That* is Dante's Inferno. Which, if I'm not mistaken, means we're both condemned to hell."

Not giving her time to react, he swept her into his arms and kissed her.

Violent heat flashed through Téa, mercurial swift and burning with white-hot need, making her forget her responsibility to her family—something that hadn't happened since she was sixteen. Her reaction to him was identical to when he'd first taken her hand, igniting where their lips melded, the fit sheer perfection. It flashed downward to the pit of her stomach and lower still until the feminine core of her throbbed with the urge to join with this man. It raced through her, tripping over sense and emotion, instinct and logic, turning every part of her inside out and upside down. And still it didn't stop.

The desperation grew so intense that if he stretched her out on the floor of his foyer, she would have allowed him to strip away her clothing and lose himself in her. Just the thought of having him on her, in her, over and around her, joined with her in the most intimate way possible… She shuddered.

"Luc…" His name escaped on a sigh, became part of the kiss, greedily consumed.

His mouth slipped from hers, following the line of her throat, scalding the sensitive skin as he drifted relentlessly downward. Somehow the buttons of her blouse had escaped their holes. The edges of the crisp material separated, giving him access to explore the gentle swells rising above the lacy cups of her bra.

"I don't think I've ever seen skin like yours before. So pale." He trailed a string of kisses along the demarcation line of silken skin and protective lace. "It seems such a cliché to say it's like cream."

She laughed softly. "Not magnolia blossoms?"

He spared her a swift grin, though his eyes remained a shocking molten gold, flaming with a passion unlike anything she'd seen before. "Definitely magnolia blossoms. Only softer."

She didn't know what had gotten into her. This wasn't like her at all. Not the joking. Certainly not the lovemaking. But one touch from Luciano Dante and she tumbled. Her cell phones began to ring and chirp and plead, and with an exclamation of impatience, Luc opened one of the doors leading off the foyer—a coat closet—and shoved her handbag and briefcase inside.

It gave her just enough time for her head to clear.

"Wait, Luc." Those cell phones were her lifeline. They were a vital link that kept her grounded and connected to her family. Besides, she owed them. She couldn't allow this sort of selfish distraction. "Those calls could be important."

"There's nothing more important than this…"

He pulled her close and all coherent thought vanished. How did he manage to do that, when she'd always been so careful with her priorities? Maybe it was because she'd never known real desire before. Not like this. In fact, she'd gone out of her way to avoid it.

Family always came first. Duty and responsibility had been her obsession ever since the death of her parents. She didn't dare let down her guard and surrender to her baser desires. Not since that one hideous occasion when she'd done just that and her world had come crashing down around her.

She'd learned her lesson well that night. From that moment on, taking care of her family was her life. Her obligation. Nothing else came ahead of that one crucial demand. Nothing. At least… Nothing until Luciano Dante exploded into her world and—with a single touch, palm against palm—short-circuited every last rational thought but one.

She wanted this man. Needed him. For so many years she'd been the one in control. The steady one. The one who looked after her family and protected them. She couldn't and wouldn't indulge her own selfish interest until she'd accomplished that. Once she received her inheritance, she'd be in an even better position to care for her family, instead of constantly scrambling to make ends meet.

But with that one shocking touch, Luc took that burden from her. It vanished from thought and awareness, replaced by a passion she'd never experienced, never even knew existed until he'd shown her the stunning possibilities.

His mouth covered hers again, inhaling her, and she simply tumbled. Duty and responsibility floated away, as did reason and intellect. All that remained was a shattering. Intense. Unspeakable. All consuming.

Without breaking the kiss, Luc swept Téa into his arms. She had the sensation of movement from living room to bedroom—a light floating, then a gentle descent, the softest of cushions at her back when they sank into the mattress and a blazing heat that blanketed her. It settled over her, pressing into her, molding hard, powerful angles against the soft, willing give of her body.

She stared up into his face, at the hard, uncompromising features, examining them one by one. He had chiseled cheekbones coupled with a tough, squared jaw. His mouth was wide and sensuous, bracketed by deep grooves that could convey both humor and displeasure depending on his mood. His hair, cut almost military short, was the darkest shade of ebony and showed a tendency to wave, a tendency he kept under ruthless control. But it was his eyes that dominated his face. He possessed the deep, ancient golden eyes of a predator. Eyes that could cut straight through to the soul and lay bare what she most wanted to keep hidden.

He could never be called handsome. Powerful, certainly. Bold. Aggressive. Blatantly masculine. His face had been carved to intimidate, yet had those elements that—despite lacking prettiness—were wildly appealing to women.

Heaven help her, but he was an impressive male specimen. Tough. A body both strong and muscular. And yet, his touch showed infinite control and tenderness. How was it possible that a man so clearly cut from the cloth of a warrior could also be so gentle?

"What are we doing?" she managed to ask. "What's happening to us?"

"Dante's Inferno."

She shook her head in confusion. "I know it's an inferno. But why is it so intense?"

She caught the smile he couldn't suppress and it dazzled her. "No, that's what it's called. What we're experiencing. Or so the legend claims." He trailed his hand, harshly callused, in a fiery path from throat to breast. She shuddered beneath the dichotomy of rough and soothing. "We call it Dante's Inferno. It happens to the men in our family when they first meet certain women."

She managed a laugh. "How did I get so lucky?"

"I have no idea."

"How long will it last?"

He lowered his head and replaced his hand with his mouth in a leisurely exploration. "I have no idea."

"If we…" She inhaled sharply, shuddering beneath his roving lips and tongue. Her thoughts scattered for an instant before she gathered them up again. "If we make love, will it go away?"

"I hope so." He shook his head with a groan. "Or maybe not. Maybe it'll continue for a while. I wouldn't mind so long as it's not permanent. We could work it out of our systems over the next six weeks."

Relief flooded through her. "But it will go away?"

He reared back, hovering above her like some pagan god. "It better. I'm not like my cousins. They ended up married when it struck. I'm not after the fairy tale or commitment, or even love. You understand that, don't you?"

"I don't understand any of this," she confessed.

He shook his head as though to clear it. "This isn't permanent." The words were filled with grit and honesty. "This is a temporary affair. It's sex. That's all. If you're expecting a fairy tale ending—"

She allowed a hint of the darkness that had shadowed her over the years to reflect in her gaze. "Don't worry. I don't believe in fairy tales. And I definitely don't believe in happily-ever-after endings."

"But you believe in this." He released the front clasp of her bra and cupped her breasts. Sunshine splashed and rippled across her skin, chasing away the darkness. He traced his thumbs across the sensitive tips, eliciting a soft moan. "You believe in the physical, the same as I do. What we can touch. Desire. Sating that desire. You believe in that, don't you?"

"It wouldn't be hard to make a believer of me," she confessed.

His mouth curved to one side and his eyes glittered like sunrays, threatening to blind her with their intensity. "Trust me. By the time I'm finished, you'll believe."

She found herself laughing, a sound free and light-hearted and utterly alien to her. She cupped his face and tugged him down, covering that wonderful mouth with her own. His taste intoxicated her and she rejoiced in the dizzying explosion of pleasure. For long minutes they kissed, slow and sultry. Deep and wet. Learning. Testing. Discovering. But it wasn't enough. Not nearly enough.

Téa tugged at Luc's shirt, struggling to find the buttons and holes and get one through the other. They resisted all efforts and impatient with her own lack of skill, she simply ripped at the edges until buttons pinged all around them. To her delight the edges of his shirt parted and she swept her hands across a broad chest, sharply delineated by gorgeous dips and ridges of toned muscle and sinew.

She'd never felt so free with a man before and she took her time, exploring this one to her heart's content. She rubbed the flat discs of his nipples and bit into his golden flesh, soothing the small mark with her tongue. A soft groan rumbled through his chest, caught within the palms of her hands, and she rejoiced in having provoked the reaction. She'd never wielded so much feminine power. It was a heady sensation.

She took a circuitous route in a southern direction, exploring all the side roads and byways of what she bared, until she hit a roadblock. She made short work of it, her fingers coordinated for a change. The belt parted, the zip of his trousers rasped downward and she slid her hands to the very heart of all that heat and masculinity.

He was hard and swollen, sliding into her hands with greedy urgency. She'd never done this before, either. Never given full rein to her curiosity and her own need to explore. But she couldn't help herself. Not this time. Not with Luc. He didn't stop her or attempt to take charge. Instead he encouraged her with soft, biting kisses and velvety, rough words.

She sensed the effort it took to control himself, could see the iron grip he maintained in order to hold himself back. Instead he devoted himself to stripping away her barriers. Bit by bit her clothes drifted away, her blouse and bra, her skirt and stockings, until all that remained was a scrap of triangular silk guarding her core. She was so caught up in her own exploration that she barely noticed.

Until he turned the tables on her.

Just as she familiarized herself with his body, he began to map hers. First her mouth and throat. Then her breasts and abdomen. Degree by degree he turned up the heat, catching her unaware until desire swamped her in great crashing waves, turning her mindless with need. She stared up at him in utter confusion.

"What are you doing?"

The laughter gleamed again. "Can't you tell?"

"We're making love. I…" Her eyes fluttered closed and she fought to draw breath, to gather her wits long enough to speak. "I don't remember this part."

"This part?" He spread her thighs and feathered a line of kisses from the curve of her knee to her inner thigh.

"No," she quavered. "Not that part."

Before she could even draw breath, he stripped away her panties. "What about this part?"

And then he kissed her, a kiss more intimate than she'd ever known before. A climax ripped through her, unexpected and violent and utterly spectacular. The sound that escaped her was part scream and part denial. She'd never…! Not ever. Pieces of her lay scattered all over the bed and it was several long minutes before she could gather them up and paste them together well enough to speak again.

"Not that part," she said. "I definitely don't remember that part."

"We'll have to do it again, just to keep your memory refreshed." He fumbled in the drawer beside him. An instant later she heard the distinctive crinkle of foil. "But not right now. Now we have other refreshing to do."

She lay beneath him, stretched in more ways than she could count. Stretched to the edge by a desire that still hadn't been quite sated. Stretched by muscles still quivering and clenching from the aftermath of her climax. Stretched emotionally by a man she'd just met. A man she'd allowed to touch her in ways she'd never before allowed. A man she'd allowed in, or who had forced his way in. She was too overwhelmed to figure out which.

Before she could analyze it further, he came down on top of her. His hands—such tender, powerful hands— slid deep into her hair, anchoring her. Their gazes locked and held, and she felt herself sink into him just as his body sank into hers, mating them together in a perfect fit. She felt herself join with him in ways that were more than just physical. Ways that upended her tidy little world.

And she gave herself to him, totally and unconditionally.

He moved within her and all thought slipped away, replaced by something far more primitive and elemental. A driving need consumed her, an urge to become one. To complete the connection that hovered so close. She strained for it. Reached for it. Grasped it eagerly.

Then the strangest thing happened. Téa felt the powerful current from their first meeting complete its circuit. Felt the undeniable melding of man to woman. Knew on some level that this moment had changed her on some irrevocable, fundamental level. Part of her shrank from that knowledge, while another part rejoiced.

She wrapped Luc up in a tight embrace, arms and legs entwined. Each thrust came more forcefully, branding her, possessing her. She rode with him while the wildness stirred. It whipped through her, tearing her apart into shiny fragments of desperate desire. She heard him call to her on the whirlwind, centering her. And with each moment that passed, each driving movement, they roared toward the center of the storm.

It was an exploding. A shattering. A freefall into the most delicious waves of pleasure she'd ever experienced. Together they soared and plummeted. Rode the wild wind. Together they clung one to the other, joined.

Melded.

Mated.

One.

Téa had no idea how long she lay there, lost in the aftermath of passion. Somewhere along the line every scrap of intelligent thought had fled, leaving behind utter confusion. But it was a delightful confusion, one that had her body glowing with pleasure and her practically purring in satisfaction.

The oddest part was that she couldn't seem to get her brain back online. Every time she tried, her thoughts would slip and slide in Luc's direction and all she could think about was how he'd taken her. Possessed her. Thrust her into a realm of sensation that had stripped her down to the bare essence of herself and then imprinted what remained with his personal brand. It was as though they'd mixed and mingled to the point where they could never truly separate out their own unique bits and pieces.

"Dear God," Luc rumbled beside her. "I don't think I'll ever be able to move again."

"At least you can talk," she managed to say.

"Okay. I'll talk. You move."

"Can't."

"'Kay. Come here." He wrapped a heavy arm around her waist and scooped her closer. "Aw, hell. It's still there."

She didn't have to ask what. She could feel it. He spooned the hard sweep of his angles against her soft curves. The press of his body cleaving to hers caused the embers to spark to life in renewed need. Every inch of her skin burned with it. Heat blazed along the contact points and she trembled beneath the onslaught.

"Yeah, it's still there." She shuddered in reaction. "Was it supposed to go away?"

"Thought so."

Or was it that he hoped so? The thought flitted in and out of her head as she turned to face him. He opened his eyes, slumberous, yet still hungry. With a soft growl, his mouth came down on hers again, blotting out thought and reason and words. Her arms slid around him just as his slid around her and their legs intertwined once again. They kissed, soft and gentle, then more urgently. An irrepressible need replaced exhaustion, one that couldn't be denied.

Téa wriggled against him. "Luc, please. I want—"

She couldn't even express what she wanted. Just him. More of him. He didn't need the words. He knew. Knew, and responded with a passion that shredded her world into bright glittering starbursts of pleasure. It was as though all the silver and gold from her company somehow melded with the unique fire diamonds from his and encircled them like a ring, creating a bond neither of them were prepared for, nor wanted.

A bond from which they couldn't easily escape.

Three

Téa awoke with a start and unlike last time, her brain came screaming online, flooding her with frantic messages and warnings. "Oh. My. God."

Luc surfaced from beneath her, rumpled and gorgeous and sexier than any man had a right to be. "Is that a please-do-it-again-even-if-it-kills-us version of oh-my-God? Or have we switched over to what-have-I-done-get-me-the-hell-out-of-here?"

"Um." She carefully untangled male parts from female and put a few precious inches of breathing space between them. It didn't help. Heat and want still pulsated across the breach, threatening to suck her back in. "The get-me-the-hell-out-of-here one."

"Thought so."

With a groan, he levered himself off the bed and limped nude in what she assumed was the direction of the bathroom. Her small gasp stopped him dead in his tracks.

"Oh, Luc. Your hip." Hugging the sheet to her, she crouched in the center of the bed, her gaze riveted on his side. "And your knee! Dear heaven, what did you do?"

His mouth twisted. "I rescued a damsel in distress. Foolish of me, I know."

It took her an instant to understand. "This is *my* fault?" Her misery increased as she took in the huge vibrant bruise that covered his entire hip and edged down his thigh toward his knee. "Why didn't you say something? You must be in pain. Maybe you should see a doctor. Have it X-rayed."

"It's not broken or I wouldn't be walking. I planned to take something for it." A swift, ravening grin came and went. "But I got distracted."

"I'm so sorry. I had no idea you were that badly hurt."

"Trust me, this isn't bad."

She recalled the photos taken of him during his military service and suspected he spoke the unvarnished truth. "And your knee?" She started off the bed, but the change in his expression glued her in place. In an instant he transformed from lover to warrior. To someone she didn't recognize. Someone tough and dangerous, who'd seen and done things she couldn't even imagine.

"Old injury. It has nothing to do with you or what happened earlier."

"But today must have made your knee worse," she said softly.

"It didn't help," he conceded. "My choice, though. And I chose to keep you from becoming cab fodder."

"Thank you." She grimaced as she considered how

blasé she'd been about it at lunch. More than blasé. As she recalled, she'd blamed him for the incident. "Seriously, thank you. When I think of how I behaved at lunch—" She broke off with a shake of her head.

"You weren't very grateful."

Ouch. No doubt she deserved that. "I didn't realize. I was distracted." She straightened her shoulders. "Not that that's any excuse. I can't thank you enough for what you did and I'm sorry I made it necessary."

It was only then that she caught the flash of amusement and realized he was deliberately provoking her as payback for her earlier behavior. And she'd fallen for it.

"No problem," he said. "Next time I'll let the cab have you."

She simply laughed. "No, you won't." If she'd learned nothing else about him in these past few hours, it was that. The words "knight in shining armor" were probably engraved on his soul.

He shook his head with a sigh. "I think it's more a matter of, no, I can't."

He didn't linger, but disappeared through the doorway. The sound of running water confirmed her guess about it being the bathroom. It also gave her an opportunity to escape the bed and gather up her clothing. She winced as she examined the garments. Well, the good news was that most of them could be worn again. Unfortunately some of the more fragile bits and pieces of silk were beyond use or repair.

Tiptoeing and not quite sure why she bothered, she disappeared into the depths of his apartment, relieved to discover that there was a second full bath adjoining his spare bedroom. She took possession of the shower and the various toiletries lined up on the counter.

Definitely a woman's touch and she couldn't help but wonder who had left her mark and whether or not she was still in Luc's life. After toweling off, Téa pulled on the salvageable pieces of her clothing and escaped the bathroom. She could hear Luc rummaging through the bureau drawers in his bedroom and paused.

She caught her lower lip between her teeth and briefly debated. She could either sneak out of the apartment, like a thief in the night. Or she could face him and deal with the situation. Since there was a real chance they would be stuck together for the next six weeks, addressing what had just happened, and doing it now, seemed the wisest course of action. Plus, she'd never been one to run from a problem. She'd learned long ago to take responsibility for her mistakes. Learned it in the worst possible manner. This one today with Luc had been a huge one.

With a sigh, she made her way to the living room. A quick glance toward the windows warned that day paused in those breathless few moments between dusk and true night. Lights from various boats dotted the bay, sweeping straight across the water to Marin County. Off to the left, the Golden Gate Bridge glittered, the suspension cables looking like glowing strands of pearls connecting the city to the northern peninsula. Directly in front of her hovered Alcatraz Island, perched like some mythical land while wisps of fog gathered in a protective mantle about its shores.

Where had the time gone? She shook her head in exasperation. Idiot. She knew full well where it had gone. She'd lost the hours in Luc's bed. No doubt if she went in there and rummaged between the sheets she'd find all those minutes just sitting there laughing at her.

Luc chose that moment to join her. The fullness of his personality exploded into the room, overwhelming it. "You hungry or should we move straight on to getting drunk and pretending none of this happened?"

She couldn't quite tell if he was serious or not, and suspected a combination of both. She swung around to face him. "I really should go. But before I do I thought we should discuss things."

"Discuss things," he repeated. He gave her an aggrieved look, one men had patented back in caveman days. Clearly the last thing he wanted was a discussion. "That definitely calls for a drink. You sure you don't want something?"

"No, thank you."

He crossed to a wet bar and pulled out ice and a cut glass tumbler. Tossing in a handful of cubes that caused the crystal to sing, he splashed a healthy finger of whiskey over the cubes. He swirled the liquor in the glass for a moment and then downed it in a single swallow before facing her. She noticed that when he pivoted he was careful to plant and twist with his left leg so he wouldn't cause any unnecessary trauma to the injury on his right.

He gestured with his glass, causing the ice cubes to chatter. "Okay. Start discussing. I assume this is the part where you say this can never happen again. That we have to work together for the next six weeks and it would be more professional if we kept things on a business footing. We'll just pretend what happened, didn't. Does that about sum things up?"

He hit too close to home. More than anything she wanted to claim he was wrong. That she was hoping for a torrid affair for the next six weeks and would be quite happy to spend every night in his bed, exploring every possible position and variation of their activities over the past few hours.

"I think I'd like a drink, after all," she announced.

"Smart choice."

"Do you have any wine?"

"Red, white or somewhere in between?"

"Red."

He poured her a glass of something dry and deliciously biting that carried the label from a Sonoma vineyard. She sipped it while considering her options and organizing her points. While he waited, he poured himself a second drink, but didn't down this one. Instead he swirled the combination of liquor and cubes. It took every ounce of effort to yank her gaze from his hand and those long, clever fingers, fingers which had done shocking and delicious things to every part of her body.

She cleared her throat, suddenly aware she'd somehow sipped her way through most of the glass of wine. "Here's the problem," she announced. "The reason we've been forced to work together is because I'm so distracted trying to juggle the pressures of my job and family life. We can't afford to have both of us distracted by this…" She lifted an eyebrow. "What did you call it? An inferno?"

"*The* Inferno," he corrected. "With a capital 'T,' capital 'I' and a whole lot of fire and brimstone in between."

She smiled at the name. Clever. "You said earlier that The Inferno, capital 'T,' capital 'I,' fire and brimstone, etcetera, is a family legend?"

"Yes," he replied, making it clear by tone and attitude that he didn't want to discuss it. "Or at least, that's the claim. Never having experienced it before—"

"Until today," she inserted smoothly.

It was like prodding a panther. Those incredible gold eyes narrowed in warning and if he could have snarled, he would have. As it was, he came close. "Hell, Téa. If it makes everything tidier to call a bad case of lust by a more acceptable name like The Inferno, go right ahead. It sure as hell makes it more acceptable to me."

"Lust." She chewed on the word for a moment and decided she didn't care for the flavor. "I thought you said your cousins all married because of The Inferno."

"They did." He threw a lot of emphasis on the word "they." Underscore. Italics. Highlight. Red flashing lights. The works.

She gestured with her glass. "I gather you don't intend to."

"I'm not very good husband material. Too much commitment for my taste." The panther sheathed its claws and he flashed her a smile that practically had her clothing melting off her body. If they could have stripped themselves, they'd be puddled on the floor at her feet. "But, I do make a terrific lover."

It was the unvarnished truth, spoken simply and without pretension or bravado. And one she readily conceded. Considering she'd been the most recent recipient, there was no point in denying facts. Unfortunately there was also no denying the fact that she would have loved to have him prove his words all over again. It took a moment, but she managed to pull herself together again, though she did spare a quick downward glance to make certain all her buttons were still safely in their holes.

Reassured, she couldn't resist provoking him one final time. "Just out of curiosity, how do you plan to avoid The Inferno when none of your other relatives have?"

She could see he'd never even considered the question before. She could also see he didn't care for her asking it…or for the fact that he didn't have a ready answer. To her amusement, it only took a moment for him to come up with one.

"I'm thirty years old and I've had extensive military training, as well as the skills I picked up running my own security business. We'll either satisfy whatever urges we're experiencing and move on, or…" He shrugged. "It's a simple matter of intellect over inclination."

She couldn't decide whether to be amused or insulted. "I believe that brings us back to our main problem. I have to confess, I can't decide which will be more distracting, indulging in an affair with you or trying *not* to indulge in an affair with you."

"Just out of curiosity. Do I get a vote?"

"Just out of curiosity. Which way would you vote?"

He approached, graceful despite the limp. He took the wine glass from her hand and set it on a nearby table along with his whiskey. Then he caught hold of her and pulled her into his arms.

"I vote to end things right now," he told her. And then he kissed her.

Want blew him apart. Heaven help him, she tasted every bit as delicious as before. Soft and sweet and yet potently female. He liked the way she attacked his mouth, like a succulent piece of fruit that she couldn't quite get enough of. And then she would sink into him, savoring him the way he'd seen some women savor a piece of rich, dark chocolate.

Everything about her appealed, from the light, crisp scent of her to the subtle silken curves that had so recently graced his bed, to the wit and intelligence that gave strength to her face and brilliance to the unusual teal shade of her eyes. He almost lost control again, almost swept her up into his arms and carried her back to his bedroom. Maybe he would have if the echo of his last words to her didn't still linger in the air. With a final hungry kiss, he put her from him.

It took her an instant to recover her equilibrium. She stared at him in fuzzy bemusement before snapping back into focus with a soft cry of outrage. "You…!" Anger sparked to life, flaming in her gaze and giving her cheeks a rosy bloom. "Why did you kiss me after what you said?"

He shrugged. "I didn't think I'd get the chance again."

He didn't give her an opportunity to reply. Didn't dare. It didn't pay to give women like Téa too much room to fully exercise their vocabulary. Not when they wielded each word with the precision of a marksman and could slice and dice a man with the skill of a master chef.

"I have some associates who can help with our problem. They can take over as your temporary bodyguard."

He couldn't have shocked her more if he'd slapped her. "And us? What about The Inferno?"

"As I mentioned, I have four cousins who described the sort of instant lust that we experienced and every last one of them ended up married. That's not going to happen to me. I don't do commitment. And I sure as hell don't do marriage."

"Neither do I," she retorted. "I have more important priorities."

"Excellent. Then we end this before it has a chance to get out of hand. Agreed?"

She opened her mouth to reply, when a muffled voice began to call, "Answer me. Answer me. Answer me, me, *me!*" Her eyes widened in horror and without a word she darted to the foyer and dove into his closet. She emerged a bit more tousled, but with her briefcase and shoulder bag in hand.

She took up residence on his couch and pulled out her cell phones, lining them up with military precision on his coffee table. The ring tone on the first phone—a shiny black one covered in neon pink kisses—switched to "Here Comes the Bride."

Téa flipped it open. "Hel— Yes, Jules. Yes, I know. I was in a meeting and couldn't be interrupted." She actually blushed at the lie, then listened for a moment. "Did you check out Divinity for your wedding gown? It won't? Why—" She listened silently for several more seconds. "No, no. I understand. It's just that I arranged for the owner... Okay. If it won't work, it won't. I'll get back to you with an alternative. I've got to speak to Vida now. No, she's not more urgent than you. But there's nothing else I can do about your wedding gown until tomorrow. I'm sorry, but that's the best I can do."

She pushed a button with smooth precision and started a new conversation. "Davida, what—" Pause. "Listen up. If you fail that course, you'll be on academic probation. No, I can't get you off again. You'll have to go in and speak to your professor. Well, why did you miss the exam? Oh, for— Yes, that was exasperation you heard in my voice. Recovering from a frat party is not an acceptable excuse for... I don't intend to argue the point. If you can't work it out with your professor, you know the consequences." A fraction of a pause this time.

"Oh, really? Well, let me spell it out for you. Colleges no longer offer BS degrees in Flirting. If you get kicked out, there's a job waiting for you in the mailroom at Bling. Why, Vida, that's brilliant. I don't know why it didn't occur to me to suggest you speak to your professor and throw yourself on his mercy."

She flipped the phone closed. It immediately began its "Answer me!" chirp.

"Téa—" Luc began.

She held up a preemptory Wait-A-Minute finger which he would have found amusing if it had been aimed at anyone other than him. "What did you do this time, Kat?" Téa asked the instant she answered the shrill summons. "Again? That's the third time you've been in detention this month. It's also the third time I've had to speak to the principal this month. Listen, I have to go. Madam needs me. I'll see you later tonight and we'll discuss it then."

Luc winced at the way she said "discuss." He didn't envy Kat that particular conversation. Téa hesitated, her hand hovering over the lavender phone that had caused them so much trouble earlier in the day. She caught her lower lip between her teeth, but didn't pick it up.

"Well?" Luc prompted. "I thought you said you took her call anytime, no matter when or where."

"Yes," she confessed. "But I really don't want to answer this time."

Amusement filled him. "Afraid she'll know what you've been up to?"

She fixed her startling blue-green eyes on him and nodded. "She can read minds," Téa answered, perfectly serious. "There's no point in trying to lie to Madam. She knows."

"She won't know."

"Yes, she will. You'll see." The response came out in a "we're doomed" tone of voice. Bracing herself, she picked up the lavender phone and flipped it open. "Hi, Madam. What's up?" she asked, sounding a shade too casual.

"It's not that she can read minds," Luc offered helpfully. "It's that you don't know how to lie."

She scowled at him over the phone and mouthed, "Shut up," gesturing to give the demand added emphasis. Then she froze, her eyes huge. Guilt stormed across her face like an invading army. "Nothing. No one."

Luc snorted. "Give it up." Crossing to her side, he snatched the phone out of her hand. "Hello, Madam. It's Luc."

There was a brief pause and then Madam said, "Luc? Are you and Téa still together?"

"Just ironing out the final details over dinner."

An almost girlish laugh came across the airwaves. "I'm so relieved you agreed to do this. Nonna was just saying she wouldn't trust anyone else with my granddaughter's welfare, and neither would I."

"Nonna's with you?" So much for palming the job off on his associates. Even if he could get Madam to agree, Nonna would put a swift end to that particular dodge.

"She's right here. The two of us made a day of it. We've been shopping. Visiting. You know…" He could almost see her airy wave. "Right now, we're sitting in Primo's garden, enjoying the night air over a glass of wine. Do you want to speak to your grandmother?"

He froze, hoping guilt didn't decide to invade his face now that it was done with Téa's. "No, no. That's not necessary."

"It's been hours since lunch. And no one's been able

to reach Téa all this time. That's so unlike her. We were starting to worry."

Luc couldn't help himself. It must have been the alcohol that gave the devil access to his tongue while preventing his guardian angel from curbing it. "She insisted on turning off her cell phones while we put our differences to bed," he explained in a bland voice.

Téa made a choking noise.

"Very wise," Madam approved. "I'm just surprised it's taken you so long to settle everything."

"You know your granddaughter," Luc replied smoothly. He fixed Téa with a hot, hungry gaze. "She's very thorough. Likes to examine every inch of whatever you put in front of her and make sure she's intimately familiar with each and every detail."

Téa closed her eyes with a groan and sank back against the couch cushions.

"She is a bit of a perfectionist," Madam conceded.

"I noticed that. And then the minute you think you're finished, she wants to start at the beginning and go over it all again."

"Well the two of you keep at it until you have it just right."

"I'll be sure to tell her you said so."

With that the connection went dead, leaving Téa staring at him with death and dismemberment in her eyes.

"Well?" Nonna prompted. "Luc is still with Téa?"

Madam nodded slowly. "Interesting, yes?"

"Very." Nonna's expression turned crafty and she tapped her finger against her lower lip while she considered the possibilities. "They could not have been discussing the job every minute of all this time, could they?"

"No." Madam drew out the word. "I didn't get that impression."

"So? What do you think they were doing?"

Madam peered carefully around to make certain Primo was out of earshot. She dropped her voice to a whisper. "I think they were having the sex."

Nonna fought back a grin, while struggling to appear appropriately shocked. "Well, we thought we saw signs of The Inferno all those years ago when they first met at the lake as children. Little baby fizzes that suggest at what is to come. The same thing happened between Lazzaro and Ariana and look how happy they are together. This simply confirms our suspicions and means we did the right thing when we set this up." A hint of satisfaction crept into her voice.

"You were right," Madam conceded. "But then, you always are."

"Once The Inferno strikes there is nothing they can do but give in to its demands. And maybe, if we are very fortunate, it will keep them too busy to ask uncomfortable questions."

"What questions?"

"You have to admit, that story about Téa needing a bodyguard will not hold up for long," Nonna said. "Luciano will soon discover that she is absentminded and when preoccupied prone to walk into walls, but is not in any real danger. We are lucky she had that little accident today or we might never have convinced him to help out."

"Lucky!"

"Now, now. It could not have worked better if we had planned it. No one was hurt and it added credibility to our story." Nonna patted Madam's arm in a reassuring manner. "Luciano is a good boy. Do not worry about your Téa."

"I have always worried about her." Madam's dark eyes glistened with tears. "No one else does. She takes so much on her shoulders. Ever since her parents died. She blames herself, you know."

"Luciano will ease her burden." Nonna's hazel eyes narrowed in thought. "So, step one is complete."

"Step two will be far more difficult," Madam warned.

Nonna lifted a shoulder in a shrug that spoke volumes. "There is always a way to get caught in the act, especially if nature is busy taking its course."

"And once caught?"

Nonna's smile grew cat-swallowing-canary smug. "Why, step three. A wedding, of course."

Luc winced at the expression on Téa's face. She stalked in his direction and snatched the cell phone from his hand. "I can't believe you did that."

"I'm sure she didn't catch the subtext."

Téa lifted an eyebrow. "And if she did?"

Luc felt dull color inch across his face. "Hell."

"You think?" She marched to her handbag and carefully began reorganizing it. "You were right earlier," she said as she arranged.

"Of course I was." He paused a beat. "What was I right about?"

"I also vote to end things right now. Two 'yes' votes… that makes it unanimous. The motion carries. As of this minute our relationship is strictly business."

He didn't bother commenting, since ending the relationship was what he wanted, as well. Though why he had a sudden urge to argue the point, he couldn't say. Instead he frowned as the cell phones vanished into her shoulder bag. "Just out of curiosity, why do you have three phones instead of just one?"

"I tried that. There were so many messages, my cell exploded."

His mouth twitched and he found himself relaxing. "Cell phones don't explode."

"Mine did." Her graceful fingers continued sorting and arranging, dancing over her possessions with all the skill of a concert pianist. "After just twenty-four hours the poor thing whimpered like a baby. Then this mushroom shaped cloud erupted out of my purse and the phone melted into a puddle of electronic goo all over everything. It made a terrible mess." She paused, a wistful expression creeping across her face. "A shame really. It was a pretty little thing. I quite liked it."

He folded his arms across his chest and propped his shoulder against the wall. "That's when you bought the individual phones?"

"Oh, no. Then I switched to one of those all-purpose PDA phones."

"And?"

"It's recovering nicely at the sanitarium. The doctors have high hopes it can be retrained as a dictionary or address book."

Luc grinned, unexpectedly charmed. "And then?"

At long last she appeared satisfied with how she'd packed her shoulder bag and flipped open her briefcase. It was one of those with endless little cubbyholes and slots and zip sections. "Organization is important to me," she said, stating the all-too obvious. "So, I assigned one phone for each need. My three sisters on one, my grandmother on the second and—"

"And?" he prompted again.

She shrugged, burying her head deeper in her briefcase. He suspected it was to avoid looking at him. "And a private line just for me."

"Ah." His focus narrowed, his hunting instincts going on full alert. "Who calls you on that one?"

For a moment, he didn't think she'd respond, wouldn't tell him whether there was someone special in her life. Then she admitted, "Sometimes work." For a split second she appeared intensely vulnerable and self-conscious. "I've been meaning to cancel it. There's really no point in keeping it since I rarely use it."

For some odd reason it took a moment to respond. "Don't," he insisted gruffly. "Don't cancel it."

Now she did look at him, all ruffled and defenseless and clinging gallantly to her dignity. "Why ever not?"

"That one will be our phone."

"*Our* phone?" She frowned. "We don't need a shared phone. We'll be together often enough that you can just tell me whatever you need to in person."

"There may be times over the next six weeks when we're not together and I'll have to get in touch with you." For some reason he found himself speaking gently. "If you'd rather not give me the number, I don't mind sharing with your sisters."

She dismissed the suggestion out of hand. "No, that won't do."

"What about my using Madam's line?"

"Not a chance." She sighed. "No. I guess it'll have to be my private cell."

He searched his pockets until he unearthed his phone. "Give me the number."

Reluctantly she relayed it and he punched it in. "Once I turn twenty-five I'm going to cancel the service," she warned. She couldn't have made herself any clearer if she'd announced, "In six weeks I'm deleting you from my phone, my work, my life…and my bed."

"Understood," he said, the word ripe with irony.

She stood, and he could tell she was intent on leaving. "Could you call me a cab?"

"Sure. Just as soon as we clarify one thing."

"Which is?"

"This."

He crossed to confront her, his arms closing around her. To his surprise, she didn't attempt to slip from his grasp. Instead her curves settled against his, fitting like a key to a lock. Only this key and this lock were filled with heat and demand. Even more important, this key and lock opened a treasure beyond compare, one he'd never believed existed. One that tempted and seduced.

One he wasn't quite certain he could walk away from in six weeks…though he'd find a way.

"We weren't going to do this again," she protested.

"We weren't going to do this again once we started working together," he corrected. He swung her into his arms. "Our working relationship doesn't begin until tomorrow."

"Your leg!"

"My leg will survive." His lips curved into a wry smile. "It's the rest of me that's questionable."

She teetered on a knife's edge between resistance and capitulation and he waited to see which way she tipped. Then her expression softened into exquisite surrender.

"Well, guess what?" Her arms crept upward and wrapped around his neck. Her lips nuzzled into the hollow at the base of his throat. "Some things may be questionable for you, but I believe I have the answers. Shall we see if I'm right?"

He eyed her with amused appreciation as he carried her to the bedroom. "If you insist."

"Oh, I do insist. In fact, I demand."

"A demand is it?" He deposited her on his bed. "I guess a man has to do what a man has to do," he said with a gusty sigh, and reached for his belt buckle.

FOUR

Four

Luc wasn't the least surprised when he woke the next morning to find Téa long gone, no doubt with her briefcase, shoulder bag and cranky cell phones in tow. Some bodyguard he was, allowing his assignment to slip away with such ease.

The apartment felt strangely empty and silent, qualities that until a few hours ago he'd not only prized, but actively sought. He glanced toward the bedside table where he'd stashed his cell phone. He was tempted to try the number she'd given him, but since he'd see her soon at work, there wasn't much point.

He rolled over, planning to get up and shower and make tracks. But something stopped him, the faintest of scents. It sweetened the air next to him, coming from the indentation that was all that remained of Téa. He snagged the pillow and breathed her in.

Her light, crisp perfume saturated his lungs and made

him hungry for her. Hungry to repeat the excesses of the night before. But there was another reaction he hadn't anticipated, one that was far worse. His palm throbbed and itched and he found himself rubbing at the sensation just as he'd seen Dante men do their entire lives.

As much as he wanted to deny it, he could feel The Inferno stirring like some great dragon waking from a deep sleep. Flames sparked and crackled, surging through his veins and heating his blood. Not good, he realized in alarm. Not good at all. Somehow, someway, he'd have to return the dragon to its eternal rest. Because if there was one thing he intended to avoid experiencing, it was The Inferno.

He refused to consider that it might be far too late.

Luc arrived at Billings less than an hour later. It was an impressive place, he decided. Thick pearl-gray carpet sucked up all peripheral noise. Not that there was much. The few people he saw spoke in hushed undertones. The furniture was all heavy wood, stained a deep, somber shade of brown. A jungle of plants sprouted from every corner, dense enough to hide a tiger if one wandered in by mistake.

It was all a bit on the stuffy, pretentious side, especially when compared to Dantes. Still, if the purpose of the decor was to give the visitor the impression of wealth and prestige, it succeeded.

The attractive, impeccably tailored receptionist seated behind an intimidating fortress of wood and electronics assured him that not only was Ms. de Luca there, but expecting him. After making a discreet phone call, she examined his identification and presented him with credentials that would allow him to breach the upper echelon of the company's executive offices.

She then escorted him to a bank of elevators and actually pressed the call button for him. He couldn't quite decide if it was the limp that made her so solicitous, or if she just thought men with limps had trouble pushing buttons.

Before he could ask, a gleaming elevator accented in mahogany and chrome and playing a soft operatic aria in the background arrived and carried him directly to the executive level where another impeccably tailored receptionist—this one male—escorted him down a heavily forested hallway. He didn't see any tigers lurking in the brush, which disappointed him. But at least this receptionist didn't have to press any buttons for him.

Instead he knocked on a door and opened it before motioning Luc into a corner office. A small break in the march of skyscrapers outside Téa's window allowed for a sliver of sunshine to creep through, along with a splash of grayish-blue water. Luc stepped inside the office and closed the door in the receptionist's face, if only to prove himself capable of that much.

"How nice," he said to Téa, squinting at the sliver of water. "You have a view of the bay."

Téa looked up from her computer screen. For an instant, he saw their last waking moments together reflected in the turbulent blue-green of her eyes. Then she smiled at his jest, robbing him of breath and making his palm throb. Other parts throbbed, as well, but he did his best to ignore those.

"Good morning," was all she had to say to make the throbbing intensify.

"You left." He didn't mean to say that, let alone growl it. For some reason, he couldn't stop himself. "You left without saying goodbye."

"I did."

He didn't quite know what to respond to such a simple and ingenuous admission. He crossed to the window and snatched at his tie, tearing at the knot that threatened to choke him. "Maybe now would be a good time to decide how this bodyguarding stuff is going to work, don't you think?"

"We were supposed to do that last night."

He released a short laugh. "We seemed to spend a lot of last night doing what we weren't supposed to and not doing what we were. How is today going to be any different?"

"We'll start fresh," she said lightly. "See if we can't get it right this time."

He spun to face her. "It felt like we got it right last night."

"Don't."

Images ripped through his mind. Téa splayed across his bed, her glorious hair captured in the final rays of sunlight turning each strand to a blazing, vibrant russet. Téa, her pale skin soaking up the moonlight and glowing with a soft, pearl-white radiance. Those silken limbs twined around him, holding him in the cradle of her hips with surprising strength. The look in her eyes when he joined with her. The sound she made when she climaxed.

His mouth twisted. "Tell me how to stop and I will."

A wistfulness crept into her expression, a hint of the want she'd expressed with such generosity the night before. He could see her swing, light as a summer breeze, between desire and her precious logic.

"Luc." His name escaped on the swing toward desire. "I—"

Before she could complete the thought, a tinny

version of "Here Comes the Bride" filled the air. Every scrap of passion vanished as though it had never been. Without another word, she took the call. From what little he caught of the one-sided conversation, Juliana's fiancée was in the military and stationed overseas, which probably explained why Téa was involved in so many of the decisions. The conversation seemed to go on forever and it wasn't only passion that drained from her face, but energy. She'd just wrapped up that call when Davida rang with an update on her college woes, followed by Madam with a series of financial questions. At least Katrina held off, but maybe that was because someone had locked her in a classroom. Or better yet, detention. He could only hope.

Completing the call, Téa snapped the phone closed and regarded him with an appealing hint of bewilderment. "I'm sorry. What were we discussing?"

Best to let it go. After all, they'd elected to avoid that particular entanglement. "It wasn't important." He tilted his head to one side and decided to probe. He doubted it was germane to the job at hand, but he wouldn't know for certain until he had all the facts. "Is your family always so demanding?" he asked curiously.

She shrugged. "I'm sort of the mother figure."

He asked the next logical question. "What happened to yours?"

"She and my stepfather were killed in a car accident when I was a teenager."

He saw it then, the curtain that whisked across her emotions, hiding them from view and could tell there was a lot more to that simple statement than she was letting on. Way more. Took one to know one. He also had an incident that he kept carefully curtained. Knew how hard she must have practiced to perfect that calm, matter-of-fact tone. How carefully she worded the explanation so it contained the clear statement: Don't go there. I don't want to discuss it.

He let her off the hook. "I gather Madam took you in."

Téa nodded. "She raised us. But it was my responsibility to fill in for our mother."

Interesting. "Who told you that?"

"Who…?" The question knocked her off stride and she blinked at him, a hint of confusion causing her brow to wrinkle. "No one told me. No one had to."

"Uh-huh." He made some swift calculations in his head and came up with…way too young. "Just out of curiosity, how old are your sisters?"

"Juliann is twenty-two, Davida is twenty-one, and Katrina is eighteen. She graduates from high school in a couple months. Maybe."

That pretty much confirmed what he suspected. "Which makes you only two years older than Juliann."

"Almost three." This time her response came with a hint of defensiveness.

He throttled back, keeping his comments gentle and understanding. "Right. But even so, it's not quite enough of a gap to make you a mother figure in their eyes." He shot her an easy, confiding sort of grin, one meant to link them in some nebulous way. "I mean, we're both stuck in the same predicament. We're the oldest. We're supposed to set the example for the younger ones. But, my sister, Gia, is six years younger than me and I guarantee she doesn't see me as a father figure. Not even close."

Téa mulled that over, no doubt searching for a flaw in his logic. Eventually she came up with something, though it took her a minute. "Probably because your father's still alive," she said with a hint of triumph. "But when our parents married, they sort of looked at me as if I were—" She broke off with another shrug, her logic running out of steam since her stepfather and mother would have still been alive then, too.

"A mother figure? At nine?" he asked gently.

"Not exactly," she conceded. "But…more mature and distant. An aunt or something. I guess it evolved into a mother figure after my parents died."

He tried not to wince. In other words, they made her feel like the odd man out, despite the fact that their father eventually adopted her. He thought back to that long-ago summer at the Dante family cabin. How she'd kept herself apart from the rest of them. Now that he thought about it, she'd been different in every possible way from her sisters. In looks—like a flame dancing in the middle of a pile of coal. In attitude—a helpless fawn flitting among a pack of rambunctious panther cubs. In action—an oasis of calm amidst a storm of juvenile turbulence.

"I remember the first time I saw you," he confessed.

"You mean in the intersection?"

He shook his head. "No, I mean the very first time. At the lake when we were kids." He tilted his head to one side, watching the play of emotions that chased across her face, the unexpected vulnerability. "Don't you remember?" he asked softly.

She fiddled with a thick file folder on her desk, flipping it open and then closed again. "Yes," she said after a moment. She lifted eyes gone dark with memories.

"You made me itch even then." The words escaped of their own volition.

She stiffened. Her fingers played across the palm of her hand, though he doubted she even noticed. "Itch?"

He wouldn't admit it might have been the early signs of The Inferno. He wasn't willing to look at it that closely. But something about her had gotten under his skin, even then. "You irritated me."

She didn't press, made a face instead, then accused, "You were a bully. You all were."

It was his turn to shrug. "It wouldn't surprise me. We were probably operating under a pack mentality back then. And you didn't fit in."

She flinched. "No, I didn't."

He leaned across the desk toward her, sweeping a lock of hair off her brow and tucking it behind one ear. His fingers lingered, stroking. "You didn't want to fit in."

"Not then," she agreed, leaning into the caress. "I wasn't used to so much noise and confusion. Before we became de Lucas, it was just me and my mom. We lived a fairly quiet existence except when my Billings grandparents descended. Then it got a bit rocky."

That snagged his attention and his hand fell away. "Why is that?"

"I don't remember much, but according to Mom, Grandfather Billings was somewhat controlling." She gave a quick half smile, confiding, "Of course he'd have been excruciatingly polite about it—not like the de Lucas who handle any disagreement at top volume."

Luc grinned. "The Dantes have been known to go at it a time or two, though Nonna will bring us to a fast stop if it continues too long."

"As will Madam. She'll rap her knuckles on the table and if there isn't instant silence…" Téa shuddered.

"She can be intimidating."

"She terrified me during those early years," Téa confessed.

It was a telling comment. "So how did Grandfather Billings take the news that your mother was going to remarry?"

"Not well. He was dead-set against it. In fact, he cut us off when she married Dad." She leaned in closer still and dropped her voice, possibly because they were deep in Billings's territory. Perhaps on some level old man Billings still infused the walls with his essence and she didn't want to chance him overhearing. "It surprised the hell out of me when he named me his successor in the will. Until then I'd planned to get a law degree."

And probably surprised the hell out of her cousin, Conway Billings. Luc decided against saying as much. "You call your stepfather Dad. And you use his name. I assume he adopted you?"

"Yes, when I turned sixteen. Six months later—" She broke off, but he caught the glint of tears in her eyes.

He gathered up her hand. Heat licked across his skin where their palms joined. It was a pleasant sensation. Reassuring on some level. It was as though what had been parted was once again joined and he could relax. "I'm sorry. Losing both of your parents like that must have been rough."

"It would have been far worse if Madam hadn't taken all of us in."

"And now it's time to pay her back for her generosity."

For some reason that provoked a smile. "Is that so wrong?"

"You're the one who almost got taken out by a cab because you were so distracted. You tell me."

"It's temporary," she whispered. "As soon as I turn twenty-five—"

"You'll take over the reins of a huge company with limited experience. Your workload will increase dramatically and you'll still have three demanding sisters and a grandmother to worry about."

"You think I should just give it all up?"

"There are options."

"None that will allow me the financial freedom I need." She broke off at the knock on her door and snatched her hand from his. He watched her fight to compose herself before calling out, "Come in."

A man in his mid-forties stuck his head through the opening of the door and gave a patently fake start of surprise. "Oh, you have company. Am I interrupting?"

A smile bloomed on Téa's face and she waved the man in. "You're never interrupting, Connie. Come on in. I'd like to introduce you to Luc Dante. Luc, this is my cousin, Conway Billings."

A man hovering somewhere in those unfortunate inches between medium and short entered the office. Out of sheer habit, Luc made a swift assessment. Conway was dressed in an expensive navy suit with a snowy white shirt, the collar held in place by pretentious gold clips rather than buttons. Matching clips decorated the cuffs of his sleeves. He wore his thinning auburn hair as short as Luc's and was painfully clean-shaven. He also sported an old-fashioned pocket watch on a real gold chain—no doubt a subtle advertisement of Billings's wares, had gold-rimmed glasses perched on the ball of his stub nose and kept his shoes polished to a mirror shine. Unlike Téa's creamy complexion, his glowed an uncomfortable shade of red that clashed with his hair.

For some reason, Luc's hackles went up. Maybe it was Conway's pretense of surprise and ridiculous opening question. The door was closed. He had to have heard their voices. Of course he was interrupting. How could he not be? But then, this man ran Billings. At least, for the moment. No doubt his position meant that no matter who or what he interrupted, it wasn't an interruption.

Luc also suspected that someone had alerted him to the fact that a Dante was in the building talking to Téa. And since Dantes was Billings's biggest client, no doubt Cousin Connie wanted to find out what the hell was going on.

Luc stuck out his hand. "A pleasure," he lied.

"Yes, it is," Conway lied right back.

Luc's eyes narrowed. Okay, at least he knew where he stood. He edged his hip onto the corner of Téa's desk, staking his claim, only to ruin the possessive maneuver with a wince of pain. Damn hip. "Nice place you have here," he managed to say.

"Thanks." Pride rippled through the single word. "Billings has been the gold standard ever since my great-uncle established it, two and a half decades ago."

He placed enough emphasis on the words "gold standard" that Luc realized it was meant as a play on words. Supplier of gold. Gold standard. Ha-ha. Luc bared his teeth in a grin. "Don't sweat it. Dantes doesn't mind doing business with newcomers like Bling."

Conway stopped laughing. Either Cousin Connie didn't care for the company's nickname, or he didn't appreciate the reminder that Dantes had been around twice as long as Billings.

"Why are you here, Mr. Dante?" he asked bluntly.

"Make it Luc." He waited.

"Luc," Conway repeated through gritted teeth.

"I'm here on behalf of Dantes." He picked up on Téa's incipient protest and turned to her. Catching her hand in his, he gave it a light squeeze. "Just six more weeks, isn't it? We've almost left it too long."

"Left what too long?" Conway asked sharply.

He hadn't missed the touch Luc and Téa had exchanged, an intermingling of fingers that could be taken as a sign of intimacy—and in this case most assuredly was. He regarded the man with the sort of patience one did a child. Good ol' Connie caught the look, interpreted it as just that and bristled in offense.

"Téa takes over Billings then, doesn't she?" Luc didn't wait for confirmation. "As your largest and most important customer, Dantes wants to make certain all our needs will be met before, during and after the transition. So, I plan to work closely with Téa these next few weeks to ensure everything proceeds smoothly."

Téa's eyes narrowed on Luc in warning before she offered her cousin a reassuring smile. "You don't mind, do you, Connie?" she asked.

Conway seized the question with grim determination, using the opportunity to regain control of the situation. "As a matter of fact, I do, Téa," he informed her gravely. "If Dantes wants my assurance that Billings will continue to provide excellent goods and service—"

Luc cut him off without hesitation. "It's not *your* assurance I'm interested in. You're no longer the one in charge. Your cousin is."

Beside him, Téa stiffened. "Luc," she murmured in protest.

A sweep of heightened color darkened Conway's

cheekbones and a protest tumbled out before he could prevent it. "Not for another six weeks, she isn't."

Luc lifted an eyebrow. Interesting. Her cousin sounded a bit possessive for a man who—how had Téa described him? Oh, right. As a man who couldn't wait to get out from under his responsibilities. It might be interesting to find out just what sort of business Conway intended to start up…assuming there actually was one.

Luc shook his head with a mock frown. "Six weeks isn't very long. It might be just enough time for Dantes to satisfy ourselves that your gold standard will be upheld after the transition." He lifted an eyebrow. "You don't have any objection to my being here, do you?"

"As a matter of fact—"

"Hey, no problem," Luc interrupted and stood. "If you don't want me around, I'm gone."

"I think that would be best," Conway said with a decisive nod. He appeared more assured now that he'd regained the upper hand. Or at least, thought he had. He smoothed his suit jacket like a bird unruffling its feathers. "I'm sure you understand, Dante. But this is my company—"

"*Our* company," Téa interrupted with a spark of irritation.

Conway started. "Right, right. *Our* company." His tone turned aggrieved. "You must agree, Téa, that it wouldn't be appropriate to have someone looking over *our* shoulders, as it were."

"Got it." Luc retrieved his cell phone from his pocket and began pressing buttons. "Let me apprise Sev of these latest developments. It's an unfortunate setback, but my cousin is accustomed to those. Very decisive and proactive that cousin of mine."

"Is this really necessary?" Conway demanded.

Luc paused. "What? The phone call or my being here?" He shrugged. "Not that it matters. I assure you both are critical to our continued good relationship."

Téa sliced neatly through the testosterone thickening the air with icy shards of feminine disapproval. "If Conway objects to your being here, Luc, then that's that. Here's what I suggest in order to straighten this out and satisfy all parties involved." She clicked off her suggestions like a general commanding her troops. "Luc, please call Sev and ask if he'll take a meeting. The three of us will go over, sit down with him and see what can be arranged. But make it clear that we'll do everything in our power to ensure the transition goes off without a hitch. Connie, since our contract with Dantes is up soon, I suggest we pull together some numbers in order to begin preliminary negotiations on a new one."

Conway stiffened and Luc had the distinct impression he wasn't used to his cousin being quite so assertive. And he sure as hell wasn't accustomed to her issuing instructions to him. "That won't be necessary, Téa," he stated. "I have the contract details well in hand." Frustration ate at his expression before he finally capitulated. "Okay, fine. Mr. Dante, if you must oversee certain aspects of the transition—"

"Luc."

Silence reigned for an entire thirty seconds until Conway bit out, "*Luc*. If you insist it's necessary to be here—"

"I do."

Conway shot his cousin a smoldering glare. "Since you'll soon be running the show, Téa, you work out all the various details, though I must insist that any changes to established routine be run by me beforehand." He hesitated, sparing Luc a suspicious glance. "As for you, Mr.—*Luc*. I think it only fair you be as forthcoming as possible about your intentions."

"My intentions?"

The question caught Luc off guard and Conway picked up on that fact. He pounced with something akin to triumph. He rocked onto the balls of his feet with a quick bounce and jabbed his index finger toward Luc. "Exactly. Are you really here to ensure a smooth transition, or is this about the renewal of our contract? If you're looking for a better price…"

Huh. Luc cocked his head to one side. "Can you offer one?"

"No, I just meant…" He eyed the two, his suspicion deepening. "I hope you don't think Téa will offer you a better deal because she's a woman, and therefore susceptible to masculine influence."

"Masculine influence," Luc repeated. He didn't need to fake how much the comment offended him. "By that I assume you mean sexual influence." He slowly stood, allowing every intimidating inch of his six-feet-three to loom over Billings's five-feet-squat. "Just who the hell do you think I am? Who do you think *she* is?"

Conway retreated toward the door. "No! I didn't mean—" A heavy flush stained his cheeks and he made a production of checking his watch. "Since I have an urgent appointment in a few minutes, we'll have to finish this discussion some other time." He fumbled for the door handle behind him. "Téa, you and Luc carry on. I'll be in my office if you need me." With that, he exited the room with as much dignity as he could muster.

Luc waited until the door banged closed before glancing at Téa. To his relief, he saw amusement glittering in her eyes. He edged his hip on the corner of her desk again, managing not to wince this time. "I'm curious," he said. "Could I use sex to persuade you to give Dantes a better deal?"

"Not a chance."

He heaved a disappointed sigh. "Didn't think so, but I had to ask. Sev would have been annoyed if I hadn't at least tried."

"I understand."

"In that case, we better do what Conway ordered."

A delightful confusion spread across her face. "I'm sorry?"

Luc grinned. "Didn't you hear him? He told us to carry on. I suggest we get started." He leaned in, feeling the pull of The Inferno and allowing it to consume him. "He is, after all, the boss."

Her smile turned grim. "Only for six more weeks."

And then she, too, surrendered to the heat.

Five

The next week passed, at moments feeling as though it were on wings. Other times Téa was certain some sadistic creature had paused the minutes in order for her to fully experience the weight of desire building with each additional day she spent in Luc's company.

It was a desire she couldn't allow. One she didn't have time to explore, not when she faced so many more urgent demands. Mostly it was one she didn't deserve, not after the destruction she'd left in her wake all those years ago—a destruction she could never fully repair even though she'd do her best to mend the few rents within her capability.

Luc kept his word. Except for the single embrace they exchanged after the confrontation with Connie, he hadn't touched her. At least, he didn't touch her the way she longed to be touched. He kept their physical interaction as brief and distant as possible, though she sensed that it was as much a struggle for him as it was for her.

His struggle wasn't implicit in what he said, but she caught his reaction in small and significant ways. The deepening tenor of his voice. The slight hitch in his movement when he reached for her, as though he were deliberately switching gears from intimate to impersonal. A flash of awareness that turned his golden eyes molten with hunger before he deliberately banked the flames.

She didn't find the process any easier. She had an urgent job to accomplish right now—to learn everything she could about her grandfather's company before assuming the reins, while still carving out enough time each day to care for her family's needs and demands… not to mention the unending phone calls. The last thing she could handle was another disruption. Unfortunately Luc excelled at disrupting her on every conceivable level—including hiding her phones whenever their constant demands threatened to overwhelm her.

She couldn't say what clued her in the first time, other than the fact that she'd enjoyed several hours of blissful silence before noticing that her phones were no longer lined up along the edge of her desk. She stared at the empty space for an entire minute, on the verge of panic, before her gaze veered toward Luc and understanding dawned.

"Give them back."

He flipped the page on the journal he read, something that had to do with electronic security. "Relax, Téa. Nothing can be that urgent. If it were, they'd call Bling directly."

"That's not the point. You can't just take my cell phones." Her voice rose and she struggled to lower it, even out the shrillness. "They're lifelines to my family. Madam and my sisters depend on me."

He shot her a dangerous look, filled with a hard decisiveness she suspected was a natural part of his personality. Until now he'd never used it on her. "It's vital to trust your team, to rely on them. But it's just as vital to be self-sufficient enough to take care of business if one of those team members is lost."

"In English, please?"

"If you take self-sufficiency away from your sisters, they become less effective on all levels, personal, as well as professional."

"My family isn't some sort of military unit," she protested.

"They'll also never learn to fend for themselves if you wipe their noses every time they sneeze. Your sisters need to learn independent thought and action." His eyes narrowed, disapproval stirring in the deep gold depths. "Unless you want them dependent on you. Is that why you do everything for them? It makes you feel wanted? Needed?"

"No!"

"Are they incompetent? Handicapped in some way?"

"Of course not," she snapped.

"Then why the obsession to micromanage?"

Her mouth tightened and she shook her head, refusing to answer.

He shrugged. "Then, barring emergency, they're perfectly capable of handling their own affairs until after you've finished work for the day. Since I'm in charge of keeping you safe and distraction free, I've made the executive decision to confiscate your phones. I'll return them at five."

"And if there is an emergency?"

"There are enough brain cells between the four of them to call through to the Bling switchboard and alert you to that fact."

She didn't dare admit that not having the constant barrage of phone calls came as a tremendous relief. But it did. And Luc was as good as his word. The moment they stepped foot in her office he took possession of the phones, returning them at five on the dot.

Realizing that she'd been staring into space for the past fifteen minutes while he watched on, she forced her attention back to the spreadsheets piled in front of her. "You're not supposed to put your feet on my desk, remember?" she said absently as she scanned the numbers.

"I vaguely recall you saying something to that effect."

"And yet, I'm still seeing an impressive pair of size fourteens sitting here in front of me."

"Elevating my feet makes my knee and hip feel better."

She peered at him over the top of her reading glasses. "That's low, even for you."

"Are you calling me a liar?"

"I wouldn't dream of it. I would dream of telling you to move your feet elsewhere while I'm working."

She returned her attention to the numbers. Something didn't add up, but despite her affinity with all things accounting, she couldn't quite figure out what was bothering her. She blew out a sigh. Maybe she'd have better luck if part of her weren't constantly distracted by the golden-eyed panther lounging nearby, one that took great delight in ruffling her tidy little world.

"What's wrong?" he asked.

It didn't surprise her that he picked up on her frustration. The man was beyond observant. "I don't know. Nothing."

He dropped his feet to the floor and leaned forward in his chair. "If it were nothing you wouldn't be analyzing the same report for the fifth time this week."

"I'm having focus issues. I'm distracted." She didn't dare admit aloud that a huge part of that distraction was due to him. "That's one of the reasons you're here, remember? To save me from my own distraction."

His mouth twitched, but he answered seriously enough. "All too well. Part of your problem is that you don't get enough sleep."

"I get plenty." She couldn't say for certain, but it was possible the testy note in her voice gave lie to her claim.

"According to Madam you get maybe five hours a night."

She waved that aside. Maybe she'd have been in a better position to argue the point if the numbers weren't doing a bizarre rumba across the page. "It won't be for much longer."

"No, it won't." He caught her hand in his and tugged her to her feet. "Come on."

"What are you doing?" she protested. "I'm working here."

He shot a sardonic glance toward her spreadsheets, then checked his watch. "It's Friday and it's almost four. In my book, that's quitting time."

"Not in mine," she retorted.

"Yeah, well, I'm expected at my grandparents soon for a family celebration. It's Rafe's birthday."

"Oh."

She tugged fruitlessly at her hand before giving it up

and leaving it captured within his. Somehow the throb in her palm didn't bother her as much when their hands were interlaced. Instead it calmed her, steadied her, even as it stirred the banked fires of desire kindling between them. She couldn't decide which disturbed her the most, not having the connection created by their touch, or dealing with the urge to tug him into her arms and have her wicked way with him.

She cleared her throat, hoping it would also clear her thoughts. Not that it succeeded. "Well, you go ahead to the party. I have a few more hours to put in here and then, I promise, I'll go straight home." She offered a reassuring smile. "I'll even pay attention to what I'm doing and dive for cover anytime I see a cab."

For the past week he'd escorted her from door-to-door, unwilling to so much as debate the issue. No matter how early she attempted to leave for the office, or how late she stayed, he was always right there to shepherd her to and fro. She had a strong suspicion that Madam played a huge part in alerting him to any unexpected changes in Téa's schedule. After a few days of attempting to circumvent their efforts, she'd given up trying since it proved a ridiculous waste of both time and energy.

"I have a better suggestion," Luc countered. "Why don't you come with me to the party. Then I'll see you home, as usual."

She spared a brief glance toward the stack of accounting reports. They held all the appeal of a root canal. She'd much rather spend the next few hours with Luc. Maybe if he hadn't used the word "party" she'd have considered it. But that word carried negative associations, pushing every last one of her guilt buttons. Duty. Responsibility. Family obligation. They were brands she wore, ones burned into her heart and soul.

Something in her expression must have given her away. "What is it?" he asked sharply. "What's wrong?"

"Nothing." Not that the denial fooled him.

"Bull. You look like someone threatened with a firing squad. Why?"

She lifted her chin and forced herself to regard him with cool composure. "I don't do parties."

He studied her for an endless moment. "How about family dinners?" he asked neutrally. "You have a family, don't you?"

"You know I do," she retorted.

"And your family has dinners, right?"

"Yes, but—"

"And sometimes those dinners are to celebrate a birthday?"

She pushed out a sigh. She could see where this was going. What she couldn't see was a logical way out of it. "It's been known to happen," she admitted.

"That's what this is. A dinner to celebrate my brother's birthday. I'd like you to come with me." And then he turned downright mean and underhanded. "Please, Téa. Come with me," he said softly.

She caved. But then, how could she do anything else? Not only did she want to, but she flat-out couldn't resist the temptation, particularly when it was issued by such a bone-melting masculine package. "Fine. I'll come." She glanced down at her tailored slacks and jacket, the combination in a dignified, somber black. They screamed, "business." "I'm not sure I'm dressed appropriately for a party, though."

"You look gorgeous, as always. Just casual it up."

She blinked at him. "Excuse me?"

"You know how women do." He gestured with his hands. "Undo certain stuff. Fluff other parts."

"Undo and fluff." Maybe if her sisters were here to interpret it would help. Particularly Vida. Téa suspected that her flirty middle sister excelled at the art of undoing and fluffing. "That's man-speak for…?"

"Here. I'll show you."

Before she could stop him, he'd stripped off her jacket and tossed it aside. Then he released the first three buttons of her blouse. While she rebuttoned two of them, he ran his fingers through her hair, releasing the elegant little knot she'd fashioned that morning and sending her hair tumbling down her back in a cascade of exuberant auburn curls.

"Do you mind?" she demanded in exasperation.

"Not at all. All undone and fluffed." He tilted his head to one side. "But there's still something missing."

He took a step back and examined her while she did her best not to feel too self-conscious. "Well?" she asked, squirming just a bit. "What's wrong with me?"

"There's nothing wrong with you. It's just…" He snapped his fingers. "Got it." Reaching out, he plucked her reading glasses from the tip of her nose and set them carefully among the papers scattered on her desk. He studied her upturned face and offered a lazy smile filled with blatant male approval. "Much better."

"I need those to read." She wasn't quite sure why she uttered such an inane comment. He just had that effect on her.

"You won't need to read at the party," he answered gravely. "The cake will say Happy Birthday, Rafe."

Her lips quivered in the direction of a smile. "Thank you for letting me know."

"Glad to help."

Téa tidied up her desk and snagged her jacket on the way out of the office. "My phones," she reminded, holding out her hand. For some reason, she felt reluctant to take them when he handed them over. That was a first.

She paused by her assistant's desk on her way out and told him to take off early, before giving in to the pressure of Luc's hand urging her toward the elevators. Five minutes later they were in his car, battling the start of rush hour traffic as they headed toward the Golden Gate Bridge. She used the drive time to deal with the accumulated calls, fighting a headache from the pressure of dealing with her sisters' latest crises. The instant she finished, Luc stole the phones.

"For the next couple hours you're off duty," he said by way of explanation.

By the time they arrived in Sausalito and climbed the winding roads overlooking the bay, late afternoon was easing toward evening, resting a gentle hand on their surroundings and gilding it with a soft glow. Luc parked the car outside a wooden gate, squeezing in among the other cars piled up there. The gate led to a lush backyard, with rambling flowerbeds that rioted in color and fragrance. Carefully pruned black acacia and bay trees shaded portions of the large, fenced oasis while a mush oak spread its protective arms over a wrought iron table and chairs. The dining area offered the perfect place for an outdoor lunch or supper, with its glorious view of the bay, Angel Island and Belvedere. Currently it was the gathering place for nearly a dozen people, all of whom were talking and laughing at full volume, some in English and some in Italian.

Luc didn't approach immediately, but pulled Téa close and murmured in her ear. "Hang on a minute.

You met the original Dante clan when we were children, but I don't expect you can put names and faces together after all these years."

"Not a chance," she admitted.

"I'll give you a quick rundown. First up are the cousins." He indicated one of the men sitting near the table. He was a couple years older than Luc and bore a striking similarity in appearance. "Have you taken any meetings with Sev, yet?"

"Connie's covering that for now." She couldn't explain why she felt so reluctant to admit as much. Nor why she hastened to add, "I expect I'll have the chance to sit down with Sev when we finalize a new contract."

"Well, you can at least press the flesh tonight." He indicated two particularly gorgeous men with dark brown hair and Nonna's hazel eyes. "Those are the twins, Marco and Lazz. And their youngest brother, Nicolò, is sitting in the grass with his wife, Kiley."

Next Luc indicated a heavily pregnant blonde snuggled in Sev's arms. "That's his wife, Francesca. She and Kiley, are due…" He made a production of checking his watch.

"That soon?"

"Oh, yeah."

"Marco's wife, Caitlyn, is talking to Lazz's wife, Ariana. And my sister, Gia, is the one pouring the wine. Come on and I'll introduce you to everyone." He offered a swift grin. "Take a deep breath…"

"And dive right in?"

"The water's nice and warm."

Téa expected to feel like an outsider, but the Dantes soon proved her wrong. Perhaps it was because the family was so large and sprawling or because there were so many diverse personalities, but they instantly made her feel like one of them.

Gia, the most outgoing and vibrant of the bunch, gave her a quick hug and pressed a glass of wine into her hand. And while the men discussed all things sports related, the women talked at length about the additions that were soon to grace the family.

"So far Nonna is batting a thousand." Ariana dropped the comment into a lull in the conversation, speaking with the lightest of Italian accents.

"What do you mean?" Kiley asked.

"Well, she said you both would have boys and that's what the ultrasound shows, yes?"

"True," Francesca admitted, rubbing the taut mound of her belly. "But then, she also said you'd have the only girl out of all these Dantes sprawled around here."

"Also true," Ariana said.

It took a split second for comprehension to sweep through the family. The instant it did, a half dozen different voices exploded in everything from cheers of excitement to a rapid-fire peppering of questions.

"When are you due?"

"Is it really a girl?"

"Why didn't you tell us sooner?"

Lazz held up his hands with a laugh. "She's due in a bit under six months. We wanted to keep it to ourselves for a while without you lot driving us crazy. And yes, the ultrasound confirmed today that it's a girl. A bit early for them to know, or so I've been told, but apparently the baby was positioned just right for the doctor to make the determination."

Téa and Luc enjoyed the added celebratory mood of the family while they finished their drinks. Then he urged her to her feet. "Let's go inside and say hello to Primo and Nonna."

They found Primo supervising the kitchen, a bottle of homemade beer at his elbow. The room was enormous, with huge bluish-gray flagstones decorating the rustic kitchen floor. Overhead, rough-hewn redwood beams stretched across the twelve-foot plaster ceiling. A long, broad table, one designed for the largest of families, took up one end of the room, while appliances suitable for a gourmet kitchen filled the other. Several more Dantes were busy carrying out Primo's orders as they put the finishing touches on the various dishes they were preparing for dinner. To Téa's surprise all of them were male.

"I'm beginning to like your family," she told Luc in an undertone.

He grinned, quick on the uptake. "Because the men cook?"

"Darn right. Makes a nice change. Of course, there aren't any men in my family, only women, so we get stuck with all the chores."

"Cooking and gardening are my grandfather's two favorite pastimes. Wait until you try his *pollo al Marsala con peperoni rossi*." Luc closed his eyes in ecstasy. "There are chefs from all over the world who'd give their eyeteeth for the recipe."

"Chicken Marsala with red peppers?" she hazarded a guess. "My Italian isn't that great, much to Madam's displeasure." She slanted him a quick, teasing grin. "Except when it comes to food."

"We'll have to see what we can do to change that."

The expression in his eyes made her feel as though she were free-falling at fifteen thousand feet without a parachute. Heat exploded deep in her belly and spread outward in waves of lapping fire. All thought vanished, except for one indisputable fact. This was her man. She didn't know how it had happened or why, but he belonged to her every bit as much as she belonged to him. Even as the crazy thought took hold, she struggled to dismiss it. It was wrong to put her personal desires first. But some thoughts couldn't be so easily dismissed.

Primo paused in the middle of barking an order to greet them. "So," he said, the flavor of his Tuscany homeland filling his words with a lyrical warmth. "This is the one, yes?"

Téa wasn't certain who appeared more alarmed, her or Luc. She'd always considered herself in control of her emotions and able to keep them well hidden from curious eyes. She hoped she'd nailed the ability, considering she'd been practicing since the tender age of sixteen. But, with Primo... It was as though he looked into her heart and laid it bare. And she didn't like it one bit. Deciding to take control of the situation, she stuck out her hand.

"How do you do, Mr. Dante. I'm Téa de Luca. Luc and I are working together. Temporarily." Though who that final word was aimed at—Luc, his grandfather, or herself—she couldn't quite say.

"Mr. Dante?" he repeated with an offended click of his tongue. He wrapped her up in a powerful hug filled with the distinctive scent of a fragrant cigar and a variety of the spices he'd used in the preparation of their dinner. "I am Primo, you understand?"

"Primo," she said, accepting the enthusiastic kisses he planted on each of her cheeks. "It's a pleasure to meet you."

He drew back in mock offense. "We met when you

were a little girl. You do not remember me? With most people I make a big impression."

She fought to control her amusement, not wanting to offend. "I'm sorry. I remember the cabin and the lake, but not too much else."

Primo lifted a sooty eyebrow and fixed her with ancient gold eyes that were identical to Luc's. "Well, no matter. I remember you. You were a pale, shy thing, overwhelmed by so many people. All bright red hair and white, skinny arms and legs." He touched the tip of her nose. "Always had this stuck in a book, yes?"

"That was me," she admitted with a laugh.

Primo turned and slapped the shoulder of one of the men behind him with a hand heavy enough to knock him to the floor. Maybe it would have if he hadn't possessed a powerful Dante build. "This is Luc's *babbo*, Alessandro."

Luc's father, Téa realized. At least, the Tuscany version of the word. "It's a pleasure."

"I'm stirring or I'd come over and say hello." Alessandro tossed a friendly smile over his shoulder. "Hello, anyway."

"You stir, I say hello," Primo instructed. He pointed to the next one in line. "This is Rafe. He is one of the pretty Dantes. We only have two, thank the good Lord above for that small blessing. One is a girl, my precious Gianna, which is as it should be. We keep the other despite his being as pretty as the girl. If he did not have a brain, I would have drowned him as a child."

"I believe you tried that, Primo," Rafe offered, "and discovered I could swim like a fish."

"I should have tried harder." Primo whacked his next helper. "And this good-for-nothing is Draco. I am not certain what use he is."

"I'm the charming one."

"Marco is the charming one. You are *l'istigatore*. The troublemaker."

Draco shrugged, not bothered by the accusation. "That, too."

"That, alone," Primo corrected before addressing Luc once again. "*Cucciolo mio*, go find Nonna and Elia and introduce Téa. Maybe she will remember your *mammina* better than she remembers me." He leaned toward Téa, confiding, "I do not let them in the kitchen until it is time to eat."

"Sounds perfect to me," Téa said with sincere appreciation.

Primo grinned. "I like you. You come back when all is ready and sit next to me."

The offer touched her. "Thank you. I look forward to it."

The night seemed to fly by after that. As ordered, Téa took the seat of honor beside Primo and surprised herself by eating every morsel put in front of her. She also discovered that Luc was right. Primo's *Marsala* was sheer ambrosia. Dinner took hours, the process a raucous occasion filled with genuine family affection and laughter.

The cake did indeed say, Happy Birthday, Rafe, and after it was consumed, the presents opened and the dishes washed, the women swept Téa off to enjoy coffee and talk babies some more. She threw a panicked glance over her shoulder in Luc's direction, but he just chuckled at her dismay. The last view she had of him was his glorious grin before it dissolved into a sudden frown. It took her a moment to understand why. But then she saw it. He was staring down at his hands. Staring at the unconscious massage of left thumb against right palm. Staring as though his hands didn't quite belong to his own body.

Staring at the undeniable proof that The Inferno had claimed another victim.

"So, it has finally struck," Primo said the instant the women had left.

Luc glanced up in confusion while his brother, Rafe, looked on with an amused expression on his too-handsome face. "Excuse me?"

"The Inferno." His grandfather gestured toward his grandson's hands. "Do not bother denying it, Luciano. The signs are all there."

"What this?" He deliberately gave his palm a final scratch and forced a laugh. "Just an itch."

Primo snorted. "What you feel is a fifty year itch, boy. Longer if you are very lucky."

"Téa de Luca is an assignment, nothing more."

Primo rolled his eyes heavenward. "Why are they always so stubborn? So reluctant to believe the truth even when it strikes as hard and dazzling as a lightning bolt?"

He crossed to one of the cabinets and pulled out a canister that read, Dried Manroot. Popping the lid, he extracted a cigar while Luc struggled to suppress a snort of laughter, thoroughly enjoying his grandfather's sense of the absurd.

"Nonna will have a fit if she sees you with that," Rafe warned, his jade-green eyes gleaming in shared amusement.

"Then we will make certain she does not see." He took a moment to prep the cigar, then light it. "Luciano, you have witnessed The Inferno every day of your life. With my beloved Nonna. With your parents. One by one, with each of your cousins." He lifted a snowy eyebrow. "Did you believe yourself immune?"

Luc set his jaw at a stubborn angle. "Yes."

Primo blew a ring of smoke skyward and shrugged. "You were wrong."

"I'm not interested in settling down," Luc protested. "I'm sure as hell not interested in marriage and children."

"Because of what happened?" his grandfather asked shrewdly.

There was no point in denying the truth. "Yes."

Luc shied from the memories, knowing if he didn't build a strong enough bulwark they'd consume him. One key lesson had come from the incident, an undeniable fact he'd learned about himself. He never wanted to give so much of himself to another person that he couldn't live without her. To trust to that extent. To risk so much. Rafe had warned him when his own marriage had ended in disaster. But the accident that had ruined Luc's knee had brought the fact home in spades.

Primo stabbed his cigar in Luc's direction. "The Inferno is not something you can simply turn off. It has happened and you will have to deal with it. You can do as your uncle did—God rest my Dominic's soul." He crossed himself, grief still haunting his black eyes. "Like Dominic, you can turn from it and destroy your life. Or you can follow your parents' excellent example. You can embrace it and discover a happiness unlike anything you could imagine."

"And when it ends?" Luc demanded.

Primo regarded him in bewilderment. "Who says it must end? What is this ending?"

"All things end," he insisted in a hard voice. "Love is a gamble, the ultimate gamble. When it ends, you don't just lose. It can destroy you. I've seen it happen. That's why I'll never give into it, why I only bet when I know I can win."

Understanding dawned in his grandfather's face and an uncomfortable compassion settled into the deep lines bracketing his mouth. "You speak of the accident, yes? That unfortunate family?" He didn't wait for a response. "Death is part of life, Luciano, just as love is. No one can control it. You witnessed that during your military service. Everything in life is a risk. But you can't win unless you play. Take the love while you have the chance. Worrying about the other does you no good."

Nonna's voice drifted in from the backyard, warning of her approach. Without hesitation, Primo snatched his cigar from between his teeth and shoved it into Luc's hand. By the time his wife entered the kitchen, he was across the room with a virtuous expression pinned to his face.

Nonna's hazel eyes landed on Luc before arrowing toward Primo. "You know what the doctor said about smoking. No more cigars."

"Do you see a cigar in my hand, old woman?"

"Do you think me a fool, old man?" After nearly sixty years of marriage, her imitation of her husband was uncanny.

Primo held his hands out. "*Che cosa?* I have no idea what you are talking about."

"You look as innocent as a wolf with a lamb between its teeth, Primo Dante. My Luciano does not smoke." Nonna planted her hands on her hips. "You think I do not know the meaning of dried manroot? I know all about that canister in your spice cabinet."

"Dried cucumber," he protested. "Just a bit of sea-soning."

"Hah! A joke at my expense, is what it is. Only the joke is on you when I tell all our friends that Primo Dante keeps his dried manroot in a jar in our kitchen cabinet!"

"You would not dare…!" He thumped his chest. "I am your husband and I am telling you—"

She lifted an eyebrow.

Primo cleared his throat. "And I am telling you that as of tonight there will be no dried manroot in my spice cabinet."

She nodded in satisfaction. "I thought that might be what you wanted to tell me."

Six

The evening didn't end as well as it began.

Téa expected Luc to join her after he'd finished his conversation with Primo. But instead, Sev Dante, the head of Dantes, the family's international jewelry empire, slipped into the seat next to hers. She offered him a smile, one he didn't return.

Her smile faded. "Is something wrong?"

He frowned, adding to her concern, and kept his voice low, so their conversation didn't carry to the other Dantes sprawled around them. "I know a birthday party isn't the appropriate venue for this discussion, but Francesca insisted I speak to you," he began on an ominous note. "She's usually right about these things."

"What things?" Téa asked warily.

"Business matters."

She stiffened. This couldn't be good, not when it involved so much frowning. "Business matters…

as in Billings's contract with Dantes?" At his nod of confirmation, she said, "I thought Connie was handling that."

He studied her with a golden gaze remarkably similar to Luc's, if perhaps a shade tawnier. "Let's just say that your cousin hasn't been very responsive to the concerns I've raised. So, if he's representing you in this matter, he's not doing a very good job of it." He hesitated, then asked, "You'll be in charge of Bling soon, won't you?"

"Five more weeks," she acknowledged.

"Then you should know there's a strong possibility that Dantes won't re-up our contract."

She fought to keep all emotion from her expression while she figured out how to deal with the unexpected—and alarming—information. All the while, a thread of panic wormed through her. If they lost the Dantes account, the company would be in serious jeopardy. Other accounts might follow suit and her inheritance would go from impressive to nonexistent.

And that meant she'd fail her family.

"Can you tell me why you've changed your mind about doing business with Billings?" she asked with impressive calm.

"It's a quality issue. Yours has gone down while your prices have skyrocketed. Conway says it's at your insistence. We've had another company approach us offering far better prices and top-notch quality."

Téa straightened in her chair. She carefully returned her cup and saucer to the wrought iron table and swiveled to confront Sev directly. "No one offers better quality than Billings."

"Once upon a time that would be true," he acknowledged. "But not any longer."

She searched desperately for a solution. "What if I can guarantee both? Would you re-evaluate your decision?"

"Your guarantee doesn't hold a lot of weight considering the quality of the merchandise we've been receiving." He hesitated, then nodded. "But since our two companies have always enjoyed such a stellar relationship, I'll give you a couple of weeks to get to the bottom of the problem."

"Thank you. I'll look into the matter and call you Monday, at the latest."

Sev inclined his head. "One last thing…"

He shot a look over her shoulder. Téa didn't need to follow his glance to know that Luc was approaching. She could feel him. Feel him as though he were a rising tide and she the waiting shoreline.

"Yes?" she prompted.

"Your…association…with Luc won't influence my decision," Sev warned quietly. And with that, he stood and returned to his wife.

Luc shot a glance in Téa's direction and grimaced. Ever since they'd left his grandparents' house she hadn't said more than a half dozen words, but had wrapped herself in silent gloom. Streetlights flickered over her, giving a harsh highlight to the tension scoring her face.

"Okay, what happened?" he demanded.

She was so lost in thought he couldn't be certain she'd heard him until her voice slipped out, soft as the night. "Nothing happened. It was a lovely evening." Then as an afterthought, she added politely, "Thank you for inviting me."

"You're welcome. Now what the *hell* is wrong? And don't tell me nothing. Something happened."

She swiveled slightly to face him. "Maybe I will tell you what happened. I realized where I've been going wrong all this time. I realized that my distraction is causing me endless problems and that it has to stop."

That was good, right? "That's good, right?" So why had his alarm bells kicked in?

"It's excellent." She managed a wobbly smile that didn't convince either of them. "In fact, it's so excellent I'm not going to need your services any longer."

His hands tightened on the steering wheel. "Good try, but... Not a chance in hell."

"Madam hired you because I was distracted," she reminded him. "I'm not distracted, anymore. I've never seen the situation so clearly."

He wished he could accuse her of having consumed too much of the wine that had flowed like water that evening. But he'd be surprised if she'd sampled more than the single glass she'd been handed when they first arrived. He didn't know who had said what this evening, but he wasn't about to let her off the hook just because a single night with his relatives had—hallelujah—given her 20/20 vision.

He used the only lever he possessed. "I'm your birthday present, remember?" Was it his fault if the words came out gravel-rough? "You can't unwrap or return me until you turn twenty-five."

She didn't so much as crack a smile. "You can insist on babysitting me for the next five weeks. It's not like I'm strong enough to turf you out, not with Madam and Nonna in your corner. But I don't need your assistance any longer. I'm more focused than I've ever been in my life."

He shot her a curious look before returning his

attention to the road. "Uh-huh. And what brought that on?"

"Tonight helped me figure out my priorities."

That was good, right? "That's good, right?" he repeated.

"That's excellent," she confirmed again. "From now on, I follow the Dantes' stellar example. I put family first. I have to if I'm going to protect them."

"Uh… Great?" Damn it.

"Yes, great." Her face settled into a grim, determined expression that set his alarm bells ringing to the max. "Because it means I put all my time and focus into taking over Billings."

That was *not* good. Not even a little. "*All* your time and attention?"

"Twenty-four/seven," she confirmed.

"That's what you learned from someone at Primo's tonight?"

"That's what I learned."

"Got it."

He didn't know which Dante was gonna die, but one of them was going down for whatever bug they'd stuck in Téa's ear. He'd been where she was, devoting his life to a cause. And it had just about killed him. Literally. It was bad enough when she was striving for some sort of balance between work and family and the teeny-tiny sliver of a piece he'd managed to coax out of her for play. Now it would only get worse. And someone would pay. Someone *always* paid the price for that sort of dedication.

He just didn't want it to be Téa.

First thing Monday, frustrated as a tiger with its tail in a knot, Luc watched Téa take the first step in her campaign. She marched into Conway Billings's office—a huge, palatial room with a prime view of the city—and slammed the door in Luc's face. The conversation between cousins went on at some length before she returned. She didn't even glance at him, though one look at her burning eyes and taut jaw warned that her conversation with "Cuz" didn't go well. She made a beeline for her own office and the spreadsheets she'd left there on Friday. She spent three straight hours poring over them, her expression more severe than he'd ever seen it.

At one point, she sent him from the room while she made a series of phone calls. Something was definitely up. He waited outside her office, glancing in the general direction of Conway's and flipped open his cell. He scrolled through the names until he hit on the one he wanted and placed the call.

"Juice? It's Luc. I need you to run a full background check on someone for me."

"What happened to hello?" his former associate complained in a rumbling bass voice. "You used to at least soften me up with a, 'how's it going?' before you started in. I feel so used when you insist we just get straight to it."

Luc felt his mouth relax into a grin. "Then you shouldn't let strangers pick you up in bars."

Juice sighed. "True enough. What can I get you?"

Luc gave him the details. "Rush it, will you?"

"That's not what they usually say."

"Yeah, but at least I'll still respect you in the morning. And I promise I'll call you soon. Honey."

Juice snorted. "Stuff it," he said before the line went dead.

Luc turned to find Téa standing there, arms folded across her chest, her vivid teal-blue eyes glaring through the sparkling lenses of her reading glasses. "If you're quite finished?"

"All done," he confirmed cheerfully.

"I'm going on a business trip which means you get the next couple of days off."

He waited a beat. "No, I believe it means I'm going on a business trip, too," he corrected.

She sliced a hand through the air. "Unnecessary and out of the question. It's a matter of confidentiality."

"I'm all about confidentiality."

"Not this time. I need to do this on my own. Connie insists and I'm forced to agree."

"Oh, well. If Connie insists…" He backed her into the office, slammed the door closed and shoved his nose against hers. Awareness shimmered through him, an awareness he did his level best to ignore. "Then I'm absolutely going."

Her eyes narrowed and he could practically see the gears spinning. Then she drew back and offered a wide, insincere smile. "Fine," she said with a careless shrug. "You can come, too."

He didn't need any alarm bells to know she'd given in way too easily. Plus, there was the small matter of her utter and total inability to lie. "When and where?"

"Wednesday morning, first thing."

"Got it." He lifted an eyebrow. "I'll pick you up at the usual time tomorrow?"

Her smile returned, sunny with insincerity. "Of course."

Of course.

Luc was right.

He'd suspected Téa planned to sneak out bright and early Tuesday morning and she didn't disappoint him.

He stood wrapped in early morning dew and shadows, and rested his hip against the brick wall that guarded the de Luca family row house. Somehow, the Italianate Victorian suited them, with its trademark gingerbread accents, top-heavy cornices and long, hooded windows. The garage door opened and Téa backed her car carefully out before the electronic mechanism engaged and slid the door closed again. He shifted until he stood directly in her path.

The instant she caught sight of him in her rearview mirror, her brakes squealed and the car bounced to a stop. After turning off the ignition, Téa erupted from the car. She made a beeline toward him, the decisive click of her heels bouncing off the concrete driveway. Somebody didn't look happy to see him. He was crushed.

"I. Should. Have. Known." She bit off each word as if they were chewed nails.

"Yeah, you should have." He held out his hand. "Keys."

"You're not coming."

He didn't bother arguing. He let his expression say it all.

She stewed for an entire sixty seconds before relenting. "If you must come, then I insist on driving."

He simply stood there, as immobile as a rock, hand outstretched.

"I'm sure there's a rule somewhere that says that bodyguards ride shotgun." When he still didn't budge, she slapped the keys in his hand. "Fine. I'll navigate."

"Excellent decision."

"It's not like I had a choice," she grumbled.

"Sure you did."

She lifted an eyebrow. "I could have canceled the trip?"

His mouth kicked up at the corners. "You got it."

He keyed the fob and popped the trunk. Picking up his duffel bag from where he'd stashed it on the sidewalk, he stowed it alongside Téa's case. By the time he finished Téa was already in the car, her nose buried in a map book.

Luc eased his tall frame behind the wheel and adjusted the seat to accommodate his long legs and cause his knee the least amount of strain. Twitched the mirrors. Did a quick check of the various controls. The engine turned over with a soft purr that spoke of a well-maintained vehicle. Knowing Téa he was willing to bet she rolled in for servicing at the exact same instant that the odometer rolled past each three thousand miles.

He didn't really need directions for getting out of the city, but if telling him where to go helped Téa come to terms with his crashing her business trip, he'd put up with it.

"How did you know?" she finally asked once they cleared the city.

"I know you." He shot her a speaking look. "Plus, you have to be the world's worst liar. Probably comes from lack of practice."

"You say that like it's a bad thing."

"It can be. I'm willing to bet every one of your sisters excels at the art."

She mulled that over before conceding the truth of it. "There are a lot of arts my sisters excel at that I don't."

No doubt it was part of the reason she'd never quite fit in. "Thank God for that." He gave her a moment to digest his comment, then asked, "Care to tell me where we're going and why?"

"Connie asked me to visit some of our smaller

accounts along the coast between San Francisco and L.A., so we can all get to know each other before I take over."

"Uh… I hate to tell you this, but Sacramento isn't between San Francisco and L.A. And that's the direction you have us headed."

"That's because I'm not going to visit those accounts."

"I'm shocked." And he was. "You're flouting Conway's authority?"

"Why, yes. I believe I am. I've always wanted to learn how to flout." Her chin took on a stubborn slant. "And today's the day."

He couldn't help himself. He chuckled. "Where are we going, instead?"

"To talk to the former manager of our manufacturing plant." She pulled out a piece of paper from her shoulder bag and checked the directions against the map book. "He retired to some small town called Polk about the time I started at Bling. It's located in the Sierra Nevada Mountains."

"Never heard of the place. Why do you want to talk to him?"

She hesitated for a telling moment. "To find out why he retired and what changes have been instituted since he left."

He considered how she'd obsessed over the accounting spreadsheets, obviously troubled by something she'd found there. It wasn't difficult to put two and two together and come up with Cousin Cunning. "I thought you trusted Connie implicitly."

Her expression threatened to rip out his heart. "So did I," she whispered.

"I'm sorry."

"Me, too."

Despite traffic, they made the drive to Sacramento in just under three hours. She spent most of the drive dividing her time between Madam's cell phone and her sisters' until he finally confiscated them. To his intense satisfaction, she turned them over without a single objection. It was a gorgeous late spring day, bright and sunny, the roads reasonably clear of traffic. Blue and violet lupine and camas lilies covered the foothills, interspersed with spindles of lemon aster. Their destination took them off the beaten path, on to twisty roads that clung to the sides of rock-strewn cliffs, but offering breathtaking vistas of the mountains.

Luc touched the brakes as he rounded one of the hairpin turns and frowned. "How much farther, Téa?" he asked.

The sharpness in his tone had her head coming around. "What's wrong?"

He gave it to her straight. "The brakes are soft. I'm not sure how much longer they're going to hold. Look for a safe place we can turn off."

"This isn't a good section of road to have the brakes go out." Other than a thread of anxiety that underscored the comment, she remained impressively calm.

"No, it isn't."

He touched the brakes again, alarmed by the way the pedal depressed straight to the floor. They needed a pull-off and fast. Unfortunately on Téa's side was sheer rock and on his side an endless drop off the mountain. The car swept around the next bend and the speedometer inched ever higher. He pumped the brakes, hoping to rebuild enough pressure to stop the car. It didn't help, but he kept trying. And hoping.

"Hold on," he warned. "I'm going to use the engine to slow us."

Punching in the clutch, he downshifted. The car bucked, shimmied. He wrestled with the wheel, fighting to keep the car on the road. The back tires slid sideways and the engine screamed in protest. Another sharp curve loomed ahead and he took it wide, dragging the car through the gravel along the shoulder, hoping the extra friction would slow the car.

"I'm going to downshift again."

"I'm okay. Do it."

Her soothing voice acted like a balm. It eased his concerns about her and allowed him to give his full focus to the task at hand. He downshifted once again, wincing at the sound of gears clashing and grinding. If he stripped them, they'd really be in trouble. The road flattened out briefly and he used the opportunity to play with the emergency brake on the console between the two front seats. He pushed in the button on the end of the stick and eased it backward. The car slowed but fishtailed so badly he was forced to let go of the lever in order to control the car.

"I need your help," he said.

"Tell me what to do."

He waited until he successfully steered them around the next bend. "I need you to push in the button on the emergency brake handle and pull it backward until you feel resistance. It'll engage the rear brakes. But if you yank too hard I'll lose control. So do it gently."

Early afternoon daylight flickered through the trees, dancing across the grim determination that lined her face. She reached for the brake handle, the slight tremor of her hand giving away her agitation. She played with the brake, first too gently, then too much pressure, before finding that sweet spot between the two. They rounded another curve, taking it far too fast.

The next instant he saw it. A straight stretch of road lined with heavy brush on Téa's side. There were trees, as well, but they were a solid twenty feet off the road. He wouldn't get a better opportunity than this.

"I'm going to crash the car into the brush. Cover your face."

She limited herself to a single word. "Damn."

Skidding onto the gravel-covered shoulder, he dragged the passenger side of the car against the thick brush. Téa instinctively flinched away. Branches slashed against the metal, tearing at it, clawing at the vehicle. The car slowed and he arced more fully into the bushes. The wheel jerked from his hand and the car spun in a sharp 180, flinging itself into the embrace of the roadside shrubs before careening into a ditch and plowing sideways against a towering fir.

The scream of metal was followed by simultaneous explosions. The first, the ringing impact of tree against car, followed instantaneously by the bang of the airbags inflating. Fine powder filled the air and he felt a sharp sting. The coating from the airbags, no doubt. Or maybe the sting came from the impact of the bags, themselves. It had happened too fast for him to be certain. He could recall the sensation from his last car wreck, though, and shied from the memory. The powder made him cough and irritated his eyes. Then silence descended, broken by the wheeze of the engine and the whirr of one of the tires that continued to spin.

"Téa?" Luc cut the engine. The car was tilted, driver side down and her weight sagged against him. "Are you hurt?"

To his relief she shifted. "I...I'm okay. I think. Dizzy."

"Did you hit your head?"

"I don't know." She felt for it. "Small bump on the side."

"The back windows blew out. Are you cut? Can you tell?"

Her sigh sounded amazingly normal. "To be honest, I can't see a damn thing. My eyes are watering from all this dust."

"Hang on." He shoved the deflated airbags out of the way until he uncovered Téa. "Hello, gorgeous."

She managed a smile. "That bad?"

"That good."

He eased a wealth of curls away from her face. He'd never seen a more beautiful sight. Unable to help himself, he leaned in and kissed her. Inhaled her. Allowed himself a full minute to lose himself in celebration that they'd survived such a close call. She wound her arms around his neck and kissed him back with gratifying enthusiasm. Finally he pulled away and cupped her face, his fingers skating gingerly over her face and into her hair. He found the bump she'd indicated, saw her wince and skimmed past it as he checked the rest of her.

"If we manage to get out of this with only a small bump and a batch of scrapes and bruises, we can consider it a miracle."

"No, the miracle is that you were behind that wheel instead of me," she replied. "If I'd been on my own—" She broke off with a shudder.

Luc's eyes narrowed and he filed the comment away for future consideration. "Any chance you can open your door? Mine's wrapped around the tree."

"I'll try." She squirmed around, wedging her shapely

backside against him while she fumbled with the door. "It's too heavy. I can't lift it."

"Okay. How about you dig out one of your cell phones so we can call for help?"

"I'm not sure where my purse ended up."

He shifted, fighting back a curse when his knee issued a sharp complaint. Great. Just what he needed. He poked around the floor of the car until he found her bag and passed it over.

"Everything's jumbled," she murmured. "Okay, here's one. Oh. It's our phone."

For some reason the comment gave him a warm, possessive feeling. "Perfect."

She placed the call and within twenty minutes the car swarmed with emergency personnel who extracted them in no time. While the EMTs examined Téa, Luc had a private conversation with one of the county deputies, whose nametag read Sandford. Together they walked the path the car had taken and the deputy shook his head in disbelief.

"That's one hell of a piece of driving. I think you picked the only stretch on this road where you could have gotten away with ditching the car the way you did." Sandford gestured farther down the road. "If you'd kept going you'd have ended up driving right off the mountainside. Sorry to say, I've seen the results of that once before. Just as soon never see it again."

"Not much choice but to ditch. The brakes went out on me."

"Bad place to have that happen."

It would have been just as bad if they'd taken the coast road Conway had requested, Luc realized. Long sections were a steep drop into the Pacific on one side and a wall of rock on the other. "I want the car checked from top to bottom." Luc spared a glance over his shoulder and grimaced. "At least, what's left of it."

Sandford's eyebrows shot upward. "You think someone messed with the brakes?"

"Let's just say I want to cover all the bases."

"I'll have it impounded, Mr. Dante."

"And the less said to Ms. de Luca, the better."

Sandford shrugged. "Nothing to tell her. Yet." He jerked his head in the direction of the ambulance. "I suggest you get that leg checked out. We're not big enough to warrant an actual hospital, but we have a decent medical center down the road a piece. They're going to want to transport you there to get checked out and I advise you to let them."

Luc didn't have the energy to argue, though the next few hours weren't the most pleasant he'd ever experienced. After a battery of tests, they were finally released. They discovered that Sandford had rescued their belongings from the mangled remains of the car and dropped them off at the medical center. Téa took the time to send text messages to her sisters letting them know she'd arrived safely—"safely" being a relative term. She was careful not to mention the accident. On their way out the door, one of the nurses recommended a nearby bed-and-breakfast over the local mom-and-pop motel where they could spend the night while they arranged for transportation home.

The proprietress welcomed them with open arms and tutted over their accident. Then she insisted on giving them her best accommodations, a honeymoon cabin tucked under a stand of pines and overlooking a small, private lake.

"Nothing better to ease your aches and pains than a view from the back deck. And if that's not enough, there's a hot tub out there that will do the trick. Just had it put in. You two will be the first to give it a whirl."

"Sounds like heaven," Téa admitted with a weary smile.

The two of them limped down the path toward the lake. Luc unlocked the door and shoved himself and their bags over the threshold. Téa made a beeline toward the bedroom, and of more interest, the king-size bed. Kicking off her shoes, she dropped face-first onto the mattress.

"Come on," she mumbled around the feather pillow. "There's enough room here for a small army."

He didn't need a second invitation. He invaded the bed, an army of one, scooped Téa into his arms and was asleep before she'd finished spooning that glorious backside up against his thighs.

Seven

Téa surfaced slowly, aware of a delicious warmth surrounding her and an intense feeling of peace and security, both of which made her reluctant to open her eyes in case it caused the sensation to vanish. She might have drifted back to sleep if Luc hadn't stirred.

"Damn knee," he muttered.

Instantly she sat up and twisted to face him. "What can I do?"

He massaged the joint. "Just need to take an anti-inflammatory."

"Would soaking in the hot tub help?"

Early evening sunshine slipped through the shaded window and highlighted the grin that creased his face. He regarded her speculatively, the color of his eyes a sleep-laden tawny gold, filled with the sort of hunger that caused her heart rate to kick up a tad.

"It would help, but only if you join me."

Her concern eased and an answering smile flirted with her mouth. "How would my being there help your knee?"

"It would take my mind off the pain," he offered hopefully.

"No doubt." She escaped the bed and winced. Bruises she hadn't even known she possessed made themselves known. "Maybe it'll take both of our minds off the pain."

His amusement vanished. "Where do you hurt? Do we need to go back to the medical center?"

"No, no," she reassured. "A few scrapes and bruises. They warned me that it would get worse before it got better. I think a soak in a hot tub is just what the doctor ordered."

"First food. We skipped lunch, if you recall."

"Sounds good. But no alcohol for twenty-four hours."

"Spoilsport." He yawned. "I wonder if there's anywhere around here that delivers."

"I'll call the front desk and ask."

There was a nearby pizza place and, after calling in an order, Téa closeted herself in the bathroom for a quick shower. She wasn't surprised when Luc joined her. He wrapped his arms around her and drew her against his chest. She tilted her head back and relaxed against him.

"You shouldn't be here."

Somehow he'd found the soap and he traced her curves with slick, sudsy hands. "Or doing this?"

She moaned. "Probably not. The pizza is due to arrive any minute."

He nuzzled the sensitive skin in the curve of her neck. "Do you want to eat it in the hot tub?"

She sank against him in clear surrender. "Probably be better than eating it in the shower."

They never made it to the hot tub. The minute Luc paid off the delivery boy, they carried the pizza to the bedroom. Téa climbed into his lap and fed him a slice while helping herself to one, as well. Somehow the box ended up on the floor, along with the terry cloth robes they'd found hanging on the back of the bathroom door.

She feathered a string of kisses from shoulder to mouth. "We weren't supposed to do this again, not while we were working together," she reminded him.

He settled her more firmly on his lap. "I won't tell, if you don't."

"Works for me."

He rolled her under him and gave her his close and undivided attention. She was soft and sweet from her shower, though the bruises she'd sustained from the car crash were already purpling her ivory skin. He kissed each and every one, wishing he could kiss away the hurt as easily. It horrified him, how close they'd come.

"If you hadn't been there…" Her words echoed his thoughts.

"But I was."

"Have I thanked you, yet, for saving my life?"

"That's not nec—"

He never finished his sentence. She inhaled the last word, drinking him in, and he sank into the mattress with her. Sank into her mouth, over her body, and into the warmth and passion she so openly offered. The Inferno hummed between them, a livewire that quietly pulsated no matter how far apart they were. But here, in her arms, in this bed together, it crackled with a deep and abiding need that drove him to possess the woman he considered his and his alone.

It was temporary, he reminded himself. He wasn't made for love or marriage or commitment. The accident five years ago had brought that fact home. But somehow, in this moment out of time, it seemed less imperative.

He sculpted her shape with his hands, lingering over the sleek, toned curves. "So perfect," he murmured.

"Funny. I was going to say the same about you."

She pushed at his shoulders and obliging, he rolled onto his back. She drifted over him, delicately. Tenderly. Massaged the tension from his arms and shoulders, then ran her fingertips across his chest. Just the lightest of touches. Sheer torture. He reached for her, but she pushed him away.

"No. Not yet. I'm not through," she protested.

"I am." Heaven help him. "Or I will be if you don't stop."

"And here I thought you were such a tough guy," she teased.

"Hell," he muttered. "So did I."

Her laugh whispered in the gathering dark. "Then, control yourself, tough guy."

She continued along her path of destruction, wreaking havoc with each new caress. He sucked in air, his hands fisting in the sheets so they wouldn't fist in her hair and yank her back into his arms. And still she continued, drifting ever lower until she found the rigid length of him.

There she paused. There she lingered. There she took him, as he'd once taken her. It was beyond intimate. Beyond glorious. Beyond thought and description. He'd never fully surrendered to a woman before, never lost control of what happened in bed. Never felt safe enough to let go of that final shred of containment. But something about Téa…

Something about this woman loosened all he'd kept wrapped up tight. Something about her slipped beneath his guard and allowed her to breach every last one of his defenses. He could feel her within him. He drew her in with every breath. Felt her sweep through his veins with every beat of his heart. Felt her feminine strength and power to the very marrow of his bones. Held her in a soul-deep grip that he'd never willingly let go.

He called to her, his voice hoarse and desperate. And she answered him, giving of herself in the most generous way possible. He didn't hold back. Couldn't. Afterward, they curled together, locked tight within each other's embrace.

He regained consciousness hours later while dark lay full around them. He eased into her, waking her in the sweetest way possible. She sighed in pleasure, wrapping him up as he gave all he had to her. Driving the storm that swirled within them before riding with her on the wild wind that swept them away.

Then once again they slept, two parts made whole.

"No!"

Téa jerked upright at the visceral shout, her heart pounding. "Luc?"

Beside her, he twisted in the bedcovers, clearly in the throes of a nightmare. "I won't do it!"

She caught her bottom lip between her teeth, not quite certain whether or not she should touch him, in case he hit out in panic. She'd read somewhere of that possibility. Instead she scooted to the far side of the bed and called to him. "Luc. Wake up. You're dreaming."

"Got to stop the bleeding."

She flinched. "Luc." This time she raised her voice, speaking firmly. "Wake up. Now."

To her relief, he came to. Unlike her, he didn't jump up, but froze, swiftly assessing the situation before his tension slackened. He scrubbed a hand across his face. "Aw, hell."

"Bad dream?" she asked in as neutral a voice as possible.

"Yeah." He levered up on one elbow, squinting at the bedside table. "Can you see what time is it?"

"A little before eight." She hesitated. "Do you want to talk about it?"

He spared her a brief glance. "Do you suppose that hot tub is still up and running?"

He hadn't answered her question. Then again, maybe he had. "Should be."

He caught her hand in his and tugged. "Can't hurt to find out."

They snatched up their bathrobes on the way to the back porch where the sun peeked over the mountaintops and skipped across the stillness of the lake. In the distance, a loon gave a startled cry, the eerie sound echoing over the water. Other than the birds and deer, the place was deserted, protected from curious eyes by a tall privacy fence. They removed the cover from the hot tub and draped their robes across a nearby bench. Shivering from the morning mountain chill, they climbed into the gently steaming water.

To Téa's amusement they both sighed in unison as they sank into the warmth. Luc pushed a button on the inset panel next to him and the water began to gently churn. Satisfied, he scooped her close, settling her in the vee of his legs. She relaxed against his chest. It was as though she'd been gifted with a taste of heaven and she savored the unexpected moment. They sat for a while in peaceful silence, simply enjoying the view and each other.

Then Téa gathered up her courage and said, "I have nightmares, too." She waited a second before continuing. "Not…not just bad dreams. But waking up screaming, in a total sweat type nightmares."

"Sounds familiar. Your parents?" It didn't surprise her that he was so quick to pinpoint the cause.

"Yes." The word was barely audible over the sound of the jets. "It was my fault, you know."

"What happened?" For some reason, the simple question sliced neatly through the scars, straight down to the source of the infection.

"I went to a party I'd been forbidden to attend. They found out and tracked me down. They were on the sidewalk outside, approaching the house when one of the girls started screaming that we were about to get busted. The boy I was with jumped in his car. He was drunk, of course." She shrugged. "It was over in an instant. He didn't see them, they couldn't get out of the way in time."

"I'm sorry."

"Aren't you going to tell me it wasn't my fault?"

"You already know that," he startled her by saying. "But I understand now why you've taken on the role of mother to your stepsisters. Why you feel obligated to put your family ahead of your own needs and wants. I can't see you doing anything else. Not until you're ready to forgive yourself."

Tears flooded her eyes and she blinked hard to hold them at bay. "What about you? What are you blaming yourself for?"

Luc sighed. "Takes one to know one?"

"Something like that." She made an educated guess. "I gather this is in some way related to your injured knee?"

"Yeah. Same incident."

She turned, curled into him, rested her cheek against his chest while the water frothed around them. It felt right to be with him, held like this. "Must have been bad if you still have nightmares about it."

He held on to her as though she anchored him against the pull and drag of a turbulent sea. "Five years bad."

She winced. "If you'd rather not—"

"You did. Seems only fair that I should, too." He took another minute to gather himself. "I owned my own security firm after I left the military. We specialized in personal protection."

"Dangerous."

"Boring," he corrected, "with the occasional splash of terrifying."

"Got it. This must have been one of the terrifying episodes."

"This was *the* terrifying episode."

"What went wrong?" Because, clearly, something had.

"There was a married couple. Sonya and Kurt Jorgen." She felt him swallow. "They had a young child, maybe five. Kurt asked me to help them disappear for a while. I knew something wasn't quite right. Hell, my internal alarm system went haywire even during that first meeting. I questioned him, but he kept insisting they wanted to reconsider the direction they were taking in life and just needed to get away from it all for a while."

She had to agree with Luc. Something didn't add up. "How did Kurt explain the need for a bodyguard?"

"He claimed to have a lot of money. That taking off would leave him vulnerable. He just wanted some protection until they settled in somewhere. Mainly, he wanted me to show him how to get lost for a couple months."

"But that wasn't the real problem." She didn't phrase it as a question.

"Hell, no. It turns out the husband witnessed an incident at work he shouldn't have, but neglected to mention that detail when he hired me. On the way to disappearing, goons of Kurt's employer caught up with us and ran us off the road. I failed to do then what I succeeded in doing yesterday."

"A controlled crash," she murmured numbly.

"A controlled crash. The husband was killed instantly." She felt the harsh swallow again. Heard the choke in the rumble of words. "The kid, too. Sonya was badly hurt. The goons managed to take themselves out at the same time they took us out. Since they weren't a problem, I worked on saving Sonya."

"She died, too?"

"No. I saved her." He waited a beat before dropping the other shoe. "Unfortunately she didn't want to be saved. She begged me to let her die so she could be with her husband and son."

Téa tightened her grip, wrapped him up in as much warmth as she could muster, hanging on tight. "Oh, Luc."

He relaxed into her embrace, though she could feel the emotional walls he erected pushing at her, trying to hold her at a distance. "When I visited the wife in the hospital she became so hysterical they had to sedate her. She just kept screaming at me that she hated me. That I should have let her die."

"I'm so sorry. She was out of her mind with grief." Téa tilted her head back to look up at him. "You must realize that?"

"Of course I realize it. Just as I realize it wasn't my fault when she attempted to take her own life three months later." His voice grew even more grim, if that were possible. "Didn't succeed."

"What ultimately happened to her?"

"I have no idea." He closed his eyes and shook his head. "I'm afraid to find out."

"You think she's gone, don't you?"

He shrugged. When he opened his eyes again they were the darkest she'd ever seen. Hard. Remote. Dispassionate. "If you're that determined to die, chances are excellent you'll eventually succeed."

"You did the right thing. You do understand that, don't you?" she asked urgently. "It wasn't your fault."

He didn't bother to point out the irony of her statement. "Trust me, I've looked at this from every possible direction. If the husband had warned me when he first hired me. If I'd hit the brakes sooner. Later. Turned left instead of right. The bottom line is…" He shrugged dismissively. "I took the job. People died. End of story. Afterward, I dissolved the business and went to work for Dantes Courier Service."

But it wasn't. She could see it wasn't. The incident had struck hard and deep, and left wounds that still hadn't healed, just as hers hadn't. "What aren't you telling me?"

He looked at her with tarnished eyes, the expression so distant. So emotionless. "I don't know what you're talking about."

She shivered despite the warmth of the water. "Yes, you do." She'd never been more certain of anything in her life. "Something else happened that day. What was it?"

He hesitated, then offered a cool smile. "Okay, fair enough. It wasn't part of the accident, merely a decision I made as a result of it. Just like you made the decision to fill in for your parents."

Every feminine instinct she possessed warned her to let it go. To change the direction of the conversation. To offer some lighthearted quip that would cut through the thickening tension. But she couldn't. Wouldn't. Not while that look of pain and grief darkened Luc's eyes. Not while the poison still swept through his veins, infecting every aspect of his life. Not while her palm itched and throbbed, warning that whatever existed between them would always be tainted by the hideous events of that day.

"Go on," she whispered. "Tell me what you decided."

"I decided that I'd never marry."

With that, he shifted her to one side and erupted from the hot tub. He padded across the deck like some great, sleek jungle cat to where they'd discarded their robes. He shrugged into his and held the other out to her.

"I gather we're done soaking?" she asked in a neutral voice.

"Since this is a bed-and-breakfast, I thought we'd go and find the breakfast portion of our stay. According to my stomach, that pizza is a fond but distant memory."

Téa didn't bother arguing. One look at Luc's face convinced her of that. She switched off the jets and hurried from the steaming warmth of the tub into the protective covering of her robe, doing her best to limit her exposure to the crisp mountain air. Luc opened the French doors that led into the living area of the cabin and picked up the phone. Téa waited while he spoke to the owner.

"It would seem that one of the benefits of the honeymoon cabin is private dining," he explained once he'd hung up. "They'll bring breakfast to us."

"I guess we should dress."

"Then I need to arrange for a rental car. We should also decide if we're staying another night or returning to the city."

He spoke calmly, as though his earlier announcement was of little concern. Maybe it wasn't to him. But she'd always been hampered by a logical nature and she didn't understand the connection between the two incidents. Deciding to bide her time, she returned to the bedroom to dress. Luc was on the phone arranging for a car to be brought in from Lake Tahoe when a staff member arrived with a loaded tray.

"There's a coffee machine in the kitchenette," he informed Téa. "I'll start a fresh pot for you. Or would you prefer tea?"

"Coffee is fine," Téa confirmed.

As soon as the coffee finished brewing, she and Luc took their breakfast onto the deck. The temperature had crept upward, warmed by the sunshine splashing down from a cloudless sky. They fell on their meal as though they hadn't eaten in a week, polishing off every bite before relaxing in their chairs to enjoy a steaming cup of coffee.

"Go on," Luc surprised her by saying. "Ask."

She didn't bother pretending. There wasn't any point. Plus, there was that small matter of being, quote, the world's worst liar, end quote. "Fine. I'll ask." She tried for an indifferent attitude, as though she couldn't care less. She suspected she failed miserably at the attempt.

"What has the accident got to do with your decision to never marry?"

He hesitated. "You have to understand my world. The Dante world," he offered on a roundabout way. "Primo and Nonna. My parents. My uncle and his disaster of a marriage."

Téa lifted a shoulder. "I'm sorry. I'm not following." Her brows drew together. "Wait. Is this about The Inferno?"

"Yes." He refilled his coffee cup and topped off hers. "All my life I've heard about The Inferno. Lived with The Inferno. Had it stuffed down my throat."

Téa attempted a light laugh. "Luc, it's just a story. A charming family legend."

He shook his head. "It's more than legend for the Dantes. You've seen my grandparents. They'll turn eighty soon and they still can't keep their hands off each other. My parents aren't any better. Nor are my cousins. And every last one of them claims it's because of this damn Inferno."

"What about your uncle?" Téa strove for normalcy. "You said his marriage was a disaster. Doesn't that prove The Inferno doesn't always work?"

He laughed without humor. "Uncle Dominic proves just the opposite. You see, he didn't marry for love, even though he was madly in love with one of his jewelry designers and had a torrid affair with her. Instead he married Aunt Laura for her money. Primo warned it would end in disaster. And it did. Uncle Dom and my aunt were killed years ago in a boating accident while in the throes of a divorce discussion. I gather he'd decided to marry this jewelry designer, after all. When my aunt and uncle died, my grandparents took in Sev and my cousins and raised them."

So much tragedy! "Oh, Luc. I'm so sorry."

"Of course, that only solidified the legend in everyone's eyes. Turned your charming fairy tale into truth."

"But it's not," she insisted.

He reached across the table and took her hand in his, intertwined their fingers so their palms met and mated. "Isn't it?"

She shuddered. "I—" She snatched an uneven breath. "What we're experiencing is just a bad case of physical attraction. Anything else would be illogical."

"I'm glad to hear you say that. Because that's what it's going to stay," he warned, even as a spark of desire caught hold and roared to life. "I won't be forced into a marriage I don't want because of a make-believe fairy tale."

"No one is forcing you to do anything," she protested.

"Aren't they?" He released her and sat back. A hint of cynicism played about his mouth and burnished his eyes. "Maybe it would have occurred to me sooner if *I* hadn't been so distracted. But there's a lot that doesn't add up. For instance, why have I been hired as your bodyguard?"

She offered a self-deprecating smile. "Apparently because I can't put one foot in front of the other without tripping over it."

"Funny." He cocked his head to one side. "In the couple of weeks we've spent together I haven't noticed that about you."

"The first time we met—" she began.

"Had me worried," he agreed with a nod. "But how many incidents have there been since?"

"Well, none," she admitted. "But I assumed that was

because you were there." She broke off with a frown. "Now that I say that out loud it doesn't make the least bit of sense, does it?"

"No, it doesn't. I've just recently concluded there's only one reason we were brought together."

She gave a disbelieving laugh. "You can't think it's because of The Inferno. How could anyone possibly know that we'd be a match?"

Luc lifted his cup and stared at her over the rim, his gaze enigmatic through the steam. "That stopped me, too, until it occurred to me that we met once before, remember?"

"That was ages ago," she said with a dismissive shrug. "We were children."

"Really? Lazz and Ariana first met as children. Primo claims that Uncle Dominic saw early signs of The Inferno even then. As a result, he and Ariana's father contracted a marriage between them right then and there."

Téa's mouth opened, then shut again, before she managed to say, "You must be joking."

"Not even a little."

"And you suspect your parents or grandparents caught something similar between us? How is that possible?" she scoffed. "We hardly said two words to each other. We despised each other at first sight."

"Don't you remember why?"

"I…" She thought back, struggled to recall that miserable, uncomfortable summer. "You kept pestering me. Teasing me."

"Zapping you," he said softly.

"That's right. I remember now. It was like you were filled with static electricity. And you loved jumping out at me when I least expected it to give me a shock." Her eyes narrowed. "Brat."

"Think about it," he urged. "Wouldn't that be a gentler, more childish version of what we experienced when we first touched as adults?"

She drew back in her chair, closing in on herself. "I thought you didn't believe in The Inferno," she accused.

"I don't."

"Then—"

"But my parents and grandparents believe implicitly."

Her eyes widened in outrage. "And because of that zapping…"

He nodded. "I'm now guessing they decided we were experiencing The Inferno. Primo made me stop and told me not to go near you for the rest of your visit. And when Primo lays down the law…" Luc lifted a shoulder. "So, the years passed. I'm willing to bet Nonna and Madam decided it was time to put us together again and see if anything happened between us. I'm also guessing they drummed up your distraction as the perfect excuse."

Téa returned her cup to the saucer with a sharp click. "Fine. Let's say for the sake of argument that the reason we're in our current predicament is because of what happened at the lake all those years ago. That certainly doesn't mean we have to act on it. And I still don't understand what The Inferno has to do with the car crash and your decision not to marry."

Darkness settled over him and she could tell he wasn't seeing her. That she'd lost him to those long-ago events. "The Dantes believe that once mated through

The Inferno, it's a lifetime love affair. One man. One woman. One love."

"Isn't that the idea with all marriages, at least going in?" she asked gently.

He nodded. "That's how it was between the Jorgens. Even I could see that much, despite the limited amount of time we spent together. One second they were a loving family. The next she was alone. Her life ended when theirs did, but she was still alive. Empty. Broken. And forced to live that way for the rest of her life—a life she appeared determined to end."

Téa struggled to put the pieces he was showing her into a logical whole. "And you're afraid that will happen to you?"

Luc focused on her. "Sonya gave every part of herself to Kurt and their son. When they were gone there was nothing left. As far as she was concerned, without them her life had ended. Someone had just forgotten to turn out the lights for her."

"Sonya isn't you," Téa argued.

"No, she isn't. Because I won't surrender that much of myself to another person. I watched Rafe do it with his wife, Leigh, and watched her gut him on her way out the door. I won't be another Sonya. I won't be Rafe after the death of his marriage." He turned his haunted gaze on her. "So, I won't marry."

Téa shook her head. "You're wrong, Luc. It's not that you won't marry. What you've decided is that you won't love. Funny thing about love." She shoved her empty coffee cup aside. "You're assuming you have some control over it."

"I do."

"That's where you're wrong." She pushed back her

chair and stood. "Unfortunately for you, love chooses. And it chooses whether you're willing or not."

With that Téa turned and forced herself to walk away from what she'd just discovered she wanted most in the world.

Eight

A couple hours later, the rental car was delivered and Luc signed the necessary papers to take possession. The owner of the bed-and-breakfast asked if they wanted the cabin for a second night and Luc glanced at Téa.

"It's your call," he said without expression.

Téa hesitated. "I don't know how long it'll take to locate the former manager of our plant and convince him to talk. Plus, Connie expects me to be gone at least two days, if not three. I'd rather he not find out I didn't go where he requested."

"There's weather moving in late this afternoon," the owner offered tentatively. "Don't want to be on these mountain roads when it hits. Should be clear again by tomorrow morning."

Téa gave a decisive nod. "We'll stay another night, if that's all right."

The owner beamed. "Our next reservation doesn't

arrive until Friday. We'd be happy to have you until then."

Téa shook her head apologetically. "One more night should do it." She spared Luc a wistful glance, one that clearly told of her preference to remain for the entire week. That look—one that said that a single word from him would be enough to have her prolong their stay— would have slayed a weaker man. He forced himself to remain impassive beneath it. She sighed. "There's a lot of work sitting on my desk. Plus I have to replace my car."

No doubt an added expense and distraction she didn't need right now. "I'll help with that."

"That's not necessary," she replied with cool politeness.

"It's the least I can do considering I'm the one who crashed it," he replied just as politely.

She let it go and turned to address the owner who'd been watching their byplay with an indulgent expression. "Could you give me directions to the town of Polk?"

Luc waited patiently while the two women inched their way over Téa's map book. A short time later they were on the road again. He shot her a fleeting glance. She appeared a shade paler than usual, her slight dusting of freckles standing out more sharply than usual, and she had a grim set to her mouth. More telling, her hands were laced together in a death grip, her knuckles bleached white.

"You okay?" he asked after the first series of hairpin turns. He'd deliberately kept their speed a full five miles beneath the posted limit.

"I'll survive."

They arrived in Polk shortly before noon and Luc suggested they have lunch before tackling the manager.

Téa settled on a local café with boxes of colorful flowers outside and a homey setup inside. The menu was varied and their lunch choices were attractively plated when they arrived.

"What's this guy's name you plan to visit?" Luc asked while they ate.

"Krendal. Douglas Krendal."

"Does he know you're coming?"

She hesitated. "I thought I'd surprise him. I called to make certain he was in. Pretended I was a telemarketer." She winced and rubbed her ear. "Mr. Krendal doesn't mince words."

"You may find that helpful when you talk to him."

"That's what I'm hoping." She hesitated, playing with her fork and pushing her lunch around her plate. "Listen, I want to speak privately with him. I suspect he'll be more open if it's just the two of us."

Luc cocked an eyebrow. "In other words, the conversation is none of my business?"

"Okay, yes."

"No problem."

"Really?" she asked skeptically. "You're not going to argue the way you have about Connie?"

He shrugged. "The situation with your cousin is different. I don't trust the guy. So, I've made a point of sticking close whenever he starts yanking on the puppet strings."

She stiffened. "I gather I'm the puppet?"

"Time will tell." He gestured toward her plate. "You done?"

"Yes." She shoved her half-eaten lunch to one side. "Let's get this over with."

They found the Krendal place without too much trouble, the cottage perched on top of one of the endless hillsides that surrounded the town of Polk. It was a small rambler on a large piece of property, tucked beneath a towering stand of pine trees. Luc pulled into the driveway and parked along one edge of the small circle of gravel on the side of the house. Téa exited the car and followed the cement walkway to the front door. He watched while she knocked and the door opened. Saw her introduce herself and Krendal's grim resistance. Caught the instant it began to fade beneath Téa's warmth. At long last, the door swung wide and she disappeared inside.

His cell phone vibrated about five minutes into the wait and he checked the caller ID. "Yeah, Juice," he said by way of greeting. "What did you find out about Billings?"

"The man or the business?"

"Okay, now you've got my attention." Luc frowned as he listened, his frown deepening with each new revelation. "Well, hell," he said when Juice completed his report.

"That was my reaction. What are you going to tell the de Luca woman?"

"Everything."

"She's not going to be happy."

"Furious would be my guess."

"Glad you're the one handing her the news and not me."

"Chicken."

"Cluck-cluck." And with that, the line went dead.

Twenty minutes later Téa emerged from the house. She shook hands with Krendal and then returned to the car, her heels rapping out a hard, staccato beat on the walkway leading to the gravel driveway. She climbed into the car and slammed the door closed.

"That bastard!"

Luc folded his arms along the top of the steering wheel and assessed the level of her anger. If he were to guess, he'd say steaming, bordering on, "thar she blows." "I hope that comment's aimed at Cousin Connie and not Mr. Krendal," he said.

"Oh, it's definitely aimed at Cousin Connie…or maybe I should say Cousin Con Artist." She gave an imperious wave of her hand. "Let's go. I need to drive off some of this mad."

Little did she know. "Okay."

He headed back toward their rental cabin in silence, giving her the opportunity to stew. Maybe once she'd come to terms with the information Krendal had dumped on her, she'd be in a better position to deal with his news. In the distance, the first evidence of the storm they'd been warned about boiled up over the tops of the nearby mountains, the clouds filled with threat and turmoil. They were a perfect punctuation mark to Téa's mood. He checked his watch, judged the distance and decided they'd get to the cabin with time to spare.

By the time they parked in front of the cabin, the sky had turned nighttime dark. Luc hustled Téa inside and flicked on lights to dispel the gathering gloom. While he went in search of a flashlight or candles in case the storm knocked out the power, Téa checked her various cell phones and frowned.

"What's wrong?"

"No signal. I hope Madam and the girls aren't worried." She brightened. "Maybe they haven't tried to call."

He set out a sleeve of candles he found in one of the drawers in the kitchenette, along with a box of matches. "What do you suppose the odds are of that happening?"

Her hopeful mood vanished. "Zero to less than zero." She released a sigh. "I need a drink."

He opened the door to the small refrigerator. "You're in luck. It would seem the honeymoon cabin also comes with a complimentary bottle of champagne. Are we cleared to drink, do you suppose?"

Téa checked her watch and nodded. "We're just past the twenty-four-hour time frame we were given by the doctor."

"Good enough."

Luc pulled out the bottle and removed the foil and wire, before cautiously uncorking it. Digging through the cupboards, he unearthed a pair of Lucite flutes and poured them each a glass. Téa took a tentative swallow and wrinkled her nose at the explosion of bubbles.

"Surprisingly good," she said with a hint of surprise. "Is it a California wine?"

"Yes. Carneros region."

"That explains it." She drank another couple sips, stalling. Then finally, said, "There's something I need to tell you."

"About Krendal?"

She waved that aside. "No. It's about the night we were at Primo's for Rafe's birthday party."

He wondered when they'd get back to that. "I gather you're about to tell me the real reason you were so upset when we left. Why you suddenly decided to put all your focus on work and protecting your family."

"Yes." She spared him a speculative glance. "Sev never said anything to you?"

"No." And Sev would pay for that small oversight. "What happened?"

"Your cousin warned me that there was a quality issue with our product."

He took a moment to absorb that, to put it together with the information Juice had provided. "I gather that explains your confrontation on Monday with Conway." Luc sampled the champagne, also approved it and topped off their glasses. "I can't wait to hear his explanation."

"He claimed it was all a huge error and he'd look into it."

"And you bought that?"

She waved her glass at him. "Don't be ridiculous. Of course I didn't buy it. The man is as bad a liar as I am."

Luc choked on a laugh. "Must run in the genes."

"No doubt. Anyway, he insisted I stay out of it and even when I pointed out that I'd be right in the middle of the fiasco in five short weeks—about a month now—he told me that was fine. In five short weeks I could handle it. In the meantime, he was in charge and he'd get in touch with Sev. That I wasn't to contact your cousin under any circumstances."

"That's when you came storming out and buried your nose in the spreadsheets."

"There was something about them…" Her eyes glittered darkly in the deepening gloom. "Once I understood the underlying problem, I knew what to look for."

"Your cousin has been cutting corners."

She nodded. "And charging more for an inferior product. That's what I didn't catch in the accounting records. You see, the price we charge our customers has gone up, but when I looked more carefully, our manufacturing costs have actually dropped, despite the fact that our overall profit remains the same."

Even without an accounting background, Luc could add that together to equal something was definitely fishy.

"If your manufacturing costs have gone down, your cost to customers increased, the profit margin should have skyrocketed."

"You would think," she agreed. "And the bottom line would have skyrocketed if that profit hadn't vanished into the cost of purchasing new equipment. On paper it appears legit."

"Huh."

She tilted her head to one side. "You look like a puzzle piece just fell into place."

"It did. First tell me what Krendal said, and then I'll explain."

"Okay." She helped herself to more champagne. "Douglas Krendal was the production manager of our manufacturing plant. He claims that Connie forced him out."

"Because Krendal caught on to what Billings was doing," Luc guessed.

"Yes. And he was rather vocal in his disapproval. He'd worked for my grandfather for years and was outraged that Connie wanted to cut corners by producing an inferior product."

"So, Conway fired him."

"Retired him," she corrected with a shrug. "But, essentially, you're right. He got rid of Douglas at the earliest opportunity."

Luc hesitated, knowing the time had come to give her the rest of the bad news. He blew out a breath. "You're not going to like this next part."

She stilled, a look of intense vulnerability sweeping across her face. "Please tell me you're not a secret operative for my cousin."

The sheer unexpectedness of her comment provoked a laugh. "No, I'm not a spy," he said tenderly. To his relief, his reassurance restored her confidence. "But I did ask a former associate to dig into your cousin's background." He grimaced. "It's not good, Téa."

She sank into a nearby chair. "Let me have it."

"Essentially, he's broke."

Her mouth dropped open. "How is that possible? I happen to know what he makes running Bling and it's a pretty penny."

"Right, except he doesn't receive a percentage of the profits from the company the way he would if he were the owner. He's on salary with modest bonuses approved by the board. And he's been funneling all available funds into this new start-up business he's about to launch." He allowed that to sink in before adding, "There's more."

"Of course there is," she murmured.

"I think I know what he's up to."

"Is he embezzling?"

"Not funds." He waited a beat. "Equipment."

"The purchases he made with the profits." She frowned. "I don't understand. What does he want with the equipment?"

"This is sheer conjecture, but I'm pretty sure I'm right. I think he's going to start up a competing business."

Téa inhaled sharply. "The poor quality merchandise—"

"—gets your customers angry. Makes them easier to steal away from Bling." Luc downed the last of his champagne and set the glass aside. "Oh, he's going to turn the family business over to you. He's just going to make sure it's nothing more than a shell when he does it. Then, when you're on the verge of bankruptcy because you've lost all your customers to him—"

"—he comes sweeping in and offers to buy me out for pennies on the dollar," she finished his sentence for him. "Connie's new start-up company then takes over the Billings name and he has everything my grandfather didn't leave him. The business, the name and all the money."

"That's what I suspect."

"And I suspect you're right." She closed her eyes and thought about it. "The question is, what can I do to stop him? He's had ages to set all this up. I still don't take over for another four and a half weeks. He must know I'm close to figuring it out. Which means he has a full month to bring his plans to fruition while I watch helpless from the sidelines."

"He doesn't know you're on to him, yet," Luc attempted to reassure. "There's still time to do something."

Téa shook her head. "Not while he controls Bling. If I could just take over now…" She froze. Slowly her gaze shifted to fix on Luc. He didn't care for the speculative gleam in her eyes. "There *is* a way I can do that."

"Well, okay." He snatched up his glass, annoyed to find it empty. "Then do it."

"I need your help to put my plan into action."

A plan. Action. He was all over that. "You know I'm willing to do whatever I can."

She smiled. "I was hoping you'd say that."

For some reason, her expression worried him. It had turned calculating, filled with the same drive and determination he'd noticed the night of Rafe's birthday party.

"I'm almost afraid to ask, but… What do you want me to do?"

"It's quite simple, really. I want you to marry me."

Luc stared at Téa in disbelief. "Excuse me?"

To her credit, she was smart enough to show a trace of

nervousness. "You heard me." She gulped champagne. "I want you to marry me. Temporarily, of course."

"Oh, of course."

She flinched at his sarcasm. "Luc—"

He cut her off without hesitation. "I believe we had this discussion already." Anger ripped through him, accompanied by the first rumbling of the storm. "What part of 'I'm never going to get married' didn't you understand? The 'never' part or the 'married'?"

"Let me explain." She approached, showing either an impressive amount of bravery or proving just how badly she'd misjudged his current mood. "There's a clause in the will that says that if I marry I inherit Billings outright, so long as I'm over the age of twenty-one."

"Outstanding. I wish you every success in finding someone to marry you."

"I don't think you understand."

"I understand perfectly," he snapped. "You're the one who doesn't understand. The answer, Ms. de Luca, is not just no, but *hell* no."

"I'll try not to be offended by that." A matching anger flared to life in her eyes, while outside lightning flashed, causing the electricity to sputter. "Don't you see that it's the perfect solution? For both of us, Luc."

He folded his arms across his chest. "Okay, this I have to hear. How is marrying you the perfect solution for me?"

"Your entire family believes we've been struck by The Inferno, right?"

"Unfortunately."

"So, we give them what they want." Thunder crashed overhead and she had to wait for it to die down before continuing. "We give them a wedding between Inferno soul mates. A couple months down the road…say six or seven…we inform everyone that it didn't work out. We divorce."

"Dantes don't divorce."

"Rafe did," she retorted, stung.

"Technically he's a widower."

That stopped her. "Oh. I didn't realize. I'm sorry."

"You don't need to apologize to me."

She waved that aside. "We're getting off track here."

"I understand where you're going with this, Téa. I recommend you let it go."

Luc turned his back on her and crossed to stare out into the stormy darkness. A bolt of lightning streaked overhead, the reflection forking across the surface of the lake, while thunder boomed, the echo from it bouncing off the surrounding mountains. He could see the logic of her suggestion, just as he could see all the dangerous pitfalls along the way.

Pitfalls like the itch of The Inferno that would only grow stronger and burrow deeper with each additional day in her company. Pitfalls like having her in his bed and discovering he couldn't bring himself to let her go. Pitfalls like pregnancy.

Or love.

He could see her reflection mirrored in the glass of the French door, picked up on her tension from the set of her shoulders and the way she fiddled with her empty flute. Despite his anger, he still wanted her, could feel the unwelcome connection pulsating between them.

With a sigh, he turned to face her. "You think that if we marry, wait a reasonable amount of time and then claim it didn't work out, my family will leave me alone. Stop forcing this nonsense about The Inferno down my throat. Is that your plan?"

She nodded eagerly. "Exactly. Since they believe I'm your Inferno bride, they won't keep nagging you about marrying again."

"No." He folded his arms across his chest. "They'll just keep nagging me about getting back together with you."

"Oh." She sighed. "I hadn't thought of that."

He smiled dryly at the bitter disappointment in her voice. "That's because you don't know my family."

She was quick to regroup. "Well, when I marry for real that will put an end to it, won't it? They'll leave both of us alone."

He stilled. "Marry for real?"

"It's possible." She lifted her chin. "More than possible. Because unlike you I'm not afraid of love. Seeing your family, seeing how happy the various couples are, it's made me think. Maybe once my family is safe and financially secure I can fall in love and get married, too. Start a family like Kiley and Francesca."

For an endless moment he couldn't think straight. Couldn't breathe. Images filled his head of Téa, heavy with a baby. *His* baby. And then the image shifted. Twisted. And suddenly it wasn't his baby any longer, but another man's. Her husband's. A man who had the right to put his hands on her. To take her to his bed. To share every intimacy with her.

To give her a baby.

He heard a low snarl fill the room, barely aware it had been ripped from his throat. One minute he stood silhouetted by the pounding storm and the next he was across the room. He reached for her, swept her into his arms.

"Luc," she gasped. "What are you doing."

"You're the one with all the answers. You figure it out."

Luc reached the bed in fewer than a dozen limping steps and dropped Téa to the mattress. He followed her down, his mouth closing over the questions trembling on her lips. He had no memory of stripping off her clothes, of stripping away his own. Thunder crashed around them while lightning bleached the ebony from the night. He had a quick flash of Téa, a stunning palate of ivory splayed across a canvas of black. Only her hair and eyes offered any color, a spill of vibrant, fiery red, and a blue-green as deep and mysterious as the ocean.

The elements tore across the night, setting flame to the explosive passions trapped within the room. They came together, a clash of masculine and feminine that somehow found a melding point, a place where they joined with undeniable perfection and became one. Their bodies mated, moving to the rhythm of the storm, echoing its power and ferocity, giving no quarter and expecting none. They followed each other into the very heart of the tempest, riding it, driven by it to an exquisite climax.

Luc felt Téa peak, heard her cry of pleasure. That was all it took. He followed her up and over. He heard his name on her lips. Answered the cry with one of his own, with her name, the sound of it a stamp of possession. It grounded him as nothing else could have. Slowly the tumult calmed. And when it was finished, he gathered her close. Gently. Tenderly. Safe within the harbor of his arms.

She pressed close, twining herself around him until

he couldn't tell where she began and he ended. He simply held her, felt the steady beat of her heart filling his palm.

And he slept.

Téa woke the next morning feeling better than she had in her entire life. She had no idea what had gotten into Luc. He hadn't given her much opportunity to ask. But she could only hope it happened again. And soon. She stretched, feeling the pull of well-worked muscles, along with the twinge of lingering bruises.

Luc stirred and groaned. "Is the hot tub still out there?"

She snuggled, finding his warmth, pleased when he dropped a powerful arm over her and tucked her in close. "It's there unless it washed away in the storm."

"Is it still raining?"

"I don't hear anything. And I think that yellow stuff coming in through the drapes is sunshine."

"Okay. Just this once I'll let you carry me out to the hot tub. But only this once."

"I'll get right on that." She paused. "Are we there, yet?"

He pulled back slightly and frowned down at her. "You're not very good at this. Considering the number of times I've hauled you around, the least you could do is return the favor."

"Very inconsiderate of me," she said apologetically.

"I'll say." He escaped the bed and dragged her out, protesting all the way. "Come on. Let's go soak before we pack up."

"What about our robes?"

"Let them find their own hot tub."

Moving quickly, they stripped off the cover and climbed into the tub, allowing the heat and swirling jets of water to ease sore muscles. Téa stirred, picking up on an odd noise coming from the interior of the cabin. "I think I hear something." She sat up and craned her neck, thought better of it and ducked lower in the water. "What if it's one of the staff members with our breakfast?" she whispered frantically.

Luc grinned. "Then someone's going to be really embarrassed. And I'm willing to bet it won't be me."

She heard it then. Heard the voices coming closer. Voices that shouldn't be here. She had a whole two seconds to stare wild-eyed at Luc before Madam stepped onto the deck, followed closely by Téa's three stepsisters. Her grandmother's distinctive voice cut across the peaceful serenity of the morning.

"*Madre del Dio!* Girls, don't look!"

But of course, they did.

Nine

Luc opened the door of the rental car and waited until Téa slid in before closing it. Then he limped around to the driver's side and climbed behind the wheel. He didn't start the engine.

"How did Madam find us?" he asked abruptly.

Téa answered readily enough. "Apparently the claims adjuster at my insurance agency called the house with a few more questions about the wrecked car. Madam took the call and then tried to get hold of me. When she couldn't—remember the service went out?—she assumed the worst. That we'd been injured in the accident." She rolled her eyes. "Though how I was well enough to call the insurance company but too badly injured to speak to her, I have no idea. Madam's not always the most logical person in the world." She paused. Flinched. "Oh, dear. I'll bet she was remembering the night my parents died."

"That still doesn't explain how she found us."

Téa shrugged, preoccupied with settling her shoulder bag and fastening her seatbelt. "I guess from the insurance company. If you recall I had to provide the claims adjuster with the location of the car. He must have passed that information on to Madam. She probably called the nearest medical facility. I know I would have. From there it would be a short hop to this place." She paused, studying him with a growing frown. "What's with the third degree?"

"Let's just say that her showing up and catching us naked in a hot tub is a bit too convenient for my taste," he said in a detached voice.

"Convenient? Convenient!" Téa leaned in, enunciating carefully. "For your information, Luciano Dante, there was absolutely *nothing* convenient about what just went down in that cabin this morning."

Time would tell. "How bad was it?" he asked.

She sat back, but he could see she was still simmering. "I'm guessing about as bad as your conversation with Primo."

"Damn."

"Oh, yeah." She released a long sigh. "What did your grandfather have to say?"

He watched her closely, interested in her reaction. "He said we're now officially engaged."

Téa's eyes widened in shock. "Tell me you're joking."

"I'd love to. Unfortunately I'm not. I'm open to any suggestions you might have for getting us out of this mess."

"Okay, here's one. Tell your grandfather no."

"That'll work." He turned the key in the ignition and

the engine started with an extra roar, echoing his own irritation. "Not."

"So, that's it?" she asked. "Now we just get married?"

"Isn't that what you wanted?"

"Well, yes, but not like this." She folded her arms across her chest. "Be reasonable, Luc. It's not like anyone can force you to marry me."

"Oh, really? And what did Madam have to say after catching us naked in a hot tub after a night of raw passion?" He cupped a hand to his ear. "What's that? I can't hear you."

Téa cleared her throat. "I said… She's disappointed."

"Me, too. I had plans for that hot tub."

"She also said it was so unlike me. Selfish. Impulsive. And worst of all, I was setting a bad example for the girls."

"I'd have said it was exactly like you. Generous. Inventive. And those three witches you call sisters don't need any help riding their broomsticks to Badville. I'd say they invented the place. Especially Goth Girl."

"That's Katrina. It's just a phase."

"Scary."

"She's not scary. She's wonderful. All my sisters are wonderful."

"Particularly the one who would have stuck her tongue down my throat if you'd left us alone for a minute longer than you did." He shot Téa a quelling look when she opened her mouth to argue. "Don't tell me. I shouldn't take it personally. She's like that with all the men."

"Davida's naturally exuberant," she retorted, stung.

"Exuberant. That's a catchy name for it. Well, Vida's *exuberance* came across loud and clear."

Téa closed her mouth again and released a long, tired sigh. Luc winced. He felt like the worst kind of bully. It wasn't her fault that her stepsisters were hellions. Or that they hadn't received the right sort of discipline, though Téa had chosen to shoulder the blame for that, as well as the death of her parents.

"You know… There's an easy way out of this mess," he suggested.

"Which is?"

"We drop your sisters off at Primo and Nonna's. My grandparents will have them straightened out within a week. Then we gag and tie Cousin Connie and hide him in a dusty closet somewhere so you can start running Bling the minute we return."

She offered a reluctant smile. "And what about our impending nuptials? How do you propose we handle that small detail?"

"Huh." He frowned. "Okay, you got me there. I don't have a clue how to handle it."

"I do."

"Great. Why didn't you say so."

"I'll speak to Primo when we get back to San Francisco. Explain how everyone leaped to the wrong conclusions."

"Wrong conclusion," he repeated. "Naked plus hot tub equals not much of a leap."

Téa grimaced. "It also didn't help that the owner told Madam we were in the honeymoon cottage. At first, she assumed we'd eloped. When she found out we hadn't…"

"I gather the conversation went downhill from there."

"Oh, yeah."

Luc's cell phone rang and he dug it out of his pocket and tossed it to Téa. "See who that is, will you?"

She flipped open the phone and checked the caller ID. "It's Primo."

"Perfect. Go ahead and answer it. You can explain to him why we're not getting married."

"Okay," she agreed, though she didn't sound quite as sure of herself as she had earlier. "Hi, Primo, it's Téa. Yes, Luc is still with me. But he's driving, so—" She listened at length, tossing in several, uh-huhs and oh, dears.

"Tell him!" Luc encouraged.

She waved him silent. "Uh-huh. Oh, dear." She cleared her throat. "The thing is, Primo, Luc and I... Well, we don't want to get married. Right. I understand. Okay. No, you're right. Lake Tahoe isn't all that far."

"What the hell are you saying?" Luc bit out. "Just tell him no and hang up!"

"Excuse me a moment, Primo." She covered up the phone. "Would you please try not to wreck another car? If you can't drive straight, pull over. You're making me very nervous."

"*I'm* making *you* nervous? Give me that phone!"

"He doesn't want to talk to you. He wants to talk to me. Yes, Primo, I'm still here." Her eyes widened and she inhaled sharply. "Um. You're sure they're planning to print that? You do understand we don't want to get married, right? I made that clear? No, no. That's fine. I guess we'll see you tomorrow. Yes, I'll be sure to tell Luc. Bye."

Jamming on the brakes, Luc swung onto a pull-off on the side of the road and cut the engine. "So?" he demanded. "Did you tell him?"

Téa's head bobbed up and down. "Oh, I told him.

Didn't you hear me tell him? I told him flat-out that we didn't want to get married."

"And he accepted that?"

She squirmed. "Sort of."

"Are we still engaged?"

"Not for long."

"Well, okay, then." He started the engine again and continued down the road. It took two miles for him to fully process her words. "Just out of curiosity, what do you mean by 'sort of' and 'not for long'?"

"It means we have to take a short detour on the way home."

"Where?"

She swallowed. "Reno, Vegas or Lake Tahoe. Our choice."

Swearing more virulently, Luc swerved into a dirt lane and killed the engine. "What. Did. You. Do?"

"You don't understand." The words escaped in a rush.

"Explain it to me so I will."

"You remember that gossip magazine that caused so much trouble for your cousins? *The Snitch*?"

"Unfortunately. What's that got to do with us?"

"Well, they somehow got hold of the story that we eloped. I have no idea how it happened," she hastened to add.

"Let me take a wild guess here. Which of your sisters is the most broke?"

"Vida, but—"

"Then that's my guess."

"My sister wouldn't…" She hesitated, her brows pulled together and she altered course. "That's not really the point. *The Snitch* is going to print the story in the morning. Primo said that if we don't marry immediately, it will have a serious effect on my future at Bling. That I'll lose the respect of both employees and customers."

Luc grimaced. He wished he could refute his grandfather's claim, but he couldn't. He had a feeling his grandfather had it exactly right, and if their suspicions about Conway Billings were correct, Cousin Connie would be all over this news and use it to Téa's disadvantage. With each new revelation, Luc could feel the trap tightening around him, edging him deeper and deeper into an inescapable corner.

"Plus," she added in a rush. "There's one other small problem."

"What's the other small problem? I think I can take it. Maybe."

"Primo said that if you wish to remain a Dante, you'll marry me. But I don't think he was serious." She turned to him. "Do you?"

"You did meet my grandfather, didn't you?"

"You know I did."

"I think that answers your question." He started the car again and pulled onto the road.

"So what now?" Tea asked tentatively.

"Now, we drive to Lake Tahoe and get married."

They arrived in Nevada by midday and made short work of obtaining the necessary license. Despite the rush and reluctance, Luc insisted they stop at a boutique for more appropriate clothing—a formal suit for Luc, while Téa chose an ivory calf-length skirt and tailored jacket accented with seed pearls. The shop owner suggested a simple Mantilla style veil with embroidered edges that suited her outfit perfectly. A short time later, Téa emerged from the boutique to discover Luc waiting for her, holding a bridal bouquet of multicolored roses in one hand, and a jeweler's box with two plain wedding bands in the other.

They made the short trip to the venue they'd selected and were given the choice of having the ceremony performed in the chapel, itself, or in a glorious flower-filled garden just behind the small stucco building. To Téa's surprise, Luc didn't hesitate, but selected the garden. She couldn't help but wonder if it was because it reminded him of Primo's backyard.

Both had large, sprawling shade trees and well-tended flower beds, bursting with a riot of colors. They took their vows beneath an arching arbor draped with deep red roses that filled the air with their lush scent. Twenty short minutes later they were pronounced husband and wife.

Téa didn't recall much of the drive back to San Francisco. She knew they kept the conversation light and casual. But she had no idea what either of them said. Awareness returned when Luc bypassed the turn for Madam's row house and continued on toward his apartment.

"Aren't you going to drop me off at home?"

He glanced in her direction. "Why would I do that? We're married, remember?" he asked with devastating logic. "I think your grandmother and stepsisters would find it extremely odd if you spent your wedding night under their roof instead of mine."

She blushed, feeling like an utter fool. "Oh. Of course. I didn't think."

Luc parked the rental car, said something about returning it in the morning and grabbed their bags while she gathered up the rest of their paraphernalia. The elevator ride to his apartment was accomplished in strained silence. The minute the doors parted, he carried his duffel through to his bedroom and then put her case just inside the doorway of the spare room.

Message received, loud and clear.

"Would you like a drink?" he offered politely.

She debated, then nodded. "I wouldn't say no to a glass of wine."

"Red?"

"Please." He poured her a glass and then fixed himself a whiskey. "It's almost identical to the last time I was here," she observed. "Except for the marriage part."

He eyed her broodingly. "That's a big exception."

She gently placed her bouquet on the table beside the couch. The flowers were already beginning to wilt, she realized with a sad pang. It seemed fitting, all things considered. Soon they'd have to return to reality, which meant putting her focus on work and family, while Luc went back to avoiding commitment at all costs. "I know you have something eating at you. Why don't you just say what you need to so we can go to bed?"

"All this worked out to your advantage, didn't it?"

She closed her eyes. She suspected that was what he thought. It hurt to have it confirmed. "You think I set it up, don't you?"

He took a moment to swallow his drink. "The thought crossed my mind."

"Let it uncross your mind," she said sharply. "You said no to marriage. I accepted that. End of story."

"And yet, within hours my ring ended up on your finger."

"Because of your family, Luc. Yours. Not mine. Madam was merely disappointed in me. I could have lived with her disappointment. It was Primo who forced the issue."

"You're forgetting that Primo pushed because someone leaked the news to *The Snitch*. There are only a limited number of people who could have done that."

She lifted an eyebrow. "All of whom are de Lucas?"

"Pretty much."

She took a step in his direction. "You always claimed I was a lousy liar. Look at me, Luc. Hear me." She spoke quietly. Forcefully. "I didn't trick you into marrying me. I didn't ask anyone in my family to get in touch with *The Snitch*. I would never do such a thing to you."

He inclined his head. "Fair enough."

"Do you believe me?" she pressed.

"I believe you."

"But you still want someone to blame."

"Yes. No." He released his breath in a sigh. "I'm as much to blame as anyone."

"Thank you for that much," she said dryly.

"I want you to understand something, Téa." His eyes glittered darkly, with just a hint of gold. "This doesn't change anything."

"What do you mean?"

"You know what I mean. This is temporary. In a few months I plan to walk away."

"I know." And she did. She'd just hoped... She set her glass down, exercising extreme care. "I don't think I want a drink after all. I'm exhausted. If you don't mind, I'll turn in."

He stopped her as she started from the room. Just a brush of his fingers along her arm. "Téa..."

The Inferno stirred, flared to life, sizzling and crackling with unmistakable urgency. She longed to turn and step into his arms. To beg him to allow her in.

To give her a chance. "Don't. I can't…" She shook her head, struggling for control. "Please, don't."

Without another word, he let her go.

She got ready for bed, moving mindlessly through her nighttime regimen. At long last, she slid between the sheets and curled into a ball. Just a few short hours ago she'd been married. This was her wedding night. Never in her wildest dreams had she imagined she'd spend it alone. Or that the man she married would have given almost anything to rip the ring from his finger, and her from his life.

Tears burned against her eyelids, slipped out and left scalding streaks down her cheeks. She buried her face in the pillow, fighting not to make any sound as she cried. She never heard the door to her room open. Never heard Luc limp across the floor. One minute, she was huddled in her bed, the next she was curled against his chest as he lifted her and carried her to his room.

"What are you doing?" she choked out the question.

"It's my wedding night," he said, echoing her earlier thoughts. "And I'll be damned if I'm going to spend it alone."

He deposited her in his bed, then joined her there. In the silence of the night, he gathered her up. Her nightgown whispered away, melting into the darkness. Then his hands found her. Stroked her. Spoke the words he refused to. With every touch, every caress, he gave of himself, allowing what he guarded so carefully free rein.

Where before they came together in clashing power, now they gently slid, one into the other. Sweetly. Tenderly. The climax, when it came, was every bit as powerful, but it contained a different quality. A need answered. Two hearts united. A consummation of not just bodies, but of souls.

Just before sleep consumed her, he wrapped her up in his arms, hands intertwined, palms meshed. From a great distance she heard his whisper. "Good night, my Inferno bride."

"Good night, my Inferno husband," someone answered. Not her. It couldn't have been her. "Oh, Luc. I do love you."

When Tea awoke, she was alone in the bed.

A quick search of Luc's apartment confirmed that he'd gone, though the scent of freshly brewed coffee drew her to the kitchen. Beside the pot, she found a note that read: *Don't go in to Bling until I get back.* The word "don't" was underlined several times. It took two cups of coffee to figure out why. If she planned to oust her cousin and assume the reins of Billings, she'd better do it with a plan. Because, guaranteed, Connie had one.

After a quick shower, she ate breakfast and drafted a press release announcing the change in management, fussing over each and every word, striving to get it just right. It took several hours to perfect. She'd just finished when Luc returned. He was accompanied by a tank-size black man whom he introduced as Juice.

She offered her hand, amused when it got swallowed up in his. "Pleased to finally meet you," he said. "Luc's had a lot to say about you."

"Some of it good, I hope."

"Good enough to make me wonder why you'd waste your time on him when I'm available."

She grinned. "Maybe if I'd met you first…?"

He waggled his eyebrows at her. "You'd be counting your lucky stars and singing praises on high."

"If you're done hitting on my wife," Luc interrupted, "I'd like to give her an update."

Téa buried a smile. "I just brewed a fresh pot of coffee. I drank the last one while drafting a press release."

"You read my mind."

Once everyone had fresh coffee, they gathered at the dining room table. Luc took the lead. "First, let's deal with the issue of the new equipment Conway has been purchasing. FYI, Juice was my top researcher when I owned my own security business. He was able to locate where Connie had the equipment stashed."

"How did you do that?" Téa asked in amazement.

"Uh…" Juice darted Luc a panicked look. "Best if I don't tell you. It's not exactly leg— That is to say…"

"It's none of your business," Luc cut in. "We also have temporarily relocated said equipment. My men should be finished moving it by noon."

"Wait a minute. You *stole* Connie's machinery?"

The two men exchanged glances. "Well, technically, it belongs to Billings since he used company money to purchase it," Luc explained. "Which means it's yours to move if you want. I merely decided that's what you wanted and acted on it."

"Of course." She didn't know why that didn't occur to her. "Will that be sufficient to keep him from starting up a competing business?"

"That's the hope."

Téa nodded in satisfaction. "Then the next step is to get Connie out with as little fuss as possible while keeping our current customers." She put the press release she'd drafted on the table. "See what you think about this."

Luc and Juice scanned it. "Oh, Connie's not going to be happy," Luc said, with a merciless grin. "Particularly when he reads the part about being a distant relative of your grandfather who, quote, has been forcibly removed as CEO for failing to maintain Billings's high standard of producing top quality merchandise, which is the number one priority for Daniel Billings's granddaughter, the company's new CEO. End quote." He shoved the release back across the table toward her. "One major error."

Téa snatched up the paper. "What? Where?"

"Your name. It says Téa de Luca. It should say Téa Dante."

The correction brought tears to her eyes. Considering how he felt about their marriage, it meant the world to her that he'd insist she use the Dante name. "Silly of me," she murmured. "I'll change it right away."

Luc nodded in satisfaction. His cell rang just then. "Yes, Sandford," he said as he left the table to take the call. "What did you find out?"

It took Téa a moment to place the name, but then she remembered the deputy who'd been so helpful after their car crash. She only caught snatches of Luc's conversation, but when he returned a grim fury clung to him. He gave Juice a nod before turning to Téa.

"Let's go," he announced. "Time for you to kick Cousin Connie to the curb."

Ten

Conway Billings didn't take kindly to being kicked to the curb.

Téa swept into his office without bothering to knock, followed closely by Luc and Juice. Conway looked up, his face darkening in outrage. "What the hell do you mean by waltzing in here without permission? You may take over in another month, Téa, but until then this is still my office."

"You're mistaken, Connie. It's now *my* office." She took a stance in front of his desk, her hands planted on her hips. "And don't call me Téa. The name is Mrs. Dante."

Her cousin's mouth opened and closed several times. "When…?"

She lifted an eyebrow. "Did I get married? Luc and I were married yesterday."

"Yesterday? I… You…" He resorted to bluster. "You

were supposed to be getting to know our clients. How are you ever going to learn what you need to—"

"That's no longer your concern," she interrupted. "As of this minute, you're no longer in charge."

"There's still another month until it's official, Téa." Luc and Juice both took a single step forward and Conway's eyes bulged. "Mrs. Dante," he hastened to correct. "You don't take possession of Billings until next month."

"I suggest you go back and reread the will, Connie." She circled the desk, putting herself on his side of it. Then she edged her hip onto the corner in a decidedly possessive maneuver. "In case you overlooked it, I also take possession of the company the day I marry. Since that happy event took place yesterday, I'm now the new owner of Billings."

"Don't be ridiculous, Te—" a quick look at Luc "—Mrs. Dante. You're not ready to assume control."

"That's quite possible. Time will tell. What I can say with absolute certainty is that you're through. I have security waiting outside the door. They'll escort you off the premises."

His breath hissed in surprise. "What's brought this on?" His gaze shot to Luc and narrowed. "He's responsible for this, isn't he?"

"No, Connie," she corrected very gently. "You are. Did you think I wouldn't figure it out?"

He stiffened. "Figure what out?"

"The equipment. Billings Prime. I did get the name right, didn't I? That's what you plan to call your new company?"

"I have no idea what you're talking about."

"Stop. I uncovered it all. The way you cut corners to save money and churn out inferior merchandise. The business you planned to start up. The new manufacturing equipment you bought with the extra profits you gained from overcharging *my* customers. How you planned to use the drop in quality to convince those same customers to switch to Billings Prime. The sale you're currently drafting so that your company can buy the new manufacturing equipment from Billings for only pennies on the dollar. That was particularly slick, Connie."

"And if I did all that, so what?" He shoved back his chair, fury reddening his face. "This should have been my company! I worked here my entire life." He didn't bother to conceal his disgust. "You're not even a Billings. You gave up your rights to this company when you let de Luca adopt you."

She straightened, faced him down. "That decision was my grandfather's to make. Obviously he didn't agree with you since he left Billings to me, not you." She tilted her head to one side. "I wonder why that is? He must have figured you out long ago."

Conway smoothed the front of his suit jacket and drew himself up to his full height, as little as that was. "It's too late for you to do anything about it. That equipment now belongs to me. I wasn't planning to bring Billings Prime online for another month, but I won't have any difficulty moving up my agenda."

"I think you'll not only find that difficult, but impossible," Téa replied. "I rescinded the sale of the manufacturing equipment between Billings and Billings Prime first thing this morning and I've confiscated that equipment. All you have left is a name. No equipment, no merchandise to sell and when my press release hits, not much of a reputation, either."

"That's impossible! I'll…I'll sue."

"I wish you would." She smiled coldly. "But I doubt

you will, considering that when all the facts are brought to light you'll most likely find yourself sitting in a jail cell."

Luc stepped forward. "And if by some chance the judge is inclined toward leniency, it won't last long. Not when he discovers that you tampered with Téa's brakes before sending her on a dangerous drive. I'm guessing you arranged that sometime Monday when her car was parked in Billings's garage. I suspect it was shortly after you ordered her to take that trip to L.A. No doubt you were hoping it would end up being a one-way trip."

Téa swung around to face her husband. She didn't even attempt to conceal her shock. "What?"

"Deputy Sandford called. Someone mixed transmission fluid in with your brake fluid. It's slower than simply cutting the lines. No doubt he wanted to give you plenty of time to get on some of the more treacherous stretches of road before your brakes went out. Might have worked, too."

Téa fought to breathe. "It would have worked if you hadn't been driving."

She turned to face her cousin. She saw his mouth moving, could hear the denials that spilled out. But her brain couldn't seem to process them. Instead all she saw was the guilt burning like acid in his unrepentant blue eyes.

"I want him out of here," she said, her voice cutting through whatever her cousin was saying. It took every ounce of self-control to keep from physically attacking him. He must have sensed it because he fell back as she approached. "Just so you know, Connie? Just so it's crystal clear. My sisters will inherit the business if anything happens to me. And every last scrap of information that my husband has uncovered about your activities is going to be turned over to the appropriate authorities. I suggest you find yourself a good lawyer."

"Screw finding a lawyer," Luc said. "Find yourself a nice, deep hole, *Cuz*. Somewhere I won't find you. Because if I ever see you again, I swear I'll take you apart."

Billings's security stepped in then and with Juice's assistance, escorted Conway out of the office, out of the building—and she sincerely hoped—out of her life. The instant the door closed behind them, Téa sank into the chair behind Connie's—*her*—desk.

"That's that," she murmured.

Luc inclined his head. "You're now the boss. Congratulations."

A tiny frown tugged at her brow. "Thanks to you."

"Happy to help." He shoved his hands into his trouser pockets and strolled across the spacious room to stand in front of the windows. "I guess my job is done now."

Maybe if he hadn't said it with such finality, she'd have known how to respond. She hesitated, before conceding, "I guess it is."

He threw her a look over his shoulder. "You okay?"

"Sure. Fine." Only she wasn't. Not even a little.

"Anything else I can do for you?"

Love me. Stay with me. Make our marriage real. She silently shook her head.

"If you're sure, then I'll push off."

"Thanks again for all your help," she managed to say.

For ten minutes after Luc left, Téa continued to sit behind the huge desk, numb. So this was it. In the blink of an eye, he'd given her everything she thought she wanted, and she owed him more than she could ever repay.

Because he suspected her cousin might be attempting something underhanded, he used his time, skill and associates to look into Connie's background. More, he and Juice uncovered her cousin's plan and moved to circumvent it. And thanks to Luc agreeing to marry her, she'd gained control of her inheritance in time to stop Connie from gutting it. With a lot of hard work and dedication, she'd turn Billings around and salvage her family's finances. But she'd lose something far more important.

Luc.

Her mouth trembled. Of course, that was assuming she'd ever had him. She leaned back and closed her eyes, fighting exhaustion. She loved her husband. Loved him with all her heart and soul. Loved him with every fiber of her being. And because she loved him, she'd let him go. Knowing Luc, that wouldn't be easy, despite his aversion toward marriage. She'd need to prove she could stand on her own two feet. And she'd have to find a way to get him out of their marriage without his looking like the bad guy.

Unfortunately she knew precisely how to do it, too. Even more unfortunate, she'd give him up, regardless of the personal cost. She just wished she could offer him something in return to show him how much she appreciated everything he'd done for her.

A light tapping sounded at the door and Juice peeked in. "What happened to Luc?" he asked.

"He's gone." A sudden idea struck her. One final way she could even the scales. She straightened in her chair, energized. "Juice, I wonder if you'd do one more favor for me."

"Sure." He stepped into her office. "Name it."

"There's someone I need you to find…"

Luc checked his watch and grimaced. He was late for his dinner date with Téa. Not badly, but more than he liked. Maybe it had been his subconscious way of putting off the inevitable. Because he suspected he knew what she wanted. She wanted to end their marriage so she could return to her default setting—taking care of her family. Of course, he wanted to end their marriage, too. No long-term commitments for him. He'd made that abundantly clear.

So, why the reluctance?

It couldn't have anything to do with those words she'd whispered on their wedding night. Words that burned a path straight to his heart. Words he wasn't even sure she remembered speaking. Words that confessed how much she loved him. For some reason they resonated, wrapped around him, through him, binding them as surely as the itch in his palm bound them.

"Luc Dante," he practically growled at the maître d'. "I'm meeting someone."

"Yes, Mr. Dante. She's already arrived. I'll show you to your table." He gestured toward the interior of the restaurant. "This way."

Luc followed the winding pathway through the various tables to a small alcove where a woman waited. It took an instant to realize that she wasn't Téa. The maître d' made a flourishing gesture, then retreated before Luc could explain that he'd been shown to the wrong table. He offered the woman an exasperated smile.

"Sorry about the mistake. I was supposed to meet my wife and—"

"There's no mistake," the woman said. She tilted her

head to one side. "You don't recognize me, do you? Would it help if I told you that you saved my life five years ago?"

Luc hesitated and looked more carefully. There was something familiar about her... Then it hit him. The car wreck. Kurt and the Jorgen boy, dead. The wife, pleading, begging him to let her die. *"Sonya?"*

Téa checked her watch and bit down on her lip. Right about now Luc and Sonya Jorgen would be getting reacquainted, assuming Luc stayed to talk after learning that his wife had set him up. A big if. Since she hadn't received an outraged phone call, she could only hope the impromptu meeting yielded positive results instead of all going hideously wrong. A distinct possibility, she was forced to concede. But if it worked... She closed her eyes and fought a rush of tears. If it worked, it would be the first of her parting gifts, gifts she could only pray would pay him back for all he'd done for her. Now for gift number two.

She let herself into the home that until recently she'd shared with Madam and her three sisters. She'd deliberately chosen a time when she was certain they'd all be together—the dinner hour. It was all part of her plan to try to put Luc's life back on track before their divorce. If he no longer had to worry about her, he'd feel free to move on.

She found the de Luca clan in the kitchen, squabbling over dinner preparations. She couldn't help smiling. Some things never changed. It took them a moment to realize she was there. The instant they did, they turned to greet her, the volume going up by several hundred decibels.

"What's for dinner?" she asked with a wide smile. "I'm starving."

"What are you doing here?" Madam demanded. "Where's Luc?"

"He has an appointment this evening, so I thought I'd have dinner with you." She eyed each in turn. "We need to talk."

"Actually," Sonya said, "it's not Jorgen, anymore. It's Thompson."

"You remarried?"

His shock must have shown because she smiled and waved him toward the chair across from her. Once he was seated she studied him with frank curiosity. "It's been five years and you haven't changed a bit, Luc," she murmured. "You still have the saddest eyes I've ever seen. You know, it was the first thing I noticed about you."

He took his time replying. "I may not have changed, but you have," he surprised himself by saying. "Your eyes aren't sad at all."

She lit up. "No, I guess they wouldn't be."

She shook out her napkin and spread it across her lap. Luc's gaze followed her movements, dropping downward. He froze. "You're—"

"Pregnant?" she asked with a lilting laugh. "Why, yes, I am."

"What's this about, Téa?" Madam asked apprehensively. "Has something happened between you and Luc?"

"Yes. We're going to be divorcing soon." She held up her hand when everyone began talking at once. "That's enough."

For some reason the quietly spoken words worked, cutting through the cacophony of feminine voices. Odd. It had never worked before. But then, she'd never been this serious or determined before.

"I'm not going to discuss it or answer any questions. I'm just going to say that the relationship didn't work out. As a result, I've decided to make some changes. A lot of changes." She eyed each in turn before settling on Juliann. "I've been a lousy wedding planner, Jules. I'm sorry about that."

"It hasn't been so bad," Juliann instantly denied.

"Yes, it has." Téa reached into her shoulder bag and pulled out the shiny black cell phone with its neon-pink kisses. She placed it on the table. "I appreciate you including me in the preparations, but I think what I'd enjoy most is just being there for you on your special day."

Juliann's eyes misted. "That's all I ever wanted, too. But you've always tried to fill in for Mom, and I figured…"

Téa closed her eyes. Of course. "You were trying to let me play the traditional mother role, weren't you?" She blinked back tears and offered her sister a wobbly smile. "Thank you. To be honest, I don't want to be your mother, anymore. But I'd love to be your sister."

For some reason, her confession caused all her sisters to tear up. Then there were hugs all around before Davida said, "I gather I'm next?"

"Yes," Téa confirmed. She nudged the phone farther away. "Stay in college or don't. It's your decision. But I'm not bailing you out anymore."

Davida nodded. "You're not going to have to. The professor whose exam I missed? He sat me down and we had a long talk. I realized that what I really want to do is design jewelry. Luc put me in touch with Sev's wife, Francesca. She's going to mentor me while I take the classes I need."

Téa blinked. "*Luc* put you in touch…?"

Davida made a face. "I'm sorry you two are getting divorced. I like him. He's nice."

Katrina held out her hand, gloved palm up. "Finish it, Téa. I know it's my turn to get cut off."

Téa slid the phone the rest of the way across the table. "Not cut off, just cut down to reasonable, although I am canceling this line."

"That's okay. And FYI? You don't have to worry about me, either. I've decided I'm going into the military. That or I'm gonna be a cop."

Téa could only stare. "You must be joking," she finally said.

"Nope. I've gotten to know a lot of cops over the past year." She shot Madam a nervous glance. "You know. Community service projects."

Madam simply narrowed her eyes at her granddaughter and let it pass.

"Anyway, it got me interested in law enforcement." Katrina lounged back in her chair and lifted a pierced eyebrow. "So, we done?"

Madam cleared her throat. "You…you haven't mentioned me," she said with heart-wrenching dignity. "You may give me my phone, too, if you wish."

Téa hastened to her grandmother's side and enfolded her in a tight hug. "Never. I'll always be there for you." She looked at her sisters and in that moment finally forgave herself for her parents' death. "I'll always be there for all of you. But as a sister. As a granddaughter."

Madam dabbed at her eyes. "I think that can be arranged."

* * *

Luc was surprised to discover he enjoyed the hour he spent with Sonya. "I assume Téa arranged this?" he said, taking a not-so-wild guess.

"Your wife? Yes. Such a lovely woman. She tracked me down and explained that you were still dealing with the aftermath of what happened all those years ago." Remorse swept across Sonya's face. "I'm so sorry, Luc. I'd give anything to take back those hideous things I said to you. I was out of my mind with grief."

"I understood." He tossed some money into the billfold the waiter had left and set it to one side. "I never blamed you."

Sonya's mouth twisted. "I'm not so sure. That's why I jumped at the opportunity to meet with you, so I could thank you."

"*Thank* me?" Of all the things he'd imagined her ever saying to him, this was bottom of the list. Hell, it didn't even make the list.

She pushed aside her decaf coffee, picking her words with care. "I was so angry with you, Luc. I wanted to die and you forced me to live. I hated you for that. I even attempted to commit suicide. Did you know?" At his silent nod, she shrugged. "Somehow I'm not surprised. Afterward, much to my amazement, I realized I no longer wanted to die. It took time and a lot of counseling, but I discovered I had a very simple choice. I could open myself up to love again, or continue to live a barren life. When I chose to open up, I found love." A radiant smile played at the corners of her mouth. "Actually I found my soul mate."

"I thought that was Kurt," Luc said, startled.

"So did I. I was wrong," she replied simply. "What I loved about my life with Kurt was being married. What

I loved was—" Her voice broke. "My son. I still miss him, Luc. I'll always miss him. But I can and will honor his memory by moving on and giving him brothers and sisters. He may never know them, but they'll always know him. I'll see to that."

Luc's jaw clenched and it took him a minute before he could speak. "I'm glad you made it through. That you found love again."

"You can, too." She leaned forward, speaking with a hushed intensity. "I'm reading between the lines here, but... Don't make the mistake I almost did. Don't turn away from life. Take the gamble, Luc, before it passes you by. Everyone experiences heartache. But that's going to happen whether you're alone or with someone you love. It's love that gets you through. Téa strikes me as a woman who can both fill your life with love, and be strong enough to ride out the heartache with you."

A short time later, Luc climbed into his car. He didn't bother to start the engine, but simply sat, mulling over the events of that evening. It occurred to him that when he saved Sonya, he'd given her back her life, but had shut down his own. She was right about a lot of things. He did have a choice. He could continue on as he had before Téa tumbled into his life or he could take a chance. He could open his heart and take the risk.

He thought about his grandparents and nearly sixty years of profound love and devotion, laughter and tears. It was the same with his parents. With his cousins. Would they avoid love if it meant avoiding the tears? He didn't even have to think about that one. They'd choose love every time.

He considered what his life would be like if he moved forward without Téa. Losing her warmth and generosity.

Her humor and passion. God help him, her love. And he remembered her murmured declaration on their wedding night and felt something hard and cold begin to loosen and break.

It was the ultimate gamble. Either he loved Téa and wanted to spend the rest of his life with her, was willing to open himself to her in every possible way. Or he let her go. Watched from afar as she moved on and found someone else to love. Someone else to give all that she'd given him.

He shook his head. No. No way in hell. As though in reaction, his palm itched and he stared at it. He was an idiot. He'd turned away from the best, most important parts of his life. And why? Because he'd been too much of a coward to take a risk. Well, screw that! It was past time that he took back his life. That he went after what he wanted most.

And what he wanted most was Téa—the woman he loved with all his heart and soul. His Inferno soul mate.

Before he could start the engine, his cell phone rang. He checked the caller ID and flipped it open. "What's up, Nonna?"

She spoke in rapid-fire Italian. "Your wife is here," she said without preamble. "You must come. Now."

He shot up in his seat. "What's wrong?"

"Téa is explaining to Primo why your marriage is a mistake. That he must not interfere in the divorce. What is this talk of a divorce, *cucciolo mio?*" she demanded. "You have only just married."

Hell. "Has Primo taken her apart, yet?"

"No, no. He is being very patient. Very understanding." His grandmother sighed. "She is a determined one, though, that wife of yours. Determined to get her head handed to her."

"Nonna, I need you to do me a favor."

"Anything."

"Break out Primo's homemade beer and *stall*." He cut the connection and immediately dialed Sev. "I need you to meet me at the Dante vault. Yes, now. She's *what?* Hell. Well, can you meet me on the way to the hospital? You're damn right it's an emergency. It's a matter of life and… And love."

Téa blinked owlishly at Primo and waved her bottle of beer at him. So far, her third gift to Luc wasn't going so well. At this rate, she'd never even up those scales. "So, you understand, right?" she asked hopefully.

Primo slanted a look in Nonna's direction, gritted his teeth and said, "Maybe if you explain one more time?"

"Oh." She suppressed a burp and lifted a hand to her aching head. "To be honest, I'm not sure I can."

"Good. We talk of other things now, yes? How do you like babies?" he asked expansively. "You and Luc will make many good babies. Inferno babies with red Inferno hair, okay?"

Téa sniffed. For some reason his question had tears welling up in her eyes. "Haven't you been listening? There aren't going to be any babies."

He leaned back in his chair and grinned. "There are always babies when your husband is a Dante." He fixed his attention on a spot over her shoulder. "Is this not true, Luciano?"

"Absolutely, Primo."

Téa swung around and almost fell off her chair.

"Oh, dear," she murmured as the room did a slow 360 around her.

"How many?" Luc asked Nonna with a sigh.

His grandmother shrugged. "Three or four."

"Maybe five," Primo offered helpfully.

"Damn. I was hoping she'd remember tonight."

"I'll remember tonight," Téa protested. "Why won't I remember?"

Luc tipped her face up to his. "Because, darling wife," he said, enunciating clearly. "You're drunk."

"Am not."

He gave his grandfather a stern look. "Coffee and lots of it. In the meantime…" He swept his wife into his arms. "Let's hope some fresh air will do the trick. By the way, you might want to give Sev a call. Francesca's in labor and they're on their way to the hospital."

Téa tipped her head back as Luc carried her into the garden. A dazzling canopy of stars glittered and burned like Dantes legendary fire diamonds. Cool spring air swirled around and over her in soft revitalizing currents. It helped clear her head and she stirred, suddenly aware that she'd somehow ended up where she most longed to be—in Luc's arms.

"Where did you come from?" she asked dreamily. "Or am I just imagining you?"

"Oh, I'm real enough," he claimed.

Not that she believed him. Having him here like this was just too good to be true. "This is so nice." Since he was a dream, she could indulge herself and she scattered her kisses across his bronzed skin, like the stars scattered their dust across the heavens. "We can pretend to still be married and have another glorious wedding night."

He smiled with breathtaking tenderness. "We don't need to pretend. We are still married."

"Not for long."

"True. Only a half dozen decades or so."

She laughed. "Now I know I'm dreaming."

He lowered her to a wrought iron bench situated beneath one of Primo's shade trees. The cold metal brought her surroundings into sharp focus. Luc really was here. And he really was holding her in his arms.

"Seriously," she said, her brain slowly coming online. "What are you doing here?"

"I wanted to thank you for arranging the meeting with Sonya tonight."

Sonya? Her brow crinkled. Oh! Sonya. "I was afraid you might be angry with me," she confessed.

"Not even a little."

"I'm so glad. I asked Juice to help me find her." She nestled against him, resting her head in the crook of his shoulder, allowing herself this one final indulgence. "How did it go?"

"She's remarried, but I guess you knew that." At Téa's nod, he added, "And she's pregnant."

Téa looked up at Luc, startled. "Is she really? That's good, right?"

"It's very good. She was…ecstatic."

"Pregnant." Téa frowned. "Wait a minute. Did I hear you tell your grandparents that Francesca was in labor, or was that part of my dream?"

"It wasn't a dream. She's in labor and Sev isn't very happy with me."

"Why ever not?"

"Because I made him stop off at the Dantes vault on the way to the hospital."

"I'm confused," Téa confessed with a sigh. "And it's all Primo's fault."

"Nonna's actually. I told her to feed you beer until I got here."

It took all her courage to ask. "Why?"

"So I could give you this..."

He held out a small jewelry box and flipped open the lid. Inside was nestled the most beautiful ring she'd ever seen. The band was platinum gold, Billings gold, Téa realized, a type her grandfather had dubbed, Platinum Ice. The band took the shape of two hearts linked together with a magnificent fire diamond set where the hearts joined.

It took several tries before she could speak. "I don't understand."

"I love you, Téa. And I want a real marriage. A permanent one."

"No," she whispered, shaking her head. "That's not what you want. You want to be apart. Alone."

"I was wrong. I can't live like that. Not anymore. Not since meeting you." She watched as he struggled to find the right words, to open himself in a way he never had before. "I can't promise I'll be perfect at it. I've spent a lot of years holding people at an emotional distance. But for you... I'm willing to give you everything I have. And with luck, we'll spend the rest of our lives getting it right."

"Oh, Luc. I came here to let you go." She gazed in the direction of the house and fought an onslaught of tears. "But I couldn't get your grandparents to listen to me. To understand and let you off the hook."

"Because they knew you were the one. My Inferno bride."

His admission melted her. "Oh, Luc. I love you so much."

"And I love you, Téa, more than I ever thought possible. My life would be empty without you and I think I've had all the emptiness I can bear." He slid the ring on her finger. It fit perfectly. But then, he knew it would. It was destiny. "It's from our new line of eternity rings. It has a name, if you're interested. It's actually the reason I chose it."

It took her two tries to get the question out. "What's the name?"

He lowered his mouth to hers. "Why, Dante's Inferno, of course."

Epilogue

Nonna touched her wineglass to Madam's. "*Salute*."

Madam smiled tremulously. "We did it, didn't we?"

Nonna eyed Luc and Téa with smug satisfaction. "That we did. Of course, it was your managing to accomplish Step Two that allowed Primo to insist on Step Three." She released a contented sigh. "And that just leaves Step Four."

"Step Four?" Madam's eyes widened in concern. "What step is this?"

"Babies. More precious Dante babies. Boys for these two." Nonna lifted her glass in the direction of her grandson. "But that step I will leave to Luc. I believe he has the matter well in hand."

From his position at the kitchen window, Rafe Dante regarded Luc and his bride, Téa, with a cynical smile. They were in Primo's garden, enjoying the party thrown to celebrate their elopement, and accepting the congratulations of all the well-wishers. Babies abounded: one from Francesca, as well as Kiley's contribution. Both sons, of course. The two mothers were comparing everything from birthing experiences to feeding schedules. Hell, they were even comparing toes.

To Rafe's amusement, Luc looked on, taking an actual interest. Unheard of! But then, his poor brother was the latest victim of The Inferno. Of all the Dantes, Rafe had always figured that he and Luc were the two least likely to ever succumb to the family plague. For some reason, it made him feel fiercely alone. Which was the way he wanted it, right? God knows, Leigh had caused him enough heartache that he never wanted to give another woman that much power over him. But watching his family…

He deliberately turned away.

Luc joined him midway through the festivities, taking the tumbler of whiskey Rafe offered. "I hear we've been cleared to return to work."

"As of today," Rafe confirmed. "Dantes Courier Service reopens first thing Monday morning. You coming back?"

"You can't keep me away."

Rafe nodded in satisfaction. "Congratulations, by the way. Téa's a beautiful woman." He paid the compliment with complete sincerity. "You're a lucky man." Okay, maybe that wasn't quite as sincere.

"Yes, I am," Luc agreed. He fixed Rafe with a speculative eye. "I know you're one of the unbelievers."

"Check mark firmly in that column," Rafe confirmed.

"I guess we have Leigh to thank for that." Luc rested his hip against the kitchen counter. "Tell me something. Did you believe in The Inferno when you first fell in love with her? When the two of you first married?"

Rafe took a long swallow of his drink. "What makes you think that?'"

Luc froze. "Wait a sec. You didn't feel…?" He rubbed his palm.

"Don't be ridiculous. Of course not."

Luc straightened. "Are you telling me you never felt The Inferno for Leigh?"

Rafe released an incredulous laugh. "You're as crazy as the rest of them. Don't you get it? *There is no Inferno.*"

Luc simply smiled.

A hint of anger ripped through Rafe. "Don't. Don't give me that smug, knowing look. You and the rest of our deluded relatives fell in love. That's all there is to it. But because of our family's ridiculous myth, you're calling this emotion that has you drooling all over your bride The Inferno. Well, I've got news for you, brother. It's illogical. Not to mention messy." He leaned forward, speaking distinctly. "In my book that means The Inferno doesn't exist."

"I'm sure that explains the itch," Luc said, straight-faced.

"That itch is called lust. Now, you want to talk lust?" Rafe downed the rest of his drink. "Happy to oblige. Been there, sated that. Moved on."

This time Luc didn't bother to conceal his grin. "Keep talking, Rafe. And keep telling yourself you're immune. But I'm giving you fair warning. Clearly Leigh wasn't the right woman."

Rafe lifted an eyebrow. "You think?"

"You're missing the point. If Leigh wasn't the one, that means your Inferno bride's still out there. And when you find her, you'll know." Luc jabbed his index finger against his brother's chest. "Then we'll see who has the last itch, pretty boy."

* * * * *

DANTE'S TEMPORARY FIANCÉE

BY
DAY LECLAIRE

To Kathy Jorgensen, my sister in spirit.

One

This time his family had gone too far.

Rafe Dante stared at the bevy of women being subtly—and not so subtly—paraded beneath his nose by various family members. He'd lost count of the number of women he'd been forced to shake hands with. He knew why they were doing it. They were all determined to find him a wife. He grimaced. No, more than just a wife.

They hoped to find his Inferno soul mate—a Dante legend that had gotten seriously out of hand. For some reason, his family had it firmly fixed in their heads that it took only one touch for some strange mythical connection to be forged between a Dante and his soul mate. Ridiculous, of course. Didn't they get it?

Not only didn't he believe in The Inferno, but he had no interest in ever experiencing matrimonial bliss-lessness again. His late wife, Leigh, had taught him that lesson in the short span of time from "I do" to "My lawyer will be in touch." Of course, that phone call had never come. Eighteen months ago his wife had chartered a private plane to Mexico to recover from the tragedy of her marriage to him and met a far worse fate when her plane crashed into a mountainside, leaving no survivors.

Rafe's younger brother, Draco, joined him and folded his arms across his chest. He stood silently for a moment, surveying the room and the glittering contents, both jeweled and female. "Ready to surrender and just pick one?"

"Get serious."

"I am. Dead serious."

Rafe turned on his brother, only too happy to vent some of his irritation. "Do you have any idea what the past three months have been like?"

"I do. I've been watching from the sidelines, in case you hadn't noticed. I'm also keenly aware that once you succumb to The Inferno, I'm next in line for the firing squad. As far as I'm concerned, feel free to hold out for as long as possible."

"I'm working on it."

Rafe returned his attention to the shimmer and sparkle and sighed. Dantes international jewelry reception possessed everything a man could ask for—wine, women and bling—and nothing he wanted.

The wine came from a Sonoma, California, vineyard just a few hours from the family's San Francisco home office. He knew the label on the bottles was as exclusive as the guest list. The women were beautiful, wealthy and shone as brilliantly as the wedding rings on display around the private showroom. As for the bling... Well, that often fell within his purview, at least it did when Dantes Courier Service transported the stunning array of gemstones and finished pieces.

And yet Rafe was nagged by a sense of utter boredom. How many times had he attended receptions similar to this one? Always observing. Always maintaining a vigilant eye from the shadows. Always the watchful lone wolf instinctively avoided by the guests, until one family member or another thrust a potential bride in his direction. It was a pattern that had repeated itself so many times he'd lost count.

This occasion celebrated the exclusive release of the latest Dantes collection, the Eternity line of one-of-a-kind wedding rings. Each was unique, combining the fire diamonds for which his family was renowned with the Platinum Ice gold from Billings, the company owned by Rafe's sister-in-law, Téa Dante, who'd married his older brother, Luc, three months earlier. Just seeing rings that symbolized love and commitment filled Rafe with bitterness.

Been there. Done that. Still had the scars to prove it.

And then he saw her.

The little blonde pixie working the reception as one of the caterers couldn't claim the title of most gorgeous woman in the room, but for some reason Rafe couldn't take his eyes off her.

He couldn't say why she attracted his attention or explain the vague sizzle she stirred. Granted, her features were quite lovely, delicate and fine boned with enough whimsy to make them interesting. Maybe it was her hair and eyes—hair the same shade as the ice-white sand of a Caribbean island and eyes the glorious turquoise of the rolling ocean waves that splashed and frolicked across those pristine beaches. Then there was that sizzle he couldn't explain, a vague compelling itch that urged him to get closer to her in every possible way.

She circulated through the display room of the Dantes corporate office building with a hip-swinging glide that made her appear as though she were dancing. In fact, she possessed a dancer's body, lean and graceful, if a bit pint-size, every delectable inch showcased by the fitted black slacks and tight red vest of her uniform.

She disappeared into the crowd, her tray of canapés held high, and he lost sight of her. For a split second he was tempted to give chase. A few minutes later, the pixie waitress reappeared with a fresh tray of champagne and circled through the guests in the exact opposite direction from where he stood.

For some reason it annoyed Rafe. Determined to force a meeting, he began to maneuver his way through the crowd on an intercept course, one circumvented by Draco's restraining hand.

"What?" Rafe asked, lifting an eyebrow. "I'm thirsty."

Draco shot him a knowing look. "Funny. I'd have said you look hungry. And with so many eyes on you, I recommend you avoid sating your appetite until a more appropriate time and place."

"Hell."

"Relax. Where there's a will…" Draco gestured toward one of the nearby display cases and deliberately changed the subject. "Looks like Francesca's latest line of Eternity wedding rings is going to be a huge success. Sev must be thrilled."

Caving to the inevitable, Rafe nodded. "I think he's

more thrilled about the birth of their son," he replied. "But this would probably rate as icing on the cake."

Draco inclined his head, then slanted Rafe a look of open amusement. "So tell me. How many of the lovelies fluttering around the room have our beloved grandparents introduced to you so far this evening?"

Rafe's expression settled into grim lines. "A full dozen. Made me touch every last one of them, like they expected to see me set off a shower of fireworks or light the place up in a blaze of electricity or something."

"It's your own fault. If you hadn't told Luc that you and Leigh never experienced The Inferno, the entire family wouldn't be intent on throwing women your way."

The fact that so many of his relatives had succumbed to the family legend only added to Rafe's bitterness toward his own brief foray into the turbulent matrimonial waters. Time would tell whether their romances lasted longer than his own. They might claim they'd found their soul mates, courtesy of the Dantes' Inferno. Rafe, the most logical and practical of all his kith and kin, adopted a far more simple and pragmatic—okay, cynical— viewpoint.

The Inferno didn't exist.

There was no eternal bond established when a Dante first touched his soul mate, no matter what anyone claimed, any more than Dantes Eternity wedding rings could promise that the marriages for which they were purchased would last for all eternity. Some hit it lucky, like his grandparents, Primo and Nonna. And some didn't, like his disastrous marriage to his late wife, Leigh.

Rafe stared broodingly at his older brother, Luc,

and his bride of three months, Téa. They were dancing together, swirling across the floor, gazing into each other's eyes as though no one else in the room existed. Every emotion blazed in their expressions, there for the world to witness. Hell, even when Rafe had been in the most passionate throes of lust, neither he nor Leigh had ever looked at each other like that.

In fact, he'd been accused by the various women in his life that his penchant for practicality and hard, cold logic—his lone wolf persona—bled over into his personal life with dismaying frequency. Possessing a fiery passion in the bedroom definitely compensated, as did his striking Dante looks, they conceded, but not when that passion went no farther than the bedroom door. Emotionally distant. Unavailable. *Intimidating.* For reasons that bewildered him, that word was always accompanied by a shudder.

What none of them understood was that he didn't do love. Not the brutal, I-married-you-because-you're-a-rich-and-powerful-Dante love his late wife, Leigh, had specialized in. Not the casual, melt-the-sheets-and-enjoy-it-while-the-bling-lasts type that characterized the women interested in an affair with him. And definitely not The Inferno brain-frying-palm-burning-happily-ever-after brand of bull spouted by his more emotional and passionate Dante relatives.

Rafe knew himself all too well. And he could state with absolute certainty that not only wasn't he hardwired that way, he never had and never would experience an Inferno love.

Which was just fine by him.

"It was annoying the first few times a potential bride was dangled in front of me," Rafe informed his brother.

"Since it was Nonna and Primo, I couldn't say much. But now everyone's gotten into the act. I can't move without having some gorgeous thing shoved under my nose."

Draco signaled to someone over Rafe's shoulder. "A fate worse than death," he said with a fake shudder.

"It would be if it were you under the gun."

"But I'm not." Draco leaned past Rafe and helped himself to a flute of champagne. "Want one?"

"Sure."

"Consider this your lucky day. The tray's right behind you." He offered a cocky grin. "And don't say I never did you a favor."

Confused by the comment, Rafe turned to take a glass and found his elusive pixie standing there, holding the tray of drinks. Close up she was even more appealing than from across the room.

He gestured to her with the flute. "Thanks."

Her smile grew, lighting up her face, the room and some cold, dark place in his heart. "You're welcome." Even her voice appealed, rich and husky with an almost musical lyricism.

Draco watched the byplay in amusement. "You know, if you want the relatives to leave you alone, there is one way."

That snagged Rafe's attention. "How?" he demanded.

Draco grinned. "Find your Inferno bride."

"Son of a—" Rafe bit off the curse. "I already told you. I'm never going to marry again. Not after Leigh."

He heard the pixie's sharp inhalation at the same time the flutes on her tray began to wobble unsteadily. The glasses knocked against each other, the crystal singing in distress. She fought to steady the tray, almost managed it, before the flutes tipped and cascaded to the floor. Glass shattered and champagne splattered in a wide arc.

Reacting instinctively, Rafe encircled the waitress's narrow waist and yanked her clear of the debris field. A tantalizing heat burned through the material of her uniform, rousing images of pale naked curves gilded in moonlight. Velvety-smooth arms and legs entwined around him. Soft moans like a musical symphony filling the air and driving their lovemaking.

Rafe shook his head, struggling for focus. "Are you all right?" he managed to ask.

She stared at the mess on the floor and nodded. "I think so."

She lifted her gaze to his, her eyes wide and impossibly blue, the only color in her sheet-white face. He didn't see any of the desire that had swept over him. Remorse and, oddly, a hint of panic, sure. But not so much as a flicker of passion. A shame.

"I'm so sorry," she said. "I started to step back so I could circulate some more and my foot slipped."

"You're not cut?"

"No." She blew out her breath in a sigh. "I really do apologize. I'll get this cleaned up right away."

Before she could follow through, another of the catering staff crossed the room to join them. He was clearly management, judging by the swift and discreet manner in which he took control of the situation and arranged to have the broken glass and champagne cleaned up. The waitress pitched in without a word, but when it was done, the manager guided her over to Rafe.

"Larkin, you have something to say to Mr. Dante?" he prompted.

"I want to apologize again for any inconvenience I may have caused," she said.

Rafe smiled at her, then at the manager. "Accidents happen. And in this case, it was entirely my fault. I'm afraid I bumped into Larkin, causing her to drop the tray."

The manager blinked at that and Rafe didn't have a doubt in the world that he'd have accepted the excuse if Larkin hadn't instantly protested, "Oh, no. The fault is entirely mine. Mr. Dante had nothing to do with it."

The manager sighed. "I see. Well, thank you, Mr. Dante, for your gallantry. Larkin, please return to the kitchen."

"Yes, sir, Mr. Barney."

Rafe watched her walk away. As far as he was concerned, she was still the most graceful woman in the room. "You're going to fire her, aren't you?"

"I wish I didn't have to. But my supervisor has a 'no excuses' policy for certain of his more exclusive clientele."

"I gather Dantes is on that list?"

Barney cleared his throat. "I believe you top the list, sir."

"Got it."

"It's a shame, really. She's the nicest of our waitresses. If it were up to me…"

Rafe lifted an eyebrow. "I don't suppose we can forget this incident took place?"

"I'd love to," Barney replied. "But there were too many witnesses and not all of our help is as kindhearted as Larkin. Word will get out if I do that and then both of us will be out of a job."

"Understood. I guess it would have helped if she'd allowed me to take the blame."

"You have no idea" came the heartfelt comment. "But Larkin's just not made that way."

"A rare quality."

"Yes, it is." Barney lifted an eyebrow. "If there's anything else you or anyone in your family needs…?"

"I'll let you know."

The two men shook hands and Barney disappeared in the direction of the kitchen, no doubt to fire Larkin. Rafe frowned. Maybe he should intercede. Or better yet, maybe he could arrange for a new job. Dantes was a big firm with plenty of branches. Surely he could find an opening for her somewhere. Hell, he was president of Dantes Courier Service. He could invent a job if one didn't already exist. The thought of Larkin's sunny smile welcoming him to work each day struck him as appealing in the extreme.

Draco approached. "So? Have you given my idea any thought?"

Rafe stared blankly. "What idea?"

"Weren't you listening to me?"

"It usually works best if I don't. Most of the time your suggestions only lead one place."

Draco grinned. "Trouble?"

"Oh, yeah."

"Well, this one won't. All you have to do is find your Inferno bride and everyone will leave you alone."

Rafe shook his head. "Apparently you're not great at listening, either. After that disaster of a marriage to Leigh, I'm never going to marry again."

"Who said anything about marriage?"

Rafe narrowed his eyes. "Explain."

"You know, for such a smart, analytical-type guy, there are times when you can be amazingly obtuse." Draco spoke slowly and distinctly. "Find a woman. Claim it's The Inferno. Maintain the illusion for a few months. Act the part of two people crazy in love."

Rafe's mouth twisted. "I don't do crazy in love."

"If you want everyone to leave you alone, you will. After a short engagement, have her dump you. Make it worth her while to go a long way away and stay there."

"You've come up with some boneheaded ideas in your time. But this one has to be the most ludicrous—" Rafe broke off and turned to stare in the direction of the kitchen. "Huh."

Draco chuckled. "You were saying?"

"I think I have an idea."

"You're welcome."

Rafe shot his brother a warning look. "If you say one word about this to anyone—"

"Are you kidding? Nonna and Primo would kill me, not to mention our parents."

"You?"

Draco stabbed his finger against Rafe's chest. "They wouldn't believe for one minute you were clever enough to come up with a plan like this."

"I'm not sure *clever* is the right word. Conniving, maybe?"

"Diabolically brilliant."

"Right. Keep telling yourself that. Maybe one of us will believe you. In the meantime, I have an Inferno bride to win."

Rafe headed for the kitchen. He arrived just in time to see Larkin refusing the wad of money Barney was attempting to press into her hand. "I'll be fine, Mr. Barney."

"You know you need it for rent." He stuffed the cash into the pocket of her vest and gave her a hug. "We're going to miss you, kiddo."

One by one the waitstaff followed suit. Then Larkin turned toward the exit and Rafe caught the glitter of tears swimming in her eyes. For some reason a fierce, protective wave swept through him.

"Larkin," he said. "If I could speak to you for a minute."

Her head jerked around, surprise registering in her gaze. "Certainly, Mr. Dante."

Instead of exiting into the reception area, he escorted her through the door leading to the hallway. "Is there a problem?" she asked. "I hope you don't blame Mr. Barney for my mistake. He did fire me, if that helps."

Ouch. "It's nothing like that," he reassured. "I wanted to speak to you in private."

Leading the way to the wing of private offices, he reached a set of double doors with a discreet gold plaque that read "Rafaelo Dante, President, Dantes Courier Service." He keyed the remote control fob in his pocket and the doors snicked open. Gesturing her into the darkened interior, he touched a button on a panel near the door. Soft lights brightened the sitting area section of his office, leaving the business side with its desk, credenza and chairs in darkness.

"Have a seat. Would you like anything to drink?"

She hesitated, then gave a soft laugh. "I know I'm supposed to say no, thank you. But I'd love some water."

"Coming right up."

He opened the cabinet door that concealed a small refrigerator and removed two bottles of water. After collecting a pair of glasses and dropping some ice cubes into each, he joined her on the couch. Sitting so close to her might have been a mistake. He could sense her in ways he'd rather not. The light, citrusy scent of her that somehow managed to curl around and through him. The warmth and energy of her body. The way the light caught in her hair and left her eyes in dusky blue shadow. He'd hoped the business setting would dampen his reaction to her. Instead, the solitude served only to increase his awareness.

He gathered his control around him like a cloak, forcing himself to deal with the business at hand. "I'm sorry about your job," he said, passing her the water. "Firing you seems a bit severe for a simple accident."

"I don't normally work the more exclusive accounts. This was my first time." She made a face. "And my last."

"The catering firm won't switch you over to work some of their smaller parties?"

She released a sigh. "To be honest, I doubt it. The woman in charge of those accounts isn't a fan of mine right now."

"Personality conflict?"

The question made her uncomfortable. "Not exactly."

If he was going to hire her, he needed to gather as much information about her as possible, especially if she didn't deal well with authority. "Then what, exactly?" he pressed.

"Her boyfriend was on the waitstaff, and…"

"And?"

"He hit on me," Larkin reluctantly confessed.

"Something you encouraged?"

To his surprise, she didn't take offense at the question. In fact, she laughed. "JD doesn't require encouragement. He hits on anyone remotely female. I hope Britt figures out what a sleaze he is sooner, rather than later. She could do a lot better."

Rafe sat there for a moment, nonplussed. "You're worried about your supervisor, not your job?"

"I can always get another job, even if it's washing dishes," Larkin explained matter-of-factly. "But Britt's nice...when she's not furious because JD's flirting with the help. I just got caught in the middle."

Huh. Interesting assessment. "And now?"

For the first time a hint of worry nibbled at the corners of her eyes and edged across her expression. "I'm sure it will all work out."

"I overheard Barney say something about rent."

She released a soft sigh, the sound filled with a wealth of weariness. "I'm a little behind. What he gave me for tonight's work should cover it."

"But you need another job."

She tilted her head to one side. "I don't suppose you're hiring?"

He liked her directness. No coyness. No wide-eyed, gushing pretense or any sort of sexual over- or undertones. Just a simple, frank question. "I may have a job for you," he admitted cautiously. "But I'd need to run a quick background check. Do you have any objections?"

And then he saw it. Just a flash of hesitation before she shook her head. "I don't have any objections."

"Fine." Only, it wasn't fine. Not if she were hiding

something. He couldn't handle another deceptive woman who faked innocence and then demonstrated avarice. *Refused* to deal with that sort of woman. "Full name?"

"Larkin Anne Thatcher."

She supplied her social security number and date of birth without being asked. He pulled out his cell and texted one of his brother's former security associates, Juice, with the request. He'd have gone through Luc, but there might be uncomfortable questions when he later presented Larkin as his Inferno bride. Better to keep it on the down low. In the meantime, he'd get some of the preliminary questions out of the way.

"Have you ever been arrested?" Rafe asked.

Larkin shook her head. "No, never."

"Drugs?"

A flash of indignation came and went in her open gaze before she answered in a calm, even voice. "Never. I've needed to take drug tests for various jobs in the past, including this latest one. I have no objection to taking one here and now if you want."

"Credit or bankruptcy issues?"

Indignation turned to humor. "Aside from living on a shoestring? No."

"Health issues?"

"Not a one."

"Military history?"

"I haven't served."

"Job history?"

Now she grinned. "How much time do you have?"

Rafe eyed her curiously. "That many?"

"Oh, yeah. The list is as long as it is diverse."

"Any special reason?"

She hesitated again, but he didn't pick up any hint of evasion, just thoughtfulness. "I've been searching."

"Right job, right place?"

She seemed pleased that he'd understood so quickly. "Exactly."

"I can't promise to offer that, but I might have something temporary."

For some reason she appeared relieved. "Temporary will work. In fact, I prefer it."

"Not planning on staying in San Francisco for long?" He tried to keep the question casual, but conceded that as attractive as he found her, he'd feel better about his proposition if she intended to move on a few months from now.

"I don't know. Actually, I'm looking for someone. I think he may be here."

"He." That didn't bode well for his little project. "Former lover?"

"No. Nothing like that."

He pressed. "Who are you trying to find?"

"That's not really any of your business, Mr. Dante," she said gently. "What I will tell you is that it won't have an impact on any job you might offer me."

He let it go. For now. "Fair enough."

His cell vibrated and he checked it, surprised to find that Juice had completed his preliminary check. Had to be a new record. Either that or Larkin Thatcher didn't have much history to find. The text simply said "Clean," but he'd attached an email that went into more specifics.

Rafe excused himself long enough to access his computer and scan it. Nothing unusual other than a long and varied work history. Considering she was only twenty-five, it was rather impressive.

"Still interested in offering me a job?" she asked.

It was the first time she'd betrayed any nerves, and it didn't take much thought to understand the cause. "How far behind are you on your rent?"

She tapped her pocket. "As I said, this will catch me up."

"But it won't leave you anything to spare for utilities or food, will it?"

She lifted a narrow shoulder in a wordless shrug that spoke volumes.

He took a moment to consider his options. Not that he had many. Either he made the offer and put Draco's plan into action, or he forgot the entire idea. He could still find a position for Larkin. In fact, there was no question that he'd do precisely that. The question was... Which job?

If it weren't for the Parade of Brides, it would have been an easy question to answer. But the unpleasant truth was, he just didn't know how much more of his family's interference he could handle. It had gotten to the point where it wasn't interfering just with his private life, but with his business life, as well. These days, he couldn't turn around without running into one of his many relatives. And for some reason, they were always accompanied by a young, single woman.

He needed it to stop...and soon.

Before he could decide, Larkin stood. "Mr. Dante, you seem hesitant." She offered an easy smile. "Why don't I make it easy for you? I really appreciate your concern, but this isn't the first time money's been tight.

I'm sort of like a cat. One way or another, I always land on my feet."

"Sit down, Larkin." He softened the demand with a smile. "My hesitation isn't whether or not I have a job available for you. It's which job to offer."

She blinked at that. "Oh. Well…I can handle most general office positions, if that helps. Receptionist. File clerk. Secretary or assistant."

"What about the position of my fiancée?" He folded his arms across his chest and lifted an eyebrow. "Do you think you could handle that?"

Two

For a split second Larkin couldn't breathe. It was as though every thought and emotion winked off.

"Excuse me?" she finally said.

"Yeah, I know." He thrust his hand through his hair, turning order into disorder. For some reason, it only added to his overall appeal. Before, he'd seemed a bit too perfect and remote. Now he looked wholly masculine, strong and authoritative with a disturbing edginess that most women found irresistible. "It sounds crazy. But actually it's fairly simple and straightforward."

Larkin didn't bother to argue. Nothing about this man was the least simple or straightforward. Not the fact that he was a rich and powerful man. Not his connection to one of San Francisco's leading families, the Dantes. Not his stunning good looks or the intense passion he kept so carefully hidden from those around him. How did the scandal sheets refer to him? Oh, right. The lone wolf who was also, ironically, the "prettiest" of the male Dantes.

True on both counts.

To her eternal regret, it was also true that he was still so madly in love with his late wife that he never wanted to marry again. Too bad he'd married a woman who, while as beautiful to look at as the man pacing in front of her, possessed a single imperative—to take and use whatever she wanted in life, regardless of the cost or harm it might do to others.

"I overheard you, you know," she warned. "I heard you tell your brother you never wanted to marry again. Not after Leigh."

"Leigh was my late wife," he explained. "And you're right. I don't ever want to marry again. But I do need a fiancée. A temporary fiancée."

She wasn't usually so slow on the uptake. Even so, none of this made the least bit of sense to her. "Temporary," she repeated.

He took the chair across from her and leaned forward, resting his forearms on his knees. Having him so close only made it more difficult to think straight. She didn't understand it. Of all the men in San Francisco, he should have been the very last she'd find attractive. And yet, every one of her senses had gone screaming onto high alert the instant he'd turned those brilliant jade-green eyes in her direction.

"You'd have to understand my family to fully appreciate my situation," he said.

Larkin fought to keep her mouth shut. How many times had she gotten herself into an awkward predicament because of her particular brand of frankness? More times than she could count. Despite her determination, a few stray words slipped out. "Your family does have a knack for hitting the gossip magazines."

To her surprise, he looked relieved. "Then you've read about The Inferno?"

"Yes." Excellent. That was short and sweet, and yet truthful. Added bonus…he seemed pleased with her answer.

"Then I don't have to explain what it is or that my family—most of them, anyway—believe implicitly in its existence."

Something in his manner and delivery clued her in to his opinion of the matter. "But you don't?"

A wickedly attractive smile touched his mouth. "Have I shocked you?"

"A little," Larkin admitted. She couldn't come up with a tactful way to ask her next question, so she tossed it out, not sure if it would land with all the explosive power of a grenade or turn out to be a dud. "What about your wife?"

"Never. We never experienced The Inferno. Nor would I have ever wanted to. Not with her."

Larkin's mouth dropped open. "Wait a minute—"

He cut in with cold deliberation. "Let me make this easy for you. My wife and I were about to divorce when she died. Any version of The Inferno we might have shared was the more literal, hellish kind, not this fairy tale my family's dreamed up."

"When you say you never want to marry again…" she probed delicately.

"It's because I have no intention of ever experiencing that particular level of hell again."

"Okay, I understand that." Considering how well she'd

known Leigh, she didn't blame the poor man. "But that doesn't explain your need for a temporary fiancée."

"My family recently discovered that Leigh and I never felt The Inferno toward each other."

Larkin was quick on the uptake. "And now they're trying to find the woman who will."

"Exactly. It's interfering with every aspect of my life. And since they won't stop until she's found, I've decided to take care of that for them."

His smile broadened. It would have turned his stunning good looks into something beyond spectacular if it hadn't been for the coldness in his green eyes. The smile stopped there, revealing a wintry barrenness that tugged at Larkin's heart. She'd always had a soft spot for strays and underdogs. In fact, some day she hoped to work full-time for an animal rescue organization. She suspected that for all his wealth and position, and despite the loving support of his large family, Rafe Dante qualified as both a stray and an underdog, which put her heart at serious risk.

"You want to pretend that you've experienced this Inferno with me?" she clarified.

"In a nutshell, yes. I want all of my relatives to believe it, too. We'll become engaged, and then a few months from now, you'll decide that you can't marry me. I'm sure I'll give you ample reasons for calling off our engagement. You dump me and disappear. I, of course, will be heartbroken to have found and lost my Inferno bride. Naturally, my family will be sympathetic and won't dare throw any more women my way." He smiled in satisfaction. "End of problem."

"And why won't your family throw more women your way?"

"How can they, since you were my one true soul mate?" he pointed out with ruthless logic. "They can't have it both ways. Either you were my once-in-a-lifetime Inferno match or The Inferno isn't real. Somehow I suspect that rather than admit that the family legend doesn't exist, they'll decide that my one shot at Inferno happiness decided to dump me. I'll then have no other choice but to continue my poor, lonely, miserable existence never having found matrimonial bliss. A tragedy, to be sure, but I'll do my best to survive it."

Larkin shook her head in mock admiration. "A trouper to the end."

"I try."

She released her breath in a gusty sigh. "Mr. Dante—"

"Rafe."

"Rafe. There's something you should know about me. A couple of things, actually. First, I'm not a very good liar."

She opened her mouth to explain the second reason, one that would not just put a nail in the coffin of his job offer, but bury that coffin six feet down. He didn't give her the opportunity, cutting her off with calm determination.

"I noticed that about you earlier. I admire your honesty. In my opinion, it's the perfect way to convince my relatives that we're in the throes of The Inferno."

Her thoughts scattered like leaves before a brisk fall wind. "Excuse me?"

"We're going to try a little experiment. If it doesn't work, we'll forget my plan and I'll find someone else. I'll still offer you a job, just a more conventional one." He eyed her with predatory intent. "But if my experiment works, you agree to my plan."

"Experiment?" she asked uneasily. "What sort of experiment?"

"First, I want to set up a few parameters."

"Parameters."

How could Leigh ever have hoped to control a man like this? Through sex, of course. But somehow Larkin suspected that would work for only so long and solely within the confines of the bedroom. She didn't need more than five minutes in Rafe's company to figure out that much about him.

"I'm a businessman, first and foremost. Before we move forward, I want to make sure we have a clear meeting of the minds."

Larkin struggled not to smile. "Why don't you explain your parameters and then we'll see what sort of agreement we can come to."

"First, I need to make it clear that this is a temporary relationship. When either of us is ready to put an end to it, it ends."

She gave it a moment's consideration before shrugging. "I suppose that's no different than a real engagement."

"Which is my next point. You don't want to lie. I don't want you to lie. So if we become engaged, from that moment forward it *is* real. The only difference will be that at the end of the engagement—and our engagement will end—I'll see to it that you receive fair compensation for your time."

"The engagement will be real, but we preplan the ending." She lifted an eyebrow. "I swear I'm not being deliberately obtuse, but I don't see how those two are mutually compatible."

He hesitated, a painful emotion rippling behind his icy restraint. "I don't do relationships well," he confessed, "or so I've been told. I suspect you'll discover that for yourself soon enough and be only too happy to end our involvement. Until then, it will be the same as any other engagement, right down to a ring on your finger and making plans for an eventual wedding day." His mouth twisted. "I'd rather it be a far distant eventual wedding day that doesn't involve actual dates and deposits."

Her sense of humor bubbled to the surface. "We don't want to rush into anything. Not after your first experience. Better to have a long engagement and make sure."

"See? You already have your lines down pat."

A matching humor lit his face and even crept into his eyes. If she hadn't been sitting, she didn't doubt for a moment that her knees would have given out. He had to be one of the most stunning men she'd ever met. It didn't seem fair to have all of that rugged beauty given to one man. From high, arching cheekbones to squared chin to a mouth perfectly shaped for kissing, it didn't matter where she looked, it was all gorgeous. Even his hair was perfect, the deep brown offset by streaks of sunlit gold. But it was his eyes that fascinated her the most, the color a sharp jade-green that seemed to darken like a shadow-draped forest depending on his mood.

"So how do we handle this?" she finally managed to ask. "Assuming I agree to your plan."

He frowned, and even that was appealing. "It may not work," he admitted. "I think we can figure that out easily enough. But you'll have to trust me."

She took a deep breath and jumped in with both feet. "Okay. What do you have in mind?" she asked.

"A simple test. If we don't pass, we scrap the idea and I'll find you a job within the organization. If it does work, we take the next step forward."

"What sort of test?" she asked warily.

"Just this."

He stood and circled the coffee table between them. Reaching her side, he held out his hand. She stood as well and took the hand he offered. Her fingers slipped across his palm. Instantly, heat exploded between them, a stunning flash that seemed to burrow into flesh and bone with unbelievable swiftness. It didn't hurt. Not precisely. It…melded. With a gasp of disbelief, Larkin yanked free of his touch.

"What did you just do?" they asked in unison.

Rafe took a step back and eyed her with sharp suspicion. "You felt that, too?"

"Of course." She rubbed her palm against her slacks, trying to make the sensation go away. Not that it worked. "What was it?"

"I have no idea."

She lifted her hand and stared at the palm. There weren't any marks, though based on the explosion of heat she'd experienced, it should still be smoking. "That wasn't…" She cleared her throat. "That couldn't have been…"

She could see the emphatic denial building in his expression. At the last instant he hesitated, an almost calculating glitter dawning in his eyes. "The Inferno?" he murmured. "What the hell. Why not?"

She stared at him, stunned. "You're joking, right?" she asked.

"I don't personally believe in it, no. But I've heard

The Inferno described as something along the lines of what we just felt."

"That was your test?" she demanded. "To see if we felt The Inferno when we touched?"

"No. Actually, I was going to kiss you."

She fell back another step, shocked as much by the statement as by the calm businesslike way he delivered it. "Why?"

"There's no point in becoming engaged if you aren't physically attracted to me," he explained. "My family would pick up on that in no time."

Larkin gazed down at her hand and scratched her thumbnail across the faint throb centered in the middle of her palm. "So whatever just happened when we touched is just an odd coincidence?"

"I sure as hell hope so."

Huh. She lifted her head and looked at him. Their gazes clashed and the heat centered in her palm spread deeper. Hotter. Swept through her with each beat of her heart. A dangerous curiosity filled her and words tumbled from her mouth, words she'd never planned to speak. But somehow they popped out, hovering in the air between them.

"I believe you were going to kiss me," she prompted.

He approached in two swift strides. She knew what he planned, could see the intent in the hard lines of his body and determined planes of his face. He gave her ample opportunity to escape. But somehow she couldn't force herself to take the easy way out. Another personality quirk…or flaw, depending on the circumstances. Instead, she held perfectly still and allowed him to pull her into his arms.

This was wrong on so many levels. Wrong because

of Leigh. Wrong because it wasn't real. Wrong because even while she wanted to deny it, desire built within her like a tide building before a storm. Waves of it crashed over and through her until she couldn't think straight and common sense fled. He hadn't even kissed her yet, and already she could feel the helpless give of her surrender.

He leaned in and she waited breathlessly for his kiss, a kiss that didn't come. "It feels real, doesn't it?" The words washed over her like a balmy breeze, stirring the hair at her temples. "Maybe it is real. Maybe this engagement isn't such a bad idea. We can figure out what all this means."

"All what?" she managed to ask.

"All this…"

The kiss when it came hit with all the force of a hurricane. She didn't doubt he meant to keep it light and gentle. A tentative sampling. An initial probing. Instead, the instant he touched her, hunger slammed through her and she arched against him, winding her arms around his neck and hanging on for dear life.

It didn't surprise her in the least to discover he kissed even better than he looked. With a mouth like that, how could he not? His lips slanted across hers, hard enough to betray the edginess of his control, and yet with a passionate tenderness that had her parting for him and allowing him to sample her more fully.

All the while, he molded her against his body, the taut, masculine planes a delicious contrast to her slighter, more rounded curves. His hands swept down her spine to the base. There he hesitated before cupping her backside and fitting her more tightly between his legs. She gasped at the sheer physicality of the sensation.

The scent and taste of him filled her and she shuddered, overwhelmed by sensations she'd never fully realized or explored before.

How was it possible that a simple kiss—or even a not-so-simple kiss—could have such a profound effect on her? She'd kissed any number of men. Had contemplated sleeping with a few of them. Had allowed them to touch her and had satisfied her curiosity by touching them in return. But they'd never affected her the way Rafe Dante did with just a single kiss.

Is this how it had been for Leigh?

The stray thought brought Larkin to her senses with painful swiftness. With an inarticulate murmur, she yanked free of Rafe's arms and put half the distance of the room between them. Unable to help herself, she lifted trembling fingers to her lips. They were full and damp from his kisses and seemed to pulse in tempo with the odd beat centered in her palm. She stared at Rafe. If it hadn't been for the rapid give and take of his breath, she'd have believed him unaffected.

"I think we can safely say that we're attracted to one another," she informed him.

"Hell, yes."

His voice sounded rougher than normal, low and edged with an emotion that was reflected in his eyes like green fire. He crossed to the wet bar and removed the stopper on a cut-glass decanter. Splashing some of the amber liquid into a tumbler, he glanced over his shoulder and raised an eyebrow.

"Want some?"

She shook her head. She didn't dare. She'd always been a frank person. Alcohol tended to remove all caution and strip her of the ability to control her tongue.

There was no telling what she'd say if she had a drink right now.

He downed the liquor in a single swallow, then turned to face her. "That was…unexpected."

"Blame it on The Inferno," she attempted to joke.

"Oh, I intend to."

She stared at him, not quite certain of his mood. She couldn't tell if he was annoyed by what had happened, or relieved. Or maybe he just didn't give a damn. Perhaps a little of all three. Annoyed because their reaction to one another was a complication and he'd been as close to losing control of the situation as she had. Possibly even more so, since she'd been the one to finally end their embrace. Relieved because that same attraction would allow him to execute his plan. As for not giving a damn…

No. She was wrong about that. He might hide the fact he cared, bury it deep, but she was willing to bet the Dante passion ran hotter in him than all the others.

She had a decision to make. She could turn around and walk out of the room and never return. She could tell him who she was and what she wanted. Or she could go along with his plan and see how matters developed. Every instinct warned her to get out while the going was good, or at the very least explain why this insane idea of his would never work. Maybe she'd have made the smart choice, the far less dangerous choice…if only he hadn't kissed her.

"I gather we just became engaged?" she asked lightly.

He hesitated. "Something like that."

"And will your family believe that you've gone from

a total nonbeliever to an Inferno fanatic after one simple kiss?"

"Considering it happened just that way with each and every one of the Dante men in my family, yes."

"None of them believed?"

Rafe shrugged. "My cousin Marco did. He's probably the most romantic of all the Dantes."

"But not the rest of you."

"It isn't logical," he stated simply. "It's far-fetched at best and bordering on ludicrous when you look at it from a serious, rational point of view."

"I think it's sort of sweet."

His mouth curved upward. "Most women do."

A distinct awkwardness settled over her. "So, what now?"

"Now I take you home. First thing in the morning we'll get together and plan our strategy."

"Strategy." She couldn't help but laugh. "Let me guess. You're one of those organized, I-need-to-mold-the-world types, aren't you?"

"Somebody has to." He released a sigh and returned his glass to the wet bar. "Let me guess. You're one of those seat-of-the-pants, take-life-as-it-happens types, aren't you?"

She wrinkled her nose. "This might be a case of opposites attract."

"Don't worry. I'll organize everything and you just go with the flow."

Her amusement grew. "Control is an illusion, you know."

He appeared every bit as amused. "Whatever you say. How about if I control us out of here and you let it happen?"

"I think I can handle that."

Larkin gathered up her purse and circled the couch toward the door. Rafe joined her, his hand coming to rest on the base of her spine in a gesture that should have been casual. Instead, it was as though he'd given her another jolt of electricity. She stumbled and her purse dropped from her hand. Turning, she could only stare helplessly at him.

"Larkin." Her name escaped on a groan and then he pulled her into his arms again.

How could something so wrong feel so right? She had no business making love to Leigh's husband. None. But she couldn't seem to resist, any more than she'd resisted his bizarre proposal. When he touched her, it all made perfect sense. Probably because she couldn't think straight. All she could do was feel.

He pulled her close, so close she could hear the thunder of his heart and the rapid give and take of his breath. Or maybe she wasn't hearing his, but her own. He covered her face with kisses, swift and hungry, before finding her mouth and sinking inward. Oh, yes. *This*. This was what she craved. What she needed as desperately as sweet, life-sustaining air. Where before he'd controlled the kiss, now she took charge, giving him everything she possessed.

She heard his voice. Heard raw, guttural words. Words of want and need. And then her world tipped upside down as he swung her into his arms and carried her back to the couch. She hit the cushions with a soft bounce before he came down on top of her, his body pressing her deeper into the silken material.

"We just met," she managed to gasp.

He shifted against her, fitting them one to the other like two pieces of a puzzle. "Sometimes it's like that."

"When? With who?"

"Now. With us."

None of this made any sense. Rafe was supposed to be the rational one. The one in control. And yet, whatever had ignited between them had swept him away as completely as it had her. She wanted him with a bone-deep need that grew with each passing moment.

He made short work of the vest of her uniform, slipping buttons from their holes with a speed and efficiency that took her breath away. Parting the edges, he tackled her blouse next, button after button, before yanking the crisp black cotton from her slacks and shoving it half off her shoulders.

Rafe paused then, his hand hovering over the delicate bones of her shoulder, his dark skin tones at odds with her pale complexion. "My God," he whispered. "You're breathtaking."

No one had ever described her that way before. But seeing his stunned expression—seeing herself through his eyes—she felt beautiful. He traced the edges of her bra, a simple, durable black cotton, sculpting the curves of her breasts. She could feel her nipples peaking through the material. An intense heat shot through her, echoed in the throbbing of her palm and sinking deep into her feminine core.

"Rafe…"

It was her turn to touch. Her turn to explore. She cupped his face and gave in to the irresistible compulsion to trail her fingertips over those amazing planes and angles. To revel in the sheer masculine beauty of him. When she'd first seen him in the reception area, he'd appeared so self-contained, so remote. Never in a million years would she have imagined herself in this position. Who knew if the opportunity would ever present itself again? When they regained their sanity she wouldn't be the least surprised if he instituted a "no touching" rule, especially when touching was so incredibly, gloriously dangerous.

Unable to resist, she wove her fingers into his hair to anchor his head and then rose to seal his mouth with hers. He tasted beyond delicious and she couldn't get enough of him. Not his touch. Not his kisses. Not the press and drag of his body over hers.

Her hands darted to his shirt and she tugged at his tie, managing after a small struggle to rip it free from its anchor. Next she tackled the buttons that blocked her access to the rich expanse of flesh and muscle she yearned to caress. He groaned against her mouth, levering himself upward to give her better access. Her hands hovered over his belt buckle and the bulge that lay beneath.

And that's when they heard it.

"Rafaelo?" A deep, gruff voice came from the far side of the office door, accompanied by a brisk knock. "Where are you, boy?"

Rafe swore beneath his breath. Vaulting off Larkin, he helped her to her feet. "Just a minute," he called.

She stood, swaying in place, dizzy from the swift transition from passion to normalcy. Or the attempt at normalcy. "Who's there?" she whispered.

"My grandfather Primo."

Her eyes widened in alarm and her hands shot to the buttons of her blouse at the same time his did. Fingers clashed and fumbled. She could hear the murmur of voices coming from the far side of the door. Not just his grandfather, she realized. A woman's voice, too.

"Nonna," Rafe confirmed grimly. He let her finish working on straightening her clothing while he tackled the mess she'd made of his. "My grandmother."

"Do not be ridiculous" came Primo's rumbling bass. "This is an office. It is not as though he is in a meeting, not this late. Why should I stand on the doorstep like a beggar?"

"Because he has not invited you in."

"Then I will invite myself in" was the indignant retort.

With that, he turned the knob and stepped into the room. Rafe must have anticipated his grandfather's intent because he stepped in front of her, shielding her from his grandparents' eyes while she finished buttoning her blouse and vest. Not that it really helped, considering that his shirt was open and hanging out of his trousers.

"I have been looking for you, Rafaelo," Primo announced. "I have someone I wish you to meet."

Rafe sighed as he finished making repairs to his clothes. "I don't doubt it. But it's no longer necessary."

Primo planted his fists on his waist. "Of course it is necessary. You must meet as many women as possible. How else will you find your Inferno soul mate?"

Larkin peeked out from behind Rafe's broad shoulders and saw Nonna's eyes widen with a combination of surprise and dawning comprehension. "And who is this?" she asked.

Snatching a deep breath, Larkin skirted Rafe and stepped into the light, wincing at their stunned expressions. She didn't doubt for a single moment that she looked as if she'd been doing precisely what she *had* been doing. Guaranteed her mouth was bare of lipstick and swollen a telltale rosy-red from Rafe's impassioned kisses. And Rafe didn't look much better, not when she compared his businesslike appearance earlier to his current rough and rumpled manifestation. And guaranteed one or both of his grandparents had caught that…and more.

Primo's gaze swept to a point midway down the line of buttons holding her vest closed and his fierce golden eyes narrowed. Either she hadn't buttoned them correctly or she'd skipped one. Maybe more than one.

Nonna, on the other hand, hovered between shock and amusement at whatever hairstyle Rafe had left in his wake when he'd plowed his fingers through the tidy little knot Larkin had fashioned at the start of her evening. She could feel part of it dangling over her left ear, while stray wisps were plastered to the right side of her face and neck.

"Hello." She gave them a wide, brilliant smile. "I'm Larkin Thatcher."

"You are with the catering service?" Primo asked, giving her clothing another assessing look.

"Not any longer. They fired me."

Apparently they didn't know what to say to that, so she hurried to breach the silence. She couldn't help it. It was another minor personality flaw. Leigh had always called it babbling, which was a fair if somewhat blunt assessment.

"It was my own fault. I dropped a tray of drinks and that's a big no-no. The good news is that if I hadn't, I wouldn't have met Rafe and we wouldn't have gotten to know each other. I don't think we've finished discussing it yet. But we kind of got engaged."

Three

"Engaged," Primo and Nonna repeated in unison. Primo sounded outraged, Nonna shocked.

"Sort of." Larkin shot Rafe an apprehensive glance, as though aware that she'd jumped the gun a bit. "Or maybe not anymore. To be honest, I'm not quite sure what we are because we… Well, to be honest…" Her hands fluttered over her hair and the mismatched buttons of her vest. "That is to say, we got distracted."

Beside her, Rafe groaned. "Hell."

Her gaze darted from him back to his grandparents. They didn't seem pleased with his response. "Actually, it was rather heavenly," she hastened to reassure them.

Rafe took charge of the situation. "Let's just say that the minute we touched, things got out of hand. Or in hand, depending on your viewpoint."

"The Inferno?" Primo demanded. "It has finally happened?"

Rafe hesitated. He couldn't help the hint of resistance that undoubtedly shadowed his expression. He'd experienced something when he and Larkin had first touched. But The Inferno? A connection that would last a lifetime? Sorry. Still not buying it. "Time will tell," he limited himself to saying.

To his surprise, the reluctance implicit in his tone and attitude sold the idea with impressive ease, and he couldn't help but suspect that a more overt declaration would have had the opposite effect, giving his grandparents pause in the face of such a dramatic turnaround from his previous attitude.

He spared a swift glance in Larkin's direction and winced. Hell. Primo and Nonna weren't the only ones who'd picked up on his reluctance. So had Larkin. But wasn't that what they'd agreed to? Wasn't that why he'd hired her? To be his *temporary* fiancée? That's all it was for both of them. A transient relationship that would be nice while it lasted and, when it ended, give them both what they wanted. He'd be left the hell alone and she'd receive a nice bump to her bank account.

So why did she react as though she'd lost out on a special treat? Why that wistful look of longing, a deeply feminine look, one that spoke of childhood dreams and magical wishes? A look that caused him to respond on some visceral, wholly masculine level, that seemed to compel him to give her her heart's desire. Not that he could, even if he wanted to. He'd been up front with her from the start. He could never fulfill her deepest desires because he was incapable of fulfilling any woman's. The sooner Larkin accepted that, the better.

"I need to take Larkin home," he informed his grandparents. "We can discuss The Inferno once I've had time to explain it to my—" He broke off with a small smile. "My fiancée."

Primo instantly began to protest, but Nonna shushed him. "We will call tomorrow and arrange a proper meeting with Larkin," she said. "I am sure your parents would also like to meet her, yes?"

"I think we should take this slowly." Rafe stalled. "Now, if you'll excuse us?"

"First you will promise to drop her off and then leave. No more of what we interrupted here," Primo demanded. "Otherwise, you will find yourself with a wife instead of a fiancée, just like Luciano."

Rafe grimaced. Damn it. He knew that look, as well as the tone. And the reminder about his brother and Téa was a timely one. Hadn't the two of them been forced to the altar within twenty-four hours of being caught in the act? "Yes, Primo. I promise. I'll drop her off in the same condition in which I found her."

"*Era troppo poco e troppo tardi*. Too late for that, I suspect. But there will be no more..." He waved his hand to indicate Larkin's uniform. "No more button mishaps until there is a ring on her finger."

"I understand."

"And agree?" Primo shot back.

Rafe sighed. He was going to regret getting boxed in like this. "Yes. *Accosento*."

"Very well. Take her home. Your grandmother will call in the morning to arrange a convenient time for your Larkin to meet the family."

Larkin stepped forward and held out her hand to Primo. "It was a pleasure meeting you."

"I do not shake hands with beautiful women," Primo informed her. He enfolded her in a bear hug, swamping her diminutive form, and planted a smacking kiss on each of her cheeks.

Larkin then turned to Nonna and the two women embraced. To Rafe's concern, he caught the glint of tears in Larkin's eyes and realized that she'd reached her breaking point. The events of the day must have caught up with her. First the stress of working a high-profile client, then losing her job, his proposition, followed by what had almost happened on the couch. It all added up to...too much, too fast.

He didn't waste any time. Sweeping up her belongs in one hand and Larkin in the other, he ushered everyone out of the office. Not giving his grandparents time for any further questions, he wished them good-night and urged Larkin toward the elevators. They made the ride to the subterranean parking garage in silence. But as soon as they were enclosed in his car, she swiveled in her seat to face him.

"What did your grandparents mean about Luciano? About his ending up with a wife instead of a fiancée?"

He winced at the memory. "They were caught in the act, if you know what I mean."

Larkin's eyes widened in horror. "By Primo and Nonna?" she asked faintly.

"By Téa's grandmother and three sisters. Madam is Nonna's closest friend," he explained. "When Primo heard what had happened, he stepped in and insisted Luc do the right thing."

"Meaning...marriage?"

Her voice had risen ever so slightly, and Rafe flashed her a look of concern. "It all worked out. They were in love. They even claim to have experienced The Inferno the first time they touched." He hadn't succeeded in reassuring her and gave it another try. "My marriage may not have been a shining example of happily-ever-after, but Luc and Téa seem genuinely in love. Hell, for all I know, their marriage might last as long as my grandparents'."

She fell silent for a moment, which he took as a bad sign. If there was one thing he'd learned about Larkin, she didn't do silence. Sure enough, she leaped into speech. "I don't think I can do this," she announced in a rush. "I don't like deceiving people, especially people as kind as your grandparents. They take marriage and this Inferno stuff seriously."

He started the car and pulled out of his assigned parking space before replying. "That's what makes this so interesting. We're not deceiving anyone." He paused at the exit and waited for Larkin to relay her address before pulling onto the one-way street. "Admit it. We felt something when we touched."

The overhead streetlight filled the car with a flash of soft amber, giving him a glimpse of her unhappy profile. She stared down at her palm, rubbing at the center in a manner he'd seen countless times before by each and every one of his Inferno-bitten relatives.

The sight filled him with foreboding. As far as he knew, no one outside the family was aware of that intimate little gesture, one that his relatives claimed to be a side effect of that first, burning touch between Inferno soul mates. God forbid he ever felt that tantalizing itch. His palm might throb. It might prickle. That didn't mean it itched or that he'd find himself rubbing it.

"Okay, so I felt something," she murmured. "But that

doesn't mean it's this family Inferno thing you have going, does it?"

"Absolutely not," Rafe stated adamantly. Though who he was so determined to convince, himself or Larkin, he couldn't say. "The point is… We can't rule out the possibility that it's The Inferno. Not yet. Until we do, that's what we're going to assume it is and that's what we're going to tell my family."

"And they'll believe it?" He could hear the doubt in her voice.

"Yes. Implicitly."

"But *you* still don't."

"I have no idea," he lied without hesitation. "It could be The Inferno. Or it could have been static electricity. Or just a weird coincidence. But telling my family that we think it might be The Inferno won't be a lie. And until we discover otherwise, we go forward with our plan."

"Your plan."

He drew to a stop at a red light and looked at her. She sat buried in shadow, her pale hair and skin cutting through the darkness while her eyes gleamed with some secret emotion. He didn't know this woman, not really. Granted, he had a mound of facts and figures, courtesy of Juice. But he hadn't yet uncovered the depth and scope of the person those dry facts and figures described. Just in the short time he'd spent with her, he'd gained an unassailable certainty that he'd find those depths to be deep and layered, the scope long-ranging and intriguing.

And he couldn't wait to start the process.

The light changed and he pulled forward. "It started

out as my plan. But as soon as you told my grandparents that you were my fiancée, it became *our* plan."

"But it's a lie."

"First thing Monday I plan on putting a ring on your finger. Will it still feel like a lie when that happens?"

He heard her sharp inhalation. "A ring?"

"Of course. It's expected." He spared her a flashing grin. "In case you weren't aware, we Dantes specialize in rings, particularly engagement rings."

A hint of a smile overrode her apprehension. "I think I may have heard that about you."

"When our engagement ends, you can keep the ring as part of your compensation package."

"When," she repeated.

"It won't last, Larkin," he warned. "Whatever we felt tonight is simple desire. And simple desire disappears, given time."

"That's a rather cynical viewpoint." She made the comment in a neutral tone of voice, but he could hear the tart edge to it.

"I'm a cynical sort of guy. Blame it on the fact that I've been there, done that."

"Maybe you were doing it with the wrong woman."

"No question about that."

"Maybe with the right woman—"

"You, for instance?" He pulled to the curb in front of an aging apartment building and threw the car into Park. "Is that what you're hoping, Larkin?"

"No, of course not," she instantly denied. "I just thought…"

He wasn't paying her to think. He almost said the bitter words aloud, biting them back at the last instant. He wasn't normally an unkind person and she didn't deserve having him dump the remnants of his marital history on her, even if the subject of Leigh brought out the worst in him.

Nor would it pay to alienate her. Not now that he'd introduced her to his grandparents. If she chose to pack up and disappear into the night... He hesitated. Would it make any difference? Would his family believe he'd found his Inferno match and lost her, all in one night? Or would they think he'd concocted the story...or worse, that it hadn't been The Inferno that he'd experienced, but a nasty case of lust?

No, better to stick to the plan. Better to allow his family to come to the conclusion over the next few months that he'd experienced The Inferno. Then Larkin could dump him and his family would finally, *finally* leave him alone to get on with his life. Until then, he would do whatever it took so that his Inferno bride-to-be stuck to the game plan.

"What are you thinking?" Her soft voice broke the silence.

"Tomorrow is Saturday. Since you've been fired from your job, I assume you have the day off?"

She hesitated. "I really should be looking for a new job."

"You have a new job," he reminded her. "You're working for me now, remember?"

"A real job," she clarified.

Didn't she get it? "This is a real job and it's one that's going to take up every minute of your time, starting tomorrow."

A dingy glow from the windows of Larkin's apartment building illuminated her face, highlighting her apprehension. "What happens tomorrow?"

"I formally introduce you to some more of my family."

"Rafe…" She shook her head. "Seriously. I can't do this."

He reached out and took her hand in his. The tingling throb surged to life, intensifying the instant their palms came into contact. "This is real. All I'm asking you to do is help me figure out what it is. If my family is right and it's The Inferno, then we'll decide how to deal with it."

"And if it's not?"

He shrugged. "No harm done. Our mistake. We go our separate ways. You'll be compensated for the time I've taken away from your search for your mystery man. And I have the added benefit of being left the hell alone."

"Is that what you really want?" He could see her concern deepen. "Is that what she did to you? She turned you into the Lone Wolf the scandal sheets call you?"

"It's who I am. It's what I want." He refused to admit that Leigh had played any part in his current needs. She didn't have that sort of power over him. Not anymore. "And it's what I intend to get."

Larkin gave it another moment's thought and then nodded. "Okay, I'll do it, if only to see if I can mitigate some of the damage done by your late wife." He opened his mouth to argue, but she plowed onward. "But it's just until we know for certain whether or not it's The Inferno."

If the only way she'd agree to his plan was by turning it into some sort of "good deed," he supposed he could live with that. And who knew? Maybe it would work. Stranger things had happened. "Fair enough." He exited the car and circled around to the passenger side. "I'll see you in."

"That's not necessary."

He waited while she climbed the steps of the front stoop and unlocked the door to the apartment building. "I insist."

He held the door open and a wide, gamine smile flashed across her face. "You think I'm going to run, don't you?"

"The thought did occur to me," he admitted.

Her smile faded. "You don't know me well enough to believe this, but I always honor my promises. *Always.*"

"So you're finally here, Ms. Thatcher. I'd begun to think you'd skipped." The voice issued from the open doorway of the manager's apartment. A heavyset man in his sixties stood there, regarding Larkin with a stern expression, his arms folded across his chest. "Do you have your rent money?"

"Right here, Mr. Connell." Larkin dipped her hand into her pocket and pulled out the money, handing it over.

He counted it, nodded, then jerked his head toward the stairwell. "You have ten minutes to clear out."

Larkin stiffened. "Mr. Connell, I promise to pay on time from now on. I've always—"

For a split second his sternness faded. "It's not that and you know it." Then he seemed to catch himself, retreating behind a tough shell that years of management had hardened into rocklike obduracy. "You know the rules about pets. In ten minutes I'm calling animal control. And somehow I suspect they'll have questions about your...dog."

She paled. "No problem, Mr. Connell. We'll leave immediately."

Again Rafe gained the impression that the apartment manager would have bent the rules for Larkin if it were at all possible. "San Francisco is no place to keep her, Ms. Thatcher. She needs more room."

"I'm working on it."

Rafe cleared his throat. "Perhaps a little extra rent will help clear this up. Would you consider a generous pet deposit in case of damages?" he asked.

Connell caught the underlying meaning and shot him a man-to-man look of understanding. Then he shook his head. "It isn't about the money. And it isn't about the late rent. Ms. Thatcher is as honest as the day is long." He broke off with a grimace. "At least, she is when it comes to paying her debts. The animal, on the other hand—"

"I didn't have a choice," Larkin cut in. "It was the only way to save her."

The landlord wouldn't be budged. "You'll have to save her elsewhere."

"I don't suppose you could give me until the morning?"

She hadn't even finished the question before he was shaking his head again. "I'm sorry. If it were just me, sure. But others are aware of the situation, and I could lose my job if the owners found out I hadn't acted immediately once I knew about the animal."

"I understand." Rafe wasn't the least surprised at Larkin's instant capitulation. She had to possess one of the softest hearts he'd ever known. "I wouldn't want you to lose your job. It'll just take me a minute to pack."

Rafe blew out a sigh. He was going to regret this,

mainly because it would make keeping his promise to Primo almost impossible. "I know a place you can stay," he offered.

Hope turned her eyes to an incandescent shade of blue. "Kiko, too?"

"Is that your dog's name?"

"Tukiko, but I call her Kiko."

"Yes, you can bring Kiko. The landlord won't object. Plus, he has a huge backyard that's dogproof."

"Really?" She struggled to blink back tears. "Thank you so much."

She turned to Connell and surprised him with a swift hug, one he accepted with an awkward pat on her back. Then she led the way upstairs. Rafe glanced around. The complex appeared shabby at best, with an underlying hint of desperation and decay. He suspected that it wasn't so much that the manager was lazy or didn't care, but that he fought a losing battle with limited funds and expensive repairs.

They climbed to the third floor and down a warren of hallways to a door painted an indeterminate shade of mold-green. Larkin fished her key out of her purse and unlocked the door to a tiny single-room apartment.

"Hey, Kiko," she called softly. "I'm home. And I brought a friend, so don't be afraid."

Rafe peered into the gloomy interior. "I gather she doesn't like strangers?"

"She has reason not to."

"Abused?"

"That…and more."

Rafe didn't so much hear the dog's approach, as sense it. A prickle of awareness lifted the hairs on the back of his neck. And then he caught the glint of gold as the dog's eyes reflected the light filtering in from the hallway. A low growl rumbled from the shadows.

"Kiko, stand down," Larkin said in a calm, strong voice. Instantly the dog limped forward and crouched at her feet, resting her muzzle on her front paws.

Rafe groped for a light switch, found it and flicked it on. *Son of a—* This was not good. Not good at all. "What sort of dog is she?" he asked in as neutral a voice as he could manage.

"Siberian husky." Larkin made the statement in a firm, assured voice.

"And?"

"A touch of Alaskan malamute."

"And?" He eyed the animal, certain that at least one of its parents howled rather than barked, ran in a pack and mated for life.

Larkin wrapped her arms around her waist, her chin jutting out an inch. "That's it." Firm assurance had turned to fierce protectiveness overlaid with blatant lying.

"Damn it, Larkin, that's not all she is and you know it." He studied Kiko with as much wariness and she studied him. "Where the hell did you find her?"

"My grandmother rescued Kiko from a trap when she was a juvenile. But the trap had broken her leg. Gran even managed to save the leg, though it left Kiko with a permanent limp and, despite all the love and care lavished on her, it made her permanently wary of people. But she's old now. When Gran was dying, she asked me to take care of Kiko. Since Gran raised me, I wasn't about to refuse. End of discussion."

Compassion shifted across his expression. "How long ago did your grandmother die?"

"Nine months. And she was ill for about a year before that. It's been a bit of a struggle since then to keep a job while honoring my grandmother's dying wish," she found herself admitting. It had her stiffening her spine, pride riding heavy on her weary shoulders. "I've had to move around. A lot. And take on whatever jobs have come my way. But we're managing. That doesn't mean I don't have goals I hope to accomplish. I do. For instance, I'd love to work for a rescue organization that specializes in helping animals like Kiko. I just need to take care of something first."

"Finding your mystery man."

"Yes."

"Larkin—"

She cut him off. "We don't have time for this, Rafe. Mr. Connell gave me ten minutes and we've wasted at least half that already. I still need to pack."

He let it go. For now. "Where's your suitcase?"

"In the closet."

Instead of a suitcase, he found a large battered backpack and damn little else. It took all of two minutes to scoop her clothing out of the closet, as well as the warped drawers of an ancient dresser. Larkin emerged from the bathroom with her toiletries and dumped them into a small zipped section.

"What about the kitchen?" He used the term loosely, since it consisted of a minifridge, a single cupboard containing dishware for two and a hot plate.

"It came with the apartment. It'll just take me a minute to gather up Kiko's stuff and empty out the refrigerator."

She attempted to block his view of the contents, but it was difficult to conceal nearly empty shelves, especially when it took her only a single trip to the trash can to dispose of what little it contained. After she fed Kiko a combination of kibble and raw beef, she bagged up the trash and put a leash on the animal. Rafe picked up her bag. He felt a vague sense of shock that all her worldly possessions fit in a single backpack. Hell, half a backpack, since the other half contained supplies for her dog. He couldn't have fit even a tenth of what he owned in so small a space.

"You ready?" he asked.

Larkin snatched a deep breath and gave the apartment a final check before offering a resolute nod. After that it was a simple matter to lock up the apartment, turn in the keys to Mr. Connell, dispose of the trash and exit the building. Once there, Larkin gave Kiko a few minutes to stretch her legs. Then Rafe installed the dog in the back of his car, along with the bulging backpack, while Larkin returned to her seat in the front.

"So where are we going?" she asked as he pulled away from the curb.

"My place."

She took a second to digest that. "I thought you said you knew of a place Kiko and I could stay," she said in a tight voice.

"Right. My place."

"But…"

He shot her a quick, hard look. "If it were just you, I could make any number of arrangements, even with it pushing midnight. But your dog—and I use the term loosely—is a deal breaker. There isn't a hotel or motel in the city that would allow Kiko through their doors. And I suspect the first place you tried would have the police coming at a dead run. Is that what you want?"

She sagged. "No," she whispered.

"Then our options are somewhat limited. As in, I can think of one option."

"Your place."

"My place," he confirmed.

Traffic was light and he pulled into his driveway a short twenty minutes later. He parked the car in the detached garage and led the way along a covered walkway to the back entrance. He entered the kitchen through a small utility room.

Larkin hovered on the doorstep. "Is it all right if Kiko comes in?"

"Of course. I told you she was welcome."

"Thanks."

The two walked side by side into the room and Rafe got his first good look at Kiko beneath the merciless blaze of the overhead lights. The "dog" was a beautiful animal, long and leggy, with a heavy gray-and-white coat, pronounced snout and a thick tail that showed a hint of curl to it—no doubt from the husky or malamute side of her family. Her golden gaze seemed to take in everything around her with a weariness that crept under his skin and into his heart. He suspected that she'd have given up and surrendered to her fate, if not for her human companion.

Larkin stood at her side, dwarfed by the large animal, her fingers buried in the thick ruff at Kiko's neck. She fixed Rafe with a wary gaze identical to her dog's. "Now what?"

"What does Kiko need to be comfortable?"

"Peace and quiet and space. If she feels trapped, she'll chew through just about anything."

He winced, thinking about some of the original

molding and trim work in his century-old home. "I didn't notice any damage to your apartment. I wouldn't exactly call that spacious."

"She regarded that as her de—" Larkin broke off with a cough. "Her retreat."

"Right. Tell me something, Larkin. How the hell did you smuggle her into your apartment in the first place?"

"Carefully and in the wee hours of the morning."

"I'm sure. And no one noticed her when you took her out for a walk? They never complained about her barking or howling?"

"Again, we made as many trips as possible while it was still dark. But I guess she did make noise, since we've now been kicked out." She shrugged. "It doesn't matter. Kiko isn't crazy about the city, and I wasn't planning to stay long. Just until I finished my search. Then we were going to move someplace less crowded."

"Good plan. You do realize that if anyone catches you with her she'll most likely be put down."

"I have papers for her."

He lifted an eyebrow and waited. "You do remember that you're a lousy liar, don't you?"

For the first time a hint of amusement flickered in her gaze. "I'm working on that."

An image of his late wife flashed through his head. "Please don't. I like you much better the way you are." He gestured toward the refrigerator. "Are you hungry?"

"I'm fine."

"What about Kiko?"

"She's good until morning."

"Come on, then. There's a bedroom you can use on this level with doors that open to the backyard."

"It's fenced?"

"High and deep. My cousin Nicolò has a St. Bernard who's something of an escape artist. Brutus has personally certified my fence to be escapeproof."

A swift smile came and went. "We'll see if Kiko concurs."

He could see the exhaustion lining her face, her fine-boned features pale and taut. He didn't waste any further time in conversation. Turning, he led the way toward the back of the house, throwing open the door to a suite of rooms that was at least three times the size of her apartment. She seemed to stumble slightly as she entered the room, favoring her left leg.

"You okay?" he asked.

"Oh, this?" She rubbed her thigh. "I broke my leg when I was a kid. It only bothers me when I get too tired."

"My brother Draco has a similar problem."

"I feel for him," she said, then turned in a slow circle. "Wow," she murmured. "This place is amazing."

"Nothing too good for my fiancée."

She spared him a swift, searching glance, but didn't argue. "Thank you, Rafe," she said.

He couldn't resist. He approached and tipped her face to his. From the doorway he caught a soft, warning rumble, one silenced by a swift gesture from Larkin.

"It'll take Kiko a while to realize you're safe," she explained.

His thumbs swept across the pale hollow beneath her cheekbones to pause just shy of the edges of her mouth. "Somehow I think it'll take you a while, too."

"You could be right."

He leaned down and captured her lips in a gentle caress. She moaned, the sound a mere whisper. But it conveyed so much. Hunger. Passion. Pleasure. And maybe a hint of regret. More than anything he wanted to pull her into his embrace and lose himself in her softness. She swayed against him, and it took a split second to realize her surrender came from exhaustion rather than desire.

Reluctantly he pulled back. "Wrong time, wrong place," he murmured.

She sighed. "The story of my life."

He rested his forehead against the top of her head. "I also promised Primo that I wouldn't unbutton you any more tonight."

"I believe he meant from now on, not just tonight," she informed him gravely. "And I also believe you agreed to honor that promise."

He released her and took a step back, allowing them both some breathing space. "Actually, what I promised was that I wouldn't unbutton you again until I put a ring on your finger." He flashed her a suggestive grin. "Come Monday, I plan to have that ring right where I need it to be. Then prepare yourself to be thoroughly unbuttoned."

Four

Larkin awoke to someone knocking on her door. Kicking off her covers, she stumbled to her feet and blinked blearily around. What in the world? This wasn't her shabby little apartment, but something far more sumptuous and elegant. Something a world away from her realm of experience.

Memory crashed down around her. Getting fired. Rafe's proposal. Their shocking first touch. Their even more shocking kiss. His proposition. Her losing her apartment. And finally, her arrival here with Kiko. The knock came again and she jumped.

"Just a minute," she called.

She yanked open her bedroom door, only to discover that the knocking came from farther away. She stumbled in that direction, realizing there was someone at Rafe's front door. A very determined someone. She hovered in the foyer, debating whether or not to answer. Better not to, she decided, considering it wasn't her house. Unfortunately, the unexpected guest had a key and chose that moment to use it.

The door swung open and a woman poked her head inside. "Rafe?" She caught sight of Larkin and her eyes widened. "Oh. Oh, dear. I'm so sorry. Nonna said—"

"What is wrong, Elia?"

Larkin recognized Nonna's voice and shut her eyes. This could not be good.

"We've come at an inconvenient time," Elia turned to explain. "Rafe has a guest."

Nonna replied in Italian, the sound knife-edge sharp. Then the door banged open and Nonna marched into the house. "Larkin? I am surprised to find you here."

"I'm surprised to find me here, too," Larkin admitted. "In fact, I'm surprised to find us both here."

"What the *hell* is going on? Can't a man get a decent night's sleep?" Rafe's voice issued from on high and he appeared at the top of the staircase leading to the second story. "Mamma? Nonna? What are you doing here?"

He stood there, hands planted on his hips, his chest bare, a loose pair of sweats riding low on his hips. Larkin stared, dazzled. Despite his obvious annoyance, she'd never seen anything more gorgeous.

"Oh, my."

The comment escaped, along with her breath, her common sense and every last brain cell she possessed. To her utter humiliation, his mother took note, suppressing a smile of amusement at her reaction.

But really… His body was an absolute work of art, sculpted with hard muscle that filled out his lean frame. His shoulders were broad, with strong, ropey arms, though she'd suspected as much when he'd lifted her in them last night and carried her to the couch in his office. His abdomen was flat and sporting the type of six-pack that she would have been only too happy to spend an entire night sampling. His mane of hair fell in rumpled abandon, the colors a lush mixture of browns and golds.

"We came over to arrange a time to meet Larkin," Elia explained. Her smile wavered. "Surprise! We met."

Rafe thrust his hands through his hair and Larkin suspected by the way his lips moved that he was swearing beneath his breath. "Let me get dressed and I'll be down." His gaze sharpened, arrowing in on Larkin. "May I suggest you do likewise?"

"Oh, right." She glanced down at her own shorts and cropped T-shirt with something akin to horror before offering Rafe's mother and grandmother a weak, embarrassed smile. "Excuse me, please."

She dashed in the direction of her bedroom and closeted herself inside. Kiko stared at her alertly from where she lay in one corner, curled up on a thick, cozy rug. "What do you say we try out the backyard again and see what you think about it in the daylight," Larkin suggested.

She opened the French doors leading outside and watched while Kiko limped into the yard. She kept an eye on the dog for several minutes to assure herself that the fence would withstand all escape attempts before taking a swift shower and throwing on the first set of clean clothes to come to hand. The fact that a night spent in a backpack had pressed a thousand wrinkles into them couldn't be helped.

Calling to Kiko, Larkin headed in the direction of

the coffee scenting the air. She found Rafe and the women in a low, heated conversation. Since it was in Italian, she could only guess what they were saying. Nonna appeared to be offering the strongest opinion, and Larkin could make a fairly accurate guess what that opinion might be. They broke off at the sight of her and smiled in a friendly manner, though Larkin picked up on the tension that underscored their greeting.

She pretended not to notice, returning their smiles with a broad one of her own before zeroing in on Rafe. "I just want to thank you for giving me a place to stay when I lost my apartment. If you hadn't, I think Kiko and I would have been wandering the streets all night."

"What is this?" Nonna asked sharply.

"I've been trying to tell you—" Rafe began.

"No." He was cut off with an imperious wave. "I wish Larkin to tell me."

"I wasn't allowed to have a pet in my apartment building. The landlord found out about Kiko last night and kicked me out. Thank goodness Rafe insisted on walking me inside. If it hadn't been for him…" She shrugged. "Obviously we didn't have the time to find a place that would accept a dog, so Rafe thought the smartest option would be for Kiko and me to use his guest room for the night. I'm just relieved that he has a Brutus fence." She offered a quick grin. "Turns out it's also Kiko proof."

Rafe grimaced. "After last night, I don't know whether to be disappointed or relieved."

"Last night?" Elia asked sharply.

His eyes narrowed on Kiko in open displeasure. "Full moon," he said as though that were all the explanation necessary.

"Would it be okay if I fed her now?" Larkin hastened to interrupt. "I have some kibble for her, but she needs a little bit of raw beef mixed in."

"No problem." He crossed to the refrigerator and rummaged through the contents. "Before you joined us, we were talking and Nonna and my mother would like to take you out today so you three can get to know each other."

With his head buried in the refrigerator, Larkin couldn't get a good read on either his voice or expression. "I thought I might look for a job," she temporized.

"Time enough for that on Monday." He emerged with a small packet of steak and carried it to the cutting board. "In fact, I might have something for you at Dantes."

"Oh, I don't think—"

"Perfect," Elia declared with a friendly smile. "This engagement is all so sudden it's taken my breath away."

"That makes two of us," Larkin answered with utter sincerity.

Elia's smile wavered. "Then this should give us time to catch our breath, yes?"

Larkin's gaze swiveled in Rafe's direction where he stood at the counter slicing up the raw meat. "Not unless Mr. Organize and Conquer plans on changing his personality by the time we get back."

The two Dante women glanced at each other and then at Larkin before breaking into huge grins of amusement. "It would seem you know my Rafaelo surprisingly well, given the short amount of time you have known him," Nonna commented.

"Perhaps that's because he doesn't bother to hide that aspect of his personality," Larkin replied.

"In case you three haven't noticed, I'm standing right here," Rafe said.

He combined Kiko's kibble with the slices of meat. The dog sat at attention, watching his every move. When he placed the food on the floor, she approached it cautiously, sniffing at the floor and around the bowl before attacking the contents.

"That's a most unusual dog you have," Elia said with a slight frown. "If I didn't know better I'd swear she was part—"

"Definitely not," Larkin hastened to say. "She belonged to my grandmother, who raised her from the time she was a youngster."

Rafe broke in, rescuing her from any further questions. "I gather I'm Kiko's designated sitter?"

Larkin turned to him in relief. There were times his take-charge personality came in handy. This was one of them. "Do you mind?"

"Will she eat me?"

"I don't think so."

He lifted an eyebrow. "Color me reassured."

His dry tone brought a flush to her cheeks. "She's very sweet natured. Very beta."

"Well, if that's settled?" Elia asked.

Not giving Larkin a chance to come up with a reasonable excuse for avoiding their girl-bonding session, Elia urged Nonna to her feet and swept everyone toward the front door. Once there, she gave her son an affectionate kiss, one Larkin noted he returned with equal affection. Then they were out the door and tucked into Elia's car. The next instant they pulled out of Rafe's drive and headed toward the city. Larkin couldn't help tossing a swift glance over her shoulder.

Elia must have caught the look, because she chuckled. "Don't worry, Larkin. We'll return you safe and sound before you know it."

Right. It was that nerve-racking time between now and then that worried her. How in the world had she gotten herself into this mess? Yesterday she'd been free as the proverbial bird. No entanglements. No men. Just one simple goal. Find her father.

And now… Larkin shot one final desperate look over her shoulder before settling in her seat. Now she had a fiancé to deal with, his family, no job and was expected to spend the day bonding. Bonding! With Leigh's former mother-in-law, of all people. Not to mention this bizarre ache centered in her palm. She rubbed at it, which for some strange reason caused Nonna and Elia to exchange broad smiles.

Larkin sighed. What an odd family. Almost as odd as her own.

Rafe stared, thunderstruck. "What the *hell* have you done to my fiancée?"

"We've been doing what women have done for centuries in order to bond," Elia said. "Shopping."

"Makeover." Nonna enunciated the word carefully, then smiled broadly, though Rafe couldn't tell if it was due to the word—one he'd never heard his grandmother utter before—or the results of said makeover. "This is something girls do together," she added with an airy gesture. "You are a man. You would not understand."

Larkin's eyes narrowed. "Don't you like it?" she asked in a neutral voice. "Your mother and grandmother went to a lot of time and expense on my behalf."

He hesitated. Damn. Okay, this was familiar territory.

Dangerous, familiar territory. The sort of territory men discovered during their first romantic relationship. Most poor saps of his gender stumbled in unaware of the traps awaiting them until they'd fallen into the first one, impaling themselves on their own foolhardiness. Having several serious relationships plus one disastrous marriage beneath his belt, Rafe had figured he'd safely skirted or uncovered all the traps out there.

Until now.

"You look lovely." And she did. Just…different.

Larkin's mouth compressed. "But?"

Behind her, Nonna and his mother also regarded him through slitted eyes and tight lips. "But?" they echoed.

"But nothing," he lied. Time to regain control of the situation. First item on the agenda…get rid of Larkin's backup. He gathered up his mother and grandmother and ushered them toward the door. "It's late. Nearly dinnertime. You've spent the day bonding with Larkin and I appreciate all you've done. I know this has been very sudden, and yet you've made her feel like one of the family."

"Of course we made her feel like one of us," Nonna said. "Soon she will be."

"Not too soon," he soothed. "This Inferno business is new to both of us and a bit of a shock. We need time to get to know each other before jumping into marriage."

Nonna turned on him. "Where will she stay until then?"

"Right here in my guest room."

She shook her head. "That is not proper and you know it."

He gave her his most intimidating look. Considering

she was his grandmother, it met with little success. "You think I'd break my promise to Primo?"

She lifted a shoulder in a very Italian sort of shrug. "The Inferno is difficult to resist."

"If it becomes too difficult, I'll make other arrangements."

Nonna gave a dainty snort. "We will see what Primo has to say about that."

No doubt. Giving each woman a kiss, he sent them on their way before going in search of Larkin. He found her in the kitchen brewing a pot of coffee. Unable to help himself, he stood in the doorway and watched, vaguely blown away by her grace.

There was a gentle flow to her movements, as though each step was choreographed by some inner music. What would it be like to dance with her? At a guess, sheer perfection. She was made to dance, and the idea of holding her in his arms while they moved together in perfect symmetry filled him with a longing he'd never experienced with or toward any other woman.

Another image formed, a picture of another sort of dance, one that also involved the two of them, but this time in bed. She had such a natural sense of rhythm, combined with a lithe, taut shape. How would she move when they made love? Would she drift the way she did now, initiating a slow, sultry beat? Or would she be fast and ferocious, pounding out a song that would leave them sweaty and exhausted?

"Coffee?"

The mundane question caught him off guard and it took him a moment to switch gears. "Thanks."

"Cream? Sugar?"

"Black."

She poured two mugs. "Do you really hate it?"

Rafe hesitated, still off-kilter. It wasn't until she ruffled her hair in a self-conscious gesture that he realized what she meant. "No, I don't hate it at all. It suits you."

And it did. Before, her hair had been long and straight, and the two times he'd seen her, she'd worn it either pulled back from her face in a braid or piled on top of her head with a clip. The stylist had cut it all off and discovered soft curls beneath the heavy weight of her hair, curls that clung to her scalp and framed her elegant features. Few women had the bone structure to get away with the stark style. She was one of them. If anything, it made her look even more like a creature from fantasy and make-believe.

"And the clothes?" she pressed.

"I suspect I'd like you better without them."

Startled, she looked at him before grinning. "There speaks a man."

"Well, yeah."

He sipped his coffee and circled her. He had to admit that his mother had done a terrific job orchestrating the change. Between the haircut, the stylishly casual blouse, the three-quarter-length slacks and the scraps of heeled leather that passed for sandals, Larkin had settled on an eclectic style that was uniquely her own. No doubt some of that was due to his mother's influence. She had a knack for seeing the true nature of a person and giving them a gentle nudge in the appropriate direction, rather than simply layering on the current fashion, regardless of whether or not it suited. But the rest was all Larkin.

"How did she convince you to accept the clothes and salon treatment?"

A hint of color streaked across Larkin's cheekbones and she buried her nose in her coffee mug. "Your mother isn't an easy woman to refuse," she muttered.

"Engagement present?"

Larkin sighed. "It started out that way. Of course I said no. After all, we're not officially engaged." She set the mug on the counter with a sharp click and eyed him in open confusion. "I'm not quite sure what happened after that. All of a sudden it was a pre-engagement gift or welcome-to-the-family gift or—"

"Or a bulldozing gift."

Larkin's mouth quivered into a smile. "Exactly."

"And before you knew it you'd had a total make-over."

"Is she always like that?"

"Pretty much. She's sort of like a tidal wave. She sweeps in, snatches up everyone in her path and carries them off. There's no resisting her. You just sort of ride the wave and hope you can slip up and over the swell before you get caught in the curl."

Larkin groaned. "I got caught in the curl. A couple curls."

He ruffled her hair. "They look good on you."

"Thanks." She picked up her mug and studied him through the steam. "Now I know where you get certain aspects of your personality. You're just like her, you know."

"Don't be ridiculous—I'm far worse."

She grinned, the tension seeping from her body. "Thanks for the warning." Kiko slipped into the room just then and came to sit at Larkin's feet, leaning against her legs. "How was she?"

He regarded the dog with a hint of satisfaction. "Let's just say we came to terms."

Laughter brightened Larkin's eyes. "Let me guess. You gave her more steak."

He didn't bother to deny it. After all, it was the truth. "The Dantes are firm believers in bonding over food. You'll see for yourself tomorrow night."

He'd alarmed her. Not surprising, considering how much had happened in so short a time. "Tomorrow night?" she asked. "What's tomorrow night?"

"Every Sunday night the family has dinner at Primo's."

She swallowed. "The whole family?"

"Anyone who's available."

"And who's going to be available tomorrow night?"

"It varies week to week. We'll find out when we get there, but I'm guessing my parents, at least one of my brothers, my sister, Gianna, and a couple of my cousins." She turned away, busying herself at the sink rinsing her coffee mug. But he could tell he'd upset her. Where before she was poetry in motion, now she moved in jerks and stops. "What's wrong?" he asked.

She set her cup down and turned. Turbulence dimmed her gaze and shadowed her expression. "Look. You don't know me and I don't know you. We jumped into this crazy idea without thinking it through. Everything's been moving so fast since last night that we haven't even had time to discuss the details or come up with a solid game plan. I just don't think it's going to work."

"Nonna and my mother must have grilled you today."

Larkin lifted a shoulder. "Sort of."

"You must have told them something about yourself."

"Bits and pieces," she conceded.

Based on her expression, he figured she'd told them as little as she could get away with. "Clearly, nothing you said concerned or alarmed them. Stands to reason I won't be concerned or alarmed, either."

She caught her lower lip between her teeth in a gesture that was becoming familiar to him. "I didn't tell them a lot," she said, confirming his suspicion.

"Here's what I suggest. Why don't we spend tonight and tomorrow getting to know each other? If we decide it's not going to work, we'll call the entire thing off." Hell. If anything, his offer had somehow made it worse. "What now?"

"Your mother spent a fortune on my hair and clothes. I can't just leave. I owe her."

"I'll reimburse her."

Larkin's chin jerked upward. "Then I'll owe you."

"You can work it off at Dantes or we can just call it even for the time you've invested."

"I'm not a taker," she insisted fiercely.

He fought to keep his voice even. "I never said you were."

He could see the frustration eating at her. "There are things you don't know about me." She began to pace. Kiko paced with her. "I got so caught up in your job offer and then your kisses that I haven't been able to stop long enough to catch my breath. To…to explain things."

He zeroed in on the most interesting part of her

comments, unable to suppress his curiosity. "My kisses?"

She whirled to face him. "You know what I mean. I understand that it's simple sexual chemistry, but I'm not... That is, I've never..." She thrust her hands through her hair, ruffling the curls into attractive disarray. "I flunked chemistry, okay?"

"Okay."

"The whole Inferno thing made me lose my focus. I got off course."

Something was seriously upsetting her and his humor faded, edging toward concern. "It's not a problem, Larkin."

"It is a problem."

She practically yelled the words, pausing to control herself only when Kiko whimpered in distress. The dog paused between the two of them, at full alert, her ruff standing up, giving her a feral, dangerous appearance. Larkin made a quick hand gesture and the animal edged closer, rubbing up against her hip.

She forced herself to relax. "I'm sorry," she said, though Rafe couldn't tell if the apology was directed at him or the dog.

Okay, time to approach the situation the same way he did a business dilemma and apply some of his infamous Dante logic. "You told me you came to San Francisco to find someone. Is that what's upset you? You feel like this job is distracting you from finding this person?"

"Yes. No." She crouched beside Kiko and buried her face in the dog's thick coat. "My search is only one of the reasons I'm here."

"That's not a problem," he argued. "There's no reason why you can't continue with your search while working for me. In fact, I might be able to help. I know someone who is excellent at finding people. He's the one who ran the security check on you last night."

"It's…complicated."

Rafe hesitated. "And you don't trust me enough to explain how or why or who."

"No," she whispered.

"Fair enough."

He approached and crouched beside her. Kiko watched him but no longer appeared distressed, and he slipped his fingers through the dog's thick fur until he'd linked his hand with Larkin's. He could feel the leap and surge of their connection the instant they touched. Though he continued to reject the possibility that it was The Inferno, he couldn't deny that something bound them together, something deep and powerful and determined.

"Here's what I suggest," he said softly. "Let's do what we told my mother and Nonna we'd do. Let's take this one day at a time. We'll also give my suggestion a shot and get to know each other a little better. You tell me about yourself. Or at least, as much as you're comfortable telling me. And I'll reciprocate."

She peeked up at him. "An even swap? Story for story?"

"Sounds fair."

She considered for a minute before nodding. "Okay. Who goes first?"

"We'll flip for it. Winner's choice." He lifted an eyebrow. "Agreed?"

She considered for an instant, then nodded. "Agreed."

Satisfied to have them back on course, he released her

hand and stood. "It's getting late. Why don't we throw together a simple meal, open a bottle of wine and sit outside and enjoy the evening? I think we'll find it more comfortable to reveal personal details in the dark."

"Definitely."

They worked in concert after that. He grilled up most of the portion of the steak he hadn't fed Kiko while Larkin threw together a salad. Then he nabbed a bottle of wine, a pair of glasses and a corkscrew on the way out of the kitchen. He set everything on the glass-and-redwood table on his patio. "There's some crackers in the cupboard and cheese in the fridge," he called to Larkin. "Oh, and Kiko will want the last of the beef that's in there. Middle shelf."

"She will, will she?"

"Absolutely. I'm sure that's what I heard her just say."

Larkin appeared in the doorway. "Kiko talks now?"

He lifted an eyebrow. "What? She doesn't talk to you? Ever since you left this morning, I haven't been able to get her to shut up."

To his satisfaction, the final vestiges of distress leached from Larkin's body. While she carried the last of the food to the table, he opened the cabernet and set it aside to breathe. Then he fed Kiko, who gave a contented grunt and settled down closest to where Rafe stood, no doubt hoping for another treat in the near future.

"You've corrupted her," Larkin accused. "You're going to make her fat."

"I'm trying to keep from getting eaten. There's another full moon tonight."

"She's not a wolf," Larkin muttered.

"And you're a lousy liar."

"I'll have to work on that."

"Don't." A terseness drifted through the word. "I was married to an expert, so you have no idea how much I appreciate the fact that you don't lie."

For some reason his pronouncement had the opposite effect of what he'd intended. She shot to her feet and faced him with a desperate intensity. "You're wrong. I am a liar. My being here is a lie. Our relationship is a lie. And I've told you any number of lies of omission. If you knew the truth about me, you'd throw me out right now. This minute." She shut her eyes. "Maybe you should. Maybe Kiko and I should leave before this goes any further."

Five

Larkin waited anxiously for Rafe's response. To her surprise, he didn't say a word. Instead, she heard him pour a glass of wine. The instant she opened her eyes, he handed it to her.

"I believe lying by omission is called dating," he explained gently. "No one is completely honest when they date—otherwise no one would ever get married. All of that changes once you're foolish enough to say 'I do.'"

"Marriage equals truth time?" Is that what he'd discovered when he'd married Leigh?

"Let's just say that the mask comes off and you get to see the real person. Since we're not getting married, that shouldn't be a problem for us. Relax, Larkin. We're all entitled to our privacy and a few odd secrets."

His comments were like a soothing balm and she sank onto her seat at the patio table, allowing herself to relax and sip the wine he'd poured. The flavor exploded on her tongue, rich and sultry, with a tantalizing after bite to it. "This is delicious."

"It is, isn't it? Primo got a couple of cases in last week and spread them out among the family to sample. It's from a Dante family vineyard in Tuscany that belongs to Primo's brother and his family."

"Huh." She went along with the drift from turbulent waters into calmer seas, even though her intense awareness of him followed her there. "And does his brother's family have that whole Inferno thing going on, too?"

"I don't know. It's never come up in discussion. Though I suspect most of the Dantes are fairly delusional when it comes to The Inferno."

Rafe settled into the seat beside her and stretched out his long legs. He was close. So deliciously close. Her body seemed to hum in reaction, flooded with a disconcerting combination of pleasure and need.

"You still don't believe it exists, despite..." She held out her hand, palm upward.

He hesitated, shrugged, then cut into his steak. "That's what we're going to spend the next month or so figuring out."

Careful and evasive. It would appear she wasn't the only one being a bit cagey. "Are you just saying that so I'll stick with the job?" she asked, tackling her salad.

"Pretty much."

She couldn't help smiling. "Devious man."

A companionable silence fell while they ate their dinner, though she could also feel a distracting buzz of sexual awareness. It seemed to hum between them, flavoring the food and scenting the air. She forced herself to focus on the meal and the easy wash of conversation, which helped mitigate the tension to a certain extent. But there was no denying its existence or the gleam of awareness that darkened Rafe's eyes to an impenetrable forest-green. It added a unique dimension to every word and interaction, one that teetered on the edge of escalation…or it would have if they hadn't both tiptoed around the various land mines.

After they'd finished eating they cleared away the dishes and returned to the patio with their wine. Larkin released a sigh, half contentment, half apprehension. "Okay. Story time," she announced. "Explain to me again how this is supposed to work."

"Winner of the coin toss asks the first question. Loser answers first."

"Ouch. That could be dangerous."

"Interesting, at the very least." He tossed the coin. "Call it."

"Heads."

He showed her the coin, tails side up. He didn't hesitate. "First question. Tell me about Kiko—and I mean the truth about Kiko. Since she's going to be around my family for the next month or two, I think I deserve the truth."

It was a reasonable question, if one she'd rather have avoided. "Fair enough. To be honest, I don't know what she is. She's definitely not pure wolf, despite her appearance. I'd guess she's probably a hybrid wolf dog." Rafe's eyebrows shot upward and Larkin hastened to add, "But I don't think she's very high-content wolf. She has too many of the traits of a dog, as well as the personality."

"Explain."

Larkin winced at the gunshot sharpness of his response and chose her words with care. "Some people breed dogs with wolves, creating hybrids. It's highly controversial. Gran was violently opposed to the practice. She considered it 'an accident waiting to happen' and unfair to both wolves and dogs, since people expect the hybrids to act like dogs." At his nod of understanding, she continued. "But how can they? They're an animal trapped between two worlds, living in a genetic jumble between domestication and wild creature. So both wolf and dog get a bad rep based on the actions of these hybrids whenever they respond to the 'wild' in their makeup."

"Got it," he said, though she could tell he wasn't thrilled with her explanation. "What about in Kiko's case? How likely is she to respond to her inner wolf?"

"She's never harmed anyone. Ever." Larkin leaned on the word. "Can she? Potentially. So can a dog, for that matter. But she's more likely to run than confront, especially now that she's so old."

"How did you end up with her?"

Larkin switched her attention to the animal in question and smiled with genuine affection. Kiko lay on the patio, her aging muzzle resting on her forepaws, watching. Always watching. Alert even at this stage of her life. "We think Kiko must have been adopted by someone who either couldn't take care of her or were living someplace where they couldn't keep her because of her mixed blood. They dumped her in the woods when she was about a year old. Gran found Kiko caught in an illegal trap, half-starved."

He shot a pitying look in the dog's direction. "Poor

thing. I'm amazed she let your grandmother anywhere near her."

"Gran always had a way with animals." She spared him a flashing smile. "And Kiko didn't have much fight in her by the time Gran arrived on the scene. The trap had broken Kiko's leg. She was lucky not to lose it."

"Did your grandmother set the leg herself?"

Larkin shook her head. "That would have been well beyond her expertise. She took Kiko to a vet who happened to be a close personal friend. He set the leg and advised Gran on the best way to care for Kiko. It was either that or have her put down. Since neither Gran nor I could handle that particular alternative, we kept her."

"And my family? How safe will they be with her?"

Larkin leaned forward and spoke with urgent intensity. "I promise, she won't hurt you or your family. She's very old now. The longest I've heard of these animals living is sixteen years. Most live fewer than that. Kiko's twelve or thirteen and very gentle. Except for the occasional urge to howl, she's quiet. Just be careful not to corner her so she feels trapped. Then she might turn destructive, if only in an attempt to escape what she perceives as a trap." Pleased when he nodded his acceptance, she asked a question of her own. "What about you? No dogs or cats or exotic pets?"

He shook his head. "We had dogs growing up, but I'd rather not own a pet."

She couldn't even imagine her life without a four-legged companion. "Why not?"

"You're talking about taking responsibility for a life for the next fifteen to twenty years. I'd rather not tie myself down to that sort of commitment."

It didn't take much of a leap to go from pets to a wife. If he'd thought owning a pet was an onerous commitment, how must it have felt to be married to Leigh? Larkin suspected she could sum it up in one word.

"I guess Kiko isn't the only one who doesn't like feeling trapped," Larkin murmured. "Is that what marriage felt like?" *Or was it just marriage to Leigh?*

"It didn't just feel that way. That's what it was." He raised his glass in a mocking salute. "One good thing came out of it. I realized I wasn't meant for marriage. I'm too independent."

That struck her as odd, considering his tight-knit family bonds. In the short time she'd known the Dantes, one aspect had become crystal clear. They were all in each other's business. Not in a bad way. They just were deeply committed to the family as a whole. And that just might explain Rafe.

"What made you so independent?" she probed. "Is it an attempt to keep your family at a distance, or something more?"

He tilted his head to one side in open consideration. "I don't feel like I need to hold my family at a distance. At least, I didn't until this whole Inferno issue came up." He frowned into his glass of wine. "I'm forced to admit they do have a tendency to meddle."

"So if it's not your family that's made you so independent, where did it come from?"

He returned his glass to the table and shook his head. "That's more than the allotted number of questions. Four or five by my reckoning. If we're playing another round, you have to answer one for me first."

"Okay, fine." She slid down in her chair and sighed.

"Just make it an easy one. I'm too tired to keep all my omissions straight."

He chuckled. "Since we're not even engaged, I wouldn't want any deep, dark omissions to slip out by accident."

"You have no idea," she muttered. "Come on. Hit me. What's your question?"

"Okay, an easy one… Let's see. You said you broke your leg at one point. I guess that gives you something in common with Kiko."

"More than you can guess."

"So tell me. What happened?"

She tried not to flinch. She didn't like remembering that time, even though everything worked out in the long run. "I was eight. I was in a school play and I fell off the stage."

"I'm sorry." And he was. She could hear it in the jagged quality of his words. "Unless someone saw you when you were as tired as you were last night, no one would ever know. You're incredibly graceful."

"Years of dance lessons, which helped me recover faster than I would have otherwise. But I was never able to dance again." She couldn't help the wistful admission. "Not like I could before."

"Were you living with your grandmother at the time?"

"Yes." Before he could ask any more questions, express any more compassion, she set her glass on the table with unmistakable finality. "It's been a long night. I should turn in."

"Don't go."

His voice whispered into the darkness, sending a shiver through her. It was filled with a tantalizing danger—not a physical danger, but an emotional one that threatened to change her in ways she couldn't anticipate. Indelible ways from which she might never recover. She hesitated there, tempted beyond measure, despite the ghost of the woman who hovered between them. And then he took the decision from her, sweeping her out of her chair and into his arms.

"Rafe—"

"I won't break my promise to Primo. But I need to hold you. To kiss you."

A dozen short steps brought him to the French doors leading to her suite of rooms. Kiko followed them, settling down just outside, as though guarding this stolen time together. Even though an inky blackness enfolded the room, Rafe found the bed with unerring accuracy. He lowered her to the silken cover. A delicious weight followed, pressing her into the softness.

Despite Larkin's night blindness, her other senses came alive. She heard the give-and-take of their breath, growing in urgency. Felt her heart kicking up in tempo, knowing it beat in unison with Rafe's. Powerful hands swept over her and she caught the agitated rustle of clothing that punctuated the tide of desire rising within her. And all the while, the flare of energy centered in her palm spread heat deep into blood and bone, heart and soul.

"Are you sure this isn't breaking your promise to Primo?" she whispered.

His hand slipped around behind her and found the hooks to her bra. One quick twist and the scrap of lace loosened. He released a husky laugh. "I'd say we were teetering on a thin line."

She pulled her arms out of the sleeves of her blouse

and the straps of her bra and wrapped them around his neck. "A *very* thin line. Maybe a kiss tonight before you leave?"

Even as the words escaped, his mouth found the joining of her neck and shoulder. Her muscles locked and her spine bowed in reaction. She'd never realized that particular juncture of her body was so sensitive. She released a frantic gasp, a small cry that held the distinct sound of a plea. How was it possible that such a simple touch could have such an overpowering effect? She couldn't seem to wrap her mind around it.

He cupped her breasts and drew his thumbs across the sensitive tips. Tracing, then circling, over and over until she thought she'd go crazy. He hadn't even kissed her yet, and already she was insane with a need she couldn't seem to find the words to express.

"Rafe, please."

She couldn't admit what she wanted. It was all twisted into a confused, seething jumble of conflicting urges. The urge for more. Far more. The need to stop before she lost total control. Or was it already too late for that? The sheer, unadulterated want to wallow in the heat and desire of his touch. This was wrong—not that she dared admit as much to Rafe. But she knew. And the knowledge ate at her. She shifted restlessly beneath him and he stilled her with a soothing touch.

Cupping her face, he took her mouth, obliterating the wrong beneath a kiss of absolute rightness. It was sheer perfection. Where their earlier kisses were filled with heat and demand, this one was far different. It soothed. Gentled. Offered a balm to the senses. The desperation eased, grew more languid, and she found herself relaxing into the embrace.

"You know I want to take this further," he murmured against her lips.

"You also know we can't. I couldn't look your grandparents in the face if—" She broke off with a shiver.

"Then we won't." She could hear the smile in his voice and feel it in the kisses he feathered across her mouth. "But that doesn't mean we can't come close."

She squeezed her eyes closed. "That's torture. You realize that, don't you?"

"Oh, yeah. But I can take it if you can." A warm laugh teased the darkness. "I think."

"We're playing a dangerous game."

"Do you really want me to stop?"

She considered for an entire five seconds. What had happened to her willpower? She'd never found it difficult to hold a man at arm's length. Until now. But with Rafe… For some reason he affected her in ways she'd never expected or experienced before. Everything about him attracted her. His looks. His intelligence. His sense of humor. His strength. His compassion. Even his family ties—especially his family ties. They all appealed. And then there was her physical response to him. She'd come here wanting something specific from Rafe. What she'd gotten in its stead had been totally unexpected.

She slid her arms downward, surprised to discover that at some point his shirt had disappeared. "What if this isn't real? What if The Inferno is causing us to feel this way?"

She sensed his surprise at the question. "Is that what you think? That your response is caused by a myth?"

Larkin attempted to control her hands, but they had a mind of their own, sweeping over the sculpted muscles of his chest. They were so hard and distinctly masculine, so deliciously different from her own body. "I…I've never felt like this before. I'm just trying to understand—"

"You mean rationalize what's happening." His laugh contained a wry edge. "Trust me, I understand completely. I'm not interested in another emotional entanglement. Not after Leigh."

She stilled, the reminder an icy one. "Emotional?"

He leaned in until his forehead rested against hers. "Hell, Larkin. Do you think I want this to be anything more than physical? Pure chemistry?"

"I can pretty much guess the answer to that," she said drily.

He rolled off her and onto his back, scooping her against his side. She rested her head on his shoulder and allowed her hand to drift across the flat expanse of his abdomen. He sucked in his breath, lacing her fingers with his in order to stop their restless movement. "Since the minute I met you, I've been telling myself it's a simple physical reaction. That's all I want it to be. That's all I can handle at this point in my life."

"But?"

"But then you told me about your broken leg and how you'd never been able to dance again.…"

"I can dance. Just not the way I did before." She shrugged. "So?"

"It just about killed me to hear you say that," he confessed roughly. "To see how it affected you."

"Is that why we ended up here?"

"Pretty much." He tugged at her short crop of curls. He blew out his breath in a sigh. "Go to sleep, Larkin."

"What about…?"

"Not tonight. I'm not sure I could stop once we got started. Hell, who am I kidding? I *know* I won't be able to stop."

Nor would she. "Are you going to stay here with me?"

"For a while," he compromised.

She hesitated, not sure she should ask the next question. But it slipped out anyway. "What happens from this point forward?"

"I don't know," he answered honestly. "I guess we take it one day at a time."

"You think this feeling is going to dissipate over time, don't you?"

"Don't take this the wrong way, but I hope so."

"And if it doesn't?"

"We'll deal with it then."

She fell silent for a moment, then warned, "Whatever this is, Inferno or simple lust, it can't go anywhere. You aren't the only one who isn't interested in a permanent relationship."

"Then we don't have anything to worry about, do we?"

She wished that were true. But once he found out who she was, that would all change.

Rafe woke in the early hours of the morning to the haunting sound of a howl. He glanced down at the woman sprawled across him and smiled. It usually took several nights to get comfortable sleeping with a woman. But with Larkin, all the various arms and legs had sorted themselves out with surprising ease. He couldn't remember the last time he'd slept so soundly.

If it hadn't been for Kiko, he doubted he'd have woken until full daylight. Speaking of which...

Ever so gently, he eased Larkin to one side. She murmured in protest before settling into the warm hollow left by his body, her breath sighing in pleasure. Desire coursed through him at that tiny, ultrafeminine sound. Is that what she'd do when they made love? Would she use that irresistible siren's song on him? He couldn't wait to find out.

Deliberately he turned his back on the bed and crossed to the French doors. A full moon shone down on the fenced yard, frosting the landscape in silver and charcoal. Kiko sat in the middle of the lawn, her head tipped back in a classic pose, her muzzle raised toward the moon.

She exhibited an untamed beauty that drew him on some primitive level. Part of him wanted to run, free and natural, driven by instinct rather than the intellectual side of his nature, a side he clung to with unwavering ferocity. To be part of that other world, the world that called to the untamed part of the animal before him.

Knowing he couldn't, that *she* couldn't, filled him with sadness. She was wildness trapped in domestication...a trap he'd do whatever it took to avoid. Before she could voice her mournful song again, he gave a soft whistle. She hesitated another moment, gave a sorrowful whine, then padded in his direction.

"It makes me so sad." Behind him, Larkin echoed his thoughts.

He turned to glance at her and froze. The moonlight bathed her nudity in silver. She was a study in ivory and charcoal. Her hair, shoulders and breasts gleamed with a pearl-like luminescence, while shadows threw a modest veil across her abdomen and the fertile delta between her thighs. Rational thought deserted him.

She inclined her head toward Kiko. "She feels the pull of the wild, but can't respond the way she wants because she's been trapped in a nebulous existence between wolf and dog, unable to call either world her own." She fixed her pale eyes on him. "Is that how you feel? Trapped between two worlds?"

He still couldn't think straight. He understood the question, but his focus remained fixed on her. On the demands of the physical, rather than the intellect. "Larkin..."

She made the mistake of approaching, the moonlight merciless in stripping away even the subtle barrier of the shadows that had protected her. "Your family is such an emotional one, but you're not, are you?"

He couldn't take his eyes off her. "Don't be so sure."

A slow smile lit her face and she tilted her head to one side. With her cap of curls and delicate features, she looked like a creature of myth and magic. "So you *are* one of the emotional Dantes?"

It took him three tries before he could speak. "If I touch you again, you'll find out for yourself." The words escaped, raw and guttural. "And I'll have broken my promise to Primo."

For a long moment time froze. Then with a tiny sigh, she stepped back, allowing the shadows to swallow her and returning to whatever fantasy world she'd escaped from. Everything that made him male urged pursuit. He knew it was the moonlight and Kiko's howling that had ripped the mask of civilization from his more primitive instincts. He fought with every ounce of control he possessed.

As though sensing how close to the edge he hovered, the dog trotted past him to the open doorway. There she sat, an impressive bulwark to invasion.

"You win this time," he told her. "But don't count on it working in the future."

With that, he turned and walked away from a craving beyond reason. And all the while he rubbed at the relentless itch centered in the palm of his hand.

She'd lost her mind. Larkin swept the sheet off the bed and wrapped herself up in its concealing cocoon. There was no other explanation. Why else would she have stripped off her few remaining clothes and walked outside like that, as naked as the day she'd been born? Never in her life had she been so blatant, so aggressive. That had been Leigh's specialty, not hers.

Leigh.

Larkin sank onto the edge of the bed and covered her face with her hands. What a fool she was, believing for even a single second that she could embroil herself in the Dantes' affairs and escape unscathed. Maybe if she'd been up front with Rafe from the beginning it would have all worked out. That had been the intention when she'd asked to be assigned to the Dantes reception.

Her brow wrinkled. How had it all gone so hideously wrong? He'd touched her, that's how. He'd dropped that insane proposition on her and then before she could even draw breath or engage a single working brain cell, he'd kissed her. And she'd lost all connection with reason and common sense because of The Inferno.

The Inferno.

She stared at her palm in confusion. She wanted to believe that it was wishful thinking or the power of suggestion. But there was no denying the odd throb and itch of her palm. She couldn't have imagined that into existence, could she?

A soft knock sounded on her door. It could be only one person. She debated ignoring it, pretending she was asleep. But she couldn't. She crossed to the door and opened it, still wrapped in the sheet. He'd pulled on a pair of sweatpants and seemed relieved to see that she'd covered up, as well.

"It's late," she started, only to be cut off.

"I'm sorry, Larkin. Tonight was my fault." He leaned against the doorjamb and offered a wry smile. "I thought I could control what happened."

"Not so successful?"

His smile grew. "Not even a little. I can't allow it to happen again." He waited a beat. "At least, not until I have a ring on your finger."

Her eyes widened. "Excuse me?"

"Let's just say that once you're wearing my engagement ring, I'll consider my promise to Primo fulfilled."

The air escaped her lungs in a rush, and she fought to breathe. "And then?" she asked faintly.

"And then we'll finish what we started tonight." He reached out and wound a ringlet around his finger. "One way or another we'll work this out." His mouth twisted. "Of course, getting whatever this is out of our systems will take a lot of work."

"What if I don't want to make love to you?"

He chuckled. The rich, husky sound had her swaying

toward him. "Somehow I don't think that'll be a problem."

He leaned in and snatched a kiss, leaving her longing for more. And then he released her and left her standing there, clutching the sheet to her chest.

He was wrong. So wrong. Making love would be far more than a problem. It would be a disaster. Taking their relationship that next step would forge a deeper connection. No matter how much he wanted to deny it, it would create a bond between them that could offer nothing but pain.

Because the minute she told him that Leigh was her sister—*half* sister—and he discovered the real reason she'd approached him, he wouldn't want anything further to do with her.

Six

"Nervous?" Rafe asked as he downshifted the car.

They climbed farther into the hills overlooking Sausalito along a winding road that led to Primo and Nonna's. Each bend showcased breathtaking views one minute and then equally breathtaking villas the next. It was pointless to pretend she wasn't nervous, so Larkin nodded.

"A little. Your grandparents can be rather intimidating. And now there's the rest of the Dantes to contend with…."

She trailed off with a shrug that spoke volumes. A far greater concern was whether any of them would somehow make some sort of quantum leap and connect her to Leigh. With such a large contingent of Dantes present for Sunday dinner, she'd be lynched for sure.

Rafe spared her a flashing smile. "Try not to worry. The intimidation factor is aimed at me, not you. I've already received a half dozen lectures from various family members who are worried about my intentions toward you. Afraid I'll corrupt you or something." Pulling into a short drive, he crammed his car behind the ones already parked outside his grandparents' home. "Other than that, I have a terrific family."

"Big. You have a big family."

He glanced at her, curious. "Is it the size that worries you?"

"Everything about your family worries me," she announced ominously.

He chuckled at that. "Just do what I do and ignore all the drama. You don't have to answer any questions you don't want to."

"I'll tell them you said that, but somehow I doubt it'll work."

She opened the car door and climbed out, smoothing the skirt of her dress—something she rarely, if ever, wore. It was new, a purchase that both Nonna and Elia had insisted on making, despite her hesitation. In all reality, it was more of an oversize shirt than an actual dress, right down to the rolled-up sleeves and button-down collar. Unfortunately, she felt as if she'd forgotten half her outfit. Still, she couldn't deny it suited her.

A dainty gold belt cinched her waist, making it appear incredibly small, while the shirttail hem flirted in that coy no-man's-land between knee and thigh, drawing attention to her slender legs. She just hoped it didn't also draw attention to the thin network of silvery-white scars that remained a permanent reminder of her broken leg.

"Stop fussing. You look amazing." Rafe circled the

car and took her hand in his. "They're all going to love you as much as Mamma and Nonna."

Despite her nervousness, she couldn't help finding the Italian inflection that rippled through his voice endearing, especially when he referred to his mother or grandmother. It was as beautiful as it was lyrical.

"I'm being ridiculous, aren't I?" She blew out a breath. "I mean, even if they don't like me it really doesn't matter. It's not like this is re—"

He stopped the words with a kiss, the unexpected power of it almost knocking her off her legs. Every last thought misted over, vanishing beneath his amazing lips. She shifted closer and wound her arms around his neck, giving herself up to the delicious heat that seemed to explode between them whenever they touched. She couldn't say how long they remained wrapped around each other, doing their level best to inhale one another. Seconds. Minutes. Hours. Time held no meaning. When he finally lifted his head, she could only stare at him, dazed. He grinned at her reaction.

"Interesting," he said. "I'll have to remember to do that anytime I want to change the subject."

"Who...? What...?" She took a tottering step backward. "Why...?"

His grin broadened at her helpless confusion. "You were about to say something indiscreet," he explained in a low voice. "I kissed you to shut you up. You never know who might be listening."

Larkin's brain clicked back on, along with her capacity for speech. "Got it."

It was so unfair. For her their embraces felt painfully real. But for Rafe... Didn't the heat they generated melt any of his icy composure? She could have sworn it did.

She sighed. Maybe that was just wishful thinking on her part, which meant she was putting herself in an increasingly vulnerable position if she didn't find a way to keep her emotions in check.

"I'll be more careful from now on," she added, as much for her own benefit as for his.

She drew in a shaky breath and aimed herself toward a large wooden gate leading to the back of the house. To her profound relief, she discovered she could walk in a more or less straight line without falling down. Rafe opened the gate, and they stepped into a beautifully tended garden area filled with a rainbow of colors and a dizzying bouquet of fragrances. An array of voices greeted them, coming from the people who spilled across the lawn or sat at a wrought iron patio set beneath a huge sprawling mush oak.

The next hour proved beyond confusing as Rafe introduced her to an endless number of Dantes. Some were involved in the retail end of the Dantes jewelry empire. Others, like Rafe and his brother Luc, ran the courier service. Still others handled the day-to-day business aspects. She met Rafe's father, Alessandro, who was as easygoing as his son was intense. And she met the various wives, their radiance and undisguised happiness filling her with a wistful yearning to enjoy the sort of marital bliss they'd discovered with their spouses. Not that it would happen. At least, not with Rafe.

"Have all of the married couples experienced The Inferno?" she couldn't help but ask at one point.

Rafe gave a short laugh. "Or so they claim." She considered that with a frown, one that he intercepted. "What?"

"Well, you're the logical one, right?"

"No question."

She indicated his relatives with a wave of her hand. "And every couple here, including your parents and grandparents, claim that they've experienced The Inferno."

He shrugged. "What can I say? I've come to the conclusion that the Dante family suffers from a genetic mutation that causes mass delusion. Thank God I was spared that particular anomaly." His gaze drifted toward his younger brother and sister. "Time will tell whether Draco and Gia escaped, as well."

That earned him a swift grin. "Mutations and anomalies aside, Primo mentioned that he and Nonna have been married for more than fifty years. And I gather your parents must have been married for thirtysomething years, right?"

"Your point?"

She suppressed a wince at the crispness of his question. "Despite your unfortunate genetic anomaly, doesn't logic suggest that, based on all the marriages you've seen to date, The Inferno is real? I'd also think that the fact that you *didn't* experience it with Leigh and your marriage failed only adds to the body of evidence."

He didn't have a chance to answer. Draco dropped into the conversation and into the vacant chair beside them. "You're not going to convince him. Rafaelo doesn't want to believe. Plus, he's a dyed-in-the-wool cynic who isn't about to allow something as messy and unmanageable as The Inferno steal away his precious self-control."

"If you mean I refuse to be trapped in another marriage, you're right," Rafe responded in a cool voice.

Draco leaned toward her. "Oh, and did I happen to mention that he doesn't want to believe?"

Despite the pain that Rafe's comments caused, Larkin's lips quivered in amusement. "You may have said something to that effect once or twice."

"Tell me you're any different," Rafe shot back at his brother. "Are you ready to surrender your current lifestyle to the whims of The Inferno?"

Something dark and powerful rippled across the even tenor of Draco's expression. Something that hinted at the depths he concealed beneath his easygoing facade. Larkin watched in fascination. *The dragon stirs* came the whimsical thought.

Draco took his time responding, taking the question seriously. "Answer me this.… If your Inferno bride dropped into your arms out of the blue, would you push her away?"

Rafe spared Larkin a brief glance. "Is that what you think happened to us?"

"To you?" Draco seemed startled by the question. His dark gaze flashed from his brother to Larkin. "Sure, okay. Let's say it happened to the two of you. Are you going to turn away from it?"

"It didn't happen to us," Rafe stated with quiet emphasis. "It didn't because there is no such thing as The Inferno, so there's nothing to turn away from."

Draco flipped a quick, sympathetic look in Larkin's direction before responding to his brother. "In that case, either you deserve an Academy Award for your performance tonight, or you're a lying SOB. I can't help but wonder which one it is."

Rafe regarded his brother through narrowed green

eyes. "You should know which one, since you're responsible for staging this little play."

"I may have orchestrated the opening scene," Draco shot right back, "but that's where my participation in this comedy of errors ended. Your role, on the other hand, appears to have taken on an unexpected twist."

Draco struck with the speed of a snake, snagging his brother's wrist. Larkin's gaze dropped to Rafe's hand and she inhaled sharply. He'd been caught red-handed—literally—rubbing the palm of his right hand with the thumb of his left, just as she'd been doing ever since they'd first touched.

"Part of the act," Rafe claimed.

But Larkin could see the lie in his eyes and hear it in his voice and feel it in the heat centered in her palm.

"Keep telling yourself that, bro, but in case you're wondering, I'm choosing Option B. That's lying SOB, in case you've forgotten." Draco deliberately changed the subject. "Hey, sister-to-be, I see I'm not the only one with an eventful childhood."

The change in subject knocked her off-kilter. "Sorry?"

He gestured to the nearly invisible network of scars along her leg. "We match. Mine was due to falling out of a tree. How about you?"

He asked the question so naturally that she didn't feel the least embarrassed or self-conscious. "Did a pirouette off a stage."

He winced. "Ouch." He nudged Rafe. "Of course, my ordeal wasn't anywhere near as bad as Rafe's."

"Rafe's?" She turned to him. "Did you break your leg, too? Why didn't you tell me?"

"I didn't break anything."

"Except a few hearts," Draco joked. "No, I meant what happened to him when I broke my leg. Didn't he tell you?"

Larkin shook her head. "No, he hasn't mentioned it."

"Oh, well, since we're all going to the lake next week, not only can he fill you in on every last gory detail, but he can show you the very spot where it went down. I'd point out the tree that started the trouble, but Rafe went crazy one year and chopped it down."

"It was infested," Rafe responded with a terrible calm. "It needed to come down before it infected other trees."

"You know, I've finally figured it out," Draco marveled. "If reality doesn't match the way you want your world to exist, you simply change your version of reality. Well, I've got news for you. That doesn't make it real. That just makes *you* delusional."

Larkin flinched at the word. She didn't know what had happened to Rafe all those years ago, but she could feel the waves of turbulence rolling off him, his impressive willpower all that held the emotions in check.

"I think we're being called to dinner," she said, hoping to defuse the situation. Standing, she offered her hand to Rafe. "I can't wait to sample Primo's cooking. Everyone I've spoken to has raved about it."

To her shock, he scooped her close. Lowering his head, he took her mouth in a slow, thorough kiss that caught her off guard and had her responding without thought or hesitation. "Thanks," he murmured against her lips.

"Anytime," she whispered back. Especially if it meant being rewarded with a kiss like that.

The kiss hadn't escaped the notice of Rafe's relatives, nor did she miss the gentle laughter and whispered comments that followed the two of them inside. She might have been embarrassed if not for the relieved delight on their faces. It didn't take much guesswork to understand why. Clearly, Leigh had done quite a number on Rafe and they were thankful that he'd finally put the trauma of his marriage behind him. She winced.

If they only knew.

"You didn't mention that we were expected to join your family at the lake next week," Larkin said.

"Sorry about that." He opened the door leading into the utility room off the kitchen and held it for her. "Is going to the lake with me a problem?"

With the exception of the few monosyllabic replies she'd offered in response to his various attempts at conversation, she hadn't spoken a word since they'd left Primo's. Rafe couldn't decide whether to be relieved or concerned that she'd finally started talking again. Clearly, something was eating at her. If their visit to the lake was her main concern, he could handle that and would chalk the evening up as a reasonable success. Otherwise…

"No. I just would have appreciated a warning."

Damn. She still wasn't looking at him, which meant her silence wasn't because of the trip to the lake. A lead-in, perhaps, or an oblique approach to the actual problem. But definitely not the problem itself. She crouched to greet Kiko, scanning the area as she did so.

"I don't see any damage in here. Maybe we should do a quick walk-through, just to be on the safe side."

"I'm sure she was fine." He stooped beside the pair and gave Kiko a thorough rub. The dog moaned in ecstasy. "Weren't you, girl?"

Sure enough, a quick inspection of the house revealed no damage. Once Larkin satisfied herself that Kiko had behaved while they were gone, he inclined his head toward the patio. "I'm not ready for the evening to end. Why don't we go outside before turning in for the night?"

She hesitated, another ominous sign. "Okay."

He removed a bottle from the refrigerator and nabbed a pair of crystal flutes, then followed her into the moonlit darkness. "Hmm. For some reason this has a familiar feel to it."

She tossed a smile over her shoulder, one filled with feminine enchantment. "Been there, done that?"

He set the bottle on the table. "Close, though a bit different from what I have planned for this evening."

She eyed the bottle and stilled. "Champagne?" A frown worried at the edges of her expression. "Are we celebrating something?"

"I guess that depends on how well this goes over." He removed a small jewelry box from his pocket and flipped it open, revealing the glittering ring within. "I couldn't wait until Monday," he explained in response to her look of shock. "Hell, I barely made it through last night."

She drew in a sharp breath. "Oh, Rafe. What have you done?"

His eyes narrowed. "You knew this was coming. I just moved up the timetable by a day or two. After last night…"

She actually blushed, which he found fascinating. At

a guess, she didn't often wander around naked in the moonlight. A shame. It suited her. It also suited him.

She took a quick step backward. Not a good sign. "It's just…" She trailed off with a shrug.

"Just what?"

He resisted the urge to follow her. Instead, he set the ring on the table beside the bottle of champagne, realizing that he'd been so focused on his own needs, he hadn't taken Larkin's into consideration. The ring and all that went with it could wait. He wanted her to enjoy their first time together, not be distracted by worries he could help ease.

"Honey, you barely spoke a word the entire way home. So either it's that, or it's the trip to the lake, or there's something else worrying you. Why don't you tell me which it is?"

He closed the distance between them and gathered her hands in his. It felt so right when he held her like this, felt the wash of warmth that flowed between them. Why did his family have to take something so basic, so natural, and wrap it up in myth and superstition? It was simple sexual attraction. Granted, the connection between them felt amazing. But couldn't they just call a spade a spade and let it go at that? Did they have to cloak a simple chemical reaction behind a ridiculous fairy tale?

"What's wrong, Larkin?"

Her gaze swept past him to fix on the table. "The only reason you bought me champagne and a ring is so you could make love to me."

He winced. Stripping it down to the bare-bones truth tarnished what he'd considered a romantic overture. "I thought—"

She cut him off without hesitation. "You thought that since you were buying my services, a bottle of champagne and a ring were sufficient. That you didn't have to turn it into some sort of big romantic gesture. I get that. It's not real, so why pretend it's anything more than sex, right?"

He released her hands. "Hell."

"I want to make love to you. But this…" She shivered. "An engagement ring is real, Rafe. It's a serious commitment, just like marriage. You're treating it like it's some sort of casual game or a fast, easy way to get me into bed."

Anger flashed and he struggled to contain it. "I'm well aware that marriage isn't a game. Cold, hard experience, remember?"

She stepped away from him, melting into the surrounding shadows, making it impossible to read her expression. "You hired me to do a job. You hired me to play the part of your fiancée for your friends and family and I've agreed to do that even though it goes against the grain to lie to them. You didn't hire me to sleep with you."

The comment had his anger ripping free of his control. "I'd never reduce it to something so sordid. One has nothing to do with the other. I wouldn't dream of putting a price tag on that aspect of our relationship. It would be an insult to both of us."

"And yet, you're only offering me that ring so you can get me in bed. Seems to me that's a hefty price tag."

He went after her and pulled her from the shadows and into his arms. "You know damn well why I offered you that ring. I made a promise to Primo, a promise I won't break. Do I want to make love to you? Hell, yes!

But I can't and won't do it unless you're officially my fiancée. It's going to happen eventually. Why not now? So I woke Sev this morning to open up Dante Exclusive and I picked out a ring for you. And not just any ring. A ring that reminded me of you. That seemed tailor-made for you."

He could tell his words had an impact. Her attention strayed to the table, her eyes full of curiosity and something else. A wistfulness that tore at his heart. "I won't be bought."

"And I'm not buying you. Not when it comes to this part of our relationship." His anger dampened, allowing him to rein it in. He didn't understand how she could rouse his emotions with such ease. He'd never had that problem with any other woman. "As far as I'm concerned, what happens in bed has nothing to do with your posing as my fiancée. If we'd met under different circumstances, we'd still have ended up there. You just wouldn't have had my ring on your finger."

She took a deep breath, conceding the point. "Show me the ring."

He took that as an encouraging sign. Crossing to the table, he collected the jewelry box. Removing the ring, he gathered her hand in his and slid it onto the appropriate finger. Even in the subdued lighting, the stones took on a life of their own.

The central diamond—one of the fire diamonds that made Dantes jewelry so exclusive and world renowned—sparkled with a hot blue flame. On either side of it were more fire diamonds, each subsequently smaller and bluer, the final one as pale and clear and brilliant a blue as Larkin's eyes. The stones were arranged in a delicate filigree Platinum Ice setting that seemed the perfect reflection of her appearance and personality.

"It's…" She broke off and cleared her throat. "It's the most beautiful ring I've ever seen."

"It's from the Dantes Eternity line."

Her gaze jerked upward. "The ones that were being showcased at the reception?"

"The very same. Every last one is unique and each has a name."

She hesitated before asking, "What's this one called?"

It was such an obvious question. He didn't understand her reluctance to ask it. But then, what he didn't understand about a woman's emotions could fill volumes. "It's called Once in a Lifetime."

"Oh. What a perfect name for it." To his concern, tears filled her eyes. "But you must see why I can't accept this."

Okay, it was confirmed. He did not—and never would—understand women. "No, I don't see. Explain it to me."

"It's Once in a Lifetime."

"I get that part." He fought for patience and tried again. "Just to clarify, you can't accept a ring from me? As in any ring? Or you can't accept this specific ring?"

A tear spilled out, just about sending him to his knees. "This one." It took her an instant to gather her self-control enough to continue. "I can't—won't—accept *this* ring."

He planted his fists on his hips. "Why the hell not?"

Now her lips and chin got into the act, quivering in

a way that left him utterly helpless. "Because of the name."

"You have got to be kidding me." He snatched a deep breath, throttled back on full-bore Dante bend-'em-till-they-break tone of voice and switched to something more conciliatory. "If you don't like the name, we'll just change it. No big deal."

She shook her head, loosening another couple of tears. They seemed to sparkle on her cheeks with as much brilliance as the diamonds in the ring she couldn't/wouldn't accept. "I'm sure you can see how wrong that would be."

"No, actually I can't." He tried to speak calmly. He really did. For some reason his voice escaped closer to a roar. So much for conciliatory. "It's a prop. Part of the job. And it's yours once the job ends."

She tugged frantically at the ring. "Absolutely not. I couldn't accept it."

His back teeth locked together. "It's compensation," he gritted out. "We agreed beforehand that it would be."

Her chin jerked upward an inch. "It's excessive and taints the meaning of such a gorgeous ring." She managed to tug it off her finger and held it out to him. "I'm sorry, Rafe. I can't accept this."

Damn it to hell! "You're required to wear it as part of your official duties. Once the job ends you can keep it or not. That's up to you."

"I won't be keeping it."

He shrugged. "Then I'll give you the cash equivalent."

She caught her lower lip between her teeth in obvious agitation. "I think it's time we amended our original agreement. In fact, I insist we amend it. When you initially mentioned my keeping the ring, I didn't realize we were talking about something of this caliber."

"If I offered you anything less, my family would know our engagement isn't real."

"Which is the only reason I'm willing to wear your ring." She drew back her hand and gazed down at her palm with a hint of longing. "Maybe a different one? Something smaller. Something that doesn't have a name."

"Sev knows which ring I chose. It'll cause comment if we exchange it." He didn't give her the opportunity to dream up any more excuses. Plucking the ring from her palm, he returned it to her finger. To his relief, she left it there, though his relief was short-lived.

"About that amendment…" she began.

He folded his arms across his chest. He should have seen it coming. Now that she had him between a rock and a hard place, she could name her terms and he'd be forced to agree. Or so she thought. He'd soon disabuse her of that fact. Just as he had Leigh when she'd pulled a similar stunt.

"Name your demands."

Larkin blinked in surprise. "Demands?"

"That's what they are, aren't they? I've introduced you to my entire family as my fiancée. We're committed to seeing this through. And now you want to change the terms of our agreement." He shrugged. "What else am I supposed to call it?"

Everything about her shut down. Her expression. The brilliance of her gaze. Her stance. Even the way she breathed. One minute she'd been a woman of vibrancy and the next she might as well have been a wax figurine.

"I don't want your money, Rafaelo Dante." Even her voice emerged without inflection. "You can keep your ring and your cash. I only want one thing. A favor."

"What favor?"

She shook her head, her features taking on a stubborn set. "When I've performed my duties to your satisfaction and the job has ended, then I'll ask you. But not before."

"I need some sort of idea what this favor is about," he argued.

"It's either something you can grant me, or not. You decide when the time comes."

He considered for a moment. "Does this have something to do with the person you're looking for?"

"Yes."

Her request didn't make the least sense. "Honey, I've already said I'd help you with that. I'm happy to help. But I hired you for a job and you deserve to be paid for that job."

She cut him off. "It's not just a matter of my giving you a name to pass on to Juice. There's more to it than that. For me, that something is of far greater value to me than your ring or cash or anything else you'd offer as compensation."

"I think I'll make that determination when the job is over. If your request doesn't strike me as a fair bargain—fair for you, I mean—then I'm going to pay you. If you don't want the ring, fine. If you don't want the money, fine. You can donate it all to charity or to the animal rescue group of your choice."

Even that offer had little impact. "Do you agree to my terms?" she pressed. "Yes or no?"

Depending on the favor, it struck him as a reasonable

enough request, though he suspected he'd discover the hidden catch at some point. There had to be one. He'd learned that painful fact during his marriage, as well as from a number of the women who'd preceded his late wife, and also those who'd followed her. When you were an eligible Dante, it was all about what you could give a woman. Once they'd tied the knot and Leigh had dropped her sweet-and-innocent guise, she'd made that fact abundantly clear. Well, he'd deal with Larkin's hidden catch when it happened, because there wasn't a doubt in his mind that it would be a "when" rather than an "if."

"Sure," he agreed, wondering if she could hear the cynicism ripping through that single terse word. "If it's within my power to give you what you ask, I'm happy to do it."

"Time will tell," she murmured in response. "I do have one other request."

"You're pushing it, Larkin." Not that his warning had any impact whatsoever.

"It's just that I was wondering about something." She continued blithely along her path of destruction. "And I was hoping we could discuss it."

He gestured for her to finish. "Don't keep me in suspense."

"What happened at the lake when Draco broke his leg?"

"Hell. Is *that* what's been bothering you all night?"

"What makes you think anything was bothering me?" she asked, stung.

"Gee, I don't know. Maybe it was that long stretch of silence on the trip back from Primo's. Or the fact that you've been on edge ever since our conversation with Draco."

He shouldn't have mentioned his brother. It brought her lasering back to her original question. "Seriously, Rafe. What happened to you that day at the lake? The day Draco broke his leg?"

When he remained silent, she added, "Consider it a condition of my leaving this ring on my finger."

Damn it to hell! "Now you're *really* pushing it."

"Tell me."

"There's not much to tell."

He crossed to the table and made short work of opening the bottle of Dom. Not that he was in the mood for a celebration. What he really wanted was to get rip-roaring drunk and consign his entire family, the bloody Inferno and even his brand-new, ring-wearing fiancée straight to the devil. Splashing the effervescent wine into each of the two flutes, he passed one to Larkin before fortifying himself with a swallow.

"Rafe?"

"You want to know what happened? Fine. I was forgotten."

Larkin frowned. "Forgotten? I don't understand. What do you mean?"

He forced himself to make the admission calmly. Precisely. Unemotionally. All the while ignoring the tide of hot pain that flowed through him like lava. "I mean, everyone went off and left me behind and didn't realize it until the next day."

Seven

"*What?*" Larkin stared at Rafe in disbelief. "They left you there at the lake? Alone? Are you serious?"

Rafe smiled, but she noticed it didn't quite reach his eyes. They'd darkened to a deep, impenetrable green. "Dead serious."

"I don't understand. What happened?" she asked urgently. "How old were you?"

She could tell he didn't want to talk about it. Maybe she should have let him off the hook. But she couldn't. Something warned her that whatever had happened was a vital element in forming his present-day persona.

"I was ten and our vacation time was up, so we were getting ready to leave. My cousins and brothers and I were all running around doing our level best to pack in a final few minutes of fun while my sister, Gia, chased after us doing *her* level best to round us up. Since she was the youngest and only five, you can imagine how well that worked."

"And then?" Larkin prompted.

He lifted a shoulder in a casual shrug, though she suspected his attitude toward that long-ago event was anything but casual. "Draco climbed a tree in order to tease Gia. I knew it would take a while for my parents to get him down, so I took off to check on this dam I'd built along the river that fed the lake. Apparently while I was gone Draco fell out of the tree and broke his leg."

She rubbed at her own leg and winced in sympathy. "Ouch. How bad a break was it?"

"Bad. All hell broke loose. Mamma and *Babbo*—my mother and father—took Draco to the hospital. Gia was hysterical, so Nonna and Primo took her with them. My aunt and uncle grabbed Luc and their four boys."

He was breaking her heart. "No one wondered where you were? They just…forgot about you?"

"There were a lot of kids running around." He spoke as though from a memorized script. "They each thought someone else had taken me. Draco was in pretty bad shape, so my parents stayed overnight with him at the hospital, which is why they didn't realize I'd been overlooked."

She could sympathize with his parents' decision, having gone through a similar ordeal. Only, in her case her mother hadn't stayed with her. Gran had been the one to stick by her side day and night. "When did they figure out you were missing?"

"Late the next day. They didn't get back to the city until then. When they went to round us all up, they discovered I was nowhere to be found."

"How hideous." Larkin gnawed at her lip. "Poor Elia. She must have been frantic."

Rafe glared in exasperation. "Poor Elia? What about poor Rafe?"

"You're right." So right. "Poor Rafe. I'm so sorry."

He reminded her of a snarling lion, pacing off his annoyance, and she couldn't resist the urge to soothe him. She approached as cautiously as she would a wild animal. At first she thought he'd back away. But he didn't. Nor did he encourage her, not that that stopped her.

Sliding her hands along the impressive breadth of his chest, Larkin gripped his shoulders and rose on tiptoe. His mouth hovered just within reach and she didn't hesitate. She gave him a slow, champagne-sweetened kiss. Their lips mated, fitting together as perfectly as their bodies. It had been this way from the start and she couldn't help but wonder—if circumstances had been different, would their relationship have developed into a real one?

It was a lovely dream. But that's all it was. The realization hurt more than she would have believed possible. He started to deepen the kiss, to take it to the next step. If the ring and champagne and engagement had been real, nothing would have stopped her from following him down such a tempting path. But it wasn't real and she forced herself to pull back.

She wasn't ready to go there. Not until she came to terms with the temporary nature of their relationship. Rafe might not realize it yet, but the "if" of their lovemaking would be her decision alone. The "when" on her terms.

He released a sigh. "Let me guess. More questions?"

She offered a sympathetic smile. "Afraid so."

"Get it over with."

"What in the world did you do when you returned and discovered everyone gone?" she asked, genuinely curious.

"I sat and waited for a couple of hours. After a while I got hungry, but the summerhouse was all locked up. So I decided maybe I was being punished for running off instead of staying where I'd been told and my punishment was to find my own way home."

Larkin's mouth dropped open. "Oh, my God. You didn't—"

"Hitchhike? Sure did."

"Do you have any idea how dangerous that was?" She broke off and shook her head. "Of course you do. Now."

"It all seemed very simple and logical to me. I just needed to get from the lake to San Francisco. The hardest part was walking to the freeway. And finding food."

Larkin couldn't seem to wrap her head around the story. "How? Where?"

"I came across a campsite. No one was there." He shrugged. "Probably out hiking, so I helped myself to some of their food and water."

She stared in disbelief. "You made it home, didn't you?"

"It took three days, but yes. I made it home on my own. Walked some. Snuck onto a bus at one point. The toughest part was coming up with acceptable excuses for why I was out on my own—excuses that wouldn't have the people who helped me calling the authorities."

"Your parents must have been frantic."

He crossed to the table and poured himself a second glass of champagne, topping hers off in the process. "To put it mildly."

"And ever since then?"

He studied her over the rim of the crystal flute. "Ever since then…what?"

She narrowed her eyes in contemplation. "Ever since then, you've been fiercely independent, determined not to depend on anyone other than yourself."

He shrugged. "It didn't change anything. I've always been the independent sort."

"Seriously, Rafe. You must have been terrified when you discovered you'd been left behind."

"Maybe a little."

"And hurt. Terribly hurt that the family you loved and trusted just up and deserted you."

"I got over it." Ice slipped into his voice. "Besides, they didn't desert me."

"But you thought they did," she persisted. "It explains a lot, you know."

"I don't like being psychoanalyzed."

"Neither do I. But at least now I understand why you hold people at an emotional distance and why you're so determined to control your world." It must have been sheer hell being married to someone like Leigh, who was a master at manipulating emotions and equally determined to be the one in control. "Did you ever tell your wife about the incident?"

"Leigh wasn't interested in the past. She pretty much lived in the now and planned for the future. Even if I had mentioned it to her, I doubt it would have made any difference."

True enough. "It makes a difference to me," Larkin murmured.

"Why?"

Because it clarified one simple fact. Their relationship would never work. His independent nature would rebel against any sort of long-term connection. Deepening that problem had been his experience at the lake all those years ago, when he'd learned to trust only himself during that three-day trek home. He wouldn't dare put his faith in someone he couldn't trust. And once he knew the truth about her, he'd never trust her. She strongly suspected that once that trust was lost, it could never be regained.

She also found it interesting that he was running away from what she'd spent her entire life wishing she could have. Family. An ingrained knowledge that she belonged. Hearth and home. Though her grandmother had been a loving, generous woman, she hadn't been the most sociable person in the world. She lived on a small farm, happy with a simple, natural existence far from the nearest town. While love and obligation had kept Larkin by her grandmother's side until her grandmother's death and news of Leigh's death had reached her, through the years she'd begun to long for more. The sort of "more" that Rafe had rejected. During the last year of Gran's life, Larkin had created a game plan for attaining that something more. First on her agenda was to track down her father. Then she intended to obtain a job at a rescue organization and pursue her real passion—saving animals like Kiko.

The only remaining question was… How did she get herself out of her current predicament? Of course, she knew how. All she had to do was tell him that she was Leigh's sister—*half* sister—and their temporary engagement would come to a permanent end. Then he'd either agree to what she required in lieu of payment, or he wouldn't. End of story.

What she really needed to know was how much longer he intended to drag out their engagement, and what sort of exit strategy he had planned. Knowing Rafe, there was definitely a plan.

"I have one last question," she began.

"Unfortunately for you, I'm done answering them. There's only one thing I want right now." He set the flute on the table with enough force to make the crystal sing. He turned and regarded her with a burning gaze. "And that's you."

How had she thought she could control this man? It would seem she was as foolish as Leigh. "I don't think—"

"I'm not asking you to think." Rafe approached, kicking a chair from his path. "I don't even care whether you choose to wear my ring or not. There's only one thing that matters. One thing that either of us wants. And it's what we've wanted from the moment we first met."

Without another word, he swept Larkin into his arms. The stars wheeled overhead as her world turned upside down. She clutched at his shoulders and held on for dear life. Her lion was loose and on a rampage and she doubted anything she said or did would change that fact.

"You're going to make love to me, aren't you?"

"Oh, yeah."

"Even though it breaks your promise to your grandfather?"

He shouldered his way into her bedroom. "I'm not breaking my promise to Primo. I put a ring on your finger. If you decide to take it off again, that's your choice. As far as I'm concerned, we're officially engaged."

"Rafe—"

He lowered her to the bed and followed her down. "Do you really want me to stop?"

The question whispered through the air, filled with temptation and allure. It was truth time. She didn't want him to stop. Just a few short days ago she'd never have believed herself capable of tumbling into bed with Leigh's husband. It was the last thing she wanted from him. But now...

Now she couldn't find the willpower to resist. It was wrong. So very wrong. And yet, she'd never felt anything so right. Every part of her vibrated with the sweetness of the connection that flowed between them. It danced from her body to his and back again, coiling around and through her, building with each passing second.

"I don't want you to stop," she admitted. "But I don't want you to regret this later on."

"Why would I regret it?" Despite the darkness, she could see the smile that flirted with his mouth and hear it penetrate his voice. "If anything, this should ease the tension between us."

"Or make it worse."

He leaned into her, sweeping the collar of her dress to one side and finding that sweet spot in the juncture between her neck and shoulder. "Does this feel worse?"

A soft moan escaped. "That's not what I meant."

"How about this?"

She shuddered at the caress. So soft. So teasing. Like the brush of a downy feather against her skin. "I mean when we go our separate ways. When the job ends. This will make it worse. Harder."

"It just gives us some interesting memories to take with us when we part."

"But it will end, right? You understand that?"

He traced a string of kisses down the length of her neck, pausing long enough to say, "I thought that was supposed to be my line."

"I just want to be clear about it. That's all."

"Fine. We're both clear about it."

"There's one other thing I should tell you before we go any further."

He sat up with a sigh, allowing a rush of cool air to pour over her, chilling her. A second later the nightstand lamp snapped on, flooding the room with brightness. "The timing's wrong, isn't it?"

Larkin jackknifed upright. "No, not at all." She twisted her hands together. "Do you think you could turn off the light?"

"Why?"

"I'd just find it easier to say this next part if the light were off."

"Okay." A simple click plunged the room back into the safety of darkness. "Talk."

"I think it's only fair to warn you. What we're about to do?"

"You mean, what we *were* doing but aren't?"

"Oh, no. It's definitely *are* doing. Or rather, about to do. Unless you change your mind."

"What the hell is going on, Larkin?"

"I've never done this before, okay?" she confessed in a rush.

Dead silence greeted her confession. "You mean you've never had an affair with someone after such a short acquaintance. You've never had a one-night stand. That's what you mean, right?"

"That, too."

He swore. "You're a virgin?"

"Pretty much."

"Last time I checked, that question required a yes or no answer. It's like pregnancy. Either you are or you're not. There's no 'pretty much' or 'sort of' involved."

She blew out a sigh. "Yes, I'm a virgin. Does it really matter that much?"

"I want to say no. But I'd be lying." He stood. "Looks like Primo didn't need to make that stipulation after all. All you had to do was say three simple words and you're officially hands-off."

She couldn't let it end like this. She didn't want it to end. She'd waited all this time for the right man and despite all that stood between them, she couldn't imagine making love with anyone else. If she didn't do something to stop him, he'd leave. Who knew if she'd be given another opportunity?

Larkin didn't hesitate. Grabbing the tails of her shirtdress, she tugged it up and over her head and tossed it to one side. She fumbled for the bedside lamp and switched it on, then froze, overwhelmed by her daring.

Her actions seemed to have a similar effect on Rafe. He froze as well, staring at her with an expression that should have had her diving under the covers. Instead, it heated her blood to a near boil.

She stood before him in a silvery-blue bra and thong that were made of gossamer strands of silk, clinging to her breasts and hips like a glittering cobweb. The set was the most revealing she'd ever owned. The bra was low cut, lovingly cupping her small breasts and practically serving them up for Rafe's inspection. Even more revealing was the thong. The minuscule triangle of semitransparent silk did nothing to protect her modesty. It just drew attention to her boyish hips and the feminine delta of her thighs. If she turned so much as a quarter of an inch, he'd also have a perfect view of the ripe curve of her backside.

It was as though he'd read her mind. "Turn around." The demand was low and guttural, filled with uncompromising masculine promise. Or was it more of a threat?

She rotated in place, feeling the heat of his gaze streak across her, burning with intent. When she faced him again, he hadn't moved from his position and her nervousness increased. Why wasn't he reacting? Why hadn't he taken her into his arms and carried her back to the bed?

"Rafe?" Anxiety rippled through the word.

"Take them off. No more barriers between us."

This was not what she'd planned. "I thought you—"

He cut her off with a shake of his head. "I want you to be very certain about this. I don't want there to be any lingering questions in your mind, now or later. If you want to make love with me, if you're absolutely certain this is right for you, then take off the rest of your clothes."

The light continued to blaze across her, ruthless

in slicing through the protective barrier of darkness. She understood his point. It wasn't that he didn't want to touch her. She could see the desire blazing in his expression, could feel the palpable waves of control stretched to the breaking point. Every instinct urged him to take her. To lay claim.

But he wouldn't. Not until she convinced him that she'd made this decision of her own free will, without his influencing her with one of his world-shattering kisses or beyond-delicious caresses.

She smiled.

There wasn't any hesitation this time. She reached behind her and unhooked the bra. The straps slid down her arms and clung for a brief instant, as did the cups. Then it drifted from her body to disappear into the pool of shadows at her feet.

A low moan escaped Rafe, and the tips of her breasts pebbled in response. "Finish it," he demanded.

She lifted an eyebrow, daring to tease. "Are you sure you wouldn't like to take care of this last part yourself?"

He took a swift step forward before catching himself. "Larkin—"

She put him out of his misery. Tiny bows held the thong in place and she tugged at them, allowing the scrap of silk to follow the same path as her bra.

"Is this enough to convince you?" She held out her hand, the one where The Inferno throbbed with such persuasive insistence. "Please, Rafe. Make love to me."

Rafe didn't need any further encouragement. In two rapid strides he reached her side and wrapped her in an unbreakable hold. Together they fell backward onto the bed. His mouth closed over Larkin's, hot with demand. She slid her fingers deep into his hair, anchoring him in place, as though afraid he'd leave her again if she didn't. Foolish of her. Now that he had her naked in his arms, he intended to keep her that way for as long as humanly possible, and hang the consequences. All that mattered right now was making it the best possible experience for her.

"I'm feeling a bit overdressed," he murmured against her mouth.

Her laugh was sweet and gentle and, for some reason, drove him utterly insane. "I think I can help you with that."

She made short work of the buttons of his shirt, yanking the edges open and sliding it from his shoulders. He shrugged it the rest of the way off and sucked in his breath when her hands collided with his chest. She had a way of touching him, of stroking her fingers across him. Just. So. This time the strokes took her farther afield, tracing the center line of his abdomen downward until she collided with his belt.

"I can take care of that," he offered. It might kill him to let go of her even for that brief a time. But considering the rewards of stripping off his trousers, he'd manage it.

"I'd like to do it." She laughed. "At the risk of totally freaking you, I've never stripped a man before."

It didn't freak him. In fact, it had the opposite effect. He wanted her to experience it all, anything and everything she wanted. Whatever would please her. He only hoped it didn't kill him in the process.

"Tell me if I do anything that makes you uncomfortable and I'll stop."

"I don't think that'll be an issue."

He captured her hands in his before she could finish removing his clothes. "I'm serious, Larkin. It could happen. I want this to be as perfect as possible for you."

She paused in her efforts long enough to cup his face. "See, here's how I figure it. It isn't the making-love part that needs to be perfect."

Rafe choked on a laugh. "No? In that case, I've been wasting my time all these years."

"Yes, you have," she retorted. "What needs to be perfect is who you're making love with."

He closed his eyes and swallowed. Hard. "Hell, sweetheart. Don't say that. I'm not perfect."

"No, you're not." He caught the tart edge underscoring her words and couldn't help chuckling. "But in this moment, you're perfect for me. Right man. Right place. Right time."

"But no pressure."

Her laughter bubbled up to join his. "None at all."

She made short work of his remaining clothing, removing the last of the barriers separating them. He gathered her up, spreading her across the bed. Moonlight picked a path into the room through the French doors leading into the yard. It was almost as though she drew the light to her. It seemed to rejoice in her presence, gilding her with its radiance and turning her skin and hair to silver. Only her eyes retained their vibrancy, glittering a glorious turquoise-blue that rivaled the most precious gem in his family's possession.

He studied her with undisguised curiosity. Had she always been this small? This delicate? How could something so ethereal contain such a huge personality?

Slowly he traced her features, finding a whimsical beauty in the arching curve of her cheekbones and straight, pert nose, her wide, sultry mouth and pointed chin. Then there was her body, superbly toned and supple.

"I don't think I've ever seen anyone more beautiful," he told her.

She shook her head. "Lots of women are more beautiful."

He stopped her denial with a slow, thorough kiss. "Not to me. Not tonight." He pulled back a few precious inches, reluctant to separate them by even that much. "Shall I prove it to you?"

Her eyes widened and she nodded, a delighted grin spreading across her mouth. "If you must."

"Oh, I must."

He cupped her breasts, their slight weight fitting comfortably in his hands. Then he bent and tasted them, one after the other, scraping his teeth across the rigid tips. Her breath escaped in a gasp and she arched beneath him, offering herself more fully. She shifted beneath him, fluid and flowing, parting her legs to accommodate him. And all the while her hands performed a tantalizing dance, tripping and teasing across him, one minute urging him onward, the next startling him with an unexpected caress.

It became a game, each trying to distract the other, their need and tension escalating with each passing moment. He discovered that her legs were incredibly sensitive, and that if he traced a line along the very top of her thigh and eased inward to the moist heart of her, she'd quiver like the wings of a newly hatched butterfly.

Their game came to an abrupt end when she darted

downward between their bodies and cupped him, delighted by his surging response. "Larkin," he warned. "I can't wait much longer."

She squirmed in anticipation. "I don't want you to wait."

He snagged the condom he'd had the foresight to stash in her nightstand table. An instant later, he settled between her thighs. He lifted her knees, opening her for his possession. But he didn't take her immediately. Instead, he slowed, making sure that the culmination of their lovemaking would be as pleasurable as the dance that had preceded it. Gently he parted her, found the secret heart hidden within and traced the sensitive nubbin.

She shuddered in reaction, lifting herself toward his touch. He slipped a finger inward, then two, and felt the velvety contraction of impending climax. "Rafe, please," she whispered. "Make love to me."

He carefully surged forward, claiming her as his own. She reached for him and he laced her hand in his. Their palms joined, melded, just as their bodies joined, melded. Heat flashed between them, sharp and penetrating, building with each thrust of his hips.

Larkin rose to meet him, singing her siren's song, calling to him in a voice that penetrated straight to his heart, straight to his soul. It lodged there. Her sweet voice. Her heartbreaking gaze. The tempered strength of her body as it surrounded him, held him. Refused to let him go.

Never before had he felt anything remotely similar to this. Not with any other woman. It was as though the mating of their bodies had mated every other part of them, forging a connection he'd never known existed.

Heat blazed within his palm, while an undeniable knowledge blossomed.

This night had changed him and he'd never be the same again.

Eight

Larkin stirred, moaning as tender muscles protested the movement.

"You okay?" Rafe asked.

She lifted her head and forced open a single bleary eye, blinking at him. "I think that depends on your definition of 'okay.' I'm alive. Does that count?"

"It counts."

"It's the strangest sensation."

"What is?"

"Most of my body is screaming, 'Don't move.' But there are a few regions that are saying, 'Again. Now.'" She decided to experiment and shift a fraction of an inch. "I'd be an absolute fool to listen to the 'Again. Now' crowd."

"'Kay."

He started to roll off the bed and she shot out her hand to stop him. "Call me a fool."

A sleepy grin spread across Rafe's face. "Call us both fools."

She went into his arms as though she belonged, which maybe she did, despite all that stood in their way. He'd been so careful with her, so attentive, determined to make certain she enjoyed her first sexual experience. No matter what happened from this point forward, she'd always have the memory of this night to cling to.

"Thank you," she told him.

He lifted an eyebrow. "For what?"

"For being perfect. Or at least, perfect for me."

It took him a moment to reply. "You're welcome."

She lifted her mouth for his kiss, shivering as it deepened and grew more intense. Kissing she knew about. She'd kissed a fair number of men. But those experiences paled in comparison to what she shared with Rafe. With the merest brush of his lips, Rafe seduced her. That's all it took for her to want him. To feel the rising tide of desire crash over and through her. One single kiss and she knew she was meant to be his. One single kiss and she knew...

She loved him.

The breath caught in her throat. No. That wasn't possible. She pushed against his shoulders and tumbled away from him, fighting to drag air into her lungs. Sex was one thing. But love? No, no, no! How could she have been so foolish?

"Larkin?" He reached for her. "Sweetheart, what's wrong?"

She evaded his hand. It was *that* hand. The hand that had started all their trouble. The one that had damned her with a single touch. The touch that had infected her with The Inferno.

She snagged the sheet and wound it tightly around herself, for the first time abruptly and painfully aware of her nudity. "How are we going to get out of this?" she demanded, her voice taking on a sharp edge.

He watched her, a wary glint in his eyes. "Get out of what?"

She shook her hand at him. Sparks from the diamond ring he'd placed there sent jagged shards of fire exploding in all directions. "Get out of this. Get out of our engagement. What's your exit strategy?"

He shrugged. "I don't know. Does it matter?" He patted the mattress. "Come on back to bed. It's not like there's any hurry."

She ignored the second part of his suggestion and focused on the first. For some reason, his admission filled her with panic. "What do you mean, you don't know? You must have a plan. You *always* have a plan."

He stilled, his eyes narrowing. "What's with the sudden urgency, Larkin?"

"I need to know how this is going to end. I need to know when."

He vaulted from the bed and padded across the room to where his trousers lay in a crumpled heap and snagged them off the floor. "You're having regrets."

She thrust her hand through her hair, tumbling the curls into even greater disarray. "I don't regret making love to you, if that's what you're getting at."

He grunted in disbelief. "Right."

Kicking the sheet out from beneath her feet, she came after him. "I'm serious. I don't have any regrets about that. None. Zero."

"Then what?" He tossed his trousers aside and cupped

her shoulders. Dragging her into his arms, he examined her upturned face, his expression hard and remote. "One minute we were kissing and the next you're freaking out about exit strategies. What the hell happened?"

She clamped her lips shut to hold back the words. That worked for an entire twenty seconds before the truth came spilling out. "I liked it."

He stared blankly. "Liked what?"

"Making love to you."

His lips twitched and then he grinned. "That's good. I liked making love to you, too."

"No, you don't understand." She attempted to tear free of his hold, but he wouldn't let her. Why in the world had she elected to have this conversation with his stark nakedness hanging out all over the place? It made rational thought beyond impossible. "I *liked* making love to you. A lot."

"I'm still right there with you."

She groaned in frustration. "Do I really have to spell it out for you?"

"Apparently you do."

"I *liked* making love with you. I *loved* making love with you. I want to do it again, as often as possible."

He reared back. "Well, hell, woman. No wonder you want to end our engagement. Who would want to make love as often as possible?"

"Stop it, Rafe." To her horror, she could feel the rush of tears. "You're supposed to be the logical one. You're supposed to have life all figured out. Hasn't it occurred to you that if we keep doing—" she shot a look of intense longing over her shoulder toward the bed "—what we've been doing, it might be sort of tough to stop?"

"Who said anything about stopping?"

Didn't he get it? "Don't you get it? That's generally what happens when engagements end. The two unengaged people stop making love." She pouted, something she hadn't done since she was all of three. "And I don't want to stop. So what happens when it's time to stop and we don't want to?"

"What usually happens is that those feelings ease up or wear off." He said it so gently that it made the pain all the worse. "It's just because you've never gotten to that stage of a relationship before. But trust me, I have it on good authority that excellent sex and mounds of bling aren't enough to make a woman want to stick around once she walks out the bedroom door."

That didn't make a bit of sense. "Now *I* don't understand." She waved her hand in a dismissive gesture when he started to explain again. "I get that you think the physical end of things will gradually grow ho-hum."

"I didn't say ho-hum," he retorted, stung.

"But what I don't get is what that has to do with the rest of it. What's bling got to do with sex, and what changes between us once we leave the bedroom? Is there a manual somewhere that explains these things? Because I have to tell you, I'm clueless."

He gave a short, hard laugh. "Are you serious? You don't know what bling has to do with sex?"

She shot him a knife-sharp look. "No. And if you do, then you've been hanging with the wrong sort of women."

He ran a hand along the nape of his neck. "I have to admit you've got me there."

"Look, I don't give a damn about bling. If the sex gets ho-hum, bling sure as hell isn't going to fix the problem, now, is it?" She planted her hands on her hips, only to make a frantic grab for the sheet when it started a southward migration. "What I need you to explain is what's going to happen after we leave the bedroom that will make our relationship turn sour?"

"I believe it has something to do with my being a loner," he explained a shade too calmly. "Too independent. Not domesticated. Emotionally distant. *Intimidating*."

The rapid-fire litany worried her. It sounded as if he was quoting someone, and she could take a wild stab as to the identity of that someone. "Is that what Leigh told you?" Larkin asked, outraged.

"She wasn't the only one." He scrubbed at his face, the rasp of his beard as abrasive as the conversation. "How the hell did we get on this subject anyway?"

"Let me get this straight.... You think that once I've gotten bored with having sex with you, I'll actually want to leave you?"

"Yes." Humor turned his eyes a brilliant shade of jade. "Though I'll do my best not to bore you while we're in bed."

"And that's your exit strategy? One day I'll be here and the next day I'll be gone and you'll tell your relatives that I got bored and left."

His expression iced over. "I don't explain myself to my relatives."

She cocked an eyebrow in patent disbelief. "Something tells me that you'll need to do a lot more than explain the situation to them if—*when*—I leave." He didn't argue, which told her that he privately agreed with her assessment. Sorrow filled her when she realized that even if he didn't have a plan, she did. "I'll tell you what. I'll take care of it for you."

He frowned. "You'll take care of our breakup?"

"Yes."

"And how do you intend to accomplish that?"

Stupid. Very stupid of her. She should have anticipated the question. "It's better if you don't know."

He shook his head and folded his arms across his chest. Standing there, nude and intensely male, she could see how some women might find him intimidating. Not her. She swallowed. Probably not her.

"I happen to think it's better if I do know your plan," he insisted. "Now, spill."

"If I explain beforehand, you won't be in a position to react appropriately."

"I won't let you cheat on me." The fierceness behind his comment had her stumbling back a step. "Nor will they believe you, if that's what you're going to try to tell them."

"It isn't," she instantly denied. "That never even occurred to me."

Her bewildered sincerity must have convinced him, because he nodded. "Okay, then." He throttled back a notch or two. "Give me some sort of idea so I can decide whether or not it'll work."

She didn't dare tell him, or he'd find out how well it would work right here and now. "Trust me, it'll work. Not only will they believe it, but they'll rally around you. You won't have to worry about anyone trying to find another Inferno bride for you ever again."

She looked him straight in the eye as she said it. Could he see the bleakness she felt reflected in her gaze? He must have, because he took a swift step in her direction.

"Larkin? What is it?" Concern colored his voice. "Are you ill? Is something wrong with you?"

"It's nothing like that," she assured him. Time to move this in another direction before he broke her down and forced the truth from her. She planted her splayed hands on his chest and maneuvered him backward toward the bed. "Why don't we table this discussion for now and in the meantime, I suggest you get busy and bore me."

His legs hit the edge of the mattress and he reached out to snag her around the waist as he toppled backward. She tumbled on top of him, laughing as she fell. It still hurt whenever she thought about the future. Hurt unbearably to realize that this couldn't last. But she'd known it wouldn't when she'd agreed to an affair. And until the moment came when he found out who she was and what she wanted from him, she'd enjoy every single second of their time together.

Would he consider it a fair bargain? Somehow she doubted it and it distressed her to think that she'd make him any more of a loner than he was already. That he'd continue to turn from people because he no longer trusted them. She'd never forgive herself if that happened. But maybe he'd understand. Maybe he'd help her and they could part on good terms.

And maybe baby pigs around the world would sprout gossamer wings and use them to fly straight to the moon.

He tunneled his fingers through her hair and thrust the wayward curls away from her face. "What are you thinking about?"

She forced out a smile. "Nothing important."

"Whatever it was, it made you look so sad."

"Then why don't you give me something else to think about?"

He didn't need any further prompting. He took her mouth in a hot, urgent kiss, one that drove every thought from her head except one. Rafe. The way his lips drove her wild with desire. The hard, knowing sweep of his hands across her skin. Those magical fingers that left her weeping with pleasure. It was an enchantment from which she never wanted to escape.

She gave herself up to pleasure, exploring him with an open curiosity that he seemed to find intensely arousing. She'd never realized how hard and uncompromising a man's body could be in some areas and how flexible and sensitive in others. But she didn't allow a single inch of him to go uncharted.

One minute laughter reigned as she painted her way across his shape with her fingertips and the next minute it all changed. "I can't imagine ever becoming bored with you." She whispered the confession.

It took him a moment to reply. "I'm not sure it's possible for me to be bored, either. Not with you."

What should have been a light and carefree exchange took on a darker aspect, shades within shades of meaning, filled with a bittersweet yearning. She kissed him. Lingered. Then she began to paint him into her memory again. Only this time she did it with her mouth and lips and tongue, sculpting him with nibbling bites and soothing kisses. Arms. Chest. Belly. He called to her, the cry of the wolf for its mate. But all it did was drive her onward to the very source of his desire.

He didn't allow her to linger as long as she would

have liked. Instead, he became the sculptor, shaping and molding her until they became one. He linked his hands with hers, just as he had before. She knew why, could see it in his eyes and in the emotions he didn't dare express. Even though he would have rejected its existence with every ounce of his intellect, it throbbed between them, giving lie to his denial.

She opened herself to him, took him deep inside her until they flowed together in perfect harmony. She wrapped herself around him, surrendering to the explosion of passion, swept away like a leaf before a whirlwind. Tumbling endlessly into the most glorious sensation, a sensation made perfect because she wasn't alone. She was there with Rafe.

The people in his life called him a lone wolf and he'd more than lived up to his reputation, to the point where he believed it himself. But there was something he'd never considered. Something he either didn't know or had forgotten. But she knew. She understood. Because she was as much a lone wolf as he was.

Wolves mate for life.

The next week proved one of the most incredible of Larkin's life. Making love to Rafe shouldn't have made such a difference. But somehow it did. Whenever she bothered to analyze the situation—which wasn't often— she realized that it wasn't the sex itself that accounted for that difference, but the level of intimacy. It deepened, became richer, added a dimension to their relationship that hadn't existed before.

They spent hours in conversation, discussing every topic under the sun, except the few she avoided in order to keep him from connecting her to Leigh. Art. Science.

Literature. The jewelry business. It all became rich fodder for the hours they spent together.

How could anyone consider him emotionally distant? Or unavailable? Or even intimidating? It defied understanding. To her delight, he'd taken to Kiko, the two becoming firm friends. Even more amusing, she'd come across him a time or two conducting a lengthy one-way conversation with the animal.

"You will let me know if she answers, won't you?" Larkin teased when she discovered him discussing the merits of raw versus cooked beef with Kiko.

"I don't know what it is about that dog, but she insists on eating her food raw."

"She likes it the way nature intended. That might not be the healthiest for us, but it works for her."

He set Kiko's bowl on the ground. "Have you finished packing for the lake?"

"I have. Not that there's much to pack. Even with your mother supplementing my wardrobe, I can still fit everything into my backpack." She winced. "I think."

"Mamma does seem intent on filling up your closet."

Larkin smiled, though it felt a bit forced. "Every time I go in there I find another new outfit."

"Don't sweat it," he reassured her. "She's enjoying herself."

"I realize that." She shifted restlessly. "But it bothers me because she doesn't know our engagement is a sham. I don't want her to spend all this money on me when I'm never going to be her daughter-in-law. It's not right."

Rafe turned to face her, leaning his hip against the counter. "We've had this discussion before." He fixed her with his penetrating green gaze, his expression one that no doubt sent his employees scurrying in instant obedience. "I don't see any point in having it again."

It was the second time she'd caught a glimpse of the more intimidating aspect of his personality. Not that he hadn't warned her. She'd just been foolish enough not to believe him. She should have known better. Rafe didn't pull his punches.

"In that case, I'll wear a few of the outfits and leave the rest," she said lightly. "You can return them after I'm gone."

He shoved away from the kitchen counter and approached. "Why all this talk about leaving?"

"Well…" She forced herself to hold her ground even though a siren blared in her head, urging a full-scale retreat. "It occurred to me that since everyone's going to be at the lake, that might be a good time to stage our breakup."

"In front of all my relatives?"

"Bad idea?"

"Very bad idea, since I'm willing to bet that the majority of them would take your side in any fight you might care to initiate."

She cleared her throat. "I wasn't thinking of a fight, so much as an announcement."

"I don't do fights or announcements. Not in public. And I sure as hell don't do them in front of my entire family."

He closed to within inches of her. No matter how hard she tried, she couldn't keep herself from falling back a pace or two. Kiko looked on with intense curiosity and Larkin suspected that if it had been anyone other than Rafe proving his intimidation skills, the dog would have objected in no uncertain terms.

"Are you bored already, Larkin? Is that the problem?"

Her mouth parted in shock. "No! How could you even think such a thing?"

If shrugs could be sarcastic, Rafe had it nailed. "Oh, I don't know. Maybe it has something to do with your wanting to break off our engagement after one short week."

"In case I didn't make it clear enough last night, I'm not bored." Images of what they'd spent the time doing flashed through her head and brought a telltale blush to her cheeks. "Not even close."

"I'm relieved to hear it. But if it's not boredom…" He raised an eyebrow and waited.

Naturally, she broke first. Would she *ever* learn to control her tongue? "I'm afraid, okay?"

It was his turn to look shocked. "Afraid?" Shock became concern. "Of me?"

"No!" She flew into his arms, impacting with a delicious thud. "How could you even think such a thing?"

He wrapped her in a tight embrace. "Hell, sweetheart." He rested his chin on top of her head. "What else am I supposed to think?"

"Not that. Never that."

He pulled back a few inches and snagged her chin with his index finger, forcing her to look at him. "Then what are you afraid of?"

She didn't want to explain. Didn't want to tell him. But she didn't see what other choice she had. And maybe if he understood, he'd let her go before it was too late.

"It's what we were talking about before. I'm afraid to drag out our engagement," she admitted. "I'm afraid that it'll hurt too much when the time comes to walk away."

Something dark and powerful moved in his gaze. How could any woman have believed for one little minute that he was emotionally distant? It wasn't distance, but self-control. Larkin had never known a man whose emotions ran deeper or more passionately than Rafe's. And because they were so strong, he'd learned to exert an iron will over them to keep them in check. Intimidating? Okay, she'd give Leigh that one. But not distant. Never that.

"I won't let you go." The words came out whisper-soft and all the more potent because of it. "I can't."

He didn't give her the opportunity to reply. Instead, he swept her into his arms. Instead of carrying her in the direction of the guest suite, he climbed the stairs to his own bedroom. They'd never made love there before and she'd understood without it ever being said that his inner sanctum was off-limits.

He lowered her to her feet once they were inside and she looked around, curious. If anything, the room confirmed her opinion of him. The furnishings were distinctly masculine, powerful and well built, with strong sweeping lines. But there was also an elegance of form and a richness of color both in the decor and the warmth of the wood accents and trim. If she'd been shown a hundred different rooms and asked which belonged to Rafe, she'd have chosen this one in an instant.

The door swung shut behind her with a loud click and she turned to discover him watching her, the intensity of his gaze eerily similar to Kiko's. "Welcome to my den," Rafe said.

She attempted a smile, with only limited success. "Am I your Little Red Riding Hood?"

He approached, yanking his shirt over his head as he came. There was something raw and elemental in the way he moved and in the manner in which he regarded her. "Not even close."

Her smile faded. The wash of emotions thickening the air between them was far too potent for levity. She responded to the scent of desire, to the perfume of want, feeling it stir her blood and feed her hunger. Her body ripened in anticipation, flowering with the need to have him on her and in her. To be possessed and to be the possessor.

"Then what am I?" she whispered.

"Don't you know?" He backed her toward the bed. "Haven't you figured it out yet?"

In that instant she understood. Knew what he was to her and she to him.

She was his mate.

She could see it in his stance and in the possessiveness of his gaze, in the timbre of his voice and the strength of his desire. By bringing her here, he'd lowered his guard and allowed her into the most private part of his home… into the most private part of himself.

Even as she surrendered to his touch, a part of her wept. He'd finally opened himself to her, and in a few short weeks—possibly in just days—she was going to destroy not just his trust, but any hope of his ever loving her.

Nine

The closer they came to the lake house over the course of the three hour drive, the more Larkin's tension increased. Rafe could feel it pouring off her in waves. It didn't take a genius to guess the cause.

"No one's going to know," he told her.

She tilted her head to one side and peered at him over a spare set of his sunglasses, since she didn't own a pair of her own. "They're not going to know that we're sleeping together? Or they're not going to know that our engagement is a sham?"

His mouth twitched in amusement at the way the glasses swamped her delicate features. "Yes."

She considered that for a moment before releasing a low, husky laugh. "You're right. Blame it on an overly active sense of guilt."

"Guilt because you're sleeping with me, or guilt because our engagement's a sham?"

She shot him a swift grin. "Yes."

"Let's take care of your first concern." He spared her a heated look. "Sex."

"I believe you take care of that on a regular basis," she responded promptly.

"I do my best," he replied with impressive modesty. "Fortunately for you, you're about to discover that the engagement ring you're wearing is magical."

She held it out, admiring the way it caught and refracted the light. "It is?"

"Without question. The minute I put it on your finger, it created a net of blissful ignorance."

"Funny. I don't feel blissfully ignorant."

He snorted. "Not you. My family."

"Ah." To his relief, she began to relax. "And I assume this magical net keeps everyone from knowing we're sleeping together?"

"Without question. They may suspect, but the ring will cause them to turn a blind eye to it."

"Even Primo and Nonna?"

"Especially Primo and Nonna," he confirmed.

"And my other concern?"

That eventuality continued to hover between them like a malevolent cloud. "The reality—or lack thereof—of our engagement is also a nonissue."

"And why is that?" she asked.

He could hear the intense curiosity in her voice, along with a yearning that he found quite satisfying. "I have a plan."

"Which is?" she asked uneasily.

He debated for a moment. "I don't think I'm going to tell you. Not yet." At least not until he figured out how to convince her it would work. It would be a huge step for both of them. Only time could prove whether that step was the right one. "My plan needs a while to ripen."

She shifted in her seat, betraying her nervousness. "You do remember that I also have a plan, right?"

"We'll consider that plan B."

"I'm not sure that'll work," she murmured.

"Why not?"

She released a sigh filled with regret. "It's sort of on automatic. Eventually it's going to go off by itself."

"What the hell does that mean?"

But they arrived at the lake before she responded, which caused her as much relief as it caused him annoyance. He filed the information away for a more opportune time to drag out the details. One nice thing about his fiancée was that she found it impossible to keep secrets from him. A single, tiny nudge and it all spilled out.

They pulled up to the main residence, a huge sprawling building. When he'd been a kid, the place had looked far different, more rustic. But in recent years the family had rebuilt and expanded it, cantilevering the newer two end wings out over the lake. They'd also added private cabins, which dotted the shoreline and were better suited for the privacy issues of newly married couples.

Larkin leaned forward, her breath catching. "My God, it's magnificent."

He smiled in satisfaction. "Maybe you can understand why we all make the effort to come here each year."

"I'd never want to leave."

He parked in the gravel area adjacent to the storage

shed and workshop. "We'll be expected to stay at the main house."

"In separate rooms, I assume."

"Guaranteed. Don't let it worry you. I know plenty of places where we can find some privacy."

She appeared intrigued by the possibility. "I've never made love in the woods before."

"Only because there hasn't been the opportunity until now. I look forward to correcting that oversight."

She shot him a mischievous look. "So do I."

The next several days proved enlightening. After an initial shyness, both Larkin and Kiko took to his family with impressive enthusiasm. It made him realize that she never talked about her family, other than the occasional reference to her grandmother, and he couldn't help but wonder why.

Where he had always found his family somewhat intrusive, particularly when it came to certain personal issues such as women and romance, Larkin soaked in the love and attention as though it were a new and wondrous experience. Over the days they spent at the lake, he noted that she blossomed the most beneath the attention of his mother and father and he remembered her mentioning that she'd been brought up by her grandmother. She'd always taken pains to change the subject whenever the conversation turned to the topic of her parents, which raised an interesting question. What had happened to them?

Toward the end of their stay, he finally found a private moment to ask. He'd arranged for a picnic lunch that he'd set up on one of the rafts dotting the lake, this one offering the most privacy from curious eyes. She laughed in surprised delight when they swam out to the raft and discovered lunch waiting for them.

"What have you been up to, Rafaelo Dante?" She knelt on the raft and opened the lid of the basket, peering inside. Freezer packs kept the chicken and Primo's uniquely spiced potato salad icy cold, as well as the bottle of white wine Rafe had tossed in at the last minute. She rocked back on her heels. "This is… This is amazing."

Something in her voice alerted him and he took her chin in his hand and tilted her face toward him. Sure enough, he caught the telltale glint of tears. "What's wrong?"

"Nothing's wrong," she instantly denied. "It's…" She gazed out across the lake, emotions darting across her face, one after another. Longing. Sorrow. Regret. Then they vanished, replaced by a grateful smile. "Thank you for bringing me here. This week has been like some sort of beautiful dream. I've enjoyed every minute of my time here."

"I gather the ring is working? No one's given you any trouble?"

She stared down at it in open pleasure. "Your family hasn't given me a moment's trouble. And they were all so excited to see me wearing it." Then the sorrow and regret returned. "I hope they won't be too crushed when our engagement ends."

Time for the first step of his plan. "There's no rush to end it," he remarked in an offhand manner. "In fact, I think it may be necessary to continue the engagement for a while longer. Would that be a problem?"

"I—I'm not sure."

He didn't give her a chance to invent a list of excuses.

No doubt she'd come up with them, but he had a plan for that, too. Hoping to distract her, he filled their plates with food. Then he opened the wine and poured them each a glass.

They sat in companionable silence, soaking up the August sun while they ate and sipped their wine. It gave him plenty of opportunity to admire the sleek red one-piece she wore and the way it showcased her subtle curves. She was beautifully proportioned. Magnificent legs. A backside with just the perfect amount of curve to it. Narrow hips and an even narrower waist. And her breasts, outlined in the thin Lycra of her swimsuit, were the most delectable he'd ever seen. A dessert he planned to savor at the earliest possible opportunity.

"Tell me something, Larkin."

"Hmm?"

He gathered up their empty plates, slipped them into a plastic bag and returned them to the basket. "Why were you raised by your grandmother? What happened to your parents?"

The instant his question penetrated, she stilled. It was like watching a wild animal who'd caught the unexpected scent of a predator. She didn't say anything for a long time, which was so out of character for her that he knew he'd stumbled onto something important. She pulled her legs against her chest and wrapped her arms around them, her grip on the stem of her wineglass so tight it was a wonder it didn't shatter.

She remained silent for long minutes, staring toward shore where Kiko chased a flutter of butterflies. "Gran raised me because my mother didn't want me."

"*What?*" It was so contrary to his way of thinking,

he struggled to process it. "How could someone not want *you?*"

She buried her nose in her wineglass. "I don't like to discuss it."

She didn't actually use the words *with strangers,* but she might as well have. If anything, it made him all the more determined to pry it out of her. Hadn't she done the same for him when it came to his relationship with Leigh, as well as those long-ago events at the lake when Draco had broken his leg? He understood all too well what it felt like to have a poison eating away inside. Larkin had lanced his wound. It was only fair he do the same for her.

"What about your father?"

She shifted. "He wasn't in the picture."

"He left your mother?"

To his relief, Larkin allowed the question, even smiled at it. "My mother wasn't the sort of woman you leave. Not if you're a typical red-blooded male. No, she left my father to return to her husband."

He couldn't hide how appalled he was, couldn't even keep it from bleeding into his voice. "That's how you ended up living with your grandmother?"

Larkin nodded. "My mother discovered she was pregnant with me shortly after she returned home. She and her husband already had a daughter, a legitimate one. Naturally, he wasn't about to have proof of her infidelity hanging around the house, or have my presence contaminating his own daughter. So Mother kept my half sister and turned me over to Gran. She even gave me her maiden name, so her husband wouldn't have any connection to me. Considering some of the alternatives, it wasn't such a bad option."

In other words, her mother had abandoned her. He swore, a word that caused her to flinch in reaction. "And your father? What happened to him?"

She didn't reply. Instead she lifted a shoulder in an offhand shrug and held her glass out for a refill.

He topped it off. "You don't know who your father is, do you?"

"Nope," she confessed. "Barely a clue."

It killed him that she wouldn't look at him. He didn't know if it was embarrassment or shame or the simple fact that she was hanging on to her self-control by a thread. Maybe all of those reasons.

He took a stab in the dark. "I gather he's the one you're looking for."

She saluted him with her glass. "Right again."

"So what's his name? If you'd like, I'll pass it on to Juice and we'll have him tracked down in no time."

"Well, now, there's the hitch."

Rafe winced. "No name."

"No name," she confirmed.

"I can't think of a tactful way of asking my next question...."

"Let me ask it for you. Did my mother even know who he was? Yes, as a matter of fact, she did."

"And she won't give you his name?" Outrage rippled through Rafe's voice.

"She died before she got around to it, although she did let it slip one time that he lived in San Francisco. And Gran remembered her calling him Rory."

"Granted, that's not a lot to go on," Rafe conceded. "Even so, Juice may be able to help. Was there anything else? Letters, perhaps, or mementos?"

"You don't want to go there, Rafe," she whispered.

"Of course I want to go there. If it'll help—"

She set her glass on the raft with exquisite care. "Remember when I told you that my plan for an exit strategy from our engagement was on automatic? If you keep asking questions, the countdown begins."

"What the hell does finding your father have to do with ending our engagement?"

Darkness filled her eyes, turning them sooty with pain. "I can explain, if you insist. But don't forget I did try to warn you."

"Fine. You warned me. Now, what's going on?"

"My father gave my mother a bracelet shortly before she left him. I was going to use that to try to find him, assuming he wants to be found. It was unusual enough that it might help identify him."

"Go on."

"It was an antique bracelet."

"Great. So we'll give Juice the bracelet—"

She cut him off. "Small problem." He could see her struggle to maintain her composure. "I don't have it."

"Did you sell it?"

"No! Never."

"Then where is it?"

"My sister took it. My *half* sister."

Son of a bitch. Did he have to drag every last detail out of her? "Okay, I really don't understand. How did she end up with your father's bracelet if he wasn't her father and the two of you didn't grow up together?"

"Every once in a while, Mom would drop by for a visit with my sister in tow. On one of the visits, Mom gave me the bracelet. My sister—*half* sister—was *not* happy. She had everything money could buy, except that one thing. And she wanted it. It ate at her. I realize now that she couldn't stand the idea that I possessed something she didn't. She threw a temper tantrum to end all temper tantrums."

"And your mother gave in? She gave the bracelet to your sister?"

"Nope. She dragged my sister, kicking and screaming, out of my grandmother's house. The few times they visited after that everything seemed fine, though one time I caught her snooping around in my room. But years later, long after Mom died, she showed up out of the blue. I thought it was an attempt to mend fences and reconnect." Larkin's laugh held more pain than amusement. "After she left I discovered that the bracelet had left with her."

"Can you get it back?"

"I don't know yet. Maybe."

"Is there anything I can do to help? Perhaps if we were to approach her, offer to purchase it?"

For some reason the kindness in his voice provoked a flood of tears and it took her a minute to control them. "Thanks."

"Aw, hell."

He swept her into his arms and she buried her face against his shoulder, her body curving into his. He couldn't understand how a parent could abandon her child. But then, he couldn't imagine making any of the choices Larkin's mother had. No wonder Larkin took such delight in his family and the way they encouraged and supported and—yes—interfered in each other's lives.

Larkin had never had any of that. Worse, she'd been abandoned by her mother, never known the love of her father and been betrayed in the worst possible way by her half sister. Well, that ended. Right now.

"We'll take care of this, sweetheart. We'll get your bracelet back and use it to track down your father. If anyone can do it, it's Juice." He pulled back slightly. "Let's start with finding the bracelet. What's your sister's name? Where does she live?"

Larkin caught him by surprise, ripping free of his embrace. Without a word she dived from the raft and struck out toward shore, cutting through the water as though all the demons of hell were close on her heels. He didn't hesitate. He gave chase, reaching the shore only steps behind her. Catching her by the shoulder, he spun her around.

"What the hell is going on?" he demanded, the air heaving in and out of his lungs. "Why did you take off like that?"

She struggled to catch her breath. Water ran in thin rivulets down her face, making it impossible to tell whether it was from her swim or from tears. "I warned you. I warned you not to go there."

A hideous suspicion took hold. "Who is she, Larkin? Who has your bracelet? What's her name?"

"Her name is…*was*…Leigh."

"Leigh," he repeated. He shook his head. "Not my late wife. Not that Leigh."

She closed her eyes and all the fight drained from her. "Yes, your late wife, Leigh. She was also my half sister." She looked at him then, her eyes—those stunning aquamarine eyes—empty of all emotion. "And I wondered, assuming it's not too much trouble, if you could give me back the bracelet she took from me."

For a split second Rafe couldn't move, couldn't even

think. Then comprehension stormed through him. "All this time you've been with me, you've kept your relationship to Leigh a secret? All so you could find her bracelet?"

"*My* bracelet. And no! Well, yes." She thrust her hands into her wet hair in open frustration, standing the curls on end. "I didn't move in with you in order to search for it, if that's what you're suggesting. But yes. I asked to be assigned to the Dantes reception in order to get an initial impression of you. To decide the best way to approach you."

She'd been sizing him up. Right from the start she'd been figuring out the perfect bait for her trap. And he'd fallen for it. Fallen for almost the exact same routine Leigh had used on him. The poor innocent waif. In Larkin's case, abandoned by her mother, searching for her father. Raised by her grandmother. Was any of it true? None of Leigh's stories had been. Or was this Larkin's clever way to get her hands on whatever valuables his late wife had left behind?

"What a fool I've been."

"I'm sorry, Rafe. To be honest—"

"Oh, by all means," he cut in sarcastically. "Do be honest. It would make such a refreshing change."

"I was going to tell you the truth the night you offered me a job."

He paced in front of her, more angry than he could ever remember being. Somehow Larkin had gotten under his skin in a way that Leigh never had, making the betrayal that much worse. "If you had told me that night, I'd have thrown you out then and there."

"I know."

"So you didn't mention it."

Her mouth tilted to one side in a wry smile. "I think it had more to do with your asking me to be your fiancée and then kissing me. That pretty much blew every other thought out of my head."

The fact that his reaction had been identical to hers only served to increase his anger and frustration. "You still should have told me."

"Then your grandparents arrived on the scene and I got kicked out of my apartment." She continued the recital with relentless tenacity. "Maybe I should have confessed then, but to be hon—" She winced. "The reason I didn't was because I didn't feel like spending a night on the streets."

"I wouldn't have thrown you out in the middle of the night." He smiled grimly. "At least, I don't think so."

"Then in the morning I got swept off by Elia and Nonna. I really didn't want to make the announcement in front of them." She captured her lower lip between her teeth and a line of anxiety appeared between her brows. "But I shouldn't have let them spend any money on me. That was totally wrong, and if it's the last thing I do I'll repay every dime."

"Would you forget about the damn money?" Rafe broke off and scrubbed his hands across his face. What the hell was he saying? Money was the reason she was here. She just had a different routine than Leigh, a far more effective one, as it turned out. "You had ample opportunity to tell me in the time we've been together. Why didn't you?"

She squared her shoulders. In her halter-top bathing suit they looked breathtakingly delicate and feminine—a fact he couldn't help but notice despite all that stood between them. "You're right. I should have told you. My only excuse is that I knew it would change everything between us." Her chin quivered before she brought it under ruthless control. "And I didn't want our relationship to change."

He did his best to ignore the chin. She might look like a helpless stray, but he didn't doubt she was every bit as conniving as her sister. *Blood will tell,* as Primo always said. Of course, he'd been referring to The Inferno. But maybe greed and deceit and a lack of honor ran in some families the way The Inferno ran in his. Like mother, like daughter.

"You want Leigh's bracelet? Fine. You'll have it first thing tomorrow. After that, I expect you to clear out."

His final comment kept her from replying for a moment. Her distress shouldn't affect him. Not anymore. But for some reason it did. "Then you have it?" she asked in a low voice. "I wasn't sure whether it had been lost when Leigh's plane went down."

"It was at Dantes at the time, having the catch repaired. Right now it's in my office safe." He whistled for Kiko, then inclined his head toward the lake house. "Come on. We're leaving. I'll tell everyone there's been an unexpected emergency."

She didn't argue. "Of course." Her tone turned formal. "I'll find somewhere else to stay as soon as we get back to the city."

The comment only served to spin his anger to an all-time high. "As much as I'd love to have you gone, it'll be far too late to find a place for both you and Kiko tonight. Tomorrow I'll get your damn bracelet and find you a hotel or apartment willing to house you both." He cut her off before she could argue. "Enough, Larkin. This discussion is over. From now on, we do things my way. And my way means you're out of my life as soon as I can arrange it."

Rafe didn't waste any time putting his plan into action. Nor did he give his family the chance to do more than express confused concern before he had the two of them and Kiko packed and loaded and flying down the road toward San Francisco.

The instant they arrived home, Larkin made a beeline for her bedroom. Rafe followed. It wasn't the smartest move, but he had some final questions he wanted answered. He paused in the doorway, struggling to see through the pretense to the woman she'd revealed herself to be—a woman ruled by greed and avarice and dishonesty.

It was as though she read his mind. "I'm nothing like Leigh." She threw the comment over her shoulder.

"No? Time will tell." He stared at her, broodingly. "Once I slipped a ring on your sister's finger she went from sweet and innocent—like you—to cold and calculating. I have to hand it to her, she put on a great act leading up to our wedding. I guess I'm an easy mark when it comes to the helpless waif type of woman. Leigh was a more sophisticated version, granted, but that changed soon enough. It didn't take long to realize she wanted what every other woman wants from a Dante, the good life and everything my money could provide. I suppose I could have lived with that. For a while."

"Then what went wrong?"

"It was the adultery that I refused to tolerate."

The fluid lines of Larkin's body stiffened and she slowly turned to face him. "She cheated on you? *You?*"

He supposed he should be flattered by the way she said that. "Hard to imagine?"

"Yes, it is."

His eyes narrowed and he approached, swallowing up the narrow bones of her shoulders in his two hands. "How do you do it?"

She stared up at him, eyes huge and startling blue, her expression one of stark innocence. Bambi in human form. "Do what?"

"Look the way you do, so trustworthy and ingenuous, when everything you say is a total lie. How do you do that?"

"I'm not Leigh." She spoke calmly enough, but a hint of steel and temper washed across her face. "You're trying to tuck us into the same little box and I refuse to allow it. *I am not Leigh!*"

"And I might have believed you if you'd been candid about your connection to Leigh from the start. Just out of curiosity, was any of your story true? Were you really abandoned by your mother and raised by your grandmother?"

Exhaustion lined her face, along with a heart-wrenching despair. "I've never lied to you, Rafe. I simply didn't tell you about Leigh and the bracelet. I even told you I had secrets. Omissions. Remember?" She searched his face, probably looking for some weakness she could use to her advantage. "You said lying by omission was part of dating. Everything else I told you was the truth."

"And I'm supposed to just believe it."

"You know what, Rafe? I don't care what you believe. I know it's the truth and that's all that matters." She lifted her chin an inch. "You should be grateful to me, you know that? I've given you the perfect excuse for staying emotionally disconnected. I betrayed you. Now you can go back to being independent. The original lone wolf. You should be celebrating."

"Somehow I don't feel like celebrating." She attempted to pull back and he tightened his hold. "I can still feel it. Why is that?"

She didn't pretend to misunderstand. A hint of panic crept into her gaze, combining with a wealth of longing. "Maybe it really is The Inferno."

"You'd love that, wouldn't you?"

She hesitated. "I'd love it if it were real," she admitted with brutal frankness. "But I'm not that thrilled about it given the current circumstances."

He uttered a humorless laugh. "There's one good thing that's come from all this."

Her breath escaped her lungs in a soft rush. "I'm afraid to ask...."

"Once I explain the facts to my family they'll finally leave me alone. No more Inferno possibilities paraded beneath my nose. Not only that, but they'll understand completely why I can't marry my Inferno soul mate. How could I, when she's Leigh's sister?"

Bone-deep temper ignited in Larkin's eyes, turning the color to an incandescent shade of cobalt-blue. "*Half* sister. And I'm getting really tired of being hanged for her crimes. You want something to be angry about? I'll give you something."

She swept her hands up across his chest and into his hair. Grabbing two thick handfuls, she yanked his face down to hers and took his mouth in a ruthless kiss. Desire roared through him at her aggressiveness. Her mouth slanted across his, hot and damp with passion.

Gently she parted his lips with hers. Teasing. Offering. Beckoning him inward. He didn't hesitate.

He tugged her closer, melding them together. Her thighs, strong and slender, slipped between his while her pelvis curved snugly against him. He could feel the shape and softness of her breasts against his chest, feel the pebbled tips that spoke of her need. And her mouth. Her mouth was as sweet and lush and tasty as a ripe peach.

He staggered forward a step, falling with her onto the bed. The instant they hit the mattress, he shoved his hands up under her shirt and cupped the pert apple roundness of her breasts. He traced his thumbs across her rigid nipples, catching her hungry moan in his mouth. The sound was the final straw.

He lost himself. Lost himself in the fire that erupted every time they touched. She wrapped her legs around him, pulling him tighter against her. Her breath came in frantic little gasps and she snatched quick bites of his mouth.

"Tell me this is a lie," she demanded. "Tell me I'm lying about what happens whenever you kiss me. Tell me this isn't real."

It took endless seconds for her words to penetrate. The instant they did, he swore viciously. "Not again."

"Yes, again." She wiggled out from underneath him and shot to her feet. "Do you think I want it to happen? You're Leigh's husband. I've never before wanted anything that belonged to her. But you—" Her voice broke and she turned away.

"I never belonged to her."

"You were married to her." She lifted a shoulder in

a disconsolate shrug. "There's not much difference as far as I can tell."

He stood, aware that nothing he could do or say would restore order to his world. He wanted a woman he didn't trust, probably would have made love to her again if she hadn't put a stop to it before it went any further. He'd already had his life turned upside down once, courtesy of his former wife. He wasn't about to let it happen again.

"I don't belong to any woman. And I never will."

"A lone wolf to the end?" she whispered.

"It's better than the alternative."

With that he turned and left. And all the while his palm burned in protest.

Ten

Larkin spent the night curled up in the middle of the bed counting the minutes until dawn.

Rafe was right about one thing. She should have told him she was Leigh's sister—*half* sister—right from the start. That had been the plan all along. If only she hadn't gotten distracted. No, time to face the truth. She hadn't been all that distracted. She hadn't wanted to reveal her identity to him because living the lie had filled her with more joy than she'd ever before experienced.

She swiped at her cheeks, despising the fact that they were damp with tears. She'd discovered at an early age that feeling sorry for herself didn't help. Nor did it change anything. Not that she had much to feel sorry about. She'd had Gran, who'd been a wonderful substitute parent.

Even so, she'd be kidding herself if she didn't acknowledge that some small part of her felt as though she were always on the outside looking in. That she'd never quite measured up. More than anything, she'd wanted to be loved by her mother. To belong. To have known the love of a father, as well. Instead, what had Leigh called her? A Mistake. Capital *A*. Capital *M*. Underlined and italicized. As a result, Larkin had held men at a distance, determined not to visit upon a new generation the same mistakes of her parents. If you didn't fall in love, you couldn't create A Mistake.

But her lack of a real family, a "normal" family, one that consisted of more than a loving grandmother, had filled her with an intense restlessness, a need to belong. Somewhere. To someone. To find the elusive dream of hearth and home and family. To finally fit in. But how did you find that when you were too wary to let people approach? Beside her, Kiko whimpered and bellied in closer.

"I know I wasn't a mistake, any more than you were," she told the dog. "We just don't quite fit in anywhere. We're unique. Special. Caught between two worlds, neither of our own making."

But no matter how hard her grandmother had tried to convince her of that fact and fill her life with love, there'd always been a part of her that had conceded there was a certain element of truth to Leigh's words. Bottom line… She wasn't good enough for her mother to keep. She'd been thrown away. Dispensable.

Until Rafe.

For a brief shining time she'd discovered what it meant to belong to a family, one who'd welcomed her with open arms. Until she'd ruined it. "I should have told him." Kiko whined in what Larkin took as agreement.

"But then he'd never have made love to me. And I'd never have fallen in love with him."

Tears escaped no matter how hard she tried to prevent them. It was worth it, she kept repeating to herself. No matter how badly it ended, the days she'd had with Rafe were worth the agony to come. If she had to do it all over again, she would.

Without a minute's hesitation.

Dawn finally arrived, giving Rafe the excuse he needed to give up on pretending to sleep and dress for work. He would have skipped breakfast, but Kiko padded out to join him, and well, damn it. He couldn't let the poor girl starve, could he?

He didn't see or hear any sign of Larkin, which was fine by him. The sooner he concluded their remaining business, the sooner he could get his life onto an even keel again. Go back to the way things had been before Larkin had stormed into his life and ripped it to shreds. Avoid further emotional entanglements and just be left the hell alone.

"It's what I've always wanted," he informed Kiko.

She gave his comment the attention it deserved, which was none at all. Aware he didn't have a hope in hell of gaining any support from that quarter, he downed the last of his coffee and rinsed the mug. Then, refusing to consider the whys and wherefores of his actions, he started up a fresh pot before heading out the door.

He wasn't expected at the office, since the entire Dante family was still officially on vacation. He'd also given his assistant the time off, which provided him complete privacy to closet himself in his office, undisturbed. He wasted a couple of hours taking care of business emails and paperwork, knowing full well they were his way of avoiding the inevitable. Finally he shoved back his chair and stared at the display rack that concealed his office safe.

He sighed. *Just get it over with!*

It took him only minutes to punch in the appropriate code and verify his thumbprint. The door swung open and he sorted through the various gemstones and jewelry samples stored there until he found the plain rectangular box he'd stashed in the farthest recesses.

Removing it, he relocked the safe and carried the box to his desk. Flipping open the lid, he stared down at the bracelet. It was a stunning piece. The setting gave the impression of spun gold, delicate filigree links that appeared to be straight out of a fairy tale. The original stones had been a lovely mixture of modest diamonds of a decent quality, and amethysts that weren't bad, if a shade on the pink side. Not good enough for Leigh, of course, but then few things were.

She'd insisted he replace the amethysts with emeralds because they were her birthstone, and the smaller diamonds with oversize fire diamonds because they were more impressive, not to mention expensive. He'd never felt either complemented the setting. But since he'd still been in the throes of lust, he'd agreed to her demands. She'd even wanted to have the setting altered, but there he'd drawn the line. It was perfect as is. Instead, she'd gone behind his back and made the adjustments without his knowledge. It wouldn't take much to return it to its original form, he decided, studying the bracelet. Sev's wife, Francesca, could do it in her sleep.

A knock sounded at the door and his sister, Gia, poked her head into his office. "Hey, you. Larkin said I could find you here."

He leaned back in his chair. "Did she, now."

"Yes, she did."

Gia entered the room and closed the door behind her. He and his sister had always been dubbed the "pretty" Dantes, identical in coloring, with matching jade-green eyes. While he'd despised the moniker, Gia had simply shrugged it off, neither impressed nor dismayed by the description. He, on the other hand, had been offended on her behalf, since his sister wasn't merely pretty. She was flat-out gorgeous.

"To be honest, I'm relieved Larkin's still at your place," she continued. "When the two of you left the lake I was a little worried you were on the verge of breaking up."

"So you followed us home?" Her shrug spoke volumes. "It's none of your business, Gianna."

"Then you *are* on the verge of breaking up. Oh, Rafe." She approached and slid a slim hip onto the edge of his desk. Leaning in, she examined the bracelet. A delaying tactic, no doubt. "Huh. Definitely not Francesca's work. Almost beautiful. Or it would be if it weren't so—" she made a fluttering gesture with her hands "—over the top. It also needs softer stones."

"Amethysts."

"Exactly." She nodded, impressed. "Good eye. Whose is it?"

"Leigh's." He corrected himself. "Larkin's, I guess." Confusion lined Gia's brow. "Come again?"

"Leigh and Larkin are sisters. *Half* sisters." Though why he bothered to make the distinction he couldn't say.

Gia's mouth dropped open. "Is this some sort of joke?"

"I wish." He gave her the short version. "Now she wants her bracelet. Once she has it, she'll be on her way. She can use it to try to find her father, or sell it, or do whatever the hell she wants with it." He flipped the case closed with a loud snap. "And that brings to an end my very brief Inferno engagement."

"I don't understand. Why does any of that put an end to your engagement?"

He glared at his sister. "What do you mean, why? Because she's Leigh's sister." He grimaced. "Half sister."

"So? It's not like she's Leigh. You only have to talk to her for five minutes to realize that much."

"She lied to me."

"Did she? She claimed she wasn't Leigh's sister?"

"Half sister," he muttered.

"I'll take that as a no." She waited for him to say more, blowing out her breath in exasperation when he remained stubbornly silent. "Fine. Be that way. But you can tell Larkin that if she needs somewhere to stay while she searches for her father—"

"Assuming there is a father and she's actually searching for him."

Gia inclined her head. "Assuming all that. She's welcome to crash at my place." She slipped off the desk. "Larkin loves you, you know."

He stilled. "She used me."

Gia shrugged. "It happens. But I'll tell you one

thing…" She paused on her way out the door. For some reason she wouldn't look at him. "I'd give anything to have what you're throwing away."

Rafe returned home to find Larkin perched on the edge of a chair in his living room, dressed in one of her old outfits. Kiko lay at her feet, the dog's graying muzzle resting on her paws. Her brilliant gold eyes shifted in Rafe's direction and she watched him with unnerving intensity. He caught a similar expression in Larkin's gaze. Beside the dog sat her backpack. It didn't take much thought to add two and two and come up with…Larkin was running. At least she'd done him the courtesy of waiting until he returned home. But then, it wasn't likely she'd leave without her bracelet.

She drew in a deep breath and blew it out. Rising, she gathered up her backpack, shifting it nervously from hand to hand. "Do you have it?"

He removed the box from his suit-jacket pocket and held it out to her. Without a word she accepted it and turned her back on him, her spine rigid and unrelenting.

"That's it?" he asked, though he didn't know what more he expected.

"Thanks." She threw the words over her shoulder. "But if it's all the same with you, Kiko and I will be on our way now."

He let her go. It was better this way. Easier. Cleaner. Safer.

An instant later she slammed her backpack to the ground. Whirling around, she came charging toward him. "Rafaelo Dante, what the *hell* have you done to my bracelet?" She shook the box he'd given her under his nose. "What are you trying to pull? You were supposed to give me *my* bracelet. Not this…this…*thing*."

"That is your bracelet."

Larkin popped open the top and held out the glittering spill of gold and gems. "Look at it, Rafe. What happened to it? It's ruined!"

How was it possible that she could put him on the defensive with such ease? "Leigh had me switch out the stones. Don't worry—it's even more valuable than it was before."

"Valuable? *Valuable!*" She stared at him as though he'd grown two heads. "What has that got to do with anything?"

"I just thought—"

Larkin's eyes hardened, filling with a cynicism he'd never seen there before. And something else. Something that twisted him into knots and filled him with shame. It was disillusionment he read in her gaze. It was as though he'd told her there was no Santa Claus. No Easter Bunny. No magic or fairies or wishing on stars. As though he'd taken every last hope and dream and crushed it beneath his heel.

"I know what you thought," she stated in a raw, husky voice. "You assumed I'm like Leigh. That it's the dollar-and-cent worth of an item that's important."

It hit him then. She wasn't Leigh. How could he ever have thought she was? It was like comparing an angel to a viper. Where Leigh had demanded and taken, Larkin had given him the most precious possession she owned—herself. And he'd thrown that gift back in her face. Accused her of the worst possible crime—being the same as her sister. *Half* sister. She'd given him her heart and he'd tossed it aside as though it were worthless, just as her mother had done.

"Don't you get it?" she whispered. Pain carved deep lines in her expression. "This bracelet is my only connection to my father. How am I supposed to use it to find him when it looks nothing like he remembers?"

Face it, Dante, you screwed up.

And now he had a choice, a choice that was vanishing with each passing moment. One path led back the way he'd come. Returned him to where he'd been just weeks ago. The other option… Well, if he chose that one, he'd have to risk everything he'd always considered most precious. His independence. His need to control his world and everything within it. The barriers he'd spent a lifetime erecting to protect himself.

But the potential reward…

He looked at Larkin. Truly looked at her. That's all it took. He burrowed the thumb of his left hand into the throbbing center of his right palm and surrendered to the inevitable. He'd risk it all. Risk anything to have her back in his life. And just like that, a plan fell into place. It would take days to accomplish, possibly weeks. It would take extreme delicacy and exquisite timing. But it just might work.

Now for step one. "I can put the bracelet back the way it was," he offered.

Tears welled up and she brushed at them with a short, angry motion. "Forget it. I don't want anything from you."

She turned to leave, whistling to Kiko. Instead of following her, the dog darted forward, snatched the backpack in her jaws and took off at a dead run up the steps to the second story.

"Kiko!" she and Rafe called in unison.

Together they raced after her, finding her crouched in the center of his bed, guarding the backpack. She barked at the pair of them.

"Looks like she doesn't want you to leave," Rafe said.

"She'll get over it." Larkin approached the bed and picked up the backpack. "Let's go, Kiko."

Though the dog allowed Larkin to take the backpack, she hunkered down on the bed in a position that clearly stated she wasn't planning to budge anytime soon. Okay, this could work to his advantage.

"Let her stay," Rafe suggested.

"What?" Larkin turned on him. "Why?"

"You both can stay here until we get the problem of your bracelet sorted out."

She instantly shook her head. "That's not going to happen."

Rafe wasn't surprised. That would have been too easy, and something told him that nothing about regaining her trust would prove easy. "In that case, Gia has offered you a room while you search for your father. The only problem is that her place isn't suitable for Kiko. Leave her here for the time being."

Tears filled Larkin's eyes. "It's not enough that you ruined my bracelet? Now you're taking my dog, too?"

Hell. "I'm not taking her," he explained patiently. "I'm letting her stay until our business is settled."

Her chin jutted out. "I thought our business was settled."

"Apparently not. I still owe you for your time and the damage to the bracelet."

"Forget it."

"Somehow I had a feeling you were going to say that," he muttered. "In that case, the least I can do is have your bracelet fixed so it's returned to its original condition. Will you consider that a fair exchange?"

She looked doubtful. "You can do that?"

"Francesca can handle anything."

"Francesca." Her eyes widened at the reminder, filling with horror. "I forgot about the engagement ring."

She yanked the ring off, holding it out to him. When he refused to take it, she crossed to his bedside table and placed it there with unmistakable finality. "If you'll have my bracelet repaired, I'll consider us even."

He wouldn't. Not by a long shot. She squared her shoulders and turned her back on Kiko. The expression on her face almost brought him to his knees. Despite the love and support she'd received from her grandmother, everyone else in her life had abandoned her. So many rejections in such a short life. And here it was happening to her again.

Well, not for long. No matter what it took, he intended to make things right.

The next couple of weeks were absolute agony for Larkin. Rafe made no attempt to get in touch. Nor did she go to the house, even though she missed Kiko fiercely. She made noises a couple of times about sneaking over while Rafe was at work so she could see her dog, but Gia informed her that her brother had elected to stay at home for the remainder of his vacation, and Larkin couldn't bring herself to confront him. At least, not yet. Not while recent events were still so raw.

Midway through the third week, word finally came that the repairs to her bracelet were completed. "Meet me downstairs in five and I'll drive you over," Gia called to say. "I think I'm almost as excited as you to see how it looks."

It wasn't until they made the turn onto Rafe's street that Larkin realized where they were going. "I thought the bracelet would be at Dantes," she said uneasily.

"Nope. Rafe has it." Gia spared her an impatient look. "You've done nothing but grouse about the fact that you haven't seen Kiko in weeks. Now you have the opportunity to see both her and the bracelet. You should be over the moon. Don't tell me you're going to let a little thing like my good-for-nothing brother spoil your big moment."

"No. No, of course I won't." Maybe not.

To her surprise, Gia pulled up in front. Instead of parking, she waved her hand toward the house. "On second thought, why don't you go ahead without me."

Larkin turned to glare. "You're setting me up, aren't you? You think if I go in there alone, maybe Rafe and I will resolve our differences."

Gia shrugged. "Worth a try."

"It's not going to work."

"Then it won't work. But at least I'll have given it a shot."

Realizing it was pointless to argue, Larkin exited the car. Snatching a deep breath, she forced herself to climb the steps of the front porch at a sedate pace and knock. A minute later the door swung open and Rafe stood there. They stared at each other for an endless moment before he stepped back to allow her past.

She didn't know what to say. Emotions flooded through her. Powerful emotions. Longing. Regret mixed with sorrow. Love and the sheer futility of that love. And overriding them all was pain. A bone-deep, all-invasive hurt.

"Where's Kiko?" she managed to ask.

"Out back." For some reason he couldn't seem to take his eyes off her, his gaze practically eating her alive. "The gentleman who brought the bracelet wanted you to inspect it before he left and I wasn't sure how well he'd take to having a wolf hovering over him."

She almost smiled, catching herself at the last instant. "But Kiko's okay?"

"She's fine. Misses you. But then, that seems to be going around."

She blinked up at him, not quite sure what to make of his comment. Not that his expression gave anything away. "I guess we shouldn't keep your associate waiting."

Rafe led the way to the den and shoved open the door. She could see her bracelet spread out across the empty glass-topped desk, captured within the beam of a bright spotlight. A man stood nearby, silent and attentive.

Larkin approached the table, her breath catching when she saw the bracelet. She swung around to glance at Rafe, tears gathering in her eyes. "It's beautiful. Please tell Francesca she did an amazing job restoring it."

The man beside the table cleared his throat. "She made a few minor changes. The fire diamonds, for instance. They're similar in size, but the quality can't be compared. And I understand she used Verdonia Royal amethysts. The color is stunning, don't you think?"

Larkin glanced at the man and smiled. "Don't tell Francesca, but I still prefer the original."

"Do you really?"

For some reason, he seemed ridiculously pleased by the comment. He looked directly at her then and she froze, riveted. He was far shorter than Rafe, maybe five foot six or seven and somewhere in his late forties. Eyes the color of aquamarines twinkled behind a pair of wire-rimmed glasses. And though his wheat-white hair was cut short, there was no disguising the wayward curls that were next to impossible to subdue. His nose was different from hers, stubbier, but they shared the same pointed chin and wide mouth. And she knew without even spending a minute of time with him that he used that mouth to laugh. A lot. Best of all, he made her think of leprechauns and rainbows and pots of gold. And he made her think of magic and the possibility of dreams coming true.

"I must confess," he said, "the old girl looks quite grand with all those fancy stones attached to her."

Larkin continued to stare at him, unable to look away. "Old girl?" she repeated faintly.

"The bracelet. She belonged to your great-great-great-grandmother."

"You're—"

"Rory Finnegan. I'm your father, Larkin."

She never remembered moving. One minute she was

standing next to the table and the next she was in his arms. "Dad?"

"You have no idea how long I've been looking for you." He whispered the words into her ear and they flowed straight to her heart.

The next few hours flashed by. At some point, Larkin realized that Rafe had slipped away, giving her and her father some much-needed privacy. Coffee would periodically appear at their elbow, along with sandwiches. But she never noticed who brought them, though it didn't take much guesswork to know that Rafe was behind that, too.

During the time she spent with her father, she discovered that her mother had called him shortly before her death. "She was horribly sick. Almost incoherent," he explained. "She just kept telling me I had a daughter but couldn't give me a name or location. By the time I tracked her down, she was gone and that bastard of a husband claimed he had no idea what I was talking about."

Larkin also learned that her name belonged to the same woman whose bracelet she'd been given. And she discovered that she had a family as extensive as the Dantes, and every bit as lovingly nosy. "You won't be able to get rid of us," Rory warned. "Not now that I've found you. I'd have brought a whole herd of the troublemakers with me, but I didn't want to overwhelm you."

When the time finally came for him to leave, they were both teary eyed. Standing by the front door, he snatched her close for a tight hug. "You'll come by this weekend. We'll throw a big welcome home party. And bring your man with you. Your grandmother Finnegan will want to look him over before okaying the wedding date."

"Oh, but—"

"We'll be there," Rafe informed him as he joined them.

The instant the door closed behind her father, Larkin turned to confront Rafe. "I don't know what to say," she confessed, fighting back tears. "Thank you seems so inadequate."

"You're welcome." He held out his hand. "I have something else I want to show you."

"Okay." She dared to slip her hand into his, closing her eyes when The Inferno throbbed in joyous welcome. "But then I'd really like to see Kiko."

"That's what I wanted to show you."

He pulled her toward the back of the house to the guest suite where she'd spent so many blissful days and nights. The door was shut and on the wooden surface someone had screwed a glistening gold placard. "Official Den of Tukiko and Youko" it read.

"You told me that was Kiko's full name. I looked up the meaning." He slanted her a flashing smile. "Moon child?"

Larkin shrugged. "It seemed fitting." She frowned at the sign. "But who is Youko?"

"Ah, you mean our sun child."

He shoved open the door. Where once had stood a regular bed, now there were two huge dog beds. The door to the backyard stood ajar and he ushered her in that direction. She gaped at the changes. In the time she'd been gone, someone had come through and transformed the yard into a giant doggy playpen. Rope pulls and exercise rings, doghouses and toys were scattered throughout the area. He'd even had a section of lawn dug up and a giant square of loosely packed dirt put in its place.

"For digging," he explained. "And burying bones. And for rolling around, if that's what they want."

Just then Kiko emerged from one of the doghouses and bounded across to her side, nearly bowling them both down in her enthusiasm. Larkin wrapped her arms around her dog and buried her face in the thick ruff.

"I've missed you so much." A small whine drew her attention back to the doghouse. Peeking out from the shadows was another animal. "And who is this?" Kiko darted back to stand protectively beside the newcomer, a dog who appeared to be part yellow Lab and part golden retriever. "Youko, I presume?"

"She's a rescue dog. Terrified of people, so I'm assuming she was abused. Kiko's helping me socialize her." He hesitated. "I'm hoping you'll help, too."

She stiffened. "A dog's a big responsibility. A long-term commitment."

"Fifteen. Twenty years, if we're lucky. Of course, Kiko's Pals will also be a long-term commitment."

Larkin stared blankly. "Kiko's Pals?"

"It's the rescue organization we're starting, if you're willing. A charitable organization to help dogs like Kiko. I'm hoping you'll run it."

"You've started—" She broke off, fighting for control. "You did that for her? For us?"

"I'd do anything for the two of you," he stated simply.

"I don't understand," she whispered. "I don't understand any of this."

"Then let me explain."

This time he took her upstairs, pausing outside his bedroom door. Another plaque had been attached. This one read, "Den of the Big Bad Wolf and his Once in a Lifetime Mate." He opened the door and stepped back, giving her the choice of entering or walking away.

She didn't hesitate. She stepped across the threshold and straight into hope. He closed the door and she turned. In two swift steps he reached her side and pulled her into his arms.

"I'm so sorry, Larkin. I was an idiot. You're nothing like Leigh and never could be. I've spent so many years protecting myself that I almost lost the only thing I've ever wanted. You." He cupped her face and kissed her, losing himself in the scent and taste and feel of her. "I love you. I think I loved you from the first minute we touched."

"Oh, Rafe." She was laughing and crying at the same time. "I love you, too."

He pulled back. "I still want you to be my temporary fiancée."

Her eyes narrowed. "You do, huh?"

"Definitely. A very temporary fiancée, followed by a very long-term wife." He swung her into his arms and carried her to the bed. "You'll have to remind me where we left off. It's been so long I can't quite remember."

She wrapped her arms around his neck and feathered a kiss across his mouth. "I'll see what I can do to refresh your memory."

"Nope. We can't do that. Not without breaking my promise to Primo."

He fumbled for something on the dressing table. Taking her hand in his, he slid her engagement ring on her finger, back where it belonged. The heat of The Inferno flared between them and even though he didn't acknowledge it aloud, she could see the acceptance in his eyes.

"It would seem this is the perfect ring after all," he told her.

"And why is that?" she asked, even though she already knew.

"Your ring is named Once in a Lifetime, which is fitting because if there's one thing you've taught me—" he kissed her long and hard "—it's that wolves mate for life."

* * * * *

MILLS & BOON®

Want to get more from Mills & Boon?

Here's what's available to you if you join the exclusive **Mills & Boon eBook Club** today:

✦ *Convenience – choose your books each month*
✦ *Exclusive – receive your books a month before anywhere else*
✦ *Flexibility – change your subscription at any time*
✦ *Variety – gain access to eBook-only series*
✦ *Value – subscriptions from just £1.99 a month*

So visit **www.millsandboon.co.uk/esubs** today to be a part of this exclusive eBook Club!

MILLS & BOON®
By Request

RELIVE THE ROMANCE WITH THE BEST OF THE BEST

A sneak peek at next month's titles...

In stores from 16th January 2015:

- **His Revenge Seduction** – Melanie Milburne, Kate Walker and Elizabeth Power

- **Secret Affairs** – Natalie Anderson, Sarah Mayberry and Chantelle Shaw

In stores from 6th February 2015:

- **The Jarrods: Temptation** – Maureen Child, Tessa Radley and Kathie DeNosky

- **Baby for the Greek Billionaire** – Susan Meier

Available at WHSmith, Tesco, Asda, Eason, Amazon and Apple

Just can't wait?
Buy our books online a month before they hit the shops!
visit www.millsandboon.co.uk

These books are also available in eBook format!

0115/05